REBIRTH

BASED ON ACTUAL EVENTS

I will bless those who bless you (Israel), and curse those who treat you with contempt ...
—Genesis 12:3

DAVE LONGEUAY

SEVEN-7
PUBLISHING

Dave Longeuay

www.rebirthofisrael.com

ISBN: 978-0-9839058-0-6
e-ISBN: 978-0-9839058-1-3
LCCN: 2011914228

DEDICATION

Rebirth is dedicated to all the men, women *and youngsters* who bravely supported Israel's rebirth in 1948. Some believed in, and were driven by biblical prophecies, some fought for their survival, others joined for the adventure; They all believed Jews had a right to have a homeland of their own.

The following persons mentioned in *Rebirth*'s story represent only a small portion of the individuals who made a contribution to Israel's success, and in no way can commemorate all who have sacrificed so much for this monumental event.

Presidents Theodore Roosevelt and Harry Truman, Senator Robert Kennedy, Albert Einstein, Vidal Sassoon, Winston Churchill, American Colonel Mickey Marcus, Theodore Hershel, David Ben-Gurion, Golda Meir, Dov Grunner, Moshe Sneh, and Corrie ten Boom.

This book is not recommended for children under the age of twelve.

SEE THE IMAGES

As you read, visit www.rebirthofisrael.com to view images and videos of the actual events that inspired the story of *Rebirth*.

ACKNOWLEDGMENTS

Special thanks to my incredible wife Sheri, who endured countless hours away from me as I spent three years to research and compose *Rebirth*.
I love you, Sheri!

CHAPTER 1

July 1945, Based on actual events.

Charles Devonshire paced the deck of the ocean liner he'd boarded sixteen days before. His shoes clacked the wooden planks while he dodged passengers and scanned the horizon for approaching vessels that might have his father aboard. Once again, he saw nothing except rippling water and frothy whitecaps under the uneven ranks of patchy clouds. He sighed; for at least today, he wouldn't be dragged to his personal prison back home.

With a slight stagger from tossing waves that slammed the ship, Charles neared the bow, where he snatched a copy of *The New York Times*, wedged into a coiled rope. He unfolded it and gripped the edges as it flapped in the cool, salty breeze.

BATTLE OVER PALESTINE CONTINUES!

World's longest feud intensifies as an influx of Holocaust survivors fill the Arab-dominant territory to claim their Promised Land, while fleeing post-war hatred generated by Nazi propaganda.

The news tightened his gut, like the time he'd been caught, six years earlier, sneaking into Father's wooden chest of anti-Semitic literature. Even at age ten, his stomach had churned when he read the ugliness in the propaganda pamphlets.

When a gust of wind sent shivers to his chest, he wadded the newspaper because the headlines confirmed what the ship's crew had warned: Palestine had become a battleground for the most volatile land grab in history. No wonder passengers had been whispering among themselves and praying more with each passing day.

Boots pounded behind him on the newly swabbed deck. The stomping halted as he turned to see a steward; the sway of the ship didn't budge the man's rigid stance.

"It's after six," the mate said, his hair fluttering under his cap. "No one under eighteen on this deck, *little sonny*."

Charles had already been fed up with jealous peers who'd taunted him with names such as "runt" because he graduated high school two years early. But instead of walking away, he pulled his fabricated passport from his pocket and struggled to hold it still.

The steward adjusted his spectacles, crouched over and squinted at the photo. His eyes pierced Charles as he straightened. "You don't have glasses like the person in this picture. And the description says red hair. Off with the hat."

Charles removed his cap and pulled his glasses from his pocket while he juggled the wadded newspaper. "Sometimes the glasses give me a headache. I don't use them for reading, mister."

Raising his brows, he hoped the steward would look into his frosty-blue eyes and see him as an innocent passenger. It worked at the train station in Los Angeles, when their attendant also disbelieved he was eighteen.

The steward gave a tight nod. "Sorry to trouble you, sir." He pivoted a half circle and left.

Watching him leave, Charles stooped to retie his shoes, which bulged from lumps of cash under his feet. The discomfort served as a nagging reminder of his escape from the hostile recruitment of Father's anti-Semitic group. When he straightened and saw the orange sun recede toward the waterline, his eyelids drooped. But it didn't ease his throbbing head while he questioned his sanity for traveling eighty-six-hundred miles to escape his parents' abuse. And there'd be no guarantee of finding wrongdoings from their past, which he'd come to suspect originated in Palestine.

Light mist prickled his face and caused him to blink faster. A Jewish father and his boy, both in black and wearing their distinctive caps and curled hair, passed by. As they disappeared around the corner, he pondered the irony of being on a ship filled with Jews: the very race Father spent his life trying to teach Charles to hate.

Since his appetite had fled, he descended to his quarters. He spiraled down a few dozen steps into the musty common area, and nodded at a young Jewish couple when he opened the curtain to his bunk. The last few weeks of the Atlantic's rough waves made rest difficult, and reading had become his best sleep aid. So he sat on his bed, clicked on his flashlight, and flipped through the preadmissions papers from the Technion University, where he hoped to earn a degree in engineering—and dig into his family's past. And though they claimed his baby pictures were lost in a fire, he'd found a hidden photograph of his parents, standing next to the university's sign, holding him as a toddler. And even more mysterious was the writing on the back: "some day we will return from whence we came—"

Beams of light sliced through his porthole, illuminating his closet-sized area. He dropped his flashlight and gazed out to sea, but intense rays forced him to look away.

Passengers in the barrack-style quarters murmured from a bullhorn muttering outside. Charles slid his curtain open and watched people stagger from their bunks. His heart raced as silhouetted bodies bumped cots, while others waved flashlights and argued with one another.

Finally, he deciphered the garbled reverberations outside: "By decree of the Royal British Government, you are ordered to shut down your engines and prepare to be boarded!" The commanding voice repeated at regular intervals while the ship's motors that had hummed for weeks faded to silence, and the vessel slowed to an eerie crawl.

Queasiness beset his stomach again. He thought he'd designed a perfect getaway in the months it took to process his grandfather's inheritance before Father could steal it. And last night's sleep-depriving nightmare had come to pass; somehow Father had tracked him all the way out at sea.

The interior lights flashed and the captain's voice muttered over the intercom, but the British accent outside and stammering voices inside overpowered the internal speakers. Charles slipped his shoes on while his new friends roused across the aisle: an elderly white-bearded rabbi named Jesse Rosenthal, his wife Elizabeth, and their grown son, Samuel.

As Charles crossed the aisle, the ship jerked and thrust him into Samuel's frail body. "Sorry, Samuel. I didn't mean to step on your foot."

"It is them again! They going to arrest us!" Samuel shrieked with a Hungarian accent, his eyes wide and shifting. "The British harpoon the ship with the grappling hook. They will reel us in like—" Something boomed liked a massive door closing in a dungeon. "Hear that? That is boarding ramps. They will take us because we are Jews."

"Samuel, quiet down." Rabbi Jesse gripped his son's shoulder. "How could you possibly know this?"

Beads of sweat ran down Samuel's milky face. "Not again."

Charles backed up and steadied himself while Samuel bumped into people who shoved their way toward the portholes. Samuel clasped his hands to his head. "We must think of something."

"Get out of the aisle." Jesse pulled Samuel's arm. "Everything will be okay. God is watching over us."

"God will watch you. Not me."

"What are you talking about, Samuel?" Charles shouted as a gaunt gentleman passed.

Elizabeth drew the rest of their curtain open. "Samuel, come back and sit."

"I tried to enter Palestine eighteen months ago, after I escape Nazi prison ... Buchenwald."

Elizabeth opened her mouth. Jesse widened his eyes and put his palms out. "You didn't tell us that."

"How could I, Father? You move to America before Nazis take Jews." Samuel whisked his finger starboard. "If we get caught by Brits, we will suffer. They treat Jews like prisoners."

Jesse shook his head. "If that is the British out there, they will not mistreat us. We are American citizens now, and allies. And you don't have to worry—you are with us."

The hall lights flashed, followed by the ship's alert whistle.

"Attention all passengers. This is Captain Williams," a shallow voice scratched over the speakers. "We are anchored two miles off the coast of Haifa, Palestine. Please have your passports ready for inspection by the Royal British Navy. Stay calm and wait to be visited by a ship's officer and a British soldier. No cause for alarm. This is a routine inspection."

Samuel's warning might be right, but Charles couldn't relax, knowing how Father could have used one of his cunning tactics to have the Royal Navy halt the ship.

5

After sitting with the Rosenthal family and watching passengers calm, a ship's officer and a British soldier entered. When the soldier's tidy dark blue coat came under the light, the area hushed and everyone's demeanor stiffened. The intruder advanced and stopped at each person's quarters, demanding papers. Charles' forged passport had held up so far, yet he battled with the image of Father pacing the top deck, his typical smirking face showing satisfaction while waiting to have him jailed. Mother wouldn't be up there; She would've remained quiet at home.

After soliciting replies to suspicious questions from his friends, the soldier turned to Charles. Charles broke eye contact and scanned the red stripes that raced down each leg of the invader's white pants. A stiff hand almost hit his chest. "Passport. Religion?"

Charles held out his identification card. "I ... ah, don't have a religion, sir."

The soldier snatched the document. "You're from Los Angeles? Where are your parents?" He'd made no previous eye contact with any Jew, but fixed an intense gaze on Charles.

"My parents?"

The soldier remained stiff.

Charles resisted swallowing the lump in this throat. "They ahh ... don't exactly fit in with the average passenger on this ship." He couldn't look at the Rosenthals after that statement.

The soldier grinned. "You should not be traveling alone, lad, especially to such a volatile place. What's your purpose for entering Palestine?"

"Actually he is with us," Jesse said. "We are watching over the boy."

The soldier shifted his glare to the Rosenthals. "Silence! I didn't address you." He thrust his finger at Samuel. "Your son is not an American citizen!" He looked back at Charles with narrowed brows. "Are you with this family?"

"Ah … yes, sir." A wave of relief warmed his chest. Jesse had only known Charles for a few weeks, yet he vouched for him.

The soldier made a note on his clipboard, then had the rabbi, his family, and Charles escorted to a stateroom, where they were told the senior officer would question them further.

Charles came close to Samuel as they followed the soldier. "It's going to be okay."

"That is easy for you to think. You are not a Jew. Everywhere I go, somebody wants to arrest me, torture my body, or kill me."

Those words resonated with Charles. He too felt anxiety from being pursued by someone with evil intentions. He could imagine the Nazis or Father inflicting harm on these Jews, but not the British. Nothing in the media had covered abuse toward people like Jesse and his family since the war ended.

With the thought of his new friends being treated like convicts, Charles tightened his jaw and stomped upward as they ascended toward the main deck: the Rosenthals had made the lonely trip tolerable, insisting he join them at mealtimes. Jesse had even offered a place to stay at his brother's home in Haifa. Jesse was the opposite of Father: kind, understanding and enthusiastic about Charles pursuing a degree. And Elizabeth recognized the interest Charles took in her husband's conversations about biblical prophecies concerning a mass regathering of Jews to Palestine. Rabbi Jesse boasted in the Scriptures as his reason for migrating to the Promised Land, she'd said.

After heading down a long corridor, they entered a stateroom with fancy walnut siding and red velvet chairs lining the edges. The commander entered and positioned himself under a chandelier like a statue. Then he inspected Charles from top to bottom. "You may enter, but your Jew friends are not going to Palestine."

Charles' heart plummeted to his stomach. Denied passage simply because they were Jews? This wouldn't do.

His rebuke died on his lips when Elizabeth faced her husband and crossed her arms. "I can't believe this. We're not criminals!" Her boldness reminded Charles how opposite she was from Mother.

Jesse crossed his arms over his chest like his wife. "I beg your pardon, sir. We have valid American passports."

"It doesn't matter. Our quota of fifteen hundred Jews expired this month. All others are considered illegal. I'm recommending Cyprus for your family until we find you passage back to the United States."

"That is prison!" The sweat on Samuel's face shimmered under the bright light above.

The commander removed his white glove and slapped Samuel's face with it. "Not another word out of you, Jew!"

Elizabeth snarled and stepped forward. Jesse stretched his arm across her chest. Samuel remained motionless as if he'd seen a Nazi.

"I'm an American non-Jewish college student," Charles said. "I'm relying on this family to sss-support me while I'm in school." He thrust his finger portside in the direction of the shore. "If they don't accompany me to Palestine, I'll make sure the American consulate opens an inquiry as to why *you* hindered an international student."

The commander raised his brows and paused. "If I allow these Jews into Palestine, what's stopping them from uprising against us? In case you haven't heard, we're sustaining attacks by Jewish freedom fighters in every sector."

Charles shook his head. "I'm just here to get an education. And the rabbi is assuming leadership at a synagogue in Haifa."

Another officer approached, clacked his boot on the wood floor and cleared his throat. The commander turned to Charles with a smirk. "Excuse us." He moseyed a short distance with the soldier. Officers in the background interrogated other Jews while Charles studied the commander's aged face. The other officer pointed at them as he spoke, his mouth hidden from Charles' sight.

Charles focused on the commander's lips: "Don't bother me with your uninsightful reasoning. The boy just raised a political threat you are not privy to. Their President Truman is constantly nagging the parliament to let one hundred thousand Jews into Palestine. That would not go well with our Arab oil suppliers. I want no incidents with this ocean blockade." He shot a quick glance at Charles. "We need to be very careful with American citizens, like that young student." He sent a stiff nod. "Process their passes."

The officer saluted the commander, did an about-face and stomped off.

Charles resisted a grin, knowing he'd been instrumental in helping the rabbi join relatives in Haifa. Yet his heart ached to watch other innocent families hauled off the vessel—Jews who'd left everything in America for some barren desert in Palestine, just because some old historical book said they would regather there in the last days of earth's history.

The commander motioned his hand and another officer came and escorted them to the dining room, where non-Jewish passengers chattered and lingered. "I told you it's going to be okay," Charles told Samuel when the officer left.

Samuel's glossed-over stare repelled his encouragement.

Before he could reassure Samuel again, two soldiers entered the room and bolted toward Charles. Their boots hit the oak floor in sync like a steady tribal drum. Charles sucked in a breath, and stared at the handcuffs in the soldiers' belt-pouches. He'd paid quite a sum to create a fictitious name and background history, and they were coming to ruin his master plan.

"Samuel Rosenthal?" the taller soldier said.

Charles let his breath out as Samuel hunched forward and looked toward his shoes. His statement about being hunted because he was Jewish made little sense to Charles since the Third Reich fell—the persecution was uncalled for. Either the British really were apprehending Jews to appease Arabs, or some other underlying plot had to be simmering.

The soldier leaned forward. "I said—"

"Yes, he's my son." Puffing out his large chest, Jesse inserted himself between the soldier and Samuel. Elizabeth joined her husband.

The soldier maneuvered around both parents and whisked his cuffs out. "Samuel Rosenthal, you are under arrest for immigration smuggling." The clicking of the prongs closing around Samuel's wrists made Charles grind his teeth.

Jesse threw his arms up, barely missing the arresting soldier. "What is the meaning of this?"

The other soldier moved his hand to his holstered pistol.

Jesse stepped back. "Why you are doing this."

The soldier eased his stance. "Come hear for yourself, *if* you can keep a respectable distance."

Jesse motioned at Charles to follow. Each officer clasped one of Samuel's arms and marched him to a gentlemen's cigar room, where other officers interrogated Jews throughout the smoke-filled lounge. They approached the commander, who stood rigid with flared nostrils. "You've been a busy man, haven't you, Samuel?"

Jesse shook his head. "I assure you my Samuel has done nothing wrong, sir."

The commander ignored Jesse; his eyes pierced Samuel. "Haven't you!"

Samuel lowered his pale face and shuddered.

Jesse and Elizabeth crowded their son. "Tell him you have done nothing wrong," Jesse said.

"Yes Samuel," the commander said with a sneer, "enlighten us."

Though he'd vowed to avoid attracting attention, Charles bristled at the commander's tone and eased closer to his friends as Jesse reached his hand out. "Please, sir, there must be some kind of mistake. Samuel hasn't—"

"Your son violated our law! And you wonder why we've restricted Jewish immigration in Palestine?"

Jesse squinted. "I don't understand. You must be confusing my Samuel with someone else."

"We caught a luggage mate with a pocket full of money concealing illegal immigrants with no passports. The mate gave up Samuel's name."

Samuel kept his head down. Elizabeth wiped sweat from his face.

"Rabbi, your son deceived you. Zionist groups in New York and abroad are smuggling thousands of Jews into Palestine via reconditioned warships. We've detained ninety-seven violators from the belly of this vessel."

"Who gave you the right?" Samuel's cuffs jingled. "You are no better than Nazis!" He glanced at his father and shrugged, then lowered his head again.

"Samuel …" Jesse took a big breath and tried to blink away tears.

"Enough sentiment." The commander waved his white-gloved hand to a soldier. "Take him."

Charles' whole body tightened while guards ushered Samuel away. There'd be no need for any further confirmation of a British-Arab conspiracy. The blockade also validated skeptics who mocked Jesse for proclaiming God's promises to possess their own land. Now the ridiculing whispers of Jews trying to topple the British and Arab forces made sense. And when Charles set aside his feelings of friendship and thought logically, the rabbi's quotes from the old book sounded convincing, but had to be a fable.

"Where are you taking him?" Jesse's voice cracked.

The commander cocked his head back. "Cyprus."

When the door opened, Charles followed Jesse to a ship steward standing in the hallway, with Elizabeth right behind them. "Where is this Cyprus? Can you sail us there so I can get my son back?"

The steward frowned. "That's a bad place, Rabbi. It's an island off the coast of Turkey, that … ah … we don't sail there." He squinted. "I can't imagine why you'd leave America for Palestine anyway."

Jesse raised his hands and widened his eyes. "In Amos, chapter nine, verses fourteen and fifteen, the good Lord says: 'I will restore the captivity of My people Israel, and they will rebuild their ruined cities and live in them; they will also plant vineyards, drink their wine, and eat their fruit. And Israel will not again be uprooted.'" He pointed his finger at the steward. "And I will tell you something else: God will rescue my Samuel, because we will pray for his release."

The steward looked at Charles and rolled his eyes. "You don't know what you're getting yourself into, sonny. The best advice I can give is to sail back to New York with us."

"I'm just going to school there. Besides, I'm used to a big city."

The steward shook his head. "Haifa is nothing like any other city." He slapped his arms to his sides. "I've told you too much. Let me escort you back to your quarters."

Elizabeth stepped in his path. "We can find our way back!"

"Sorry, ma'am. Jews are not permitted to be unescorted while the British are present."

When they returned to their bleak quarters, an unnatural quiet loomed as the day's first sunrays crept through the portholes. Charles sat on his cot, rubbed his head and weighed the perils of entering the proclaimed "battle zone" against discovering the mystery behind that long-ago-hidden photograph behind his mother's mirror. And if traveling across the planet was far enough to hide from his father's toxic influence, it would be worth the risk.

Just when he was about to lie down, the ship's speaker blared a distorted call to disembark. Jesse and his wife approached, eyes red and puffy; they motioned and he gathered his luggage and followed them up the staircase. Halfway up he turned to look back, still thinking about the admonitions he'd received, when a woman advancing up glanced over her shoulder. "Martha's going to be devastated when we inform her of Joseph's arrest," she told her companion. "I knew if my best friend survived the death camp, he'd survive anything," an elderly man replied. "But another incarceration is going to kill him!"

Charles surfaced to the quiet deck and passed more somber faces; The first view of the Palestinian coastline glistening under the rising sun ran goose bumps up his neck—he'd finally put an end to his miserable upbringing. He wanted to raise his hands and proclaim his newfound freedom, but that would've been inconsiderate.

Seagulls squawked above as passengers inched forward, and when he came into view of the busy Haifa dock, he saw something stirring the water that put his jubilee on hold.

CHAPTER 2

With a barrage of indistinctive port sounds meshing, Charles squinted at two guards on a makeshift pier, hovering over divers who were bobbing around a British destroyer. His hand shading his eyes, he turned to a deck mate. "What are those divers doing?"

"They're sweeping for mines."

"Mines? As in explosives?"

The mate shook his head. "You've got much to learn about this place. Let me see your identification." He glanced at Charles' papers, then handed him a red card. "Hold this so they know you're not a Jew, and stow your passport in your suitcase. Someone could pickpocket you and sell it on the black market."

Charles nodded, and then peered at the docks, where people moving in all directions gave the appearance of a teeming Hollywood movie set. An ambulance with the Star of David on its side puffed smoke from its tailpipe, while nurses lingered. Dockworkers flexed their arms while they piled luggage onto a wagon. Policemen directed traffic laced with street marketers peddling everything from beads to handbags.

The bird's-eye view also revealed curious faces looking upward; some had the aimless eyes of the homeless, others displayed a hardened, criminal-like cast. But some had dipped brows with the familiar look of concern, waiting for loved ones to appear. Obviously, no one had informed them of the British invasion the night before.

Scraping noises revealed dockworkers dragging a ramp, and when Charles stooped over the rail, he saw the deck officer loosening a chain that had covered the exit. When passengers descended the gangplank, authorities herded Jews through a corridor of policemen leading to a refugee camp surrounded in barbed wire. Charles turned to speak with his friends, but they'd already ushered Jesse and his family down the line.

The racket on the wharf grew to a multilingual barrage as Charles put his feet to solid ground, gripping his luggage and bracing his elbows to ward off strangers who pressed against him. Peeking through a small opening in the crowd, he searched for the Rosenthals. He cringed at a piece of wood posted over a barbed wire gate labeled "Quarantine." Inside, children removed their clothes to be washed for disinfection, while others dipped their tin cups into a pot and sat at wooden tables. Many refugees were slouched over, moved slowly and stared at the ground. It reminded him of how unjustly the southern states of America segregated Negros.

When frantic voices called out names in various accents, he looked back and saw the ship's line had ended. A glaring official pointed him toward the main square, but he couldn't leave until he found his friends. His stomach sloshed from strangers bumping him; each one added ripples of pain to his already-throbbing head.

At the sound of a merchant's goods crashing to the ground, someone's fingers painfully dug into his shoulders. A cloth pressed against his mouth while his suitcase and knapsack were yanked away. He tightened his abdomen and shouted, but the smothering cloth muted him, while a scratchy fabric tightly wrapped around his upper body. Then a muscular person yanked and dragged him; his kicking feet no longer held him up.

When the abduction halted, the cloths whisked away and spun him into a stumbling daze. A bulky figure shoved him to the ground and Charles froze, seeing a grubby man flaunting a dagger. The noisy port behind the shipping containers tempted him to holler.

"You yell? I will knife you." The man showed his rotted teeth while he thrust the blade forward. "Give up your money or today you die."

The thief's smug expression resembled Father's evil grin each time he'd plunged Charles's head into a hot tub to apply scalp medicine. The smelly red liquid stung, but it didn't compare to the near-death experience of being held underwater when he rebelled against Father's coercion to hate Jews.

Charles gasped while another thief rummaged his suitcase. Then the bristle-faced man jerked him to his feet and yanked his billfold from his back pocket. The attached chain snapped and forced Charles face-first toward the dirty concrete. His glasses cracked on impact and cut his cheek, while the thud sent waves of pain through his skull. He rolled to his back, ears ringing.

The mugger stretched a grin. "Not bad, boy." He turned to his accomplice and flashed the bills. "He got seventy-nine American dollar." He smirked at Charles. "Just for that you not get beat up today."

If the thief had only known about the jackpot resting uncomfortably in his shoes, one thousand in cash and another forty thousand in a bank draft, his wicked grin would've been bigger.

The man loomed over him. "But if you report this to authority …" He rammed his dirty boot into Charles' side.

Charles doubled over as his insides exploded; darkness framed his outer vision.

A shadow crept over him. "I forget, welcome Palestine to you. Stupid American."

Charles struggled to rise, but fire in his ribcage constrained him and wheezing followed. He'd been used to bruises inflicted by Father, but this injury could be the end of him if he couldn't get up.

He waited until the thugs faded into the distance, then he stretched his shaky fingers on the concrete toward the dock. Every move snapped jabbing stings to his side. Through a crack in the shipping crates, he saw the crowd and whispered for help. He should have stayed on the ship like the steward suggested. What a waste to plan such an elaborate escape, only to die at the docks on the first day. Father might finally win: join his sinister group, or die.

Charles resisted his fading eyes, but they prevailed…

≈≈≈

Charles sensed the motion of the sea moving under the bed. When the room came into focus, he realized he wasn't lying on his cot aboard the ship—the journey was too vivid to be a dream. He tried to get up but his burning side wouldn't let him. The thought of Father bursting through the door for the bad-boy punishment increased his breathing. If Father were gone, Mother would be in soon to apologize for his injury.

He gazed around the room again, but didn't recognize the yellow walls and flowered bedspread. With effort, he slowly inhaled. "Hello?" He inhaled again. "Anybody here?"

Shortly after, a little girl poked her head in, then she darted out of sight. Not long after, the door opened to Jesse and his family.

Charles looked up at the people who encircled the bed: Their smiling faces showed resemblances to each other. Then, flashes of conversations with Jesse concerning ancient prophecies reminded him about Palestine, which made his stomach jitter.

"Welcome back, Charles." Jesse's tone cheerful, but his soon-after frown reminded Charles of Samuel's arrest.

He blinked his eyes, his hand reaching to the nightstand. "Where am I? Where are my glasses?"

"Try not to move. You have a few cracked ribs," Jesse said.

Charles looked at each of their nodding faces as Jesse introduced the family. He stretched to look at the floor, but the movement felt like a knife piercing his side. "Ugh. My suitcase. Where is it?"

Elizabeth put a red-stained bottle to the light. "This is all that's left from the crime scene. It's not yours is it? It stinks." She scrunched her nose just like Mother used to when Father would snatch it from her hand.

"It's my scalp medication," Charles replied. "So, where am I?"

Jesse set his hand to Charles' arm. "You're at my brother Jacob's. You will need to reapply for a passport at the American Embassy. It must have been in your suitcase. Good thing you dropped your knapsack in the crowd." Jesse held it up.

No one had shown him such kindness other than his only friend back home, David Walker, who'd enrolled at New York University just after Charles escaped. The family's gestures confirmed that real love wasn't just a fantasy he'd read about.

"Annie, where are you?" Jacob turned toward Charles. "She's a bit shy. Annie's brother Jonathan is not here, but you will meet him later."

Annie came in with a cute, but timid smile, and handed Charles a cup. "I'm eight years old."

"Thank you, Annie." He looked in the cup and flared his nostrils. "What is this?"

"It's *tnuva*," she said.

Sipping it, he scrunched his nose. "Nuva?"

"It's Hebrew for warm milk," Jacob said. "I'm sorry, many of the American luxuries are scarce in Palestine."

"It's okay." At least it soothed his scratchy throat.

Jacob's wife, Ruth stepped forward. "Be sure not to drink the water. Not from our faucet, or at the restaurants. You'll see locals drinking it, but they were raised with it. We boil ours first."

"How did I get here?" He blinked his eyes again and looked at the nightstand. "Where are my glasses?"

As Jesse finished relaying what had happened, Jonathan arrived, and Jacob introduced his son. Jonathan was a tremendous help in the days that followed. When he saw Charles stiff and hunched over, he'd unexpectedly come up under his arm and be his crutch so he could join the family for meals.

Each day, Charles asked to visit the Technion University. Knowing his parents were probably students there made him anxious for answers about their dealings back home—what language the foreigners spoke at their meetings—and the reason for the cash exchanged. Each time he pleaded with Elizabeth, she'd put her hand on her hip. "The doctor left me in charge. No leaving the house until I see you walk upright without pain on your face."

He could've left, but he owed the family the respect of cooperating, since they'd showed him uncommon hospitality.

A few days later, he approached Elizabeth in the living room and asked to travel across town again, when an inhuman wail broke the conversation. Elizabeth put a hand to her face. "Oh my, what now?" She scurried toward the front door.

Within seconds, everyone in the house bolted to the source of the screaming out front, nudging Charles out of the way one by one. Each painful bump caused flashes of the mugger's hideous face. He peered out outside, but couldn't see anything except the family huddled around the weeping rabbi.

His alarm turned to joy when the entire family locked arms, sang in Hebrew and danced the hora while circling around a frail but smiling Samuel. A lone tear dropped down Charles' face; he'd never seen Samuel smile. Unable to join the dance, he could still bob his head to the singing. Though he didn't believe in miracles, he couldn't deny how much this looked like one, because Jesse said God would rescue Samuel. Charles sensed he was supposed to see this event, as if something out there had tried to show him why others had faith.

The singing and praising of God ensued for at least twenty minutes. Then Samuel motioned to the family to sit on the lawn. "When the British soldiers bring me to their ship, I see flashing light in the ocean. Like a signal."

Jesse flung up his arms. "You see, God took care of you."

"Father, it was Jews in a boat, not God." Samuel pushed his hands forward. "So I push the two soldiers and I jump. The drop hurt when I *slapped the water*." He smacked his hands together, and little Annie jolted back. "I was freezing. Then, a little boat paddle near and they help me, while spotlights search the water. They tell me they are from the Irgun of Palestine."

Jacob crossed his arms. "Samuel, do not get involved with the Irgun. They're a *dangerous* group of Jews."

Samuel squinted at him. "They save my life, Uncle Jacob."

Jacob shook his head. "You must realize Samuel, they brutally attack the British. The Jewish Agency and the Haganah both condemn their violence."

Jesse put his hand to his beard. "Who are the Haganah?"

Jacob turned to his brother. "You know what Haganah means: the defense. They're the Jewish military in Palestine. Their objective is to keep us safe and defend our Promised Land. But the British despise them, so they operate in secret much of the time. If it weren't for the Haganah's presence, we couldn't ..." Jacob looked upon his children.

Charles came over and eased down on the lawn, fighting a groan. "Couldn't what?"

Samuel smirked. "The Arabs. They think this is their land. We say it is ours. They have millions of acres. We have no land! Our battle will not stop because they are friends with Nazis. They say their duty is to—"

"Samuel!" Jacob removed his hat and shook his head. "We have children present. And many of our Arab neighbors are good friends, who want nothing to do with violence. You will not be residing in my home if you continue to speak like this."

"My brother." Jesse stood. "This is our home now too."

Elizabeth stood and cleared her throat. "Charles is well enough to see his new school. Who wants to join him tomorrow?"

CHAPTER 3

When several crows cawed outside his window, Charles fluttered his eyes open and grunted, but the lingering pain couldn't quell his excitement. Soon, he might learn why he'd been brought up under such ghastly conditions, perhaps even why his father wanted to steal his inheritance that his grandfather had left him. He stretched upright, traveled to the kitchen and restrained an urge to wince when he saw Elizabeth. "I'm ready to go."

"I think the doctor would approve." She raised her index finger. "Just in time," she turned to the counter and handed him a small black box. "Your new glasses arrived this morning."

He opened the box, put them on and looked around the kitchen. "Finally. I can see detail again."

She put her hand to her chin as her husband often did. "Can I ask you a favor?"

"Sure. Anything you want."

"Ruth and I are having a dreadful time helping Jonathan with his schoolwork. Would you look over his assignments?"

Her request warmed him. He hadn't known what it was like being needed, until he met this family. "I would be happy to review them. I am a high school graduate."

"You are?" She raised her brows.

He took in a breath and tried to stretch taller. "Yeah. I'm eighteen."

She chuckled and covered her mouth with her fingers, then leaned in. "I'm sure you have your reasons, but you're not passing yourself off as an adult to me. You look ... maybe fifteen, sixteen at the most."

He wanted to flex his chest and protest, but it hurt too much.

Elizabeth relaxed her face. "No need to concern yourself, I'm not going to say anything. It's clear you're not the criminal type."

He looked around. "I'll be seventeen next month. I would be grateful if you kept that between us."

Jesse entered the kitchen with Jacob. "We'll give you a ride to the university if you like."

Soon after, Jacob's four-door black Chrysler putted up a hill and passed a sign that read "Carmel Valley." Jacob took the long route to bypass Arab villages, and weaved in and around horse carts that shared the streets with numerous British officials.

"This is like being thrust back in time," Charles said. "But at least the Hebrew signs are also in English."

Jacob nodded. "If it wasn't for the dual signage, I'd be entering an appliance store to get my suit tailored."

Charles and Jesse laughed.

"Why are there so many British soldiers?" Charles expected more bad news like what he'd heard on the ship.

Jacob cocked his head back and opened his mouth. Then he turned back around. "Yes, they're ... everywhere."

Turning the corner revealed several men on foot, their supplies loaded onto mules and camels walking beside them. The deep age lines on their faces and sluggish steps made them look tired. "Those are the farmers, Charles," Jacob said. "Many of them don't have the luxury of an automobile. You'll see them every day, stocking our markets with goods."

The tires hit every bump of the poorly maintained roads, which caused Charles to keep holding his ribs. "You didn't tell me. Why so many soldiers?"

Jacob remained silent while watching the road. Jesse turned. "Charles asked you a question."

Jacob glanced at Charles from the rearview mirror. "You've been a bit stressed ever since you got here. Why add to it now?"

Jesse narrowed his brows. "You would be stressed too, if you were robbed and beaten just minutes off the ship. Why are you being evasive?"

When they stopped at a light, two officials crossed the street in front of them. Jacob nodded. "How about those fuzzy Russian-looking snow caps? Different from California, right Charles? But I forget what they're called."

Charles leaned forward, deciding not to press Jacob for now. "I think it's strange that they carry swords on their sides. They look like they're on a lunch break from filming a movie."

When the light changed to green, Jacob accelerated and turned into the university's parking lot. Charles pulled the door latch before the car stopped. "It looks just like the picture I've seen."

The men tried to keep up while Charles strode to the front university sign, thinking about the photo that had led him to Palestine. He pictured his father and mother posing and holding him as a baby in that very spot. If their records were in the school, he might find out why they traveled to America in the first place.

When they entered the admissions office, Charles scurried to the counter, where a middle-aged woman addressed them in Hebrew.

Jesse replied in the same language, pointing at Charles.

She turned to Charles. "You speak English. Why are you here?"

"My name is Charles Devonshire, and I'd like to apply for your structural and mechanical engineering courses." He scanned the filing cabinets behind the woman, saw the "D" section, but realized his parents might have used another name if they attended there.

The woman pulled a binder out and set it on the counter. Charles lingered and glanced at the cabinets behind her again.

The woman peered over her glasses. "There was something else?"

One wrong decision, and his parents could get a telegram stating someone had inquired about them. "No, that's it for now." He led the way to the exit, his face staring at the marble floor.

"You can still spend time at the university library," Jacob said as they walked toward the courtyard. "I hear it's well—"

"The library!" Charles lifted his head. He still felt the pain of having to give away his duffle bag filled with his literary collections he had hidden from Father.

They stopped next to the courtyard garden. "How about we pick you up in an hour, we have a few appointments at the synagogue," Jesse said.

Charles nodded. "Why don't you make it two or three hours?"

Jesse tugged his watch chain. "We'll be back by three."

Charles headed to the library and pulled the giant mahogany door open, to see where Albert Einstein had given lectures as their first society president. His mouth opened when he assessed the medium-sized room with polished mahogany walls, cathedral ceilings and oak flooring. A sparkling chandelier lit the center quite nicely, while elegant wall lights and huge beveled windows illuminated the outer perimeters. He marveled at the plethora of books and tried to picture the famed professor at a desk when a woman standing on tiptoe, reaching for a paperback, halted his wandering eyes. His gaze ran up a pair of shapely legs to a trim waist. When she twisted to set a book on the counter, he tried to look away from her curvaceous form, because his pumping heart assaulted his healing ribs. She selected another volume, turned around, and their eyes locked.

He gasped, then averted his stare. He'd determined long ago not to treat a person as an outcast like he was, and wouldn't just because part of her chin had a jagged scar. Jitters ran up his chest as he refocused his eyes on hers, hoping she hadn't caught his shallow initial reaction. The wax-like edges running below her lips to the right of her jaw probably averted everyone's eyes at first glance.

Nothing could have prepared him for her grin turning into a wide smile, since women never gleamed at him that way. Certainly her next gesture would be a smirk when she got a better look at his hair; schoolmates back home had it in for redheads.

She extended her hand. "You coming in, Charles?"

He exhaled. "Ha … how did you know my name?"

"You are American." Her smile turned vivacious. "I am psy-kick. I know all names here."

He narrowed his eyebrows, fighting an urge to tell her the myths of telepathy were unfounded and not logical.

She placed her hand on the countertop and giggled. "I am kidding to you. The office … they ring me and say maybe you come. Want to tour the library?"

Her broken English charmed him as he gazed at her imperfect but inviting face, a gorgeous face otherwise with a pert nose, high cheekbones and winter-blue eyes. Most girls back home treated him with contempt, but at least she was trying to be kind—of course, that was part of her job.

The tilt of her head caused her brown hair to caress her shoulders. "A tour? You would like to see the books?" She stepped a little closer and waved her hand in his line of sight. "Hello, you are there?"

"I would love to tour you—" He shook his head. "I mean, I would like a tour."

She extended her hand. "I am Gladia."

He shook her hand, whiffed her sweet perfume and reminded himself not to fixate on her scar. Instead, her piercing eyes under lengthy eyelashes caused his heart to race again: he dropped his admissions papers. He had no idea how to tame his racing hormones, so he cleared his throat. "I am gladia to meet ... I mean, it's nice to meet you, Gladia." While bending to assemble the papers, he looked up over his glasses, while she put one hand on her hip—her pose made him fumble all the more.

Her raised brows probably meant she was mentally chastening him for scanning her slender body. Yet, she gracefully knelt and gathered his mess; her grin widened as she rose, then she pivoted and *tap-tapped* the edges against the countertop.

When she extended the neat stack, he rose and received them with only one thought: dig a hole and jump in. Certainly her next word would be "klutz" or "dunce."

She stretched her palm outward. "Come, let me tour you. We have books for every person."

He had no idea if her open hand meant she wanted him to hold it, or to walk with her. What a stupid thought; of course it meant to follow her. He walked next to her down the main aisle.

Her shoulder bumped him as they strolled. "Are you to attend next semester?"

It took some concentration to process her question. "I wanted to enroll in this semester, but I was too late."

"Sorry you miss it. Tell your subject to me and I show you where it is."

"I'm applying for engineering. But first I want to inquire about some previous students who attended here many years ago."

"*Engineering* ..." She swayed her shoulder. "I am depressed."

He hoped she meant "impressed," since her tone didn't sound negative. Girls back home hadn't cared about engineering, and the last words he remembered from one beauty were, "Get lost, bookworm."

She stopped at the edge of a bookcase. "Young, but interested in—"

"I'm not that young, I'm eighteen."

"Eighteen?" She glanced him over. "Hmm. What type of engineering?" She pointed down the "E" aisle. "We have many engineer course."

"How old are you?" He waved his hand. "Sorry, I'm out of place."

She smiled. "I am nineteen. Almost twenty." She must have noticed his blushing cheeks; but she resumed her pace without a negative expression.

He cleared his throat and stretched tall. "I might triple major since I like mechanical, structural, and electrical engineering. But I—"

"Triple major? Wow, that's going to be … what do you call it?" She looked up and squinted. "A *tall order*? You say that in America, yes?"

He nodded. "Yes, we do. You know American slang."

Her eyes narrowed. "What is sling?"

"I'll explain later."

She stopped in the middle of the aisle. "You like books?"

"I love books. All kinds. I've read five hundred and eighty-seven."

She turned to him. "Pages?"

"Books," he said emphatically.

She broke eye contact, which made him sigh inwardly.

"I love books." She pointed to a sign labeled "Travel." "I want to see America and Europe. Maybe we read together and you tell me about your country?"

There was no way he heard her correctly. After all, she was taller and older and way too beautiful to be interested in him. On the other hand, he'd never met a pretty gal who was enthused about engineering.

She raised her palms. "Are you okay?"

"Did you say read together?"

She broke eye contact again. "Do you like travel?"

"Are you kidding me?" He crossed his arms. "Europe is the second smallest continent with four million square miles. Technically, it's a vast ..." He pondered David's warning not to bog down girls with technical jabber. "Yes, I love travel. Would you like to read a book right now?" What a stupid question. Too soon. Now she'd probably tell him to scram.

"Yes," she replied. "On my lunch. Maybe you show me better English?"

A group of young men passed with deriding stares at her. She bowed her head.

Charles sneered at them as they passed. Still looking down, she grinned.

Charles was surprised they didn't visually mock him also. "Where are you from?"

She straightened. "Jerusalem. I move to Haifa in nineteen hundred thirty-seven. My brother Dov give me a place over the hill. Before I leave, my neighbors say, '*Yihiye tov.*' Everything will be okay. But I feel ..."

Charles sensed he struck a nerve. "You're Jewish?"

"Yes, but not what you call, umm ... devit. I mean ... how do you say not serious with faith?"

"Not devout?"

She nodded. "That is it. You see? You can teach me." She looked down again. "If you want." She glanced about. "Nobody else will talk to me."

"That would be wonderful! I speak good English..." He closed his eyes for a moment. Time to change the subject. "I'm curious, do you mind if I ask you a question?"

"Sure, you ask."

"During my passage here, several American Jews called this place their Promised Land. Are you of this belief also?"

Her radiance fled. "Come."

She grabbed his arm and rushed him to a door marked "Private." Upon entering, she closed the door. "You look like nice boy, but ... I not know you." She placed her hands on her hips. "You do not speak that!" She pointed her finger toward the library. "Arabs. They are in the room."

He stiffened his stance, but liked the fire in her face.

"You are new to Palestine, yes?" She motioned her hand with the question. "How long since you arrive?"

He raised his shoulders and dropped them. "A couple of weeks. I didn't mean to upset you, I was just asking a simple question."

She took a deep breath. "I am not upset. I get lunch in one hour. We can talk in the garden more." She raised her brows. "You understand? Umm ... what is the word?" She paused, her eyes wandered. "Culture lesson?"

He nodded. "That would be great." Wow. Self-conscious one moment, fire in her spirit the next, and then calm. What a bundle.

She opened the door and placed her hand on his shoulder. "You can sit over there by my place and fill out the papers if you want."

"Okay." He looked at her hand on him, wondering if her affection was a cultural mannerism, or a gesture that she liked him.

She walked him to a lone table and pointed at the window. "We will talk in the garden?"

He sat, wide-eyed, and lipped "Wow." "*Ahh* ... sure." He thumbed through the stack of admissions papers and tried to keep his face lowered, but his eyes drifted to the window overlooking the garden; he pictured them walking, laughing, talking, and then kissing. The garden fantasy evolved to dating, which turned into a wedding, then he got hold of himself just short of the honeymoon.

Later, when she approached, he made sure his eyes were on the applications.

"You ready, Charles?" She bent over and placed her hand on his arm. "We can walk if you like." She turned toward the side door.

Her scent was like standing in the middle of a botanical garden.

If he knew she was sincere, it'd be the ultimate opportunity to hold hands, but he couldn't take the risk of looking like an idiot again. He rose with his papers in both hands and slightly extended his elbow. She placed her hand on his inner arm and they walked out the door—plenty of contact to put his senses into overdrive.

After the usual pleasantries of a new acquaintance, she informed him of Palestinian mannerisms, and especially warned him to guard his speech. She also taught him Hebrew words, like "Shalom (hello)," which he already knew, and *"Be' Seder* (okay)," and *"Habub* (friend)."

She spoke with her hands motioning up and down as they walked. "I can tell you have much thought. You like interesting things like art, travel, history and famous persons. I have not met anyone like you. Where did you find this knowledge at the young age?"

"I'm not that young." He saw his hands mimicking hers as he talked. "I read a lot because I was caged in growing up, so books was all I had. But now, I'm relieved to have my freedom."

"Your home was like a cage? Do you not miss your parents?"

Even though he hated thinking about his parents, it would have been nice to tell someone about his life back home. "Not exactly."

She dipped her eyebrows. "Not exact?"

"Yeah, you know, like … I dislike them, I'll leave it at that."

"Why do you not like them?"

"It's difficult to explain. Another time, okay?"

She shrugged. "Okay."

31

Charles saw Jesse and Jacob in the parking lot. He hoped she'd feel the same way about him tomorrow, but that was unlikely. "I see my friends. Will you be here tomorrow?"

"No. I work Monday to Friday between class time."

"You attend school here?"

"That is why I work the library. I get better cost on class."

"What's your major?"

She beamed. "I want to be a math professor." She lowered her gaze. "If someone will hire me."

He balanced forward on the balls of his feet to raise himself a little. "I'd hire you. Especially for math: my favorite subject. If you ever need help, I would be glad to tutor you."

She tilted her head. "That is nice offer, but I hope … I do not make you sad. I am in second year of college. You are not in college yet. American high school math is not higher than college."

"I actually have a professor's level of math skills."

She furrowed her brows. "That is nice, but I am okay."

Her questioning expression should have alerted him to stop while he had a little dignity left. "I'll look for you Monday since I plan to study here." Though she'd probably avoid him.

"I will look for you too." She smiled. "Meeting you is a delight. Maybe you teach me better English and I will teach you Hebrew, yes?"

"I would love to teach you anything. I'm good at English." He dropped his head, remembering he'd already said that. "I'm really delighted to meet you too, Gladia. Till Monday." He walked away, disgusted with himself.

He got into the car and looked back to steal one last look, but she was gone.

CHAPTER 4

Looking at Jonathan's light blue bedroom walls, Charles smiled while emptying his knapsack. Since the Rosenthals offered him the room indefinitely, he wouldn't have to present his papers to the British and be scrutinized every time he came and went from a lonely hotel room.

Jonathan walked in. "Would you like a drawer to put your clothes in?"

The question made him study Jonathan's face. He'd found it difficult to accept kindness ever since Father surprisingly brought home a Christmas tree when Charles was eight. For the first time, he ran to claim his gifts on the day everybody else enjoyed presents, only to find empty boxes under each wrapping. Father laughed hysterically and said, "That should teach you! Never trust anyone, you foolish little boy."

"Charles? Do you want a place for your clothes?" Jonathan pulled out the top drawer.

"I would, thank you." He lifted his clothes from his cot and organized them into the drawer. "Come on, I'll make you a sandwich."

Walking down the hall, Samuel brushed by, followed by Jesse. "Where are you going, Samuel?" Jesse asked. "You promised to help build a pulpit."

"Out," Samuel said. A few seconds later, the front door shut.

"I'll make you lunch next time, Jonathan." Charles tried to hurry, but side aches reminded him to slow down. "Samuel, wait." His voice echoed across the front lawn.

"No." Samuel quickened his pace down the walkway.

Charles took a few steps and cupped his hands around his mouth. "Are you sure? I'm feeling cooped up."

Samuel turned and threw his palms up. "I said no!"

Charles had observed Samuel's nervousness all week, and assumed his Holocaust memories were still fresh. During their trip to Palestine, he'd awakened other passengers with screaming nightmares. Charles knew about nightmares, but couldn't imagine a death camp experience. He watched Samuel's figure shrink in the distance, and decided to follow. Pursuing Samuel through a vacant alley, he could hear Jacob's warnings in his head. His destination ended at the back of an old factory on the edge of town.

Samuel glanced about before entering, then Charles ambled to the shabby tin structure and put his ear against the cold door. When he entered, his nostrils flared from inhaling grimy vapors in a cobwebbed break room. A window illuminated crooked stairs that led to a door buried in a shadow; leaning his ear in, he heard muffled voices up there. He tried breathing deep to calm his pounding heart while he crept up rickety steps.

Reaching the top, he pressed his ear to the wooden door and heard voices murmuring in broken English, and others muttering foreign languages.

"Fellow Jews, I am Borus Yousofiv." A German accent towered over the others. "I introduce my inmate bud-dee who escape me from Buchenwald Nazi camp. Samuel Rosenthal!"

The crowd clapped.

"We are even now, since you save me from Cyprus."

Charles recognized Samuel's voice.

"How you climb the ship with rope, I cannot know. How many times did you stab the soldier who guard me?" Samuel chuckled. "I think you kill him ten times—good thing we have the ocean to wash the blood."

Charles gasped. He latched his hand over his mouth, hoping the door wouldn't open.

"It is good to make sure he is dead," Borus said. The group laughed.

Charles pictured the gory scene, and shuddered. He didn't like the Brits either, but likely, the soldier who hauled Samuel off had only been a few years older than Charles. And the fact that Samuel hadn't been hunted for the murder yet confirmed the governmental chaos he'd heard about.

"That's enough!" A new voice quieted the room. "For those who don't know me, I am Commander Dov Grunner. We are not here to murder or laugh about killing. Let us remember our objective: to destroy British assets, and avoid killing whenever possible. I am understood? I will read the code 'Purity of Arms' every meeting, because the Irgun are receiving a bad reputation."

Charles jolted when he heard the name "Irgun." Jacob had labeled them terrorists.

"'The soldier shall make use of his weaponry and power only for the fulfillment of the mission.'" Dov's English was better than anyone he'd heard in Palestine. "'The soldier shall not employ his weaponry in order to harm noncombatants or prisoners.'" His stiff British accent sounded like he was scolding the group. "Let us get into business."

"Charles?"

Startled, he spun around, squinted and made out a woman's silhouette. It sounded like ... "Gladia?"

"Why are you at this door?" She dropped papers on the upper steps. "How do you know this place—?"

The door behind him whisked open. Rough fingers dug into his shoulders and yanked him in; his glasses flew to the ground. "Wait a minute!"

One man pressed him against the wall while another shoved a gun against his stomach. "You spy on us! Who you are?"

Gladia walked in. "Let go. I know him."

Samuel stepped forward, eyes bulging. "*What* are you doing here?"

"You both know this person?" Dov stood tall and carried himself like a western rancher. "Take the gun out of his gut."

Charles put his hand to his wounded ribs. Dozens of eyes pierced him, with looks as if he'd just raided their homes.

"He is friend of my family." Samuel shook his head. "Maybe he followed me. Charles, you should not be here."

A short man pointed a stubby finger at Charles. "Menachem, our leader, will not be happy about this."

"It is okay, Borus. He will not tell." Samuel narrowed his brows. "Right?"

Charles froze. Bands of stress coiled down his throat as he recalled Samuel and Borus bragging about killing a sailor. Other than Gladia and Dov, the attendees had an aura that resembled Chicago gangsters.

Borus waved his arm. "He is American. We need to know he stay quiet."

"He is with Samuel and Gladia. He joins us now," Dov said. "Gladia my sister, you stay too."

"I can stay?"

Dov motioned his hand. "Sit. It is time you learn more about us."

She looked around the dusty loft, walked to the back and slid two chairs out. She looked at Charles and swayed her head, then gave the chairs a quick dusting.

Dov sat at a table below a pull-chain light while the others sat on wood benches under hazy shadows. "Because of hunting season, we double our efforts and meet here from now on."

Samuel sat across from Dov. "What is hunting season?"

Borus creased his face. "The Jewish Agency—our leaders—they arrest us. Many Jews condemn us, but they not mind results. We blow oil pipeline, chop telephone poles, destroy bridges and train track, because only force will drive our enemies out. This is why Irgun exists."

He stood, his boots clunking toward a drafting table used as a podium. "We tried peace, talk to Arabs and Brits, but we get mockery." He raised a newspaper. "Now I read from Histadrut Council: 'The perpetrators of terror, who call themselves the Irgun, are traitors!'"

The group booed.

"'They must be removed from our classrooms, banished from our workshops, and taken off our streets.'" Borus disturbed a cobweb when he rocked the podium. "Our own people, against us because we fight strong for this land."

Charles scanned the room without moving his head, eyed the door and then ran his hand past the bruise on his stomach where they'd shoved a gun into it. He wanted to walk out with Gladia and never return, but he also wanted to hear what they'd say next.

Dov stepped to the podium. "There is much division, but we desire alignment with the Jewish Agency and Haganah, to gain national independence." When he crossed his arms, the light revealed scars on his forearms. "Our leaders negotiate for peace in vein, because our Islamist enemy are still in partnership with Hitler's loyalists. *This* is why the Irgun exists."

Borus pointed to the volunteers; "'This is why the Irgun exists,'" they repeated.

Gladia grabbed Charles' wrist. In disbelief that her soft fingers were on him, he sat up and flexed his torso. But as soon as he did, he slowly exhaled to ease the tenderness.

Dov stiffened. "God gave us this land thousands of years ago! He called it 'a land flowing with milk and honey.' But in Leviticus chapter twenty-six, He warned our ancestors if they did evil, He would desolate the land and scatter our forefathers all over the world. Why do you think you all come from so many different counties?" He slammed the podium with his fist and Gladia flinched.

He held a chunk of dirt. "Much of this area was wasteland, not long ago. Even Mark Twain, in 1867 wrote: "Palestine is a desolate country given over wholly to weeds.... Even the olive and the cactus, those fast friends of the worthless soil, had almost deserted the country." Dov crumbled the clod and pebbles plunked down. "But our kinsmen have planted lush crops, because nobody can take barren desert and beautify it like God! He promised to draw a remnant of Jews back to this land and prophesied we'd plant gardens and eat our fruit." Dove shot his finger out. "You are that remnant!"

The fighters cheered. Charles had heard this from Rabbi Jesse, but thought it was only a zealous man's opinion; he was a big fan of Mark Twain.

Dov nodded firmly. "The Irgun will continue an offensive until we discourage the Brits to leave our land, just as our forefathers did to the Philistines in biblical days. We are David and they are Goliath!"

Everyone cheered. Charles had never been allowed to visit a church, so he marveled at how Dov's preaching motivated the hardened underground fighters.

Dov pointed northward. "The Brits have a land, the Arabs have even more. Not us. That is why God drew us here: to fulfill His promise in Ezekiel thirty-eight." He pointed toward Gladia. "My sister has brought scriptures called 'valley of dry bones.'" He nodded. "Please Gladia, pass them out, so everyone understands our mission."

Gladia passed a stack in each direction. Charles glanced at his copy and leaned in. "What is the valley of dry bones?'" he whispered.

Her lips touched his ear. "God say in Ezekiel, He will bring back Israel like raising a dead man from the grave."

Samuel fixed his gaze at Charles. "I think Charles needs to go home, right?"

Charles cleared his throat. "Well ..."

"No." Dov raised his hand like a traffic officer. "He knows who we are and what we do." He squinted at Charles. "Will you help us rid Palestine of the Brits?"

Charles looked into numerous piercing eyes; their bodies were bony. They had to be fresh out of the Nazi camps. He pondered the rumors about Palestine turning into a second Holocaust at the hands of an Arab leader, Al Husseini, along with his followers, the Muslim Brotherhood.

Samuel shook his head at Dov. "I don't—"

"It's okay." Dov motioned toward Gladia. "My sister is a good judge of character ... Charles?"

Charles swallowed to moisten his parched throat. He didn't want to appear weak in front of Gladia, but found it unimaginable to join such a fierce group.

"Dov my friend, he is not a fighter." Samuel looked back at Charles and motioned his eyes toward the door.

Dov shook his head. "He can work with Gladia as a messenger. He has no look of Irgun, perfect to avoid suspicion. He'll be safe with her."

Charles' heart surged. Now they were talking.

Dov came near him. "Do you want to join the Irgun?"

Charles clamped his jaw to hold back what he really thought: Between Arabs outnumbering them, Nazi's on the loose, and opposing British controlling everything, there'd be no chance of this ragtag group winning a nation. But working with a dame like her? "Count me in."

"Splendid!" Dov walked to the podium, curved two fingers and wiggled them back and forth. "Come."

Charles raised his eyebrows.

"It's all right ... come." Dov pulled out a Bible from a drawer and placed a pistol on it. The book resembled the one Rabbi Jesse carried.

Charles rose, his sight fixed on the gun, while he forced his rubbery legs forward. Borus lit a menorah and leaned over the table to click-click the pull-chain light off. Only the faint glow of noses and cheeks could be seen behind the candlelight.

Dove sent a piercing stare, then nodded at the gun. "Raise your right hand and repeat after me." He took Charles' hand and placed it on the pistol.

The gun was ice cold and different from any of Father's pistols.

"Charles. Your right hand?"

He raised it.

"I Charles," Dov paused. "What's your last name?"

Charles opened his mouth but nothing came out.

"Devonshire," Gladia said, standing behind him.

"I, Charles Devon-shire …"

Gladia moved forward and stood shoulder to shoulder with him. "Charles, you repeat," she said softly in his ear.

Too late to say no. "I … I Charles Devonshire." His mind flashed through all the warnings he'd received about Palestine's mayhem. "Give my body, my mind, and my being, without reservation or qualification to the freedom fighters of the Irgun. Under torture even unto …" Charles gulped. Did he just say death?

He looked at Gladia and gulped. "Under torture even unto *death* …" The words slipped from his lips. "I will never divulge the name of a fellow member of the Irgun." He'd have to have his head examined later.

Dov lifted two chalices of wine and stretched one to Charles. "L'chaim!"

"L'chaim," they all shouted.

Charles squinted at Gladia. "It means, to life," she whispered. "You know, like 'cheers'?"

Borus pulled the light chain and blew out the candles while Dov adjourned the meeting. As the room thinned out, Charles followed Gladia downstairs. "Thank you," he said as they reached the bottom.

She turned. "Why do you thank me?"

"You vouched for me when they suspected I was a spy."

She pointed upstairs. "I think it is good ... or ... luck to you, that you know me and Samuel. After Nazis and Arabs and British hunting them, they do not trust very easy."

He frowned. "I wouldn't be here, but Samuel has been so troubled, I wanted to see where he was going."

"You would have trouble too if you live in a death camp. These Jews deserve a home and that is why I help the Irgun. Not because I like what they do, but I must help our people." They locked eyes. "You depress me you are American and you help." Her eyes gleamed. "I like that!"

"Did you mean I *impress* you?"

She giggled. "I am sorry, wrong word. You *impress* me. I hope you keep teaching me."

He smiled. "I'd be happy to."

"I will teach you more Hebrew. Yes?"

"I don't know ... I can't seem to get my mouth to pronounce those words."

"Here. I show you the secret...." She put her supple fingers on his lips, and formed a round shape. She drew closer and puckered like she was going to kiss him. "Say, *Zu, Yan.*"

What was she doing puckering her moist, rosy lips inches from his? He restrained his urge to kiss her to avoid being slapped.

She dropped her hands and stepped back. "Something is wrong?"

"No," he said, breathy. "Ahh ... what sort of help do you do for the Irgun?"

"Many things. Deliver message, pick up something for Dov, teach English battle words like 'charge' and 'retreat.' It is important for fighters to know orders in one language for une … um …" She looked up again with her lips wide open.

Her pose made him look away. "Unity?"

"Yes, thank you, uniteen."

He turned back. "You teach English?"

She rolled her eyes. "Yes, but not good."

"I thought you would teach them Hebrew. Why English?"

"Jews come from fifty-six countries. Some of them, they know a little English. And Hebrew is not yet known to many; Our language was lost when our nation fell from the Roman Empire."

He raised his brows. "How is that possible? Successful battles require extensive communications."

"It is not easy, but we do it."

A newsreel from Father's collection flashed: horrific images of Nazis piling dead Jews into graves. He felt obligated to enlighten her about the reality of their impossible war, yet she didn't appear naive, and if he watched over her, maybe she wouldn't become a casualty. "I don't understand how foreigners can come to Palestine and know this is their Promised Land."

"Jews grow up with the Torah and prophets: Like Ezekiel, the paper I hand out."

Charles felt her pamphlet in his pocket. "So people from around the world come here because of some old book?"

"Yes, the scriptures. They guide them here. Americans, they call it Old Testament. You know this book, yes?"

Charles looked down. "I know what the Bible is, but my parents wouldn't let me read it."

"We believe it is God's promise to bring Jews here. Americans, they teach children Noah's ark. We learn the Promised Land and keep it for our memory. It is Ezekiel eleven, verse seventeen."

"What does it say?" He knew the prophecies well, but feigned ignorance to keep their conversation lively.

"It says, 'I will gather you from the countries that you were scattered to; I will assemble you and I will give you the land of Israel.'"

He squinted. "And you think from that verse that all these men, women and children have risked everything to come here?"

"Yes."

He was about to change his mind about her naiveté. "I hope this God is alive, because it will take a divine act to get you out of this—"

She put her hands to her hips as her forehead tightened.

"I still don't understand something: According to my rabbi friend, Israel hasn't existed in almost two thousand years. How can Jews know Palestine is the place?" A strange sensation came over him when he asked—as she opened her mouth, something already told him: God is the magnet, who draws His people.

She smiled. "Jerusalem is written six hundred times in scripture. That is how we—"

"Gladia, Charles, I take you home. Dov tell me."

They turned to see Borus at the warehouse door. Charles didn't want to get in the car with him, but it was less risky than walking home through Haifa after dark.

Borus stopped at Gladia's place first. Charles was thrilled to see her small cottage close to Jacob's.

After saying goodbye, she got out and began walking. Charles leaned forward, recalling he hadn't asked to see her the next day. By the time he rolled the window down, she'd already walked inside.

CHAPTER 5

The sun beamed through the early coastal clouds the following Monday, and Charles enjoyed the fresh breeze as he walked to the Technion. Though he passed a massive British tank and a few dozen soldiers, his apprehensions about staying in Palestine subsided. And with his new connections in the Irgun, he might be able to gather intelligence about his parents without them being alerted.

He entered the library and saw Gladia leaning from a stepladder to shelve books, her brown hair flowing. He recalled her soft fingers on his lips, and the exhilarating sensation it caused. Finally, something more than his troubles occupied his mind.

When she descended, two young men glared at her scar, but when she grinned at him instead of looking downward, he returned her smile. He stepped into their path and scrunched his face.

When she turned to straighten some magazines, he considered their common interests: They both loved books, valued education and wanted to see Europe. And over the weekend, he'd begun to believe she liked him. Still, he had no idea how to handle a female relationship.

Nerves fluttered his belly. "Gladia, s-shall we go to the cafeteria today?"

She turned and squinted. "Cafa-terr?"

"No, caf-a-ter-ria."

When she shook her head, he turned toward his desk. It must have been too soon to ask her to share a meal.

"What is caf-a-ter-ri?"

With her question, it occurred to him that a university in an underdeveloped area might not have food on campus. He turned back. "*Ahh* … it's a place where people eat. Like a restaurant."

She reached behind the counter and held up a sack. "Lunch?"

Charles loved how she fluttered her long lashes when she didn't understand something. "Oh. You already have … that's a nice lunch … sack." Warmth filled his cheeks along with an urge to crawl under a table.

She bent her lips upward. "You teach me better English at lunch, yes?"

He sighed from within. "Sure. But whatever we do? I just want to spend time with you." He turned to regain control of his blushing cheeks, but he lost his breath, so he headed to the technical books section.

From that day on, they met in the garden daily. Despite their communication gaps, she was the first person to show interest in his passion for exotic destinations and famous people. Even David would tire from his vast knowledge accumulated from reading.

As they walked their usual garden route scented with honeysuckle, she beamed with a wider than usual, gleaming smile, as if she had a new reason for happiness. "Charles, I like the English lessons. You have big knowledge of math too. Other Americans I meet, they are not like you."

He took in slow breaths and determined not to stutter. "I think, I'm … mmm … falling for you."

She stopped in front of a patch of pink roses and placed her hand on his wrist, which made him separate his fidgeting fingers. "Are you okay? When we walk, you breathe … not normal. Your face, it gets red. Are you having headaches?"

"I'm okay." Except for her touch that ran chills up his arm. He resumed their pace. "No headache today. And I really appreciate your Hebrew lessons. Though I still can't pronounce those words." He hoped that didn't seem like a shallow attempt at getting her fingers onto his lips again—although it was. "I, uh, wanted to ask you—"

She stopped again. "That is right. Yesterday you look like you want to ask me."

His nerves jittered as he scanned the area, ready to ask the big question. "I've learned why the British opposed Jews. But why are so many Arabs hostile to you?" He grunted inside at another frustrating, cowardly moment.

Her face reddened. "It is not right. It is like Dov say." Her eyes scanned the area too. "Arabs have millions of land units. But we have nowhere to live but here. And they will not listen when Jews ask for peace."

"They remind me of my father. He's so ... so black-and-white!"

"You are angry. I do not see you this way before. What do you mean, he is black and white?"

"I'm sorry, I shouldn't have mentioned him. Let's talk about something else." He walked toward the library.

Following, she glanced at her watch. "I have to work. We should talk more about your father. Maybe it will help you feel better."

He crossed his arms. "I feel fine. He's out of my life now and I don't need to speak about him."

On their walk back, more students sent the kind of looks he used to get when he'd entered high school senior classes as a freshman. Her pretty lashes flickered as she paced faster. He took a chance and lightly bumped shoulders.

≈≈≈

Thursday morning, Charles looked up from his studies to see a middle-aged man walk toward Gladia and place a book on the teak countertop. His graying beard made him look too old to be a student. Charles moseyed closer and began to inspect the magazine rack.

"The book was informative." The man spoke good English. "If you ever visit Tel Aviv, come to my deli and have a sandwich." He tipped his hat and left.

Gladia peered around the room and spotted Charles, then stuffed the book into her purse. During lunch, she mentioned nothing about it. "You like to come to Tel Aviv tonight? I will purchase a hat."

His heart leaped. "I'd love to go." He tried to discern if it was a date, or just an errand. No matter, it was a major breakthrough.

After she went back to work, he engulfed himself in his studies of structural engineering until five o'clock, when she came over carrying her bulky purse. "I can ride you home, then I will come back at seven."

He raised his eyes above the book and prepared himself to ask her to dinner. "I'm ready." He slapped his book closed.

At seven sharp, Gladia knocked at Jacob's door, and Charles brought her into the living area. The family welcomed her with hugs: especially twelve-year-old Jonathan, whom Ruth had to detach from her. Charles thought it was strange how Gladia pretended not to know Samuel, until he realized she wasn't supposed to know him; the Irgun was detestable to conservative residents. Her polished undercover performance impressed him.

Elizabeth came out of the kitchen with a tray of cookies. "And where are you two going?"

"We will travel to Tel Aviv. I am to purchase a hat."

"It's almost dark," Jacob said. "You really shouldn't be out at night."

"It is okay, we will go, then come back. I shop alone, but since I meet Charles, I ask him to come."

Neither Jacob nor Jesse relaxed their faces.

≈≈≈

As they left, Jonathan peeked out the window. "She speaks pretty good English for a native. What happened to her chin?"

Ruth placed her hands on her hips. "Jonathan. You don't comment on people's physical aspects like that. It's not polite."

Elizabeth stood behind Jonathan and watched the car doors thump shut. "I wonder if they like each other."

Jonathan kept his nose to the window. "I *know* Charles likes her."

"And how would you know that?" Ruth asked.

"Ah ... I just know it, that's all."

≈≈≈

A half hour's drive down the coast, and Gladia parked in front of Zlotnicki's Kosher Deli. Charles looked at the quaint red booths through the tall glass panes. "I thought you were going to buy a hat. Why are we stopping here?"

"I am hungry. Do you want food?"

Darn. The dinner invitation would have been easier than he'd thought. "I ate already, but I'll get a soda." They walked in and he pulled his billfold out, but she insisted on paying. His discomfort at letting her buy vanished in his enthrallment at how her hands animated when she was insistent.

She pulled the book out and scooted it across the counter. Then she pulled out money that looked fake, reminding Charles he hadn't converted his US currency to grush yet. She cracked a sly smile, and by the time she turned back to the counterman, her face straightened. "I think you lose this book, sir."

The man picked it up, and she slid her food bill to him. He glanced at the book. "Thank you ma'am, I was looking for this." Then he scooted the money back. "On the house."

Charles analyzed her swift motions, like an actress on a stage, while she scooped up her currency and slipped it back into her purse. Instinct told him not to question her. But if she was on an assignment, she should have told him; they were supposed to be working together.

After she ate, they climbed into the car and she laughed hysterically. Charles couldn't help laughing also. "Why are we laughing?"

She extended her hand flat, beaming a big smile. "Congratulations, Charles!"

He touched her hand, not thinking it was a handshake, but she shook it with vigor. "What?" he said.

"We do our first mission together!" She flung her hands in the air. "You did it, my friend."

She'd called him "friend." That was nice, but he was annoyed. "Why didn't you tell me?"

"I know you nervous." She put her hand up. "Wait. I know you *would get* nervous. Right?"

"Your English is improving." So much for the date idea; the outing had obviously been business only.

"I hope you do not get mad. I want you to see, it is easy." She looked down. "We need this land, and if we believe, God will give it to us."

He held back pessimism, but if those ancient promises were true, why would some god bring Jews to a land filled with people who despised them? "I could never be angry with you. But what was the purpose of this delivery?"

"They do not tell. They can-not get caught with messages, so I do it for them. They like me because I do not look Irgun." She ginned at him. "And you do not look Irgun. After we do more, then you do some alone. Only if I tell them you are good … comrade." She smiled, her eyes gleaming.

She reached into her purse. "We need to get you a driver license and one of these."

He jolted his head back. "What are you doing with that?"

"You know we need a pistol. Yes?" She gripped the brown handle, her muscles flexed as she locked her arms just above her knees.

His heart rushed while he waited for her to load the chamber. That was what Father used to do. Except it would be pointed at him when he cocked it. "Is it loaded? You haven't shot anyone have you?"

"Only a fake-man at the field." She pierced him with a haunting stare. "I would if I had to save a life." She retracted the gun and put it back in her handbag. "We all carry one. You will too."

His neck tightened with tension: "Is it loaded? I … I don't want one!"

"Hopefully, you will not need it, but Dov will tell you to have one." She started the car.

As she drove north up Highway 2, he still wanted to ask her on a date, but now he couldn't understand why. She gave every impression she could use the gun without hesitation. "I had a nice time with you," he said.

"Me also. I mean, me too." She parked the car in front of Jacob's house. "Charles? I want to ask you."

Charles swallowed. "Ss-sure. You can ask anything."

"Maybe you will think it is strange."

"Ask me anything, really." When she cut the motor, his heart raced. Maybe she'd invite him to her house for dinner or possibly kiss him.

"Your hair. Why is it half red and part black?"

He slid next to her and looked in the rearview mirror. "Oh no. They don't have mirrors in Jacob's house, except Ruth's handheld. I forgot to apply my medicine."

She moved her face close to his. "Medicine?"

He scooted back to avoid doing something prematurely. "Ever since childhood, the doctor said I'd lose my hair if I didn't apply this medicine to my scalp. It's stinky and turns my hair red."

She shrugged. "I have not heard of that. I will see you tomorrow?"

"Yes. With my hair completely red again."

As he strode to the house, he saw a silhouette disappear from the front window. Judging from the size, it was Jonathan, spying. When he walked in, Jonathan stood at a distance with a wide grin. Charles narrowed his brows. "Why are you standing there grinning?"

Jonathan looked both ways. "She's ..."

"She's what?" Charles crossed his arms.

Jonathan blushed. "She has nice hair."

"Oh? You like her hair, do you?"

Jonathan nodded. "But she's ... I think she's too old for you."

Charles began walking to their room. "You don't know what you're talking about."

CHAPTER 6

October 1945

With over a month of trying to ask her out, Charles tapped on the library doors before opening hours, his breath forming fog on the glass.

Gladia clicked the lock. "You are early. Nice to see you." She latched the door behind him. "I clean windows until we open."

"I'll help." He followed her to the large beveled glass that showcased the garden. "Today, I'm going to teach you contractions."

"That is nice, thank you. What is contrat-yuns?" She picked up a rag and wrung it out in a bucket.

He picked up a towel, yet could only watch, as she stretched her slender body to wipe the glass. Her arms moved efficiently, but her face showed distress by the creases on her forehead.

He dipped his cloth in the bucket and wrung it. "What's wrong?"

She stared out the window. "I guess you know my face. You watch me. I know."

His mouth hung open. He must have looked her body over too many times for her liking, and now she was ready to scold him.

She turned, her rag dripping, and relaxed her stance. "It is okay. Everybody watch me. But you watch me ... nice. Others? They do not look at me like you." She sighed. "Dov tell me at breakfast he is traveling to Tel Aviv. The Irgun and Lehi commanders ... they get notice from Haganah to meet."

Charles put his cloth down. "I know who the Haganah are, but who are the Lehi?"

"They are freedom fighters, but more, *ah* … violent. You remember Dov talk about hunting season? It started when Lehi assassinate a British official." She crossed her arms. "They got arrested and hanged. Now, punishment for all Jews is worse. We can go in jail for being Irgun if our own people turn us in, or the Brits catch us."

A chill engulfed Charles. "We can be imprisoned?" Hopefully she was misinformed. "What type of sentencing do Irgun messengers receive?"

"It is hard to explain because you have law to protect you in America. We do not have that. Jews are not equal, so any punishment can be given. That is why we fight. I believe your people do the same when the British rule your country. Did they not resist at the Boston Tea Party?"

He smiled. "You know American history. *Impressive*. I never thought of the parallel, but you're right, there is a similarity how both our peoples contended with the same rulers."

"Now I get afraid because Dov could be arrested. He is my only family." A tear dripped from her eye.

Her face tugged his heart—he'd never met anyone who lost their entire set of relatives to brutal murders. He'd never held a woman either, but wanted to comfort her, so he awkwardly circled his arms around her. "There is hope," he whispered. "Look how America turned out." He pulled her in a little tighter. "Your nation could be mighty too someday." He cringed as soon as he said those words, but they just came out.

Her head remained lowered, arms dangling. He didn't want to betray her with empty words. Jesse's analogy about some deity working miracles for those who put their faith in God, just wasn't logical. It was time to come clean and tell her the truth. "I need to—"

"Thank you." She lifted her face; her soft eyes stared into his. "I am going to love you for being my friend. I have a bad dream they will hang my brother and now you make me better."

He closed his eyes, not believing what she just said. He'd have to wait for another time to be honest so he wouldn't discourage her. And though part of him had wanted out, something more than just being close to her compelled him to at least try to help Jews birth a nation.

≈≈≈

Charles looked up to see Samuel walk into the library. With his strange talent for not making any noise when he moved, he sat across the table.

Gladia walked over, while Samuel placed his scarred hands on the table. "Dov. He wants to meet you both tonight. Usual place."

"He is okay?" Gladia's tone perked up.

Samuel looked at her. "Of course."

At quitting time, she looked at him. "Maybe you can come to my house and I cook dinner? Then we see Dov."

"Dinner? Yes." He turned his head and mimed, "yes!"

≈≈≈

Just before dark, they entered the warehouse and climbed the rickety stairs. Charles leading, he halted midway and stared at the door, feeling his stomach, where a bruise had formed a few weeks before.

Gladia tapped his back. "You going?"

"*Ah* … yeah."

Walking in, they saw Dov thumbing through documents on the round table. "Great. I've been expecting you." He stood and shook Charles' hand. "You are treating my sister well, yes?"

Gladia handed him papers. "We treat each other fine."

Dov slapped Charles' shoulder. "There are developments with the Irgun that concern you, my new friend."

Charles didn't like the sound of Dov's words, but as usual, he was intrigued with espionage because it required intelligent planning.

"The Haganah commander, Moshe Sneh, shared disturbing news." Dov paced. "Decades ago, the British Labor Party declared support for a Jewish state with their Balfour Declaration. But the war has ended and they've reneged. David Ben-Gurion, whom we hope will be prime minister, tried to negotiate a compromise, since their ridiculous blockade caused thousands of Jews to perish."

Charles knew Dov wasn't exaggerating, having seen the British behavior, much like their ancestors' brute force toward the Colonies in pre-America. Each week he gained a little more insight why Jews were so adamant to fight to the death for their own nation, as the American pioneers did.

Dov slapped the podium. "We're tired of being treated subhuman, while Brits make concessions for Arab oil. Thus, Ben-Gurion secretly met with an American military advisor, Colonel Mickey Marcus, who pressed him to unite our forces. They announced all fighters to be one striking force." He grinned. "The hunting season is over!"

Gladia clapped.

Charles found it unthinkable how the Jews divided themselves in the first place. Various groups were scattered throughout Palestine, some non-violent, others vicious. One band within the Irgun, not acting under Dov, retaliated by hanging a British sergeant in the street, a warning attached to his chest about a booby trap waiting for anyone who tried to cut him down. On the other hand, there was the Jewish Agency, which had exhausted peace plans with the Arab Legion.

"Uniting our forces will be the turning point." Dov's emphatic tone jolted Charles out of his thoughts. "The commanders are discussing strategies to fight all three Goliaths: the British, the Arabs and Nazis."

Charles raised his finger. "With Hitler dead, I thought Nazis were in hiding."

Dov shook his head. "Arab nations gave those war criminals new identities to blend in. Loyal Nazis are still trying to carry out their Fuhrer's dream, and they're all around us."

Gladia's eyes moistened. "Nazis help the Arab riots that kill my parents when Dov save me. He was a British officer then."

Charles looked at Dov and stepped back. "You were a British officer?"

"Relax, my friend. Thirty-two thousand Jews fought in the British army to defeat Germany. That's where we gained our military experience and knowledge of how they operate. Soon we will strike much more effectively! And this is where you come in."

Charles leaned forward. "You saved Gladia?"

"Another time. Listen. Commander Sneh is searching for a covert operative to deliver secret plans to our Zionist posts abroad. We need someone intelligent who won't arouse suspicion."

Charles paced. He should urge Gladia to leave Palestine with him, so she won't end up like her parents. "You must have other qualified men to carry out this initiative." He loved the attention, and Dov's trust, but he'd already experienced more violence than any normal person should endure.

"Yes, but we don't have a young American with your gifts." Dov crossed his arms and shot a glance to his sister. "Gladia bragged about your memory skills."

Charles looked her way and they smiled at each other. That knowledge just made it easier to ask her out.

"The commanders want to test your photographic memory, because our secrets are too sensitive to be written. Couriers have to deliver critical messages verbatim, from memory—the slightest detail missed could cost lives."

Charles' thoughts turned to his original goal: an advanced position with the Resistance could grant him better access to investigate his parents. He'd had no opportunities so far.

Gladia examined Charles' face and put her hand on his back. "Maybe he does not want to use his mind like that. It sounds dangerous."

Dov shook his head. "No more danger than living in Palestine. Americans are enemy number two around here." He turned his eyes to Charles. "I heard your passport was stolen. Those are usually sold on the black market, so you're already at risk."

Charles' heart dropped. The last thing he needed was unnecessary attention by the sinister inhabitants of Palestine.

Dov gathered documents from the table. "You think it over."

Charles looked at Gladia and cleared his throat—he loved her concern. "I will do it."

Clumps echoed up the steps, so Dov took his position behind the podium. "It's time for our meeting." He pointed his finger at Charles. "You have honored us today."

Gladia tightened her face at Dov. Charles cupped his hand to her ear as the room gathered with volunteers, "You said, we all need to do our part."

Chills prickled his neck as she put her lips to his ear. "I do not like it."

While the freedom fighters filed in, Charles eyed each of them, wondering if they were all killers, until he spotted young women who were only a few years older than himself.

Dov motioned for them to sit. "Some have asked me what is a Jew's crime? Being Jewish? Entering our Promised Land? According to some, it's living and breathing. God caused the fall of the Nazis, and the demise of the Roman Empire when they attempted the same genocide almost two thousand years ago. The Crusaders from the first millennium are gone too. So are the Philistines, Jebusites, the Amorites, and every other nation that ever tried to exterminate Jews. Yet we remain." Dov grinned. "We must fight hard every day to prevent our enemies from exterminating us. And today, we have a new ally to help undermine our foes."

He thrust his hand out. "Charles, you bring us great honor as the first American youth to volunteer in the Irgun. We hope many will follow your example."

Everyone applauded. Charles felt pride since he'd never been recognized for anything other than straight A's in school. But now, regret deepened from harboring lies with people who trusted him. From that point, he'd look for an opportunity to confess his true reason for coming to Palestine.

"Charles," Dov whisked his hand. "Come up here."

Charles turned to Gladia and raised his brows. She shrugged. He rose, took a few steps and stopped short of Dov's reach.

"Charles has a unique advantage." Dov extended his hand toward him. "He looks and talks nothing like any of us. He can go places we cannot." Dov turned to a desk drawer and pulled out a pistol.

Charles stared at the firearm and reassessed the decision he'd just made. He thought Gladia was exaggerating about all members possessing weapons.

Dov held the barrel and extended the handle toward him. "It is with great honor I present you with this Beretta pistol. May you never need it."

The room fell silent while Charles wiped his clammy palms on his trousers, remembering how Father used to point a gun at his head; Pulling the trigger, he would claim he couldn't remember if a bullet was in the chamber.

Dov stretched the gun farther. "Go ahead, take it."

Charles imagined a bullet in his leg after discharging the firearm accidentally.

Then, he caught Gladia's eyes. She grinned, looked down and slightly shook her head. Looking up, her grin morphed into a wide smile.

Dov stepped forward, giving Charles no choice but to accept the pistol. "Don't be troubled, it's not loaded yet."

After the meeting ended, Dov came over. "Charles, I want Gladia to pick you up at ten o'clock tomorrow morning. She will bring you to a rendezvous point in Haifa port." He leaned in. "Bring your pistol. We won't load it until we train you to use it. From the port, we'll proceed to Tel Aviv to meet with Commander Sneh."

Charles hated the words "Haifa port." His tender ribs still reminded him of the cruel welcome to Palestine.

≈≈≈

Charles woke the next morning to pings of dancing rain on the roof and performed his morning ritual of reading several pages of Einstein's theories.

"Charles, your ride is here," Ruth shouted at ten sharp.

Jonathan hurried toward the window, while Annie placed her hands on her hips. "Watch out Charles, Jonathan wants to *steal* your girlfriend."

Jonathan stopped and Charles halted. "What are you doing, Jonathan?"

"Nothing." He backed away from the window.

Charles left and entered Gladia's car. "Hi."

"Hello." She grinned when his eyes gazed at her lightly beach-tanned legs. "I am proud of you, Charles. You have come far in little time."

"It's because I have a great teacher."

"I hope you make the good decision today." She tried to smile by bending her lips upward. Charles loved how genuine she was. He could never tell what Mother felt because Father always scolded her for making honest expressions when she didn't think he was looking.

Gladia turned down Highway 2 toward the docks and shook her head. "I still not ... I don't like it. I will miss our lunch together. I need more English teaching and—"

"No one has ever needed me. Do you realize how this makes me feel? I admit, I'm divided over this assignment, but I've been getting this pressing feeling to at least try and help create a nation—and I don't know why."

He stared at the raindrops that melted over the windshield and wondered why he said that aloud. She obviously liked him, so he should ask her on a date instead of climbing the ranks of the Resistance. "Gladia, I want to ask you …"

She glanced over and bit her lower lip, which completely derailed his focus. "Yes?" She looked back at the road. "You do that often."

"Do what?"

"You say, 'I want to ask you something.' Then you are quiet. Like in a trance."

"I do want to ask you something, but …" If she said no, it could ruin everything.

"You act strange. You are nervous to meet the commander?"

"Yeah, a little I guess."

As they arrived at Haifa port, he closed his eyes, annoyed with himself.

"Are you getting the headache?"

"I'm okay."

She stopped the car, slid over and hugged him. "Luck to you, Charles."

"That's good luck to you," he said with a smile. Even a headache couldn't keep him from reciprocating her affection. If it weren't for his jitters, he would just kiss her and get it over with.

Borus' car lights flashed; He'd parked a few hundred meters from where Charles had been mugged. "What about the question—?"

"Thanks for the ride. Maybe we can talk tonight." He trotted to Borus' car and climbed in the backseat.

Dov turned around and stretched a cloth between his hands.

Charles' throat tightened. "What's that for?"

"Nobody knows this location until they've been a member for long time."

"I put it on you." Borus received the cloth from Dov and tied the black fabric around Charles' head.

Winding along the coast, Dov coached Charles with the proper way to greet the commander and what to expect from the interview. When they parked, Charles removed the blindfold and cleaned his glasses to take a second look at an old house with faded pink stucco. When Dov opened the door, a fresh Mediterranean Sea breeze rushed in. "Why are we stopping at someone's house?"

They chuckled at him.

Borus stayed behind while Dov walked Charles inside. The roar of ocean waves faded when he shut the door. The scent of ink and paper ran up his nose. His mind went to work, taking mental snapshots of men and women casually dressed, carrying stuffed folders and writing on chalkboards. Red-hued Persian rugs covered most of the dark wood floors, with the walls populated with notes, charts and maps. An elderly woman approached and led them under an archway to a study with dozens of books lining shelves, then motioned to an antique red-velvet sofa for them to sit.

After Charles had read the spines of every book, a tall, stout man walked in. "Dov, Charles, sorry to keep you waiting."

Dov rose and stretched his height up to match the man's. "That's okay, Commander. Thank you for seeing us."

Charles stretched his body, his head barely coming to the men's shoulders.

The commander placed his hands on his wide hips. "Charles, I've heard much about you. I want you to know you are welcome here." He shook Charles' hand with the firm grip he'd expected.

"Thank you, Mr. Sneh … ah, Commander."

"You can call me Moshe in private, and Commander in public."

"Yes sir," Charles replied.

"No, it's *Moshe*," he said, chuckling.

The commander's unexpected friendliness caused Charles to recall what he'd heard about Jews having an appreciation for high achievers.

Moshe extended his hand to Dov. "We are grateful for your service and referring this fine young man. Carry on."

"Thank you, Commander." Dov nodded at Charles. "Enjoy your stay."

Charles liked being recognized as a young man. The Irgun always referred to him as a boy.

Moshe put his hand on Charles' back and motioned to walk. "Charles, there are things I can disclose, and things I cannot. Right now, we have a new problem, and I think you might be able to help us." Moshe paused in the hallway. "Are you interested?"

"Yes, sir. I mean yes, Moshe."

They entered a messy office with folders and files piled high. Moshe pointed to a chair as he sat at his desk. "Please sit. Let me explain our problem. Then, we can assess if you are right for the job. But first I must ask you something...."

Moshe leaned forward, his hand on his chin. The silence caused Charles to twist his fingers, while Moshe stared like a bullfighter facing off an adversary.

Charles knew that look and recalled Father's daily scrutiny. The importance he'd felt left as a bead of sweat made his temple itch. The distant shortwave radio chatter also reminded him where he was: the Haganah's intelligence office—if Moshe knew his secrets, he could be handed to the Brits and deported immediately.

Moshe finally sat back. "Charles, we have to be cautious of who we work with. We have many questions."

If Moshe resembled Father at all, he'd have tough inquiries, like why he really left home, where his money came from, and why he entered Palestine with a fabricated passport. The concealment exasperated him.

"Charles. Will you answer honestly?"

"Yes, Moshe." They couldn't be that smart and know everything. But then again, Elizabeth had seen right though him when he lied about his age.

Moshe escorted him down to a basement, past a communications room filled with radios and wiring, and ended up on the far side where a lamp illuminated a corner. An elderly man and woman reclined on red mats at a round table, inches off the ground. An assortment of unleavened bread, dipping bowls, and bottles of wine sat atop a white cloth with blue stripes. The couple plied him with endless questions. And though he didn't like lying to nice people anymore, he still feared giving up secrets, and risking deportation.

After a buzz from the vino, his eyelids wouldn't quit tugging downward. The couple brought him back through the chatter-filled communications area and up to Moshe's office.

"So you will be there?" Moshe said into the telephone receiver, then shook his head. "Okay, we will expect you at seven o'clock tonight, thank you." Moshe slammed the phone down. Charles flinched. The receiver already had a nice-sized crack on it. "That will be the sixth peace meeting we have initiated with the Arab League. There's no reason to believe they'll show this time, but we'll be there." He leaned back in his chair. "I'm sorry, have a seat. You look tired. Shall we continue tomorrow?"

Charles stared at the pile of documents on the desk and wondered what they contained. "We're not done?"

Moshe shook his head.

He shrugged. "We can proceed."

Moshe stood. "Okay, come this way so you can rest before we begin phase two."

"I don't need to rest." His head rushed when he stood to follow Moshe. "And those charts we passed in your communications room? They're not laid out efficiently."

Moshe stopped in the hall and lowered his chin. "What are you talking about? Nobody would have let you into that room except to pass through it."

"I couldn't help notice how your charts lacked ease of readability. I can rearrange them with color-coded annotations to direct the viewer to high-priority sectors faster. For example: red would stand for urgent matters, orange for medium, and so on. That way, decisions can be made quicker when your commanders radio in, and it could save lives."

Moshe put his hand to his forehead and chuckled. "Amazing."

He analyzed Moshe's face, but couldn't read him. While other kids played outside, he'd learned to read facial expressions from psychology books—that way he'd know if Father was suspicious to his sneaking through the forbidden zones of his home.

Moshe led him to a padded room next to his office and handed him a stack of papers. "Please read and sign these confidentiality agreements. I will be back at zero-three-hundred." He patted Charles' back and chuckled again. "I guess we have to watch what we expose you to."

Moshe smiled as Charles entered his office yawning. "Thank you for your patience. I'm sure you are wondering why you are here."

"I am."

"A nation is at stake here and our work is critical to the survival of Jewish people and our culture; Thousands of lives will depend on your successes or suffer from any failures."

"I … I understand," Charles said, trying to steady his voice. He thought about Gladia to soothe his nerves, but her life depending on his actions only made it worse.

Moshe grinned. "I have to say, I really like you, Charles. Come back tomorrow and I will reveal our offer."

Charles stiffened. "Tomorrow? I'm ready now."

Moshe laughed. "Just testing your spirit. Here is our problem: We have critical secrets, and vital instructions that need to be relayed around the world. We were surprised when Dov told us about your memory skills and your extensive knowledge of geography. That's a God-given talent and will serve you well. But you possess something else of equal value."

"Dov said my youthful appearance and American accent would be helpful."

"Right. There's no one like you in our network." Moshe placed the agreements he'd signed in a folder labeled "Courier 84." "You read the hazards of the job, yes?"

"I, *ah* … did." He flinched as he remembered Father yelling at Mother, "How many times have I told you not to let Charles out of this house? I will break him of his friendship for that pig-headed Jew, David!" The risks couldn't be any worse than Father catching up with him.

Moshe's voice faded in. "And our agreements make everybody nervous. However, your risk of capture is minimal if you follow protocol. That's why preparation is essential." He held up a bulky burlap sack with a rope tied around the top. "I have documents and packets that need attention. We'll spend a few days training you, then you will travel to our Zionist headquarters for one week and meet our president, Chaim Weizmann. Hope you like London."

Charles raised his brows. "London would be amazing! But I couldn't possibly travel roundtrip in a week's time on a steamship."

"No ships on this job. You travel by air."

"But why do I have to carry a *sack*? Why not a briefcase?" He immediately regretted asking another boyish question.

"Think on that, Charles. A young person flying alone with a briefcase?"

Charles rolled his eyes. "I understand."

Moshe hit the table with his hand. "Okay, we have a deal!" He extended his hand and Charles shook it. "We will have to get you another passport under the wire. We'll work that out if you pass your training exam, then we can explore a permanent assignment."

Charles frowned.

"Is that a problem?"

"I'm planning school next semester. And I don't want to miss school or leave my ... friend."

"I know it's plenty to take in." Moshe stood. "Give it some thought after you return."

"Okay."

He escorted Charles to the door. "On behalf of a grateful future nation, thank you."

"You're welcome, Mosh—" He realized they were now outside. "You're welcome, Commander."

Moshe smiled. "Yes, you will do quite well."

Nearing Jacob's home, Charles saw Dov's car out front. It had to be Gladia. His hope was confirmed when he entered the foyer and smelled traces of jasmine. That was it! She liked him. Time to take their relationship to the next level.

"Oh Charles, *your girlfriend is here*," little Annie said in a singsong tone.

Gladia rose from the couch and clutched Charles, her soft body pressing his revived him.

She pulled back. "You look tired; Your clothes, they are wrinkled."

"Let's talk in my room." He led her by the hand down the hall and opened his door. "Jonathan, may we have some time alone?"

Jonathan gawked at Gladia, nodded, and left.

"You'll have to excuse him. He's only twelve and a little odd around girls."

"I see that. He is cute."

Charles closed the door and trembled from being alone with her in tight quarters. She moved close, "How was the meeting with Commander Sneh?"

"It was okay, but—"

"Okay ...?"

He blew out a breath as they sat on his cot. "Exhausting. They wanted to know my entire life. Then I had to read and sign a stack of agreements."

"What was the commander like?"

"Nice, but very military—big and strong too. He stared like he was trying to see through me."

She leaned close to his face. "Did they torture you to talk about your parents?"

"Very funny."

She huffed out a breath. "Why don't you tell me something? You tell them, but not me?"

"I told you. I have to forget about them."

"But family is important. Please, say something."

"Okay, okay. I'll tell you about them soon, but not tonight. I'm tired. I *ahh* ... drank wine for the first time."

She laughed. "They must like you. That is special for friends only."

"It's that way in America too."

"So what was the come out?"

He loved the charming way she misused basic phrases. Another kissable moment, but he was too worn out.

"Charles?" She waved her hand. "The come out?"

He grinned. "It's outcome. I don't know. He really liked me. Said I'd be perfect for the job. He was even going to send me to London but—"

"London? That is where we want to visit!"

"I didn't know regular travel was required. I'd love to see London, but I can't take the assignment. I'd miss school and …"

She studied his face. "Me?" she asked with a sensual smile.

Tired or not, her gestures sparked his hormones into high gear.

"I am glad you don't go. I feel wrong about it. Like maybe you get hurt." She placed her hand on his wrist. "Something else is bothering you?"

He looked down at her hand on him. "My head hurts, it's pretty bad."

"A headache *again*? I can take care of it." She scooted behind him and started rubbing his temples. "My doctor say when I get a headache, to breathe in and relax. Have someone rub the head. Go ahead, you breathe slow."

He should have sent her home. Instead he shut his eyes and fantasized them tumbling back onto the cot, but managed to pull himself back before it got out of hand. "You get headaches?"

"Yes. The doctor say … he wants me to talk about my parents to a rabbi. But I cannot go into a temple because—"

He moved his head away because she started rubbing too hard.

She moved her face near his. "You feel better now?"

"Uh … I'm okay. Thank you." Eyes closed, he held the sides of his head and took a deep breath.

She stood. "You should sleep now. I will see you tomorrow? Then you can tell me about your parents." She took the blanket from the end of the cot and unfurled it. "You feel better, okay?"

"Yeah, I'll see you tomorrow." Too tired to don pajamas, he laid his head back on the pillow as she spread the blanket out. "Thank you." He tilted his head up. "Gladia?"

"What is it?"

"Something really big has happened inside me today. Tomorrow, when I feel better, I will tell you."

She beamed. "I cannot wait to hear it."

CHAPTER 7

After some afternoon shopping, Charles hailed a cab to the library, timing it to arrive before closing. Hopefully, Gladia had forgotten her last request to talk about his parents, because he was finally over them. He had more important things to engage in. On his way there, he whispered under his breath a speech to finally tell her how he felt.

He entered the library and almost did a U-turn as he neared Gladia's backside, while she cleared shelves. "I guess it's too late for reading," he said.

She ducked under the counter and then popped up with a rag and wiped circles on the counter. "I did not think you are coming. I worried, and think maybe your bad headache, it didn't leave you." She looked at her watch. "It is time for me to go soon."

After cleaning, she picked up her purse and they walked to the side exit. He pointed toward the garden. "Let's walk this way so we can talk."

She stopped. "You seem different and you come late. You are okay?"

"Sure." Except for sweaty palms and a pounding heart.

"Charles, I want you to take the assignment. Dov say at breakfast you will not be in danger. And you get to see London," her eyes gleamed, "maybe other parts of Europe. Wish I could go."

Regular travel could jeopardize their relationship. He shook his head. "I don't want to miss school, or you. I've already decided not to accept the mission."

She stopped him and placed her hands on his shoulders. "Look at me. We must keep our mind clear and remember why we fight."

"You sound like Dov."

"He says we must take this land now, or we will never have it."

Charles nodded, but the pledge meant nothing if he had to leave her.

"Go. You will be back soon. Then we can go on more missions and keep teaching each other. And ..." She tilted her head. "I will miss you too."

"You'll miss me?" It was hard to say no to her. London would have been a dream destination. "I don't know. My feelings for you are ... plus, with training, I'd be away more."

"They will teach you *great things*. How to speak and act to foreign person. Things you cannot get from a book. Then you teach me." She raised her palms out. "You see? It is good!" She smiled. "Come, I will give you a ride home."

He desired everything she said, but by the time she turned down Main Street, he kicked the floorboard from failure to share his heart.

≈≈≈

Gladia's encouragement along with the opportunity to change history convinced him to take one assignment. And now, with three vigorous days of Haganah training, he walked into the library massaging his temples, looking for her. She wasn't at the counter, and that calmed his swirling butterflies. But when she emerged from an aisle with a stack of returned books, nerves assaulted his stomach again. When he left Los Angeles, he thought it would be impossible to find another friend like David, but meeting Gladia confirmed Palestine had been a great idea. And somehow, loving her decreased his desire to resolve his painful upbringing.

She hadn't seen him yet, so he diverted his route from the counter and went to his usual spot. He opened a structural engineering book, when something yellow filled his peripheral view.

"You didn't say hello." She placed her hand on his forehead. "Something is not right? You have sweat."

"It's lunch already?"

She straightened. "Yes, are you coming?"

Within a few steps into the garden, he looked about and stopped in front of her. He pulled a black box from his pocket and saw how perfect it looked against her canary-yellow dress. She looked at it rattling in his hand and then stared at him, brows arched.

He opened it and revealed an antique ring. "W … will you?"

Her eyes opened wide as she stared at the swirling circle of gold wrapped around a half-carat diamond, shimmering in the sunlight. She rounded her lips. "Will I…?"

His throat tightened. "Wear it?"

"What do you mean?" Creases ran along her forehead.

Obviously their culture gap was larger than he'd thought. When he couldn't recollect his rehearsed speech, he recalled a high school senior's pledge. "When a guy buys a girl a ring? That means …" He swallowed. "It's a promise ring."

"What is the promise?"

"When he gives her a ring, he's promising …" He closed his eyes, fearing what every guy regrets. "Accepting this ring means she's promising to be his girl … friend."

Her mouth opened farther, her eyes moved between him and the sparkling stone. If she could just say something: "Not now." Or "Maybe later in life."

When her lips moved with nothing coming out, his eyes burned. He was certain she would accept the ring; She'd never been speechless before.

"Why do you give me this?"

"I want to be—" His tense neck choked him.

She stared at the shaking box on his palm. "I not know … I not sure what to say."

He cringed, hearing her revert to poor English. Her enlarged eyes and loss of words tempted him to walk away so he wouldn't have to hear nice excuses. Yet his feet wouldn't budge; he owed her respect now that she understood.

"I am old to you," she blurted.

"No, you're not old."

"I mean. I am older."

"But you're only—"

"I know. I am one and a half years ahead. But I feel many years past you. Are you understanding that?"

"No." He regretted deceiving her about his age, but that didn't seem to matter—like Elizabeth, she must have sensed the three-year gap between them. He dropped the box to his side, the gold ring pinged on the sidewalk.

She hugged him while his arms dangled. Her wet cheeks moistened his: "I do love you."

Not breaking the embrace, he leaned back. "You do? I love you with all my heart!" Emboldened, he pulled her tight.

She let go. "I love you like, like Dov."

He backed up. "You love me like your brother?" David's words resonated: *Don't even try to figure women out.*

"I am sorry. My love is different."

He shook his head. Her face blotched red when she shed more tears. "I feel awful, Charles."

He staggered away. Moving to Palestine was a painful mistake. A long list of stupid things he'd said in response to her endearing gestures ached his chest.

"Charles, wait."

He glanced back and saw her blurry image through tears.

She pointed to the ground. "Your ring!"

He whirled back around and wandered off. After a few miles of meandering, it became apparent, he was the only white person among huts and crops.

He plopped down in the dirt and watched villagers dressed in loose garments plowing a field beyond several tin-roofed sheds. When a breeze swept away some of the dust and grain in the air, he recognized a brother and his twin sister from the library. The sister moved in his direction and the brother followed.

"Why you here?" the brother said.

"You not see? He is hurting," the sister said. "You okay?" She stooped down and looked him over. "You can get hurt in this place."

Charles looked away. "I don't care."

"What is your name?" she asked.

He stood, dust falling from his clothes. "I need to go home."

The girl pointed toward the sea. "Haifa is that way."

He walked in the direction of her pointing finger, then turned. "I know you from school. Right?"

She nodded. "No," the brother said.

He found Jacob's house by nightfall. When he entered and removed his filthy shoes, little Annie ran to him. "Mommy, something is wrong with Charles!"

Family members rushed to the entryway, but Charles, head down, began his trek toward his room. Jesse raised his hands. "What's wrong? How did you get so dirty?"

"I'm going to my room." He trudged past Elizabeth and Ruth.

"Gladia was here," Ruth called after him. "He looks heartbroken," Elizabeth muttered as he continued down the hall.

He fell to his cot with the sensation of a knife in his heart. He heard Jesse's loud voice outside his room. "Elizabeth, what did you say about Charles?"

"I think he got his heart broken."

"What do you mean?"

"Haven't you been paying attention? Can't you see he's in love with that Jewish girl from the library?"

"You mean Gladia? Why would she hurt Charles?"

"Never mind. This is women's work."

CHAPTER 8

Gladia rubbed her sore eyes, a result of lack of sleep and another pressing day of inventory at the library. She stood behind the counter and applied nail polish, to keep from biting them since she hadn't seen Charles in a week. She couldn't eat all day so she left work early, drove to Jacob's house and knocked on the door.

Jonathan cracked it open and smiled. "Hi, Gladia."

She forced a return smile. "Hello, Jonathan. Is Charles home?"

He turned his head. "Charles, your girlfriend is here!"

Her heart sank, remembering Charles' teary eyes. She clasped an envelope she had sealed with perfume, knowing he loved jasmine.

Jonathan opened his mouth wide. "Char—"

"Jonathan! Your manners." Ruth opened the door all the way. "I'm sorry, Gladia. Please, come in."

She wiped her feet and entered. "He is here?"

Ruth frowned. "Yes, but he's not talking much. We've been praying for both of you."

She patted her chest and took a breath. "Thank you. I am mis … ah, mis-er-ble."

Elizabeth came into the foyer, crossed her arms and looked Gladia over. "Hi, Gladia." She pointed to the envelope. "Is that for him?"

Gladia pulled out a handkerchief and dabbed the corner of her eyes. "Yes. My note. I had it translated to English."

"I'll give it to him." Elizabeth held her hand out.

She clenched the envelope tighter. "I wanted …" Ruth leaned forward, and the overhead light revealed worried-looking lines on her face. In that instant, Gladia remembered her mother's worried face, for the first time in many seasons. Nine years had passed since … then, quick flashes of knives, blood and screams jolted her into a suffocating frenzy. She whisked her hand to her throat and wheezed, then stooped and put her other hand on her knee.

"Oh my!" Elizabeth braced her shaky body.

"I'll get Charles." Jonathan's voiced trailed down the hall.

Elizabeth yelled for Jacob and Jesse as they cradled her to the floor.

"Breathe, honey." Elizabeth placed Gladia's head on her lap while Ruth prayed in Hebrew.

Things went dark, but she could still hear: "Jacob, get the car started! Jesse, Charles, help us carry her to the vehicle."

"Gladia what's the matter?" Charles' voice sounded far away.

When they lifted her, the jolt caused Gladia to gasp. "Bring me down!" she blurted. They hurried her to the couch.

"What happened? Are you okay, Gladia?" several voices clamored at once.

She sat up, pushed her palm forward and looked at Charles. The memories must have returned because he had pressed her to talk about her parents.

≈≈≈

When Charles saw Gladia taking deep breaths, he did the same. Her chest fluttered less and she stood to approach Ruth. "I saw my mother's face on you." That was all she managed before convulsing into tears.

Ruth embraced her trembling body and looked at Charles, who shrugged in response.

Charles walked Gladia into his room and sat her on his cot. "You scared me ... what happened?"

Gladia pulled her hair back. "I come ... to give you my sorry note. Then I see Elizabeth and Ruth, how they worry. And because I forget my mother's face, I hate myself. I use to cry at night because I cannot picture her and Papa anymore. Then, I meet you. After that? I stop crying and no more bad dreams. You make me feel ..." She blinked several times. "I don't want to miss you. The note. You can read it when I go." She stood.

She looked so beautiful, even with her makeup smeared. He hadn't noticed her amplified happiness over time, compared to the early months of their friendship.

"I must go now." She walked toward the hallway.

He followed her to door. "Maybe you should lie down for awhile." He heard whispers from the living room, but ignored them.

"No. I am okay. You read the note and I hope we talk later." She opened the door and left.

Charles would have preferred to be locked up at home again than to see Gladia suffer. He'd built resilience from Father's tortures, but had no idea how to deal with the heart-wrenching pain of being in love. No woman could ever compare. He'd turned toward his room when Elizabeth put her hand to his shoulder. "Charles. Gladia brought this." When she handed him the envelope, the sweet scent of jasmine sent bittersweet chills down his back.

He retreated to his room, and stuffed the paper under a pile of clothes. He tortured himself that night with scenarios of what he'd done wrong to spoil her romantic affections.

He opened his eyes in the morning to the pile of clothing where her note was concealed. Breakfast was offered, but he declined and began drawing a chart to analyze the dates and places he went with her.

Jonathan woke and quietly left.

After refusing lunch and having no logical conclusions for his dilemma, he decided fresh air might clear his mind. After he left home and reached the end of the street, Dov's car crept up along side him. He kept walking and fixed his gaze straight as the car motor stopped.

A door shut. "Charles, wait!"

He stopped, but kept his back to her. She faced him. "I was on my way to see you. Did you read it?"

"Are you better now?" Her English certainly was.

She looked down and shook her head. "I'm afraid I will forget her again. And, I miss you."

He lifted his hands and dropped them to his side. "I'm sorry, about everything. I feel really stupid. My hurt feelings made you feel bad about your mother. It tore me up inside to see you agonize like that."

When she placed her hand on his shoulder, it reminded him how much taller she was. She stroked his cheeks, and then went in for a loose hug. "No. You do good for me. You didn't read my paper? It says I feel love with you. Nobody talks to me except Dov, but, he is my brother and he is busy."

His arms dangling, she stepped back. "I do not look at people in their eyes, because they watch me with bad faces. But I look at you."

Knowing his friendship transformed her life made the back of his neck tingle. At the same time he wanted to scream, because he had no clue what to do next. But he couldn't tell her about his predicament without making her feel worse.

He met her intense stare and shook his head. "I just ... I can't—"

Screaming sirens raced down the one-way street toward Jacob's house.

Gladia's body jerked as she whirled around. "Come, I will take you home." They ran to her vehicle and followed the squad car.

CHAPTER 9

Charles and Gladia dashed to Jacob's porch as two Palestinian policemen were banging on the door. Jacob opened it and squinted. "What's wrong?"

The lead officer held his hand out toward Charles and Gladia. "Step back. This is police business."

Jesse stepped up from behind Jacob. "It's okay. He lives here. Come in, officers."

The men removed their hats, walked inside, and faced the anxious family. Charles and Gladia followed.

Charles looked toward the adjoining room and noticed Samuel, half-hidden behind a doorjamb.

The lead officer raised his clipboard. "Which of you is the father of Jonathan Rosenthal?" His voice boomed off the mosaic tiles.

Jacob stepped forward. "I am. What's wrong with my boy?"

The officer frowned. "We are sorry to inform you of the death of Jonathan Rosenthal."

Jacob collapsed amidst others wailing. Little Annie clung to her father; Gladia, sobbing, put her head to Charles' shoulder. Charles wept for the little brother he'd never had, and now understood why Jews risked carrying firearms illegally.

Since the noise overwhelmed them, the two uniformed men put their hats on and promised to come back. Charles assumed the circumstances were war related; the Irgun had enlightened him about Arab snipers. He looked for

Samuel again and wondered why he wouldn't join his grieving family, but then remembered Samuel's escape from British custody.

≈≈≈

When the officer returned, the family gathered in the living room, but Ruth stormed forward and clung to his arm. "My boy, he's only twelve. Take me to him!"

The officer removed his hat and eased from her grasp. "Please ma'am, let me explain the attack that took your son."

She vigorously shook her head. "He can't be gone. I won't believe it until I see him."

Gladia, on the couch next to Charles, raised her head from his shoulder.

The officer shook his head. "We do not recommend anyone to see the body except his father."

"I'm his mother!"

The officer tightened his lip. "No one sees him until we have identification from his father."

Charles glanced toward the kitchen—Samuel's shadow lingered. When he thought about the rising tension in the region, he knew Jonathan's death could have been his, or Gladia's. He had another urge to talk her into leaving Palestine, so they wouldn't be next.

"What about the attack, sir?" Jesse asked.

The official stooped down toward Jacob. "Mister Rosenthal, can you stand please?"

Jesse tapped him on the shoulder. "Not now," he said quietly. "About the incident?"

The official straightened. "There was a strike against our station. Members of a Jewish terrorist group attempted to steal weapons, and a stray bullet made its way across the street to the victim's school. That's all I can tell you."

Jesse pinched his beard with his thumb and index finger. "Hmm."

The officer glanced at Charles, took a few steps, and looked at the doorway where Samuel's shadow had just been.

"I have a list of descriptions I'll leave with you. When we have more information, we will share it. In the meantime, we need the public's help to bring these killers to justice." He looked at Jacob and shook his head, and then turned back to Jesse. "Rabbi, would you be willing to come to the hospital and identify the body?"

Ruth grabbed Jesse's arm. "I must come with you!"

The policeman stood behind Ruth and shook his head at Jesse.

Jesse swayed his head at Elizabeth. "Later, Ruth. Let me go with him." Jesse met Charles' eyes. "I want him to come. He shared a room with Jonathan. Will you join us, Charles?"

Jesse's shielded expression hinted foul play. Charles looked at Ruth, who nodded. He looked back at Jesse, who loved him like a son, and nodded.

The officer drove them to the hospital. When they arrived, his radio began chattering. "Please step out of the car while I take this."

Somber faces on the hospital staff confirmed how local tensions increased the murder rates in the heat of what the rabbi called "the longest-lasting feud in world history."

The officer came in and a nurse led them down steps to a corridor, where a sign labeled "Morgue" hung by two chains. As they neared the sign, a rotten-egg stench permeated the dank brick-walled repository of the city's dead. The nurse pushed the swinging door open and walked to a table where a sheet-covered corpse lay on a cold steel table under a hanging light. She pulled the covering back to body's waist.

The officer whipped the cloth back to the shoulder line.

Jesse glanced toward the body, but turned away. Patches of fog emitted from his exhale while Charles studied the lumpy figure under the sheet, shuddering at the idea of Jesse identifying *him* on that table someday.

Jesse paced and murmured prayers. Charles remained in the shadow, gazing along the moist dungeon-like brick design. A cold chill ran down his spine when he thought about Samuel's lurking at the house, and the Irgun's reputation of stealing weapons.

Jesse moved quickly and pulled the sheet down to the body's stomach. "Oh my!" He turned away and faced a corner, bobbing his head. The officer eased the sheet back to the shoulders again.

"Rabbi. Is this Jonathan Rosenthal? We need positive identification."

"He's only twelve!" Jesse covered his face with his hands and retreated toward the door.

The officer shifted his gaze to Charles. "Are you up for it, lad?"

"Me?" Charles gulped. "*Ah* ... I don't know." Then he recalled his and Jesse's earlier suspicions. This might be his only chance to view evidence of what really happened.

Charles went to the pasty wax-like body and saw bloodstains around the neckline. He pulled the sheet back to see more, but an urge to gag forced him to step back. "Oh my goodness!"

The policeman stomped forward and pulled the sheet back up again.

Charles nodded. "It's him. But I—"

"Let's go," the officer said. He stretched the cloth over Jonathan's face and hurried toward the door.

Charles squinted. "Wait a minute. At the house you said Jonathan caught a stray bullet. And on our way here, you said the gang used pistols." He stepped up, pinched his nostrils and ripped the cloth off Jonathan's bullet-riddled body. "I count seventeen tight-pattern bullet wounds on my friend. Only an automatic gun could do this damage."

The officer walked back and flung the covering over Jonathan's body and face. "Are you a forensics expert?"

Charles' lower lip trembled. He couldn't answer the officer without giving away his training with the underground movement.

"I have what I need," the officer said. "We're leaving."

Jesse blocked the doorway. "Wait a minute. My friend here just made an important observation."

"Rabbi," the policeman pulled his nightstick and put it to Jesse's face, "we are investigating! If you want this inquiry *to go well*, I suggest you step aside and leave this matter to us." He leaned in. "Do you understand?"

"I understand quite well." Jesse moved. The officer slid his nightstick back in his utility belt.

Charles sat behind Jesse with balled fists; Jonathan wouldn't be able to ask him numerous questions before bedtime, or interact with Charles on books they shared. Regardless of the officer's false testimony, Jonathan didn't deserve to die.

When the officer parked the squad car at Jacob's house, Jesse inclined forward. "Why are more authorities at our house?"

The policeman turned his head and smirked. "By the look on your face, I think you know."

"I don't know anything, except my nephew is lying on a cold table riddled with bullets—from an *automatic gun*."

"Hah!" The officer uttered. "You think we're stupid? Neighbors have identified a middle-aged man residing at your home, who matches our description."

Shaken, Jesse pointed his finger at him. "He didn't do anything."

They entered the house and walked into the living room as Gladia emerged from the kitchen with a tray of vegetables and unleavened bread.

The detective grilling Samuel stopped and turned. "Do we have positive ID?" Silence prevailed as the family stared at Charles, Jesse, and the officer.

The officer removed his hat. "Affirmative."

The family's sobs began anew.

The detective closed his notepad and nearly shoved it in Samuel's face. "We'll be back when we have more evidence. You and your comrades are going to hang for this."

Seconds later, the front door shut.

In silent accord, Jacob's family moved opposite of Samuel, who remained in front of the fireplace, pale and sweating. And now Charles believed the rumor about the Irgun destroying Samuel's arrest record for immigration smuggling.

Jesse latched on to Samuel's arms. "Tell me you had nothing to do with this!"

Gladia put her lips to Charles' ear. "Maybe we should leave?"

Charles watched Samuel and Jesse maintain their aggressive stance. Blurred in the background were Jacob and Ruth, who handed Annie off to Elizabeth.

Samuel's glossy eyes and sloped shoulders revealed how terrible he was at hiding guilt. Jesse paced. "I know that look. Your cousin's blood is on *your hands!* Jacob told you not to get involved with those terrorists."

Samuel gritted his teeth and looked at Charles. "We are not terrorists!"

Charles couldn't look at Jesse, who looked his way. Even though he'd known nothing of the attack, he cringed at being part of a group responsible for Jonathan's ill fate.

Jesse took small paces and waved his hands. "This is not God's way. He does not need the help of aggressive Jews to grant us freedom. I forbid you to carry on with those killers! Tell the authorities what you know."

"Killers?" He thrust his hands up. "You foolish old man. You think God will give us Palestine with no fight? Do you not understand the mind of our enemy? You read the news. They will not even attend peace meetings!"

"Samuel." Elizabeth's voice cracked as she came back in. "You don't question God, or yell at your father."

Samuel pointed. "You both sleep. We are at war, and blood will spill. I am sorry for Jonathan, but Arabs want us dead, and we have to fight with real weapons."

"Silence!" Face red, veins popped on Jesse's neck.

Samuel crinkled his face. "My days of *your* silence are over."

Gladia sprang up, looked at Charles and nodded at the door. He felt obligated to stay in case Samuel became violent. She left, and the front door shut seconds later.

"You give up everything and move us to Palestine." Samuel paced while Jesse faced the wall. "I told you this was a bad place. You want the land, but you do nothing to get it. Well … I am doing something!"

He stopped pacing. "We have to accept *collateral damage*." He cocked his head and pointed at Charles. "He teach me those words."

Charles sank into the couch a few more inches.

Samuel's face reddened. "Jews like you wait for God to smite the enemy. The more you wait, the more Jonathans die."

"Samuel, stop," Elizabeth said.

"You want *me* to stop while another holocaust come here? While we get punishment for being Jews again?" Samuel glanced at this mother. "No Jew gun down Jonathan. The policeman shoot him."

Elizabeth put her hands to her wet cheeks and shivered in a breath.

"That foolish boy." Tears washed Samuel's face. "He scream my name and run in front of the bullets aimed for me."

Sobbing, Elizabeth covered her ears and fell to her knees.

Looking at Jesse and Elizabeth, Charles cried. In part he understood Samuel's intense frustration, but he had no right to deny responsibility for Jonathan's death. He rose to help Elizabeth, but paused and fell back onto the couch.

Samuel didn't acknowledge his mother's collapse. "I will not stop until our enemies leave!"

Jesse tore his own sleeve and turned his back to Samuel. "You are not my son."

Samuel pushed on Jesse's back. "That is right. You do not known me since you leave me in Germany for a good life in America. And now ... you act American."

Jesse pointed at the door. "Get out!"

Samuel kicked a table and knocked a vase over. "How many more Jews must die? We are hated people, and I am tired of it." He thrust his finger toward the floor. "This land is our last chance to live with dignity! I will leave. But not until you know...."

"I said get out!" Jesse turned, his face reddened.

Samuel pushed his father again. "I am a Holocaust victim."

"I know, but you survived," Jesse cried. "I'm sorry we couldn't come to get you! There. Are you happy? I said it."

Samuel thrust his finger near his father's face. "I am not a survivor. I am the victim."

Oh God, please make him leave. Charles never imagined himself praying, but then he saw Samuel's red face return pale.

Samuel froze like a wax figure, as though he was slipping into a trance. "They say I was lucky when they do the experiments.... 'The Angel of Death,' they name him. The Nazis want to know how long a person will go with electricity shocking him. Soldiers bet the doctor."

Charles lowered his head to his hand after Jesse and Elizabeth looked like they were watching someone die; Their faces wet, her hair messy, and Jesse's shirt ripped.

"My friend, Joseph … he went sixteen hours and forty-seven minutes they say. They make me watch his eyes roll back and the hair burn."

Charles closed his eyes and tried to think about Gladia. But Samuel's voice was so believable, it caused him to envision the scene too—except Father was doing the torture.

Charles opened his eyes. "Samuel, you should leave," he whispered.

"My test was easier. The doctor hook me up to wires to see my reaction, while I watch them kill my friend with the other wires."

Just then, Charles remembered a buried memory of his father's voice: "You will die like those Jews if you don't conform."

"Then they bring more people in and put a knife in my hand. Now they bet each other ten German marks. Many times they yell at me to put the men out from misery so they can die sooner. When I do not do it, they bring in women and children. They say more Jews will suffer until I stab someone or myself."

"No, Samuel," Elizabeth begged. "Stop."

Charles began to comprehend more about those who'd survived the Holocaust; he knew how a tortured person's rationality could be tainted. And Samuel's memories must have been ten times worse than his own.

Jesse helped Elizabeth to stand, and then led her toward the hallway. "Please, just leave," he said over his shoulder.

Samuel walked to the couch. "You are ready, Charles?"

Charles lowered his face as he saw Jesse's feet stop in his peripheral vision. He slowly raised his eyes and cringed when the couple turned and peered at him.

He shook his head at Samuel.

Jesse tore his other sleeve and pointed to the door. "Out, Charles! And don't come back!"

Charles bowed his head and walked out behind Samuel. Crossing the lawn, he balled a fist. "Why did you do that?"

Samuel walked down the street, his back to Charles. "You are with us, and we have work to do."

"I'm not involved." Charles raised his voice to Samuel's backside. "I didn't have anything to do with Jonathan's death."

Samuel stopped and stared at him. "Yes, you did. What do you think was in the book you and Gladia deliver to Tel Aviv?"

Charles bent over and held his stomach. He'd already disliked the Irgun, but foolishly hadn't thought about their missions affecting the innocent. The overbearing desire to work with Gladia clouded his judgment. Joining a group that seemed so similar to his father's made him want to throw up.

"Come, it is getting dark," Samuel said.

Charles followed, but wouldn't walk with him. When they came to Gladia's house, he remained at the edge of her yard while Samuel struck the door with a three-strike coded knock.

The curtains moved, then she opened the door and Samuel went inside. She saw Charles. "Why are you both here?"

Her face was red and eyes puffy. He shook his head. "Samuel decided to implicate me, so Jesse disowned me. I didn't even remember to get my stuff."

She sighed. "Come in. I will get your things tomorrow when I bring them flowers."

Her eyes were even more bloodshot than when she left Jacob's house. He followed her to the sofa. "What else is wrong?"

"My brother Dov did not come home last night. The hospital send a messenger and say he was shot in the face. They will not let me see him." She peered at Samuel. "Why my brother was shot?"

Samuel squirmed in his chair. "He is not your real brother, right?"

She made a sour face. "Not a relative, but more than a real brother!"

Samuel rose and sauntered to a table in the corner. "Let us hear the radio. Maybe there is news."

"I try that already. It is broken!"

Charles eyed Samuel's movements and observed how unusually nice he was acting. He walked to the table. "I'll have a look at it." He removed the back cover and began probing.

"Samuel if you know something, you better tell," Gladia said.

Charles found a loose tube, reseated it and flipped the switch. "Here it is, it's warming up."

After interrogating Samuel about his whereabouts from the last twenty-four hours, Gladia shouted, "Listen. I hear something about shooting."

> We have more on the brutal attack at the Ramat Gan Police Station. A military vehicle let off a dozen Irgun fighters disguised as Arab prisoners. Escorted by Dov Gruner, who posed as a British soldier, the gang took out revolvers and ordered police officers into a cell.

Gladia choked. Charles ran to her and patted her back.

> When they took weapons from the armory, a police officer on the upper story noticed, and directed machine-gun fire. Tragically, an unidentified male student got caught in the crossfire and was cut down.

Gladia put her hands over her face and sobbed. Charles embraced her and hoped Samuel had lied about the book delivery containing the mission's instructions.

She broke from Charles, walked to a basin by the door and splashed her face. "I will bring them flowers tomorrow when I get your things." She pointed to a door next to the toilet room. "Tonight you can sleep in Dov's room."

Charles stood while straining to keep his eyes open, convinced he'd have to leave in the morning. He hated Palestine again.

CHAPTER 10

Charles woke to the sound of a rooster crowing and while the sky was still deep blue, he walked to the local phone station and called the Haganah headquarters. When the taxi arrived, he'd convinced himself the mission in London might lessen his tension.

He climbed in with no luggage, ready to leave the God-forsaken land, as some called it, but an urge to say goodbye nagged him. "Take the next left into the driveway, sir." When the taxi stopped in front of her home, his heart palpitated. He left the vehicle and raised his knuckles to knock, but she pulled the door open first.

Her eyes still swollen, she hugged him like a girlfriend would. Just the fact of them tightly embracing all the time, without being lovers, confirmed David's warning about women confusing men.

She pulled her head back. "I thought you leave me for good." She looked past him. "Why the taxi? You are taking the assignment?"

He nodded, freed himself from her arms and turned toward the cab.

"Charles ... Charles?"

He climbed into the cab and struggled not to turn his head back. He didn't have the strength to tell her a Haganah courier would retrieve his belongings. He hated leaving her, especially with Dov injured, but he couldn't stay another minute.

The cab hugged the coast toward Tel Aviv, and loneliness already clutched his heart, far worse than when he'd boarded the train out of Los

Angeles. When he returned, he'd look for a different method to garner her affections; If he returned.

Arriving at Gatsby's restaurant in Tel Aviv, an older woman came and drove him to the airport. When he saw the planes through a fence at Lydda airport, his insides jittered. If caught helping Zionists, a prison cell awaited. He channeled his thoughts to the better times with Gladia and the Rosenthals, but that brought more heartache.

They drove past the back gate guard with nothing more than an inconspicuous signal from the driver's hand. Bouncing down a dirt service road brought them near a plane, its spinning propellers kicking up dust. She climbed out and tapped his window, but he stared at the delivery sack and wondered what secrets he was risking his life for. She pounded the window, her hair blowing in a flurry and her thumb over her shoulder. He stepped out toward the sputtering racket of the United Airlines plane.

She looked him over. "Your pistol," she yelled. "Where is it?"

"I left it at home in my sack." As soon as he said that, he remembered there was no home anymore.

"Is that what your training taught you?"

"A courier was supposed to deliver my things from Haifa. Besides, I can't take a firearm on a plane."

"You can and you will." She casually looked about and dug into her jacket pocket. "Here, take mine, and hide it in your …" she leaned in, "*private area.*" Her nose scrunched.

"I can't hide it down there …"

"You can—"

"I know. And I will."

She crossed her arms and smiled. "You learn fast. And thank you for your service to the Haganah." She pointed her finger upward. "Oh. I almost forgot. The code word is 'master.'"

He nodded, stuffed the pistol in his pants and pushed through the hefty draft toward the steps leading up to the plane. While ascending, he thought about seeking a trashcan to throw the gun in, but he knew they'd ask for it if he returned. Then he remembered: Father often had various bulges in his clothing too. The similarity sickened him.

As the plane bounced onto the runway in London, a film of sweat broke under his clothes. While stepping off the runway, he didn't expect a pudgy man, with an Alfred Hitchcock face, to call him "master" as the code word.

As they drove, the gun down his pants, the silent driver and his sack of who-knows-what, all resembled a cloak-and-dagger mystery film. Yet, the adventure helped lessen the pain and having been away from Father's manipulative voice for months now, he repelled the notion of deserving a life of turmoil.

The driver pulled in front of the Grand Terrace Hotel. "Check into the hotel. Then return with your delivery items."

Amazed the fellow actually spoke two sentences, Charles stepped onto the noisy sidewalk and looked up at the massive hotel that seemed to tower into the stars. It reminded him he had no idea what he was doing.

When he climbed back into the limo, they drove to a stark alley where tall brick buildings standing at attention multiplied his pulse rate. His mind flashed a scene of Father storming the vehicle—he really needed to rid himself from the paranoia. He peered out. "Why are we stopping here?"

"Proceed straight, turn right at the second walkway and knock. Follow your memorized instructions."

He eased out; The clacking of his shoes against the cobblestone was the only sound after the limo's engine faded away. He regretted not saying a proper goodbye to Gladia. If he lived through the mission, he'd break protocol to send her a telegram.

After knocking with a code of three successive strikes, Charles handed over his sack and they replaced it with files labeled "confidential." Five minutes later he left, but it seemed too easy. And though it was certainly nice to conduct a mission without gunfire in the distance, something didn't seem right.

Later he was given his promised tour of London, but even with all the distractions, he couldn't stop thinking about how to attract Gladia romantically. During his life's quest for vast knowledge, he'd never learned much about women. And even if he had, she was like no other.

After a wakeup call the next morning and a quick Danish, his travels to Naples Italy, was the same as London, and by the end of the week, he loved and hated returning to Palestine.

≈≈≈

After the eight-hour flight, he reported back to Moshe's office and handed over the sack of confidential items with a smile of satisfaction. Moshe took the bag and turned it upside down; the folders and packages plunked into the trashcan. Charles squinted at the full wastebasket. Lots of anxiety had gone into transporting the contraband overseas.

Moshe crossed his arms and fixed a piercing eye on him. "What's on your mind, Charles?"

Charles mentally backtracked through his dealings, but couldn't think of any mistakes he'd made. Dumbfounded, he shook his head.

Moshe grinned and sat behind his paper-filled desk. "Relax Charles, it was a test."

"A test?"

"You don't think we're going to give a *seventeen-year-old* our most trusted secrets, do you?"

"I'm … *ahh* … nineteen now."

Moshe invoked his "bullfighter" stare. There was only one way Moshe could have learned his true age. Charles looked at the door and expected Father to come bursting in. He had to be agonizing about Charles' disappearance, and eager to drag him back to the cell that was inappropriately called "home." Nobody ever got one over on Father.

"How old are you?"

He'd lied so many times, he almost convinced himself of his adulthood. "I told you, nineteen."

Moshe laughed. "Excellent, Charles. But you'll need a lot more practice lying if you are going to be a *real* courier." He shook his head. "Heavy breathing, your eyes are open too wide, and stop fidgeting. Didn't you learn anything in training?"

Charles dropped his hands. "You don't seem as agitated as I thought you'd be."

Moshe opened a folder. "You were born October seventh, 1928, in an Arab home in Haifa, Palestine." He glanced up. "Happy birthday as of two months ago."

Mouth open wide, Charles sprang up. "I was born in …" Chills engulfed him. His whole life was a lie?

Moshe bobbed his finger to sit back down. "Your parents moved to Los Angeles, California, in 1931. You know them as Roger and Victoria Devonshire, but nobody from Palestine has names like that."

"My parents are from Palestine?"

Moshe slapped the folder on his desk. "Come on Charles, you can't be here by coincidence! You must have known your parents originated here." He leaned in. "We can make this easy, or difficult. Did they send you here? Are you on assignment for the Arabs?" He stood as if he was about to apprehend him. "I'm sure you've heard the term double agent."

Charles remained stiff. Moshe advanced and waved his palm near Charles' face. "Hey, I'm talking to you!"

Charles backed up and dropped into the chair. "Honestly sir, I knew they'd been here, but had no evidence they lived here. I figured they did because I think they were students at the Technion. But I sailed to Palestine to escape their mistreatment, and uncover their secrets." He shook his head vigorously. "There's no possible way I'd work for them. *I want to hate them!*"

Moshe walked behind his desk and sat. "From the look on your face and your age, I believe you. I'm going to take an educated guess that you have been Americanized growing up in Los Angeles, and your parents didn't see that coming. That's one of the biggest blunders covert Nazis and Arabs make. They underestimate how great freedom and democracy is. It's so good, some of *them* defect." Moshe pointed to the file. "If you are going to work with us, we'll need full disclosure. I don't appreciate dishonesty."

Charles couldn't believe Moshe would still consider keeping him. "I'm really sorry, sir."

"Are you willing to be totally honest from this point? We need to know who your parents really are. So we're going to need your testimony again."

"Yes sir. I want to know who they were more than anything!" Other than winning Gladia's heart, which would never happen if he were discharged from the Resistance in disgrace. He stood. "How did you obtain that intel?"

"We went through your things during your last training session, and found the photo, the copy of your grandfather's will, and the receipt of payment." Moshe tilted his head. "You're a wealthy young man. For such a brilliant youngster, it was not wise to carry revealing documents in your knapsack."

Charles tightened his lips in frustration because of his carelessness, but in the same moment, he felt relieved his secret had surfaced.

Moshe grinned. "Don't feel too foolish. I'm impressed you made it to Palestine undetected. You even fooled us. A fake passport, the money you obtained … none of that fits your profile. You are obviously far more complex than you lead others to believe, and those are traits we can use around here." Moshe put his hand on his chin. "But we can't figure out why your skin is so light and your hair is reddish."

Charles scrunched his face. "Why would that matter?"

"I want to send you to a doctor." Moshe pointed upward. "He's upstairs waiting."

Charles squirmed stared at the exit. He'd been used to being deceived, and Moshe's quick acceptance of his story seemed too easy—and no wonder the mission seemed that way too.

Moshe nodded toward the door. "You can leave if you want. We're not your enemy. But we can help you find answers about your heritage." He crossed his arms. "I have to admit, you baffle us."

A light knock tapped the door, followed by a woman's head and shoulders appearing. "They're here."

Charles grabbed the chair arms as Moshe stood. "Charles, this is Agatha, our legal assistant." He turned toward the door. "Send them in."

Agatha pushed the door wider. Gladia entered, while Samuel lingered in the background. She beamed a smile and embraced Charles. "I missed you."

"I missed you too," he mumbled against her tight hug.

Agatha smiled at him. "It's nice to meet you, Charles."

"Oh … you're American. It's a pleasure to meet you, Agatha." Charles let go of Gladia to shake her hand.

When Agatha turned to Moshe and introduced Gladia as her longtime friend, Charles raised his brows.

Moshe put both of his hands around Gladia's extended hand. "I'm sorry about Dov. We have offered him Agatha's legal expertise, but he refuses our help and insists he's useless to us because of his bullet wound. He won't allow visitors either, because it would compromise our cover. His valor is impressive, but we're disappointed with his refusal of help."

Gladia looked down. "He won't see me either. He tries too much to protect." Then she raised her hands to her hips and eyed Charles. "You are seventeen?"

Moshe and Agatha looked at each other and walked to the door. "We have to attend a meeting," Moshe said. "It's an honor to meet you, Gladia." He pointed. "You two can talk in the next room until I return."

Charles entered the padded side room and kept his back to Gladia.

"Now you will tell about your parents and why you lie about your age?" Her voice sounded staccato from the cushioned walls.

"My head is swirling." He sat across from her and looked down. "I don't—"

"You have to talk about your parents. And why you lie?"

He rubbed his eyes. "I don't have it in me right now."

She crossed her arms. "We are friends, yeah? Do not shut me off. I have nobody but you now." She leaned forward. "I feel bad for us, but we must … work in this."

"Work *through* this."

"I do not want English lesson! I want to know you." Her voice rose. "I see the pain on you. It will keep hurting, if you do not let it out." She ran soft fingers up his arms. "I know what that is like."

"I told you I don't have a problem with my past. I've read enough psychology books and learned to overcome my setbacks."

"That is not true. Tell me, I will listen."

Convinced it wouldn't do any good, he gave in and explained the surface of his problems and liked how it felt. He intended to omit how he ate his meals alone in the kitchen while Father and Mother dined at a nice table, but that confession too, cascaded into others. But he refused to unfold the traumatic bathtub tortures, and he'd gotten over those issues anyway. And of course he couldn't tell a Jew how Father forced him to recite anti-Semitic chants.

Her eyes moist, Gladia frowned. "Your parents. I am getting angry to them ... with them. You have a bad life. But you are ... you are ..."

Charles hung on her pause.

She interlaced her silky fingers with his. "You are *so good*."

He snapped his hands back and covered his face.

"What is wrong?" Her look of concern melted him.

How could he tell her she was stimulating him into high gear without sounding like an idiot?

She stood. "Somehow I know you can-not be eighteen when we meet. And you have a seventeen birthday and not tell me?"

"I'm really sorry about that. I feel stupid." He stood. "But I can't help how I feel about you, and ... everything I learned about human psychology ..." He sat back down. "The signals you send ..." He stood again and faced the window. "Never mind, I don't know what I'm saying."

"I do not know what I am to say."

"I know!" He sat on the arm of the chair. "I'm seventeen and you're twenty." He exhaled. "But that shouldn't matter. I'm going to grow taller."

She stood in front of him. "Please do not leave our friendship."

He stood and moved toward the window to evade her next embrace.

"Please, Charles?"

He raised his hands and looked upward. "Why can't I just say no?" By saying yes to friendship, he'd have to endure a whole new life of torture, and explain how she'd have to avoid being affectionate.

The padded door opened and Moshe walked in. "You have quite a story, Charles."

"Story?" Gladia looked around the walls. "You listen us? This was private talking!"

Agatha walked in behind Moshe. "I'm sorry. It was my idea to record your conversation. Charles' parents are under top-priority investigation."

Charles couldn't blame them for trying to extract information, since he'd deceived everybody. And now he was elated to have a leading intelligence agency investigating his parents.

Gladia scowled. "You *use me* to record my best friend?" She grabbed Charles' hand and stormed toward the exit. Nearing the door, she gave Agatha a tight-lipped frown as she blew air from her nostrils.

Charles stopped her and broke hand contact. "It's okay, I was going to tell them everything anyway." Everything except the deep-dark parts. He loved hearing her say "best friend." It gave him a shimmer of hope.

She puffed a breath. "Come on, we need to eat."

Moshe raised his hand. "Charles, I still want you to see my doctor."

"He is not needing that kind of doctor, sir," she spewed through clenched teeth.

"Gladia!" Agatha said, brows dipped.

Moshe put his hand up. "It's all right. We invaded their privacy."

Charles extended his hand and shook Moshe's. "Another time, sir. I promise I'll see him."

≈≈≈

Charles returned to the library upon Gladia's multiple invitations. He tried to resume his engineering studies as she piled books in front of him, but the information didn't leap out like it used to. The environment had too many memories for him to stick around much longer.

Shortly after lunch, he recognized the twin Arab brother and sister entering the library. They walked right to him. "Hi Rich-ard," the sister said.

Charles narrowed his brows. "Why did you use that name?" None of his new acquaintances addressed him by his fake passport name.

"You not remember?" She pushed her finger out. "I point to Haifa and say that way."

"Yes, I remember you. But I don't remember giving you my name." He'd been distraught when they met, but hopefully not that confused.

"Yes," the brother said. "You say it was Rich-erd—"

"Charles, there is a phone call in the office," Gladia interrupted.

"There is?"

She crossed her arms. "Yes, *there is*."

As they entered the office, she quickly shut the door. "Why are they talking with you?"

"*Ahh* … I met them before." He hoped she wouldn't inquire further; his first encounter with the twins was embarrassing.

"You met them? What are they saying to you?"

He shrugged. "Why so many questions?"

"Because they do not come to this library until you do. They could be irregulars."

"So all Arabs are bad people now?"

"No! You know I do not think that. My boss Regina, she is Arab. I love her. I told you that."

At that moment, he realized her passion and concern was the epitome of his attraction to her. Maybe he could figure a solution for their romance by learning more about her zeal.

"Charles. Are you listening?"

"Irregulars? I don't think so." He stretched his finger toward the door. "Look how young they are. They're very nice to me. And, *the girl* is pretty."

Gladia squinted. "She is not pretty!"

"You should let me introduce you." He opened the door and began walking toward them.

She grabbed his arm. "Our work cannot afford new friends like that," she whispered. "We trust no one. You know that."

He eased his arm from her grip. "Well, I'll just have to be careful."

As he approached the twins, he glanced to see if she was watching. "What is your name?" he loudly asked. He didn't pay attention to their answer, because Gladia quickly turned, her high heels clicking the wooden floor toward the main counter.

CHAPTER 11

Charles wiped sweat from his forehead as he snapped out of a nightmare; Father strangling Gladia in his bathtub back home. When he looked down the line of bunk beds at the Haganah training facility in Tel Aviv, he wondered how he'd get through another day. The term "lovesick" finally made sense.

Ten days after he began, Moshe summoned him to his office. His customary smile absent, the commander pulled a small brown sack from his drawer. "It's not a test this time, Charles. These documents must be carried overseas tonight."

"I won't let you down." Charles raised a finger. "Sir? I know there's more intelligence about my parents."

Moshe grinned. "That's what I like about you, Charles. You see things others don't. You're going to be a tremendous asset. We disclose what needs disclosing. It's all for the benefit of this nation, which is bigger than any of us."

Charles frowned. "One more thing, sir. I tried to obtain information about my parents through Gladia at school. She *ahh* ... looked in their archives. Was it you who directed the records' removal?"

"Like I said ..." Moshe rose. "Agatha will be in momentarily with your instructions."

However illogical, Charles hoped Gladia would come bursting in. It had been an agonizing month since he last saw her—actually thirty-four days and about seven hours. And there would be no time to say goodbye.

Agatha entered and handed him an envelope. "Your driver is here. Read this, then hand it to the driver for destruction. We'll see you in three weeks."

≈≈≈

Arriving in London, Charles still wasn't sure if the contents he carried were real or trash. While delivering them, the Zionist leaders asked if he was familiar with Cyprus. Shuddering inwardly, he thought about Samuel's near fate on the original voyage, and said he'd heard of it.

To his surprise, they disguised him as a Mormon missionary and flew him to Istanbul, Turkey, where he sailed the Mediterranean and docked in Famagusta Bay on the Island of Cyprus. On his voyage there, he thought about Samuel's theatrical description of the place. Now he could verify for himself if it was a ploy for sympathy, or if Jews were really being detained in a miserable prison for merely trying to find a home en route to Palestine.

The answer came when his bus bumped down a dusty road, along a barbed-wire fence that held thousands of thin men, women and children, some still wearing the Nazi-forced Star of David. Many of them bowed their heads, reminding him of a newsreel he'd seen of a Nazi concentration camp. When the bus stopped, only a nurse and a nun joined him toward the camp's entrance. After passing a barbed-wire gate entry and two armed Brits who never looked at him, a crooked wooden shack was all that separated him from masses of Jews. A soldier escorted the nurse to another small shack, while the nun stood behind him.

A man peeked out the shack's glassless window. "Hello little fella … ma'am." He obviously wasn't British, and looked like many of the Jews Charles had met in Palestine: still quite thin, but nothing like the ones in the dusty camp.

His speech was ready. "Hello. I'm a Mormon missionary. Can you direct me to the main office so I can check in?"

The man laughed, "And what main office would that be?" He looked up at a faded, cracked sign labeled "Office." "Hate to damper the mission, kid, but you won't be converting these Jews."

Charles looked at the other shack labeled, "Jewish entrance," and heard the familiar sounds of British voices with their snide interrogating tones. Several Jewish men carrying physician's bags, and women with red crosses on their arms, were being interrogated. One officer snatched a camera strapped around a doctor's neck. The man in front of Charles nodded toward the entrance. "I guess you can go in. Nobody's running over here to question you."

When he entered the main yard, soldiers interrupted his path with dozens of sunburned Jews following; they'd just climbed off an open-back truck. Charles froze as they passed by, knowing if his cover was blown he could be walking a line like that.

He entered the camp, the Book of Mormon and a Torah in one hand, while he removed his hat and wiped dust that clung to his forehead. He couldn't walk far without maneuvering around someone in need of a bandage or a clean towel. He stooped down and used the last clean corner of his hanky to wipe filth and snot from a cute toddler's face. The little fellow ran freely about with no parents in sight. He'd thought Palestine was backward, but at least it had buildings, trees, and better sanitation.

His heart felt like it sank to his knees from seeing hundreds of people either hunched over or displaying faces like they'd received news of a death. When he came to the main path, he couldn't gauge the end of the tents that lined up seemingly miles long. Their canvases flapped in the arid breeze while the tent stakes shook in rock-strewn soil. He trudged onward to the camp's southwest corner, his tongue parched already, but he didn't dare drink anything.

He maneuvered past more helpless Jews sitting outside their dust-infested tents, and cringed because Americans had been deceived to believe the Jews were free from this type of persecution. No wonder the British officer confiscated the doctor's camera; their facade would shatter if news of the atrocity went public.

When he reached the coordinates he'd been given, an elderly rabbi stood in his path. "Why do you remove the hat often?" The broken English matched the man's wrinkled, dusty, black European attire.

Charles tipped his cap. "It's because I have a perspiration problem, *my good fellow*." Saying the code words made him feel silly.

"I am Aaron Bartimus. I wait to meet you." The rabbi hunched over, cracked a little smile, and shook Charles' hand. "Come show me the book." He released his feeble chapped hand and dragged his worn shoes across the dirt toward his tent. "Please come out of this scorching sun."

Charles' heart ached when he saw the old rabbi taking baby steps into his living area. Inside the tent, the air smothered him like an oven, yet he had to know. "How many Jews are in this place?"

"One is too many. The dump holds thirty thousand. There is maybe about three-fourths of that now. It is difficult to know since new Jews come, and some go out in a box. Then, many more come. And thousands are born here too."

Charles could barely fathom those numbers. "That's too many stolen lives."

"Most of us think if we survive Nazis, we survive anything. But our crime of being Jewish has much broader hatred than your press lets you believe. And they use Nazi war criminals to care for this rotten place." He pointed southward. "They live in barracks near the sea. Why would anybody with a heartbeat do this to us?" He grabbed Charles' shirt collar. "Guess who pays for this dump?" He let go and stepped back. "I am sorry, I get angry from the screaming every night; Mostly the children. They have nightmares about Nazis who sneer at us from across the fence and say horrible things like, "we are breaking out tonight so we can get you!"

"Who pays for this?" Charles held the center tent stake when his head rushed from dizziness. Sweat stung his eyes and his filthy hanky was useless.

"Taxes are paid by Jews in Palestine."

Charles placed his hand on the man's bony shoulder. "I'm very sorry."

Aaron cracked a half smile. "It is no fault of yours. We like Americans." He shifted his eyes left and right. "More of you come here helping us. But a few, they were caught."

Charles didn't need to hear that, or the penalty for Americans helping Jews. "Were you arrested out at sea?"

"Yes. We would step onto anything that floated. That sea has become a new trap for our people."

If Charles had needed more confirmation about doing the right thing, hearing Aaron's testimony justified working for the Haganah. The Zionists were wise to send him, so he'd know why they fought so diligently for freedom. What decent human wouldn't be indignant with all this tragedy done in secret from the rest of the world?

"I hope you get out of this dreadful place soon," he said. "I wish I could take you with me."

"Thank you, that is a good thought." Aaron pointed his bent index finger. "That book will help."

Sensing a sermon coming like the ones Rabbi Jesse gave, Charles handed the Torah over.

Aaron shook his head. "Not the good book, the other one."

Confused that a rabbi would ask for a Book of Mormon, he exchanged them. Aaron began ripping the back cover, almost like a kid opening a gift. When he was done, he extracted a folded paper hidden inside. "No Jew would ever rip a Torah, you see."

Charles leaned over the cot as Aaron sat and unfolded the parchment. "What is that?"

Aaron looked up. "A way out." His gleaming face was in stark contrast to the hopelessness of moments ago. "We are planning—"

"Wait." The possibility of Cyprus becoming his new home made Charles' pulse rise. He walked outside and looked around.

When he returned, Aaron finished unfolding the concealed paper. "We are planning a dig to escape this God-forsaken place. I am glad you will never understand what a death camp is like. This is second worse place, and I am sorry you have to see it."

If you don't obey My commands, I will set My face against you so that you will be defeated by your enemies; and those who hate you shall rule over you. Leviticus 26:17. How odd to think of such a timely scripture. He wondered if that's what Jesse meant when he couldn't explain how God speaks to people.

Aaron looked up with soft eyes. "I have repented of my sins. I can-not die here."

Charles' eyes moistened as he sat next to Aaron. How foolish to think his mission was to report the conditions of the camp and give a poor rabbi something to read.

Aaron placed two fingers up. "Two hundred fighting men will escape for the Haganah. These plans show where to dig a tunnel...." He convulsed into a hacking cough. Then he pointed to the Book of Prophets on his flimsy cot and wiggled his fingers. Charles handed it over. Aaron flipped the pages and pointed to Ezekiel 35:37. "Look at what God said concerning the Promised Land: 'I will increase their men like a flock. Their men will populate the desolate cities. And they will know I am the Lord.'" He hacked another cough.

"You're coughing up blood." Charles tried to clean his soiled hanky, but it was disgusting. "Here, take the edge of my shirt."

"No," Aaron whispered, out of breath.

Charles stood. "I'll look for a doctor."

"Attention, I-do-not-need," Aaron said through another choking cough. Wheezing, he pointed to a dirty canteen atop a bloodstained rag. "Besides, getting a doctor here is like getting a steak supper."

Charles handed him water and the dirty towel. "I don't know ... that's a lot of blood. You need a doctor *right now!*" He rose.

Aaron grabbed Charles' shirt with strength far greater than his feeble demeanor implied. "Listen, sonny, I survive worse than this hell-hole." He placed his chapped palm on Charles' hand. "I will not expire in this rat cellar. I pleaded my case with God and I will die in the Promised Land. That is my last covenant." He nodded firmly.

Charles dropped a tear onto the print as Aaron crinkled it over his lap, then Charles sat and analyzed the drawing. "These plans are wrong."

"No, they are good—"

"The idea is good." Charles slid his finger across the drawing. "But that tunnel is in the wrong place."

Aaron coughed on the map. "You are but a youngster. How can you know this?"

"I've read numerous books on archeological digs, and I'm studying structural engineering." He dabbed blood spatters off the map with the edge of is shirt. "Who's in charge of this? I'll show them the fault."

Aaron held his wrist out. "Help me up. I will take you."

He led Charles to a nearby tent and introduced him to several middle-aged men. Charles spent the rest of the day revising the plans, then stood and stretched. "It's almost dark, and I'm required to leave. I hope you make it to the Promised Land."

Eyes wet, Aaron hugged him. "It is great people like you that God uses to win our nation. No one else has been able to bring these plans." He pinched Charles' cheek with his coarse fingers. "You avoid suspicion. Nice work."

Walking toward the checkout gate, Charles pondered all the comments people had made concerning God using him. He reasoned within about being on a divine mission, but upon careful consideration, he'd chosen his own path.

≈≈≈

After returning to London with a greater understanding about the people he'd worked for, Charles was escorted to Zionist National Headquarters. He walked into a surprise celebration dinner for notable Zionists—including him.

A couple approached his table. The man wore a tuxedo with tasseled shoulders and the woman, a white ball gown. "Hello, Charles, I'm Doctor Chaim Weizmann and this is my wife Doctor Vera Weizmann. I'm the president of the European Zionist Organization, and my lovely wife heads the Women's International Zionist Organization."

Charles stood. "I'm honored to meet you both." His voiced cracked in the middle of his sentence, but they were gracious enough not to react to it.

"The honor is ours, young man," Vera said.

Chaim smiled. "We are pleased to have you working with us. You're the first operative we've successfully infiltrated Cyprus with. I can tell by your expression, you might not realize what you accomplished."

"Are you okay?" Vera asked, glancing at his untouched plate. "Is your food not to your liking?"

"I'm sorry, I'm sure it's fine. I now have a better understanding of why the Zionist organization exists." His voice cracked again, so he cleared his throat and sipped his tea. "I haven't had an appetite since I left there."

Vera nodded. "I'm sorry you had to see that place, but it certainly brings perspective to our predicament. We need the world to see this before it happens in Palestine, but nobody will report it." She shook Charles' hand. "Please excuse me, I have an appointment to keep. I'm glad I had a chance to meet you."

Charles bowed his head. "It was my pleasure to meet you too."

Chaim put his hand on Charles' shoulder. "I can't begin to express how refreshing it is to have another American who can fathom our plight. When you're finished here, we have an offer prepared for you."

"An offer?" He was still surprised how quickly he'd risen in the ranks, and he wasn't tired of being needed. "I'm done now, sir."

Chaim grinned. "Well then … come with me."

He followed Mr. Weizmann into a private room populated with older men and glaring crystal lights. Persian rugs covered the floor and vertical walnut moldings bordered red-velvet walls. Charles felt out of place as usual, so again, he pondered old times with Gladia so his face would look pleasant. But it saddened him when he remembered her confessing how he was her only friend.

"Charles, we spoke to your commander and he agreed." Mr. Weizmann came into focus in front of him. "We want to send you to America for an extended assignment."

His heart skipped. "America? *Ahh*, well, I don't know. I … I had my heart set on attending the Technion in Haifa this semester."

Mr. Weizmann sent him a reassuring nod. "It's a very important assignment in New York, and not many individuals qualify."

"What's the *assignment?*" His voice cracked again, but worse this time.

The older men grinned and nodded at each other. "I'm sorry Charles, you know the rules."

He also knew the risks. But they may not have known the additional liabilities against him. If caught, his plan to find out about his past would cease. And the thought of being absent from Gladia for along duration was unbearable.

"You don't have to decide at this moment," Mr. Weizmann continued. "We can discuss it after the ceremony." He patted Charles' arm. "I know how important your education is. It's important to us as well. If you decide to sacrifice another year for our nation, I will make sure you get the education you deserve. And, if I am able, when I visit New York this summer, I will introduce you to someone I heard you admire: Albert Einstein."

"You know Professor Einstein?"

"Yes, he's a good friend of mine. I'm sure you know he's Jewish. He lives nearby the New York assignment, in Princeton, New Jersey."

"Is Einstein a Zionist?" Charles asked.

"Not directly like you and I, being as busy as he is, but he does support us wholeheartedly. And that makes him a Zionist." Mr. Weizmann pointed, and walked Charles toward the wall. "We framed that plaque with one of his quotes."

> We foster the hope to create in Palestine a homeland for our people. The Palestine community should aim to approach the social ideal of our ancestors as it is set down in the Bible. A spiritual center for the Jews of the entire world.

"Einstein is one of many famous supporters," Mr. Weizmann said, his pride evident. "There's another plaque over there from Winston Churchill."

Meeting the famed professor would be an opportunity of a lifetime. David attended school in New York too, so he could see his best friend. "I'll do it." Just for a short time hopefully and then back to Gladia.

Mr. Weizmann smiled. "Splendid, I will make the arrangements."

Each man in the room shook his hand and thanked Charles for his sacrifice. After, he slipped over to read Winston Churchill's comments.

> Smiling orchards. We conquered Tel Aviv when it was sand dunes and swamps. Now, over a decade later, it's overwhelming to see how the Jews have transformed the desolate places to lush orchards and initiated progress instead of stagnation.

Charles stepped back and marveled that a Brit would state such a thing publicly—obviously their government had opposing sides about Jewish support like the Americans did. It made him recall Rabbi Jesse's prediction from Ezekiel 36:34–36, from his old Book of the Prophets—although Charles heard others call it the Old Testament:

> The desolate land will be cultivated instead of being a wasteland, in the sight of everyone who passes by. They will say, "This desolate land has become like the garden of Eden" ... then the heathen that are left round about shall know that I the Lord built the ruined places....

Mr. Weizmann picked up a black box from a nearby table. "Now for more good news." He opened the box and held up a gleaming solid gold medallion. "Charles, it is with great pleasure that we offer you a promotion in the Zionist organization. If you accept this award, you will be promoted to field supervisor."

Charles widened his eyes. "I would be honored, sir."

Mr. Weizmann handed him the award. "You are the first American, and the youngest lad, to receive this prestigious recognition. Congratulations." Everyone applauded.

Charles needed some cheering up. If he could just adapt some of the positive attitudes from these great leaders, he'd be able to relax and sleep better at night. "Thank you, but I don't understand the promotion: I've only completed a few missions."

"Yes, and you exceeded our expectations. You saved lives! We understand that you discovered a serious flaw in the Cyprus tunnel plans. Please enlighten us."

Charles cleared his throat. "The escape tunnel was routed to cross under a ravine. I warned them if they dug under it, the passageway would collapse and bury anyone inside it."

"And how did you know this?" Mr. Weizmann asked.

"I love archeology, and I've read books that illustrated the pitfalls of excavations. Digging near canyons is risky, so I suggested a reroute, along with using additional support systems like tent poles to triple-support the cave. I also showed them how to redistribute the soil, to avoid detection, and to use an assembly line method I learned from reading Henry Ford's production papers."

"Impressive, young man," one of the men said. They applauded him again. "Bravo, Charles, bravo!"

Charles took a step back and grinned.

Mr. Weizmann shook his head. "Well done! *That* is why you are being promoted. A typical courier would have delivered the plans and unknowingly left our men to a disaster. God is going to bless you for contributing to His people in such a mighty way."

"I know you've been trained and briefed about confidentiality." Mr. Weizmann walked Charles out, his voice low and somber. "But I feel compelled to tell you, if this assignment leaks to the wrong people, it will greatly diminish our chances of rebirthing our nation." He led Charles into an elevator, waited for the door to close, and faced him. "Thousands of Jewish lives will be depending on *your* success."

CHAPTER 12

December 1945

After the plane screeched down in New York, Charles approached a waiting cab. The driver opened the back door and extended his hand. Charles clenched his sack, but handed over his suitcase before climbing in. The cabby hit the gas pedal, throwing Charles against the seat.

He was used to unhurried traffic due to horses and donkeys lacing the streets of Palestine, so the swerving and weaving past tall buildings and masses of people were perfect recipes to bring on a familiar headache. He examined the long rows of cars and taxis behind them. "New York University, please." Seeing David could take the edge off his reverse culture shock.

The cabby craned his neck back. "You sure? The instructions say the docks."

He sighed, knowing his orders were to report to Yaakov Dostrovski upon arrival. "*Ahh* ... yes. Stick to the location you have."

The cabby seemed to hit every pothole until he stopped in front of a beaten-down metal building with a sign above the door labeled "Acme Shipping Company." "Are you sure this is the address?" Charles asked.

"This is it. Don't know why anybody would want to go in there."

Charles tipped the driver and walked toward the dented warehouse, glancing back at the disappearing cab puffing fog from its exhaust. He slid and danced to keep balance on the transparent ice that shimmered in the morning sun. Clouds formed from his breath as he knocked on the shabby door and watched chunks of ice fall. He shook his stiff hand: gloves and a warm jacket would be his first purchases.

"Welcome to my office, Charles."

The familiar accent from behind revealed a stocky man wearing a ski jacket, scarf and cap. The man held out his gloved hand. "My name is Yaakov Dostrovski, former Haganah chief."

"You're the commander's predecessor? Pleased to meet you, sir." He put his frigid hand out and shook Yaakov's glove. "You recognized me."

"You are known well. Your reputation is preceding you."

Charles smiled. The vote of confidence almost warmed his shivering body.

"Come in my friend. You need to warm yourself." The commander opened the door and nodded for him to enter first. "You are not dressed for the New York winter." Yaakov peered about before closing the door. The small dingy office only had a desk, two chairs, a walnut filing cabinet, and a brown couch next to a potbelly stove. Yaakov stretched his hand out. "Please, sit." He sat across from Charles behind the desk. "You look pale. Your trip was not good?"

"It was okay. I'm just not used to snowy weather." The stove began to emit a little heat, which warmed his skin but did nothing for his chilled bones.

"Your assignment. Lately, immigration to Palestine is standing still. Our last Aliya Bet, that is, voyage to Yisrael, which you call Palestine, was ..." He looked up, snapped his fingers. "A disaster. We need Americans like you to help improve the effort. We must bring more Jews to our homeland and fortify our troops, or our enemies will prevail."

When the coffee percolated, Yaakov rose, poured two cups and handed one to Charles. "Charles, my new friend, I give you example of why you come. A few years ago, eleven hundred Jews hiding from Hitler, sail from

Vienna toward our land, but the British forced them to dock in Yugoslavia. Not long after, the Nazis invade that place and kill nine hundred and fifteen Jews from that ship. The Nazis do the shooting, but the Brits ... they are the killers." Yaakov frowned. "Those Jews should be living in Yisrael today. Five of the victims were my brother Josiah, his wife Emily and their children: Josephina, Matyanne and Joshua."

Charles shook his head. "I'm sorry to hear that." His voice cracked, so he touched his throat and cleared it. "I'm sorry sir, it must be the cold."

Yaakov smiled. "It is the change."

Charles nodded. "Yes, the dry air."

Yaakov shook his head. "No, it is the change in life. You are turning to a man." Yaakov looked at the glowing coals in the stove. "The boy voice ... it is changing to a mans."

"Oh! That makes sense." Charles grinned. "Finally, no more little-sonny-boy comments. The doctor said I should've had a growth spurt a long time ago."

"That is it!" Yaakov grinned and thrust his finger out. "No more small boy. Congratulates to you." Then his smile faded. "What we do here will save thousands. Everyone thinks the war is over and Jews are safe. But our people are dying because no country will accept them in large numbers. Except one time, President Roosevelt rescued nine hundred and eighty-seven Jews, to be his guest at Fort Ontario, in Oswego, New York. He saved them from Hitler."

Charles warmed his hands on his coffee mug. "Why can't the others go back to the homes they had before the Nazis invaded?"

"That is what everybody ask. But when Jews go back, hostile neighbors took their homes and businesses because Hitler's propaganda made things worse! And the Arabs? They set up hate radio in Germany." He pointed his finger upward. "They had the Fuhrer's money to curse us in Arabic over the airwaves, so thousands more join the hatred."

Although the room had warmed, a chill ran through Charles. "That explains the extreme Arab hatred, they heard propaganda in their own language." Gladia had tried to explain it, but with their translation gap, he didn't fully understand. If he could just send her a telegram and receive one back, maybe his longing for her would ease a little. She was probably at the library, sad and alone.

Yaakov leaned in. "What is it, my friend?"

"That same poison spread around the world, into my father's heart." His eyes moistened. "He made me … I'm sorry. I only meant to say, I know those lies verbatim."

Yaakov rose and sat at the edge of his desk. "You do not have to be sorry. Everybody I speak with loves you! Now that you understand more, allow me to explain a new position to you." He motioned his hands with his fingers spread. "We have thousands of Machal."

"Machal?"

"You call them volunteer. We spread a word by mouth only to American Jews, asking them to help as seamen. Happily, we also get many others like you." He smiled and spread his arms wide. "They have big hearts of compassion. Others? They come for adventure. And we get church people who know about Israel from their Old Testament too. They share our belief that God will reestablish our land. So, we will send thousands of displaced survivors from Europe to Palestine in old reconditioned warships. And because the Machal are many, we need your help."

He stood, tapping his finger to his temple. "We need smart English-speaking supervisor to coordinate. We train them to sail. You show them Palestine culture, and what they need to know for the Resistance. We choose you because they need to learn from an American. You will also obtain equipment for ships we prepare." He waved his hand across the air. "You will be master coordinator. Second to my command only."

Charles moved his head back. "You don't feel I'm a bit young?" As soon as he said that, he remembered how young some of the freedom fighters were.

"I tell you this. Chaim Weizmann only sends the best. You are young on the outside," he tapped Charles' chest, "but you are older on the inside. I am a leader of men. I know."

Charles marveled about having a reputation that would make a former commander state such a compliment. Yet, a leadership position would take a strong attitude. It was time to gird up, act manlier. Fortunately, he had Moshe and Dov to emulate. "I must say, I'm overwhelmed with the Zionist network. You're everywhere. And your plans are brilliant."

Yaakov raised his hands. "We are everywhere because God is our network. He made promises, and we humbly ask Him to fulfill them. You know the scriptures about the rebirth of Israel, yes?"

"I do. Every Jew I encounter sounds so sure of that ancient guarantee." He shrugged. Once again, he didn't want to tell a Jew what he really thought, but he took an instant trust to Yaakov. "How can you be sure it will come to pass? It's just a book. A profound one, but it's only pages of information."

Yaakov chuckled. "It is not just a book. It is God's auto-bi-ography. Where do you think we get the smart plans? His wisdom spoke through the prophets and gave us instruction how to live. When we obey, we prosper. When we sin … well, you see what has happened. Reading scripture is like reading a person's mail. If the letter is not written to you, then you will not understand it. Imagine you read a letter to my nephew, Joseph. Dear Joseph how is your mother, Augustina? You see? It would not make sense for you. But if you get the letter from your best friend, you understand the contents … yes?"

Charles nodded.

"The scriptures, they are love letters from God, written to us who believe. So we understand it more than you. It can look foolish to those who don't believe. *Until you have faith in God,* and He resides in your heart." He placed his index finger on Charles' chest. "When you have this, you understand it, because now it is written to you too."

Charles bobbed his head. "I've never heard it explained that way. Simple. Yet profound." He contemplated having faith in something written, even though he couldn't reason with it logically. On his voyage to Palestine, he dismissed the notion as foolishness just like Yaakov just said; but after months of witnessing uncommon valor and determination to fulfill prophecy, such faith was difficult to argue with: especially when he witnessed numerous prophecies fulfilled, along with Jews worldwide, banding together for one cause—those were either miracles or flukes that were too hard to explain.

But a moment later, Father's relentless chants interjected: *God created Jews for labor—they were not supposed to procreate and venture on their own.* Disgusting phrases like those still badgered him every time he considered exercising faith.

"Your face … something is not good."

Yaakov's comment brought him back, but he wouldn't dare tell him what he was thinking. "Soon I'll want to go back to Palestine. I have school and … a special friend."

Yaakov smiled. "*Ahh* … special friend. You have a woman there."

"Yes, I miss her terribly."

He shook his head. "Chaim does not want you in Palestine. Your file says you were beaten before you get off the dock, so you know it is a treacherous place. I agree. We need you here. This is your homeland, you belong here—"

Charles stood. "I belong with her!"

Yaakov grinned and hugged him. "Okay. I understand, my friend." He slapped Charles' back. "A man will die for a woman he loves. Come, I will show you where you sleep."

Yaakov brought him to a loft in the back of the warehouse, just big enough for a single bed between a nightstand and a dresser. While he unpacked, Charles thought about Gladia's routine. He looked at his pocket watch, calculated the time difference, and figured she was probably stacking books, looking amazing as usual. He hoped someday he'd bring her to see America. After Father was dead or jailed of course.

His stomach was still on European time, so he approached Yaakov for a snack. "I'd like to go to New York University tomorrow."

When he explained why, Yaakov came near him. "It is good you have a friend here, but you must be careful not to tell him about our work."

Charles smiled. "Actually, he's a Zionist." Which was one of the biggest surprises of their friendship. Just before Charles escaped the country, David had revealed his family's faith. At first, Charles was hurt that David hadn't told him before, because of his anti-Semitic father. But after thinking it through, he understood: Jews were persecuted in Los Angeles too.

Yaakov nodded. "*Ahh*, what group? Chalutzim, Habonim?"

Charles shrugged. "I don't know."

"I want you to go and see your friend, but we have training first, and much work. You can go on Sabbath, yes?"

Charles paused. "All right." After eating, he went upstairs to settle in, but when he tried to sleep, he ruffled the sheets for hours; in Palestine, it was only two in the afternoon.

He opened his eyes to "Good morning," and a blurry outline above him. He reached for his glasses. Yaakov stretched a cup in his direction. "Each morning I will wake you a little earlier, until you adjust to the time."

Charles took an elongated sniff of the Columbian blend, and sipped.

Dave Longeuay

Yaakov motioned his head. "Come outside, there is something you can see."

They walked down the steps through the messy warehouse, past dozens of crates labeled "Clothing for the Needy." Usually boxes like that contained arms and military supplies. Yaakov turned a giant metal wheel to open the back cargo door. Charles widened his eyes, but not from the cold gust blowing his hair back.

Yaakov smiled. "I thought it might impress you. She sailed in late last night."

Charles took in a crisp breath of air and examined the massive, beat-up vessel. "I'm surprised it's still floating. How big is it?"

"Nine-hundred-seventy metric tons. Two-hundred-eight by thirty-three meters. It will be named the *Balboa*."

"That's a lot of men out there." He looked at Yaakov. "I'm in charge of all of them?"

Yaakov nodded. "Not to worry my friend. I will help you. In a short time you will not need me." He stepped forward. "Come, it is time you meet your crew."

Charles had already learned nautical terms and maritime equipment specs, necessary for sailing the rigorous Atlantic. But turning battered warships from South America into seaworthy cargo/passenger vessels would be a challenge: lives would be at stake in turbulent waters.

While surveying the ship with his men, he looked at the city backdrop. The Statute of Liberty rested on the edge of the horizon. His mind battled between Father having David tailed and the math equations needed to calculate the heavy equipment so the ship wouldn't sink mid-sea.

For the first time, when he crawled into bed that night, his eyes shut prior to thinking about Gladia.

≈≈≈

124

Footsteps clumped up the stairs as Charles woke. A dark, blurry image stood in the entryway. "Charles, it is Sabbath day."

Putting his glasses on brought a smiling Yaakov into focus. "I know." He sat up with a week's worth of excitement and anxiety about walking the campus to find David.

Yaakov bent over. "You do not look happy to see your friend. You are too tired?"

He planted his feet on the floor and stretched. "I'm very excited, but … I'm kind of nervous." An urge to tell Yaakov about his fugitive status burned in his heart. The former high-ranking commander deserved honesty.

"When you see him you will feel better. Old friends, they are good to the soul. And, I understand the woman, she make you a little crazy, yes? I see it on you." He grinned. "You must love her very much." He cupped his hand on his ear. "I make calls yesterday and locate the dorm to your friend. Are you going?"

"Yes. I haven't seen him in seven months. He'll be quite surprised."

"Okay, that is more like it! I will call the cab. Do not forget the new coat I buy you."

After Yaakov yelled, "The cab is here," Charles peered out the window before going outside. Nerves made it hard for him to breathe while the cabby raced him New York style to Washington Square, Manhattan.

CHAPTER 13

Charles found his way to David's dorm room, but it was empty. He walked the campus, looking back constantly, when a young couple holding hands left a sorority house. They strolled across the grassy plaza and he pictured Gladia walking out to embrace him. It had only been six weeks, but he missed her as if they were dating. Lack of contact with her, due to spies monitoring communications to and from Palestine, was the worst part of the trip.

He noticed another couple to his left, leaving a theater with friends. A closer look revealed David with his arm around a girl, talking and laughing with friends. The group moseyed in his direction, so he followed procedure and hid. If Father had David followed, his buddy could be arrested for abetting a fugitive.

His growling stomach reminded him it was past lunch while he watched David from the shadows of buildings. When the group entered a diner nearby, the whiff of frying hamburgers enticed him. After surveying the area for suspicious characters, he opened the door to a medley of tantalizing aromas. His parents had never let him enjoy that kind of food.

When the group seated, he slipped the waiter a dollar to let him serve drinks at David's table. "Okay, who has the Coke?"

David fixed puzzled eyes on Charles. Then he whispered to his friends and they left. He grabbed Charles' shirt so he'd quickly sit. "My goodness, little buddy! How did you...?" He embraced Charles. "You've grown! And what happened to the red hair?"

"Why'd you send your friends away so quickly? He's not here is he?"

"Give me a minute." David took a breathe and handed him a menu. "Let's get you some food."

"You didn't answer my question." Charles looked about. "Tell me he's not here...."

David put his hand up. "No. But I'll tell you about that in a minute. I've never been so worried in my whole life. The way you left so suddenly ... watching you board that train, all that cash in your shoes, not knowing where you were headed." He leaned in. "Where have you been?"

Charles summarized his journey while they ate burgers, fries, and consumed multiple Cokes. David hung on every word, especially when Charles shared his mixed-signals experience with Gladia.

"I know your persistence. You'll win her over, but you're going to need my help." David pointed at him. "You're a book expert. I'll get you a book from the university library about romance."

Charles didn't have the heart to tell David how ridiculous his suggestion sounded.

David scanned the diner again. "Do you know how rare it is to be a Gentile in the Haganah? The American Zionists revere their courageous acts." He leaned back. "But I'm not surprise. You'll do mighty things for God with them. I bet you've seen the real thing, rather than what the press writes."

Charles looked down and nodded. "It's a rollercoaster ride. There's jubilee one day," he glanced upward, "and death the next. Many are scarred emotionally." He wasn't in the mood to go any further than that.

"Did you see a lot of action?"

Charles looked down and took a deep breath; the fatalities were more painful than his upbringing. "I had no idea what I was in for. Finding that photograph really changed my life." He removed his glasses and rubbed his head, ready to change the subject. "So, are you going to tell me what's wrong?

And what are you doing for the Zionists?" He set his glasses on the table. "These frames give me headaches. I wish someone would invent a way to see without these bulky glasses. Like little miniature lenses that could be placed directly on your eyes."

David laughed. "You have the wildest ideas. To answer your question: I keep important people safe. At my first interview, they looked at my size and questioned me about bullies." He pointed to Charles. "I even used you as an example, when the seniors used to harass you. After hearing that, they offered me a security position for Zionists who visit New York."

Charles smiled. "That fits you. I'll have to tell Yaakov."

David looked around again. "I'm glad you were careful, following me. Your parents, and the Los Angeles authorities, questioned me for hours before I moved here. They know about the money, and they want it back." He eyes shifted left-to-right. "Sometimes I feel like they're still following me."

Charles quivered, picturing Father's perfectly straight teeth gritting at him. "They know your location?" David nodded. Charles clenched his jaw tight. "How did they find out? Did they mention the photo missing?"

"No. They found the attorney you contacted through your phone records."

"Oh no. Julie." He rested his forehead on his palm. "How stupid of me."

"Yeah Julie, that's her name. They kept asking me if I knew her."

Charles raised his head. "Did she get in trouble?"

"She went to jail for forgery. And they threatened that I was next."

Charles shook his head. "I'm so sorry."

"Forget it. Who was Julie?"

"The legal assistant for the estate attorney. I found an inheritance from a grandfather I never knew, along with the photo. My grandfather's lawyer asked too many questions when I inquired about redeeming it early, so I left his office in a hurry. But when I reached the bottom of the stairs, Julie approached me and said she could help for a small fee."

"Don't worry about me, you did the right thing." David grinned. "I admire your courage. And it's good you never told me how you obtained the money."

"How angry were they?"

He didn't reply until Charles asked again.

"Your father pounded on our door with a face like Doctor Jekyll." He frowned. "After insulting me with all kinds of accusations, he insisted I'd regret not disclosing your whereabouts. So I followed your instructions. I held out for awhile like you said, then told him you went to Florida for schooling. That was a brilliant ploy to stall time while you left the country."

Charles' heart burned. "He didn't leave you alone, did he?"

"Now I know why you left. Within a few weeks, our lives turned into hell. First, Dad lost his job. Then, everybody in town knew we were Jews."

Charles compressed his napkin in his fist. The long list of Father's nasty quotes from Hitler's pamphlets came to mind—father enjoyed spreading poison throughout Los Angeles.

"A few neighbors were tolerant, but many shunned us like we had a plague."

The silverware began vibrating from Charles' foot kicking the table leg. Hopefully David was finished.

"It got worse. We received death threats over the telephone, and rocks with hate notes shattered our windows. People wrote political stuff on our property like, 'Pig Jews will take over the world and crush America if we don't put them down.' The wording resembled ..." David's face looked like he bit a lemon. "Remember the Nazi propaganda littered all over the city?"

Charles couldn't tell him he had to spread that trash. A belt of stress spiraled, and his breath hissed through his firm-set jaw.

129

"My father told me this was why we were Jews in secret. He wanted to spare me from this very thing: I never thought about gossip being so harmful." David's lower lip trembled. "But when the lies are about *you* ... all of a sudden, you *understand* how terrible it is."

"I did this to you and your family!"

"You're not at fault. I hated your father!" David scowled. "But I admired my father's response. He taught me it's not God's will for us to hate in return. 'Then we become like them, and hatred consumes us.'"

Charles read similar things in his psychology books: let go of bitterness and be free of its power over you.

"What was that scripture he used?" David looked up. "'Vengeance is mine saith the Lord.'" His face reddened. "But they lost their home over this!"

Charles slammed his fist on a plate; the silverware went airborne and pinged the tiles below. "Dang it! It's my fault." He jostled in his seat. "I swore I wouldn't let him get to me!" He stood, teeth gritted, no longer able to hold back a lifetime of suppressed anger. "I hate that man!"

"Whoa, buddy, sit down."

He smashed his Coke against his plate, which he imagined was Father's face. David covered his face as shards flew. Eyes bulging, Charles looked at his bleeding hand, his chest pounding. The rush was like standing on top of the world. He saw his hands around Father's neck for the first time ever.

David bolted up, clamped Charles' arm, and whisked him to the back of the diner while many sets of wide eyes followed.

Charles wanted his father dead for ruining David's family. He was a real friend, and they were hard to come by. A few breaths later, he dreaded mentally killing Father, but Father's angry face and evil phrases that were stuck in his head had to stop. Father's prejudice was alive in his thoughts, badgering him daily, and he had to stop denying the toll it took on him.

David kicked the bathroom door open and rushed Charles in. Blood from the cut dripped on the gray tiles, as Charles' breath hissed. David wet a towel and wrapped Charles' hand. "Your face is on fire. Calm down buddy. Breathe."

The door flung open and smacked the wall. A man with a manager's badge on his white shirt halted at the threshold. "Do I need to telephone the police?"

David held his palm out. "That's not necessary, sir. We're sorry. I'll pay for the dishes."

The manager stared at the blood on the floor. "You've got two minutes." He disappeared.

"Time to go, Charles." David hurried him out. Customers murmured while he slapped a five-dollar bill on the table and herded Charles out back.

They scurried down First Street. "What was that?" David asked. "I've never seen that side of you."

"I haven't either." Charles paused next to a shoeshine booth to catch his breath. "I thought a faraway place like Palestine would rid me of Father's ... but it follows me everywhere. Every Jew who confides in me? I hear Father's hatred in my head." He pulled David close. "I almost repeated one of his insults to a complaining Jew last month," he whispered. "Why do I think like him? I'm not—"

A police car ripped around the corner and sped past them toward the diner. Charles resumed his pace. "I was convinced I could overcome his ranting in my mind." He stopped and looked at David. "Will I ever find relief?"

David sighed. "Give it some time."

"Time? I've been battling this all my life!"

David patted his shoulder twice and resumed their pace down Fourth Street. "You see? You've had this torture for almost eighteen years. You've only been away from him for a short time."

"What?"

David put his arm around him. "You can't bottle it up inside. Each time it bothers you, talk about it, so you don't explode."

"Gladia said the same thing, but I couldn't tell her what I just told you."

As they continued walking toward the university, Charles pressed his head with his hands.

"You're still getting those headaches?"

"Yeah, and they're worse."

"You better see a doctor. It could be serious."

"I know." Charles pointed to a cab in front of Macy's. "It's getting late, I better get back."

"I sure missed you." David gave him a hug. "I'm happy you're here."

Charles grinned. "Sorry for the outburst. Shall we meet next weekend? I promise not to break any dishes."

David stopped and stared at him. Charles raised his palms. "I'm fine. Go. I'll contact you Friday and we'll spend the weekend together."

"One little thing comes up? You're calling me!"

Charles nodded. "Of course."

CHAPTER 14

April 1946

Months passed and several close calls with police added to Charles' anxiety that stemmed from the battles in his head; and he desperately longed for Gladia.

Coming back from a weekend at David's dorm, Charles saw Yaakov quickly stashing ammo crates in a truck with it's motor running. "Charles, help me get these boxes out of here. The police came, saying you are wanted for fraud and a runaway crime? I told them no." They hurled the last crate onto the truck and Yaacov waved the driver off. "I vouch for you. They say I will be arrested if I hide you."

Moshe wasn't exaggerating when he said his family secrets were highly classified. "I'm sorry for violating protocol. I got careless, and should have told you the truth." Charles relayed his whole story to Yaakov. "I didn't think they were watching David anymore. I wouldn't blame you if you decided to turn me in. My stupidity has jeopardized your whole operation, and put a future nation at risk!"

"You don't worry, Charles. Preparing ships for Aliya Bet is not illegal in America. Though we do it quietly, because British eyes and ears are everywhere. Of course, they don't know we have arms and TNT to load at the last minute before we sail."

"But harboring a fugitive is illegal," Charles said.

"Maybe so. But you sacrifice for us. And you flee your parents for good reasons. I would do the same. I will hide you in the ship. You can sail back to Palestine when it leaves."

"I'm not looking forward to waiting five or six weeks."

"You can continue working from the captain's quarters. We cannot risk you getting caught through public transport."

"What if the police search the ship? My father's bound to come."

"The police will not search it. It is an international ship in water. Not in their jurisdiction. I will send Moshe a message. I guess Palestine will be your destiny after all." Yaakov put his arm around Charles. "Quickly, let us get you on the ship before the police come back."

Charles peeked out from the back seat of Yaakov's car and saw the ship, *Number 106: Biriah*. It was the third ship that he'd prepared: a two-hundred-ninety-four-ton, single-smokestack, pile of ugly steel. Sailing to Sete, France, and arriving in Haifa, early July. It would be tight quarters, sailing with eleven hundred refugees in a ship barely seaworthy for seven hundred, with two, maybe three experienced seaman. The urgency to rescue hundreds of thousands of displaced Jews from tents in the freezing fields of Europe was part of the lifeline for the Jewish nation to be born.

Yaakov smuggled him in a trunk while another steamship blew its horn nearby. Several bumps later, Yaakov unlatched the door and helped him out in the cargo bay. "Charles, I'm going to miss you." He hugged him, pulled back and revealed glossy eyes. "I fly to London tomorrow. I will not see you again. Your friendship and service has been remarkable."

"Thank you, Yaakov. You …" Charles took a deep breath. "You've been amazing. I will always consider you a great friend and commander."

Yaakov ruffled his shoulder. "Okay. You go and get that girl. Bon voyage!"

"I plan to." Charles looked out at sea instead of watching another friend walk away. And now that David would be under surveillance, there'd be no goodbyes to him.

≈≈≈

Just prior to *Biriah*'s docking in France, Charles was ferried ashore at midnight. Two men in dark trench coats briefed him about being too valuable to risk prison for abetting Jews through the blockade of the Mediterranean. So he boarded a plane to Lydda, Palestine, and touched down seventeen hours later, his mood dark. With no communication for ten months, Gladia probably moved on and lost desire to remain friends.

Exiting the plane, Charles saw a black car waiting. The same woman who saw him off drove him toward headquarters, but halted several blocks from the Haganah house. He jolted forward. "Why are you stopping here?"

"That's right, you've been gone awhile. New security measures don't allow us to drive HQ." Her pointed finger stretched across his chest. "Proceed down that walkway and you'll see yellow rosebushes. Make an immediate right, clap three times and walk straight through the shrubs. A guard will escort you."

Charles got out.

"Oh. Be prepared for big news when you are debriefed," she said.

CHAPTER 15

Charles sighed when the corner of the headquarters building showed through the shrubbery. When he entered, the staff lined up and patted his shoulders as he made his way toward Moshe's office. "Shalom, Charles," each one said. He nodded and returned greetings, loving being around people who had no pretenses.

Moshe walked out and gave him a powerful hug. "Charles, what a delight to see you." Seeing Moshe's gleaming face soothed him. He'd never imagined himself in the military, but being accepted and appreciated by the Haganah filled a void he never realized was there.

Looking him over, Moshe widened his eyes. "Wow, have you grown! I barely recognize you." Moshe stared at Charles' black hair and opened his mouth, but he shut it quickly. No more comments about being small and ruddy. Hearing Moshe confirm it made him chuckle, yet as he got a better look at his commander, he noticed deeper wrinkle lines and nearly twice the gray hairs.

Moshe pointed to his office. "Let's sit. We'll address your troubles with the American authorities later." Before entering his office he yelled down the hall, "Josephina. Can I trouble you for two cups of tea with honey?"

Right on cue: Charles' favorite.

They entered Moshe's office and sat. "You're a popular young man. Chaim asked for you again, but we told him we need you here. Will you be ready for work in a few days?"

"Yes sir, I can't wait to see … everyone."

Moshe chuckled. "Would everyone have the name of, Gladia?"

"Is it that obvious?"

He winked. "When a man's in love, it's always obvious my friend. I hope things work out for you two. She's a fine woman." He raised his brows. "A passionate woman at that."

Charles grinned. "That's part of what I love about her."

"I know you're anxious to see her. But first, you need debriefing. I would've assigned you to Dov Grunner again, but he's still awaiting trial."

"They haven't tried him yet?"

"No, and it's looking like a potential death sentence, I'll have to tell you later."

Charles' heart sank. "Gladia must be devastated." He was ready to comfort her.

"I hope she can pull through this. Agatha's been concerned."

Charles was glad others looked out for her, but he wanted the honor.

Moshe pulled folders from a drawer. "Some critical events have taken place since your absence and we've assigned the Irgun to handle one in particular."

Charles' heart leaped every time he heard the Irgun's name. As far as he was concerned, they were just as responsible for Jonathan's death as the Brits.

Moshe dropped a folder onto his desk. "With our increased efforts to discourage the Brits, they raided the Agency building and confiscated records that hold the info of all our personnel including me, you, and all we know about your parents. David Ben-Gurion has accordingly authorized retaliation."

"They have my profile?" He tried to swallow the lump in his throat. If arrested, he'd never see Gladia again and father would gloat in victory.

Charles couldn't find a comfortable spot in his chair as Moshe relayed more British crackdowns and curfews that made Jerusalem a ghost town at night.

"The records are in code, so we don't believe they've deciphered them. But it's only a matter of time. This could send us all to prison, which is exactly what they want." He looked up. "We must destroy that information immediately."

A quivering chill coiled down Charles' spine. "If they contact my father … he'd be on the next plane here."

Moshe sighed. "That should be the least of your worries."

No. That would be the worst of his troubles. He looked at Moshe and tried to figure out how to tell him about Father being a formidable enemy.

"Because of your expert advice on the Cyprus tunnels, we're adding you to a team of structural engineers. You will be assigned under the leadership of an Irgun commander."

Charles stood, his face contorted. "You're sending me to the Irgun?"

Moshe took a breath. "I know you're bitter toward them. I read the tragic report about your friend, Jonathan." He frowned. "I'm very sorry about what happened to him."

"I'm not the only one. In the American newspapers, Albert Einstein referred to them as a gang of terrorists. How am I supposed to work with a group like that?"

"I don't like working with them either, but they've agreed to tame their methods of violence and take orders directly from me. It's part of our campaign to curb that kind of terror. And, we need them to complete this mission."

Much of Charles' bitterness about Jewish tactics of war had eased after learning of their continual persecution on a worldwide scale. It wasn't just

Arabs, Brits and Nazis; it was most of the world who hated them. No wonder they fought for their lives against all odds.

Moshe picked up the *Palestine Post*. "Hopefully this will help you understand our strategy."

> Recent sabotages in Palestine stirred the British public. They demand their government to give up Palestine, and stop the violence against their soldiers.

Charles looked up and blew out a breath. "A lot has transpired in ten months."

"Yes, and turmoil accelerates as we near our goal." Moshe eyed him. "Brace yourself. You will be asked to contribute to a task you're not going to favor." He shook Charles' hand. "You'll be briefed as soon as we're ready."

CHAPTER 16

Charles left headquarters, with flashes of Gladia's many smiles. He asked the driver to drop him at the library. When he entered her workplace with a rapid heartbeat, her boss, Regina, said she'd left early to see her eye doctor. Disappointed, he decided to visit Haifa Pharmacy to see if he could refill his scalp medicine. The bottle had been empty for months, which caused his hair to revert to black.

The pharmacy had a man at the counter and a woman sitting in a chair half covered by a magazine rack, her face buried under a yellow hat while she flipped pages. He approached the man, trying not to stare at the woman's exposed legs crossed under her blue dress. "Hi, I'm trying to refill this scalp medicine, but I don't know what it's called."

The pharmacist leaned in. "Scalp medicine?" He lifted the bottle and squinted. "No label?"

Charles shrugged.

The pharmacist uncorked it, sniffed the brim, and swabbed a little residue onto a piece of paper. He crinkled his nose. "This is hair dye." The pharmacist pointed. "In the back, right side."

Charles glanced back to the woman; her face was still buried in a magazine. He turned and half-smiled. "You must be mistaken, it's medicine for my scalp."

"No sir, see my swab?" He held it near Charles' face. "This is number-three red hair dye—in back."

140

Charles glanced at the woman. "I, ah, don't wear dye. My parents have applied this treatment since I was young."

The pharmacist shook his head. "Maybe your mother does not like black hair."

Charles' neck tensed. "That can't be ..." He turned and glanced at the woman. She raised her head briefly and lowered it again.

"Gladia?"

She looked up without her glasses on. "Yes, I'm Gladia."

Adrenaline surged through his body. "How are you?"

"How am I? I'm ... fine." She didn't get up.

A car might as well have hit him. Thoughts of rejection from school kids back home assailed him. She'd changed, just like he'd thought.

"Who are you?" she asked.

He raised his hands and dropped them to his side. "Gladia, it's me, come on." His eyes watered. "I'm sorry for not contacting you. You know it's prohibited."

"I'm sorry, I didn't mean to make you cry."

He wiped his eyes with his sleeve. "I'm not crying. Whatever I did to offend you, I'm sorry!"

"Why do you know my name? Who are you?"

"It's me ... Charles ... Charles Devonshire?"

"Charles? Oh my ... oh my ... Charles?" She bolted to her feet; the magazine flew. Her yellow hat fell her as she rushed him, almost knocking him over as she clenched him and kissed his cheek. "I missed you!"

They both burst into tears.

"I missed you badly." She continued kissing his damp cheeks as a customer passed them in the entryway. "I was afraid, I hear you had police trouble in America." She pulled a handkerchief from her dress pocket. "It made me start praying again. No one said you were back."

"I missed you too," he said as she dried his eyes. "I thought about you every day!" She'd said everything he wanted to hear except one important endearment.

She pulled back. "I do not recognize the new look." Her fingers dug into his biceps. "You grow big. Your hair is dark and your voice ..." She widened her eyes. "Is a *man's voice*. You look ... *what is this?*" She rolled her fingers under his chin.

"Yeah, whiskers. Finally."

They laughed, but then she shook her head. "Your doctor was not kidding. You have a *big* growth. I cannot believe you are in front of me." She put her lips to his ear. "Ten and a half months ... this is a gift to me."

"Yes, it—"

"Gladia?" An annoyed voice muttered a sentence in Hebrew from behind Charles at the doorway.

She stiffened and separated from Charles. "Yokauve! Hi ... hello."

Charles cringed at her nervousness. He'd never seen her like that.

Dressed in all black, the intruder contorted his face like a boxer dog and spattered out more Hebrew.

"Oh ... ah," her hands stiffly moved about. "This is, Charles."

Watching the puzzled man, he loved hearing the excitement in her tone when she said his name, but wondered if this was the moment he'd always dreaded.

"You know, Charles Devonshire. The one I tell you about. My best friend in the whole world."

Hearing those words exhilarated him, but as soon as he refocused his eyes on the perturbed man, his excitement faded. The rugged young man's demeanor made him think of the romance book David had borrowed from the library—the book described jealousy, but it didn't warn Charles how intense the hurt would be.

Yo—whatever his name was, maintained his rigid stance and before he could muster another word, Gladia cut him short: "English, Yokauve."

"This is him? You say he is a boy!"

"He was. He grew fast." She spoke proudly as she put on a smile Charles could tell was not her own. She pulled at her fingers while she stared at the irritated young man. "Charles this is … *ah* … this is …"

"Yokauve," he said.

Charles stepped forward and extended a hand. "Yo … kauve, nice to meet you."

Yokauve glared at Charles' outstretched hand.

"Where are you from?" Charles asked, lowering his hand.

"Where I am from? Here. Where you from?"

"He's from America, you know that," Gladia said. "Charles meant, where are you from originally?" Yokauve obviously didn't understand Gladia's question as he paused with a blank face. "Yokauve," she turned to Charles. "He worked for Dov. I see him at Irgun meetings. That is why we meet. Now we work with Borus."

Charles was aghast seeing her like this. As far as he knew, she'd never had a boyfriend. When she mentioned her brother with sadness, he turned away from Yokauve's piercing stare, his heart aching. He admired her love and dedication to Dov. What a great wife she would be. "Moshe told me about Dov. I'm sorry, Gladia."

"I have been very sad." She crossed her arms. "And angry because he is stubborn." She uncrossed her arms. "But today, I will be happy. Let us celebrate with dinner tonight."

"Celebrate what?" Yokauve asked.

"Charles is back from a long assignment. He worked hard for our nation in New York." She raised her brows at him. "You are back for good, yes?"

Charles nodded. "I think so." Her voice perked when she spoke to him again, and that was all he needed.

She slapped her hands together. "Good, then we will feast tonight!"

"We can-not." Yokauve stepped out of the pharmacy to the front walkway. They followed. "Why not?" Gladia said.

Yokauve put his back to Charles. "You help me tonight."

"Help what?"

"You know, help."

She shook her head. "No. I don't know. It must wait." She moved into Charles' view. "My friend is here. We will have dinner in Jerusalem at the King David Hotel."

Charles was relieved she still wasn't a pushover.

"That is fancy. You do not have money for it." Yokauve turned and smirked at Charles, then placed his muscular hand on her arm. "Come, we must go now." He moved her down the walkway, yapping in Hebrew.

Charles held back his desire to interfere while Yokauve still chattered at her. He blurted the only civil words he could think of: "I'll pay for it!"

CHAPTER 17

Charles smirked at Yokauve while he watched them leave. Gladia wiggled out of his grip as he raised his voice in Hebrew. Charles took a few steps forward, and then halted. They argued all the way to a car, their hands moving about. After several exchanges between them, she hurried back to Charles. "I am sorry. He had a bad day. We can pick you up at five."

She deserved better. Charles nodded. "That's great! And I'm buying."

"Can you wait in front of my house, on the swing?" Her smile looked genuine this time.

"Okay, I'll see you there." Watching her climb in his car was disheartening.

Charles began walking toward her home, and when he passed Jacob's house, he tried to forget about great times: Helping Jonathan with homework, sitting at the dinner table passing food, being cared for by two real mothers. But when Samuel came to mind, he channeled his thoughts back to Gladia.

When he arrived at her house, he sat on the swing where they used to talk for hours. After pondering conversations they had about Europe and Einstein, Yokauve finally drove up at twenty past five.

When he climbed into the car, Gladia tried to force a smile. "You will love this place we are going to." He appreciated her attempt to smooth out the cold mood generated by Yokauve's refusal to look at Charles, but it also hurt because she'd never faked emotions.

He'd barely got in when Yokauve shifted into reverse and hit the gas. "I need a box," Yokauve blurted while he screeched his tires on the road.

Gladia turned to Yokauve with narrowed brows. "Where are you going?" She pointed in a different direction. "Jerusalem is that way."

"Ayalon Kibbutz by Rehovot. To get a laundry box for Borus."

Charles scooted behind the driver's side to see Gladia squirming in her seat while Yokauve continued speeding toward the Tel Aviv coastline. Charles was hungry, and annoyed at Yokauve's detour, which looked like an excuse to avoid dinner. All of this for a laundry box. It made no sense, unless it was code for something else.

"This is the long way to Jerusalem, why are you going here now?" she said. "We are hungry."

"I get a message ... to deliver tonight. They say ur-gunt." He jerked the wheel and turned onto a dirt road, knocking Charles and Gladia against the doors while gravel pinged against the wheel wells.

The dusty road ended and Yokauve stopped in the midst of a tiny village. "Do not leave. I will come back." He left the car and strutted through the dust to a tiny brick dwelling in the deserted village center. The sun was turning orange at the horizon, and the villagers must have been in for the evening.

Charles glanced again at the dwelling and saw an empty clothesline extending from the brick. "That's strange."

She turned and faced him. "Yes, he acting odd. And I do not like his driving fast."

He hoped her troubled demeanor was from regret in dating him. He leaned forward and placed his hand on her shoulder. "He stepped into a small laundry room next to that little brick bakery. But I don't see him."

She nodded. "Let us go see."

They left the car and entered the quiet room. Charles put his hand on the washing machine. "I saw him walk in here...."

She peered at the mini-bakery across the way. "He can't be in there."

He heard a faint boom echoing. "Look at this." He stooped. "There's a little hole under this laundry machine." He knelt down to look inside the crack in the ground. "I hear things down there." A gentle breeze emitted a sulfur odor out of the crevice.

Gladia stooped. "Do you see anything?"

The sweet smell of jasmine made him close his eyes and take an elongated whiff. He was determined not to turn his face toward hers, knowing it would only entice him further. Too late, he opened his eyes and stared. Just a few more inches and they'd be kissing.

She stood. He rose too and tried to muscle the laundry machine to open the crack wider, but it wouldn't budge. He saw her staring at his flexed arms, but she quickly averted her gaze. He didn't care about buffed muscles, but David's comment concerning women being attracted to strong men came to mind; Yokauve was certainly well built.

He looked around. "Maybe there's a switch, since the machine legs are attached a floorplate." He found a lever on the wall, pulled it downward, and the trap door started humming. The machine began moving sideways and the crack grew larger to reveal a steep ladder.

Gladia hastily stepped down. "Gladia, wait." He eased himself down after her.

At the bottom, they came upon stacks of wooden boxes with handwritten markings that read, "Laundry." Teenagers operated noisy machines along a narrow corridor. As they proceeded along the wall toward the other end, no one paid any attention to them. He paused when he realized the shiny little objects on the conveyors were bullets. He watched, fascinated, as they rolled down the belts and dropped into bins.

The smell of gunpowder and burnt metal thickened as they moved farther down the narrow pathway. When they reached the end, they both ducked at the sound of rapid gunshots. When the firing ceased, they peeked around the corner. Yokauve, earmuffs on, stood at a counter and let off more rounds from a nine-millimeter pistol into an insulated wall. Five automatic Sten guns were piled on the counter.

Charles cringed when he recognized the weapon that killed Jonathan: the British-made machine guns were cheap to make and plentiful in Palestine. His training required him to load, shoot, and clean the firearm, but he hated that part, preferring his specialties of intelligence, communications and engineering.

Yokauve turned and revealed his teeth while he threw his ear protection onto the floor. "What are you doing?" His face reddened as he advanced with the gun waving. "I said wait!"

"We didn't know where you went," Gladia yelled over the racket of machines punching metal sheets into bullet shells.

"How did you get here?"

Charles pointed at the ladder.

"I close that!" He walked to a table and slammed the gun onto it.

Charles shook his head. People had been killed from similar misuses of a weapon.

"No one can know this place." Yokauve marched back and thrust his finger in Charles' face. "If you tell ..."

Charles puffed his chest and tightened his lips. Gladia stood between them. "He works with us! He is not a spy."

Yokauve peered over her shoulder. "We can get death if caught."

"I told you—"

"Yeah, yeah. I hear you." Yokauve stepped back and looked upward. "British soldiers bring their laundry up there in the daytime."

Charles' nostrils flared. Then what fool had left the trap door cracked open?

Gladia stiffened and flung her hand at him. "Next time, don't leave it cracked open."

Yokauve stormed toward the small crates of ammo by the ladder.

She turned toward Charles. "Sorry." They caught up with Yokauve. "You work here?" she asked.

"I deliver to the Irgun and Lehi. Come, we take the boxes to Jerusalem."

Gladia handed Charles a box of ammo, and he passed it up to Yokauve, who stacked them. After dozens of boxes were moved, Charles' muscles were tight, so he imagined how Gladia must have felt.

Yokauve ordered them up the ladder. When they loaded the trunk, the back of the vehicle sagged. Yokauve turned to Charles again and opened his mouth.

"I told you," Gladia raised her hand, "don't talk to him like that." She yelled as if they were still inside the noisy bullet factory.

"How long has this place been here?" Charles asked, trying for peaceful conversation.

Yokauve turned forward. "You don't know this place."

"How long, Yokauve?" Gladia asked.

"Nineteen-forty-five, last year. They make forty thou-man."

"Thousand?" she said. "Bullets?"

Yokauve started the car and crammed it into gear. "Yes, that many each day."

"Forty thousand bullets a day is astonishing," Charles said. "What an amazing place. And the workers are young."

Yokauve stepped on the gas. "We need fuel." The engine revved higher to get the heavily burdened vehicle moving out of the dirt.

When they pulled onto the main highway, a truck loaded with Arab farmers and a motorbike appeared behind them. Yokauve kept glancing into his mirror. When they pulled into the service station, the rear bumper scraped.

Gladia spun back to track the Arabs. The truck proceeded down the road blowing a trail of smoke, while the motorcycle followed them. The service attendant approached, pointed to the back of their car and commented in Hebrew.

Yokauve replied in their language and nodded toward the fuel spout. Then he aimed his gaze at the motorbike, a pistol cocked in the front seat.

The bike's motor fluttered and backfired. "Looks like trouble with the motorbike," Charles said.

"Dumb Arab, he run out fuel again," Yokauve said.

"Maybe it's a mechanical problem. I might be able to help."

"No, he is dumb. That thing run out last time."

Charles had enough of Yokauve's bad attitude, and now he struggled with enduring his prejudice, both traits similar to Father's. Even though many Arab irregulars masqueraded as innocent farmers, Charles decided not to make a judgment based on appearances. Rabbi Jesse's quote from Proverbs 15:1 made sense: *A gentle word turns away wrath, but a harsh word stirs up anger.*

Charles popped the back door open.

"Charles, where you going?" Gladia said.

"He might need help."

Yokauve slapped the wheel. "No! Get back, he is enemy."

Charles stepped out shaking his head. "Not all Arabs are enemies." He approached the motorbike while the Arab bickered with the station attendant in what sounded like a cross of Arabic and Hebrew. Since Jews and Arabs coexisted for decades under less violent terms in the past, they probably knew fragments of each other's dialect.

The attendant looked at Charles and spoke a few Hebrew words.

"No money, no fuel, he say." Gladia raised her voice from the car.

"Charles, get in," Yokauve shouted through the open window.

Charles enjoyed ignoring Yokauve's plea. "How much to fill the little tank?" Charles asked the attendant.

"Eleven grush," the attendant said. "Half an American—one American dollar from you."

Charles reached in his pocket and slapped a bill on the attendant's hand. "Here you go." He still needed to convert his money to grush.

The Arab dropped his jaw and his eyes widened. "Thank you too much. I do not forget a good person."

"Charles, in the car," Yokauve commanded with less fervor.

Gladia beamed a wide smile, the back of her head to Yokauve. And though he didn't quite know what to make of the whole God-thing that Jesse preached, he was impressed with the wisdom of the prophets: It felt right to help an Arab. Climbing back into the vehicle, he thought about another verse from Isaiah: *Cease to do evil—learn to do well—relieve the oppressed.* He wouldn't forget the Arabs' expression of shock and joy.

Yokauve paid the attendant, started the car, and turned to Charles. "You do not do that! You bring the enemy's eye to us."

Gladia slanted her head. "He was just helping someone."

"We should offer kindness whenever we can," Charles said.

"You have a problem. You do not understand Arab," Yokauve said. "Attention like that can be trouble."

Yokauve pulled out to the highway, scraping the driveway again, then glanced in the mirror at Charles. "An Arab? He will smile just like that man, while his knife is in your belly. They do that to my friend—I see it."

Charles was hungry and tired and could lose his temper if Yokauve made one more derogatory statement; On the other hand, maybe his entire family had been brutally murdered too.

Yokauve chugged his car up the hill to Jerusalem when a huge branch fell from a hillside and blocked the road. He fought the wheel, but the overloaded car swerved over a bumpy shoulder. Hitting the brakes, everybody thrust forward before stopping face-to-face with a massive tree. Several masked men emerged through the dust and surrounded the car with pistols drawn. The edge of the farmers' truck that had passed earlier jutted from behind bushes.

The men pulled the car doors open and yelled a single command in what sounded like Hebrew, then yanked them out. With pistols shoved in their backs, they were forced behind the shrubs. Their Arabic rhetoric sounded angry and chaotic.

"You shoot because we are Jews?" Yokauve bellowed.

Gladia held Charles' arm. He wished he had some tape for Yokauve's mouth.

The assailants uttered more Arabic while pointing to the car. Yokauve was bound with rope and forced to stand at the trunk.

The roar of a motorbike echoed through the canyon while the Arab leader yelled and stretched his hand out. Gladia spoke Hebrew to Charles and he thought she referenced ID cards. She returned Arabic words to them.

"Mine's in the car, in my—" Gladia whisked two fingers to her mouth and as soon as she did, Charles remembered not to speak English in the presence of hostile Arabs. As soon as he'd spoken, they conversed with a heightened tone. "American" was the only word he understood.

Two of them tied Charles' hands, then threw him to the ground, his face parting dust everywhere. The leader rammed a pistol against his head which made him eat dirt, the cold barrel adding pain to his already throbbing skull.

He cut his cheek on a rock, reminding him of his first assault. His heartbeat pulsing the ground, he dreaded Gladia having to watch his execution. With another breath of dust, he could hear Rabbi Jesse's voice: *God is watching over you.* Then Yaakov's: *God is going to do great things with you.* Then, David's voice resonated: *God will do mighty things in you.* Strangely, an unexplainable calm soothed him.

Gladia wailed a scream in a few Arabic words that must have meant *stop* or *die*, or something like that, because the gun lifted suddenly. The ear-piercing shriek even startled Charles as it echoed through the entire canyon.

"American," the gunman said, "you die!" The cold barrel returned and forced his face into the soil, while the vibration of the gun's cocking made him shut his eyes tight.

The motorbike's roar increased, then it died. Charles watched the motorcyclist from the station emerge from the swirl of dirt. The rider shouted, pointed at Charles and pushed the gunman aside.

Gladia broke free from another man's grip to help Charles up. The Arabs argued and waved pistols at Charles. "American" was mentioned again while the other Arabs tied Yokauve to a tree and looted the trunk. The motorcyclist pulled his knife out and walked to Charles.

Gladia stood in his way. "No!" Charles maneuvered around her to face the young man.

The motorcyclist raised the blade toward Charles, spun him around with his free hand and cut the binding rope. "You go now ... quick!"

"What about my friends?"

"They are Jews."

Standing rigid in front of Gladia, he balled his fists. "I will fight to the death for her. You must let them go!"

The motorcyclist turned, waved his knife and argued with the group. Then he looked at Gladia and nodded at Yokauve. "Untie him and go too."

He walked them to the car. "I tell them, you kill the American, more Americans will come. Kill his friends, more Americans come." He looked at Charles with wide eyes. "They do not want the American army." He flung his blade toward the car. "Hurry."

"Thank you," Charles said.

"I said, I do not forget your help." He stretched his knife at Yokauve. "But only this time."

Charles was relieved Yokauve had the sense to keep his mouth closed.

They hurried into the car and Yokauve started it, shifted, and screeched away. Without the ammo, the vehicle moved quickly up the road.

Gladia turned back, her hair ruffled; She grinned at Charles and handed him her scarf. Then she smirked at Yokauve when he glowered at Charles in the mirror.

Charles' heart pumped overtime as he brushed dust from his face and clothes. The scripture verses about helping others proved to be the saving factor from his execution; and no telling from what it had saved Gladia from.

CHAPTER 18

Whipping around a corner, they passed a "Jerusalem" sign. Just when Charles began to think about food again, a British checkpoint ahead suppressed it. "I suppose we don't report this?"

"No!" Gladia and Yokauve spoke in unison.

Gladia turned. "If they ask, Yokauve is a student at Technion. That is what it says on his card. Yokauve, your pistol?"

"The Arabs. They take it."

"Charles?"

"You know I don't carry mine."

She turned back and shot a precarious grin at him. "I put mine in a hole in the seat. The British arrest Jews for gun possession, but not Arabs. Remember, say nothing other than what they ask of you." She faced forward.

Charles touched the back of her shoulder. "I know the routine."

Yokauve brought the car to a smooth stop inches ahead of the dashed line. A guard with a sniffing German shepherd circled them. The sight of a British tank and the mighty display of munitions reminded Charles how fearless Jews were to rile the Brits.

"Identification," the soldier said. He stacked their cards, then spread them in his palm. "Hmm ... Yo-ka-vay, Gladia, and *Richard Anderson?* He stooped and shifted his narrowed eyes. "You're American."

"Yes, sir."

"What are you doing with these Jews, and how did you get that cut on your face?"

Charles bristled at the soldier's demeaning tone. Everywhere he went, people scorned at Jews as if they were actually responsible for the trashy gossip spread about them. "They're my friends from school and we're going to dinner. Yokauve turned a corner too fast, I hit the door lever."

The soldier alternated his stare between the front and back seats. "Step out of the car, lad," he said, looking at Charles.

"Why? I didn't do anything wrong."

The soldier whipped his pointed finger away from the car. "Out!"

When Charles climbed out, the soldier led him away and patted him down. "Why are you so dirty? Have these Jews recruited you into the freedom fighters?"

"Freedom what?"

"You heard me." He crossed his arms.

The British must be aware of Americans joining the Resistance. Charles tried not to imagine what a lengthy stay in Acre Prison would be like. "I heard you, but I don't understand. What are freedom fighters?"

The man rolled his eyes. "Never mind. Either you're already in, or you're the dumbest American I've ever seen. I suppose you have no idea how they sneak around blowing up our assets?" His tone sang with cynicism. "As long as you keep this type of company, you will be on our watch list." He wrote Charles' fake name on a clipboard. "Jews trying to topple the might of the British army is like a lamb defeating a wolf. Consider yourself warned, lad!" He shooed him like someone would a dog.

Charles got in the car. "The British seem jumpy—and rude."

Yokauve and Gladia looked at each other. The soldier tossed the cards onto Yokauve's lap while another guard raised the drawbar. Charles had another taste of British prejudice and how it resembled American history, when the British lost the colonies by their abuse to frustrated pre-Americans.

After a few minutes of deep breaths, they arrived at the King David Hotel. Spotlights accented scrolled pillars that had been built into the walls of the seven-story concrete building. "What a beautiful hotel. It reminds me of Los Angeles."

"That is right," Gladia said. "This is your first time to Jerusalem."

"I like it. It's fancy for Palestine."

Gladia stuffed her pistol in her purse. "Important people come here."

As they walked through the glass-door entry on top of red carpet, they dodged an entourage of tuxedoed men and a few women in flowing evening gowns. Charles' stomach growled from the tantalizing scent of beef stroganoff. A maître d' approached with his arm extended. "Please wait over here so you don't get in the way of our special guest."

Gladia gasped when she saw a woman in a black dress standing in the center of other dignitaries. "That is Golda Meir," she whispered. Yokauve continued to stare at waiters carrying food.

"I've heard her name, who is she?" Charles said.

"She is head of the Jewish Agency. I see her face in the *Palestine Post*. The Arab leaders say to her, 'Don't be in a big rush to declare a Jewish nation.'" Gladia smiled. "Then she said, 'We have been waiting two thousand years, is that slow enough?' After that, she went to America to raise millions to arm the Haganah. Since then, David Ben-Gurion make it law that all Jews train for defense." She glanced at Yokauve, who was oblivious to the conversation. "When we have a nation, she should be the next prime minister after David Ben-Gurion."

Charles raised his brows. "A woman president?"

Gladia placed her knuckles to her hips. "A woman cannot do the job?"

He smiled. "Of course a woman could, it's just a foreign thought to an American." He looked at Golda again. "I wonder why they're gathered around those dirty clay jars on the table."

Gladia squinted. "Let us go see." When they approached, a bodyguard dressed in black moved into their path and folded his hands in front of him. "That's far enough."

"They're just youngsters, Bill. Let them through." Golda smiled. "Hello, I'm Golda Meir." She extended her hand to Gladia first and then to Charles. They both shook her hands and said hellos.

Golda pointed toward the canisters. "I bet you're wondering what these old pots are doing in such a nice place like this."

Charles nodded. "We are curious. Did you dig them up from around here?"

Golda nodded. "Actually, a young shepherd found them in a cave above the banks of the Dead Sea, just outside of Qumran. Inside these containers are ancient copies of the Torah and Books of the Prophets." She smiled at Charles. "Being American, you might know them as parts of the Old Testament. Experts think they date back a few thousand years, to the time of Solomon's Temple."

Charles widened his eyes. "Fascinating! Will you be exhibiting them here?"

A rabbi stepped forward. "I'm sorry. As I explained to Golda, we are waiting to secure a private room because they have to be handled with the utmost care so we don't damage them."

Charles nodded. "I understand."

The rabbi lifted his hands over the jars. "If these scrolls are as old as we think, they will predate our oldest copies of the sacred scriptures by a thousand years. You are probably looking at the most important archeological find in world history. We think these manuscripts were hidden in AD seventy, the same time that Israel perished by the Romans—they slaughtered a million Jews and the rest were scattered all over the world."

Charles was astonished. If the parchments were evidence of the scriptures and had been hidden when Israel perished, then rediscovered in the same era of rebirthing the nation, it would be an undisputable sign of God orchestrating tangible evidence of His authorship.

"Table is ready." Yokauve's impatient tone rang across the expansive entryway.

Gladia gently elbowed Charles, who smiled at Golda. "Thank you for sharing this."

Golda nodded. "You are welcome. It's nice to see young people interested in historical findings."

After a host showed them a table, they both grabbed Gladia's chair, but Yokauve muscled it out. At that moment, the aroma of food lost its appeal. Charles looked back at the door, but took a breath and determined to endure the evening.

When he sat, Gladia peered over his shoulder. "That is strange." She squinted. "Ten months, I don't see them." She looked at Charles. "Now you are back, and they come here?"

Yokauve stood. "I see the Irgun. I'm going to the toilet and tell them no ammo."

Charles turned and remembered the friendly Arab brother and sister, so he waved them over.

The sister approached first. "Hello. I am surprised I see you."

"Yes, surprise," the brother said, standing behind his twin.

Charles turned the rest of his body toward them. "I just got—"

"I'm sorry, we are going to order," Gladia said.

"Okay," the sister said. She pulled her shiny black hair back. "We will see you another time." They began to leave, then she turned. "Will you come to my birthday on Sunday?"

"Okay. Where is it?"

Her dark brown eyes lit up. "My home, where you get lost."

He didn't remember seeing her house and was too embarrassed to ask. "What time?"

"Anytime," she said.

He smiled and nodded. "Then I will try and see you Sunday." He had no interest in going since her gathering would be filled with Arabs like her brother who scoffed at Americans. He didn't even know their names, and if Gladia were right about them being irregulars, it could be a trap.

Gladia leaned forward. "You should not have accepted the invitation."

"Why not?"

She puffed a breath and looked about. "Do I have to keep saying your training?"

"They don't seem like irregulars," he said.

A waiter came and took their order. Gladia added a steak for Yokauve.

"I never see them, you come back and now they here? This is no good." She squinted. "And now her English gets better?"

Charles wished he had a camera to capture her expression. He loved it when she showed concern for him. "Maybe she *likes me*."

Gladia dropped her hand on the table. "She does not like you! I saw her eyes."

"How do you know?"

"Her face. She not … *she does not* like you that way."

He rolled his eyes. "So a girl cannot like me?"

"I am not saying that."

"Then what are you saying?" He tightened his lips to hide his bemusement.

She sat back as Yokauve returned. "Dov will not accept any visitors at the hospital for safety," she said.

"We must leave soon," Yokauve said. "The Irgun. I need to get them bullets."

The food came and Yokauve shoveled his steak and potatoes down like a prison inmate. He kept staring at each bite Charles took, bringing the temptation to linger over the last few bites. Maybe wave his fork around while he and Gladia reminisced, but the stale mood made him gulp it quickly.

Yokauve wadded his napkin. "It is late, Char-loos."

Charles leaned in. "It's Charles."

"It is time." Yokauve's narrowed eyes silently said, *don't mess with me.*

"It is only ten-thirty," Gladia said.

"Yeah, it's only ten-thirty." Back home, Charles would have been locked in his room by seven-thirty. Some nights he fell asleep, but most evenings he jimmied the lock on his window, snuck out, and read his parents' lips through the sliding glass door while they folded pamphlets, met with foreigners and exchanged cash.

"Okay. You should go now—find a place to sleep." Yokauve mimicked the Brit by shooing him.

Charles stood and resisted telling Yokauve what was at the edge of his tongue.

"We're not leaving him in Jerusalem." Gladia stood. "He can stay with me." She tilted her head and grinned at Charles.

"I can?" Charles couldn't conceal his wide smile. Another sliver of hope nuzzled into his heart, and seeing Yokauve squirm made the entire evening worthwhile.

"Stay with you?" Yokauve compacted his face like a grumpy old man. "No, that is not good."

She turned to Charles. "You can have Dov's room." She nodded. "It would make him happy."

"Time to go." Yokauve put his leather jacket on and stepped toward the door, but abruptly stopped and turned. "You coming, Gladia?"

She remained standing at the table. "I need to get a key for Charles at home."

Yokauve took a breath and slowly puffed it out. "Okay, I give him a ride."

As they headed toward the exit, Yokauve butted in front of Charles and put his arm around Gladia. She deftly turned with her shoulder dipping away from his reach. "Wait. I have to go to the toilet room." She waved at Yokauve. "Go ahead. I will see you outside."

Charles sighed at Gladia's thoughtfulness and walked outside while Yokauve waited inside by the door. Looking in, he assessed Yokauve's restless pacing and again took into consideration he might be a Holocaust survivor like Samuel. Regardless, his treatment toward Gladia annoyed him.

When Gladia appeared, she and Yokauve exchanged words on the other side of the glass, their hands moving rapidly and her face showing her typical fire. Charles tried to read their lips, but they must have been speaking in Hebrew. Yokauve put his hand on her shoulder but she jerked it back, stomped toward the door and pushed it open. "Yokauve, I'm tired. I'm going to give Charles a key and stay home."

The quiet ride home seemed to last for hours, but Charles' tension had eased seeing the strain between them. He gave up trying to figure out what Gladia could possibly see in a man like Yokauve. Yet he still grappled with David's comment about women being attracted to men's physical strength. Yokauve was taller and had larger muscles, but Charles wasn't far behind thanks to the hard work at the docks—and at least he'd grown to Gladia's height.

The drive remained silent until Yokauve whipped the wheel and turned the car into Gladia's driveway. "I will pick you up in the morning for work." He glared at Charles while they got out. Somewhere in his thick head, he must have figured out not to extend affection in front of Charles. It would have been unimaginable to see his lips on hers.

Gladia looked in the window. "I will see you tomorrow, but not too early."

Yokauve spun his tires in the gravel and the wheels chirped on the street by the time they closed the door to her house. A few steps inside, she stood in front of him and crossed her arms. "You need to tell the girl you cannot go."

"Why?" He was dying to know if she was jealous or just being cautious.

"You don't think it's a ... I can't say the word." She looked at him intently. "What is the word?"

He shrugged.

She eased her shoulders. "You know the word."

"Coincidence?"

"Thank you. You cannot think it is coincidence they see you at dinner?"

Her rounded eyes and wrinkled forehead had been the look she displayed when they first worked together. He almost chuckled from being so happy to see her this way. "All right, maybe the invitation is suspicious," he said.

"More than sus-pic-ious. I told you they never come unless you are here. I think they're reporting you."

"Reporting me? You mean spying?" His gut tightened.

"Do you remember what Dov say if you get caught by irregulars?"

"Yes. And it scared me. 'Have a cyanide pill ready or save a bullet in your pistol for yourself.' Was he as serious as he looked?"

"You do not want to be interrogate by them. They will do bad things." She frowned. "Three Irgun members—friends of Dov—they get beaten, stabbed, and dumped into a trash holder two weeks ago." Her eyes moistened and she sniffled. "I cannot find you in the trash."

"Why would they care about me? I'm not an actual freedom fighter."

"You don't think you are. But they do. And you have something they want. That makes you a bigger target."

"Like what?" He knew what she meant, but he missed the engaging conversations they used to have.

"Information." She pointed her finger to her head. "Intelligence. That is the biggest weapon. And they hate Americans almost as much as Jews—you know these things. I was terrified to see the gun at your head." Sniffling, she came close and dug her fingers in his arms. "You cannot die. My parents, our friends, and maybe Dov." She hugged him. "Everyone I love, dies." Her voice broke and her lips quivered.

He hated seeing her like that, but enjoyed what he'd missed for the last ten months. He also noticed she didn't mention Yokauve when the Arabs ambushed them. A kiss would complete the night, but he'd have to get rid of the obstacle first. He smacked her glossy cheek with his lips, then nodded. "If you think I shouldn't go, I trust your judgment. You know these villagers better than I do."

"Thank you," she sighed. "We cannot take chances."

He had to let go of her. "I know, you're right. But how do I tell her? She will probably extend other invitations."

"You know."

"I can't do that." He shook his head.

"You learn it in the social manual, you know how."

"Sure, I know how, but I can't be rude and obnoxious."

"Okay. You tell her I am your girl, and I will be mad if you go."

He raised his brows high. "Okay."

"Good. We can go to sleep now." She pointed behind him. "You remember Dov's room. I ... can't go in there."

When he laid his head on the pillow, images of Gladia and Yokauve tortured him for hours as he rustled in bed.

When a stiff knock at the front door opened his eyes, he realized he'd finally dozed off at some point. He got up and peeked through the shutters and saw Gladia walking to Yokauve's car. She sat in his car facing the house and spoke English, so he honed in on her lips.

"He's my best friend. He can live here," Gladia said. Her invitation to move in surprised Charles, and he again took great satisfaction in its consequence on their relationship.

"You say Char-loose is little. And his hair red. He is not little and he has dark hair. You lie."

"No, of course not! He was little, and his hair was red. I told you already. He must have ran out of medicine for his head and ... he grew to be like a man now. I didn't recognize him when he come back."

Yokauve turned his head toward the house. "It look like you recognize fine."

The car started and Yokauve backed out of the driveway. Charles walked to the kitchenette and saw Gladia had left him a muffin on the oak counter. When the morning sun rose to about four fingers above the horizon, he headed to the library encouraged.

When he entered, the scent of old books brought back mostly pleasant memories. She stood in front of the counter, looking beautiful as usual. "Hi, Gladia. Isn't that the same yellow dress you wore when we first met?" She had to be aware it was his favorite.

She looked upward, her index finger stretched over her cheek. "Hmm ... I do not know." She laughed. "So maybe it is." She hugged him, then stepped back. "I have been sad for Dov, and now you help me feel a little better. I will protest if you want to leave again. And since it gets worse with," she scanned the area, "Arab attacks, they can use your smart mind at headquarters."

"Protest. You learned another new word."

She smiled and nodded. "I learn lots of new words so I can talk to you better." She put her finger up. "Oh. Wait. So I can communicate better to you."

"Impressive!" He pointed toward the side door. "I thought we could have lunch in the garden today."

Wrinkles shot across her forehead. "I am sorry, Yokauve will come for lunch."

Charles smirked. "He doesn't like me."

"He is going through a time of anger because his parents die in Auschwitz. He just needs time to know you." She put her hand on his arm. "It will get better."

He crossed his arms. "I'm sorry about his parents, but I doubt we'll ever get along."

She squeezed his bicep. "I am not used to your arm having muscle."

He chuckled. David was right. "My arms have always had muscles."

"But they are big now." She stared at his shoulders.

"I guess I'll be at my table reading, while *you two* go to lunch. Can you bring me the book I left off with?"

"I have it already there." She pointed to his table and expressed her usual sensual smile, but he didn't reciprocate. "We will all do dinner again tonight okay?"

"Uhh ... I don't know."

"You must come. I will tell Yokauve to act good."

He shrugged and half nodded. "Sure, why not." This could be a dreadful night, but he knew being mature was the right thing to do.

Charles tried to read while students came and went. The front door opened with rays of sunlight surrounding Yokauve's black attire. Charles lowered his eyes back into his book.

"Why is he here?" Yokauve said as he walked in.

"*Shhh* ... he is always here," Gladia said. "Remember? This is where we meet."

"You ready? Only us, right?"

"Yes I am ready, and yes, just us." She looked back, but Charles tipped his head down prior to making eye contact.

Every five minutes or so, he set his eyes on the door. And an hour and five minutes later, Yokauve walked her back in while Charles was coming out of the toilet room. He paused behind a bookcase and peeked through an opening in the books. He saw Yokauve follow her stare at Charles' table. "What are you looking for?"

"Nothing," she snapped back.

"I see you tonight for dinner. Gladia? Tonight for dinner?"

"Yes ... and Charles too."

He walked toward the door.

"And Charles!" she repeated.

He waved his hand while walking out the door. "Yes, and Char-loos."

CHAPTER 19

Charles watched Yokauve advance up Gladia's driveway, wrestling once again with her having a boyfriend. Since he couldn't take them embracing, he shifted his thoughts to formulate an exit plan if she gave in to Yokauve's advances.

The ride to Jerusalem was mostly filled with her attempts at trying to connect the two men in conversation. But Yokauve loved guns and fixated on killing the enemy, while Charles favored intelligence to accomplish missions.

With another quiet ride home, they all stepped out of the car, but Yokauve halted with Gladia at his side. Charles slipped his house key back into his pocket and caught Yokauve gawking at his hopeful wife-to-be; His open mouth and eyes glassy. Charles curled his fingers into a fist.

"You go in Char-loos, Gladia will come later."

She stepped forward. "I don't feel well, I think dinner is not good in my stomach. I will see you tomorrow morning, okay?"

He took a breath and puffed it out. "Hmm … I see *you* in the morning." He turned to Charles, eyes narrowed. "Good-night, Char-ulls."

"Goodnight." Hiding his delight, Charles pulled his key out.

She entered the living room and put her purse on the table. "We have not had time to talk. Why did the police try to arrest you?"

"You know I don't like to talk about my parents."

"You had trouble with your parents? Tell me more about them." She stepped closer and held his hand, but he retracted it. Just as he thought there could be a chance for love, some jerk entered her life. And he couldn't tell her about Yokauve without starting an argument.

"Please tell me something." Her tapered brows and soft eyes had caused his last confession, and he felt the same enticement as she sat on the sofa.

"I will if you tell me about your parents," he said while sitting on the other end of the couch.

"That is not the same. My parents—"

"I'm sorry, you're right." He sighed. "It's complicated, so I don't even know where to start."

"The police. You don't commit crime, so why the trouble?"

"Well actually, I did break the law."

She tilted her head, brows dipped.

Hours passed like minutes while he shared some of his embarrassing experiences, like the time a fellow student mentioned seeing Babe Ruth at an All-Star game with her parents. In ignorance, he asked the group if all families went to events together, and they laughed at him. It was a tough way to find out how normal families not only had regular outings, they also ate meals with each other daily.

Gladia swallowed and sent a firm nod, which meant she wanted to know more. He'd still underestimated how uplifting it was to share terrible experiences with someone trustworthy. But darker secrets couldn't be mentioned, and he noticed deep blue creeping behind the window shutters, indicating the sun's rising.

"I still don't understand," she said. "Why did you run here? The last time you tell me things, I know you don't tell everything."

"I … don't know if I want to go that deep."

"I hear an American say to get it from your chest so you feel better."

"Actually it's, 'get it *off* your chest,'" he said.

"Maybe I can help if you tell me more."

She'd just made him love her all the more, staying up all night to help him through what he finally admitted were deep emotional issues. Mother tried once, but Charles lost respect for her as he grew. And she wouldn't leave father when Charles begged her to.

Gladia's half-opened eyes still radiated from the first morning light, shimmering through a sliver in the curtain. Her long lashes and thick almond-hued brows beckoned his undivided attention, regardless of his tiredness. "You look nice when ... ah ... you look like this." He cringed inside, like when they'd first met since he could only come up with shallow compliments. He closed his eyes to rest them, hoping they'd both fall asleep.

"Tell me more," she said.

"It's too embarrassing." He reopened his eyes.

"You know you can say anything to me."

"I want to hate them! And I know ... it's more stressful to hate than to forgive." He tried to slow his breathing and think about the wisdom Jesse passed from 1 Kings 8:34: *Please forgive the sins of Your people Israel and bring them back to the land You gave to their ancestors.* Charles wondered if the sins of the ancient Israelites caused their decimation in AD 70, and that same rebellion had passed down through the generations. Regardless, he knew it would be uplifting to forgive the sins of his parents someday.

"And if it wasn't for my problems back home, I wouldn't have known you." A tear almost dropped. "You're the greatest thing that's ever happened to me. I guess Rabbi Jesse's reckoning was true about God doing things for good reasons." He couldn't believe he just said that.

"Me too. You are the best for me." She blushed and looked down. "What scripture is that from?"

He knew her expressions well, but didn't know what to make of her red face. "I don't remember the exact reference, but He said, 'God will work everything out for good to those who love Him.'"

"You are loving God now?"

He shrugged. "Well … I'm trying to figure Him out."

"Good luck to that." She chuckled. "You must tell me more about your father. What part of you is like him?"

"We're complete opposites. I'm going to tell you something, but I don't … I know you won't. He's anti-Semitic and a jerk!"

She opened her eyes wide. "He is a hater of Jews?"

"Yes, passionately. And he—"

"What is jerk?"

"A jerk is like that Arab man who was mean to his wife at dinner last night."

Gladia nodded. "Your father yells at women and makes them walk behind him?"

"Yes. He would yell at my mother, and almost everybody else: except his foreign friends. They would drink liquor, smoke cigars and laugh at disgusting films of—"

"What foreign friends?"

"I don't know, I never got a chance to hear them or find out who they were. I used to sneak outside and read their lips through glass. But most of his comrades spoke a foreign tongue, so I only got fragments of broken English."

"Your poor mother." She squinted again. "But I hear American women don't accept jerk treatment."

"I found out recently she wasn't originally born there. But she looks and sounds American."

"Your father did things you did not tell me about, yes?"

He looked down and nodded.

"What else did he do?"

He scooted close and placed his trembling hand on hers while they locked eyes. He knew baring his soul would make him fall even deeper for her. "He would tie me to a washboard faceup and dip my upper body into hot salty water to apply my scalp medicine. He always had something evil to say. Like, 'I'll drown you if you don't obey me.'"

She put her other hand over her mouth.

"And he meant it, because he'd hold me under until I blew bubbles out." He took a deep breath. "Then I'd come up gasping, with the saltwater burning my eyes, and the first thing I'd see was his wicked grin." Then Charles smiled with a tinge of satisfaction. "As I grew older though, I practiced holding my breath and could hold it twice as long." He patted her hand. "So I'd blow bubbles and squirm for his amusement." He chuckled. "Seeing that strategy work, I applied the same technique the other ..." He slipped his hand back and cleared his throat.

"Your mother. She would not help you?"

"I think she tried when I was young. I could see her wavy image through the water standing behind him. But he'd tell her she'd be next, if she didn't shut up."

Gladia began to tremble, though her tears dripped in silence.

"I think he adopted the washboard technique from one of his Nazi papers. I ... I don't have to say any more. You get the idea, right?"

She squared her shoulders. "Okay, you stop now." She leaned in and embraced him. "I'm sorry I make you tell."

"It's okay. It felt good." He tightened their hug and put his lips to her ear. "Especially telling someone like you." In that painful moment, their bond deepened. He pulled back. "There's something else I haven't told you."

"You don't have to—"

"I want to. The real reason I came here was to find out who they really are. So I could come to terms about why they treated me so badly. And I always hoped to find some incriminating evidence to have father jailed." He got up and walked to his bag. "I found this in an envelope with other documents taped to the back of my mother's mirror." He extended the crinkled photograph to her.

She held it close to her face and squinted at the faded image. "This is your parents? Is that you?"

"Yes. I'm probably about a year-and-a-half old."

She continued scanning the photo. "That is our school. And they have books by their feet." She looked between him and the photo. Then she pulled her head back and averted her eyes.

"What do you see?"

She examined his face again. "Your mother, she looks like you." She moved her face near his. "But your father, he does not." She looked down with her hand to her chin and drew in a sharp breath.

"What?"

She tilted the picture into his view. "Look at your mother's face, the way her hair is wrapped. The shawl … the …"

"What is it?"

"You said your father is a jerk, like the Arab man at dinner. That he is anti-Semitic, he copies Nazi torture. And look how your mother stands away from him. Her eyes look angry, but …" her voice cracked, "she is an Arab irregular."

He gulped. "How could you possibly know that from a photo?"

She pointed to the picture. "She wears boots with low heels."

"What does that mean?"

"Traditional Arab women cannot wear that. Today, it is different. Back then, Jews can spot Arab irregular women by how they dress. Foot covering like that means she had to march in the wilderness."

Charles' tightened throat constricted his breathing. He was long-used to the idea of Father's deep hatred of Jews. But the thought of Mother conspiring against families like David's....

"Are you okay?" Gladia said.

Moaning, he bent over and vomited.

CHAPTER 20

Gagging at the mess on the floor, Gladia ran to the kitchen and heaved before reaching the sink. She came back with a milky face and knelt with a towel. Her dress fouled, she plugged her nose while trying to clean the stain.

"Here, let me." Charles stooped down and took the rag from her, but paused. "I'm really sorry about this."

She arched her lips upward. "It is okay. You have been through a lot. Some got on your shirt and pants." She rose, put her hand out and glanced at the toilet room. "Let me wash it."

She couldn't have meant what he was thinking. He took her insistent wiggling hand and walked into a room he'd never shared with a woman.

She removed his shirt and rinsed it in a wooden bucket under the water pump, then washed his chest with a cool cloth. Her intimate and nurturing care sent chills in all directions.

With unhurried movements, she stared at his chest as she removed her dress and rinsed it in the sink. Even though her slip looked like another dress, but shorter and tighter, he looked away after she bent forward to hang her dress on a hook.

"You can put your pants on the bar up there." She motioned at the shower curtain. He couldn't believe she'd told him to remove his trousers. She pulled her pink robe from a hook, stepped back, and looked down. "Now you can take them off."

175

"I'm so stupid." He removed his pants and wrapped the robe around him, then started pumping the water handle to fill an empty porcelain basin. He sloshed his pants into it and scrubbed the stain.

"Stupid? No, you are very smart." She grabbed a white sheet from the closet and wrapped herself.

"Shouldn't we trade? I'll take the sheet and you have your robe." He hung up his pants, still battling his arousal.

"No. You look nice in my robe."

She must not realize the torment he was enduring. "How could I not know this about my own parents?"

"Arab irregulars are … what is the word? Cunning. They send agents to foreign countries like we do. They also have training from Nazis to disguise themselves."

"It's sickening how my parents conspire against your people." He saw the couch behind her, the curvy image under her slip still mentally visual. He glanced at the tiled bathing area; the wise thing to do would be to kick her out and pump cold water.

She walked toward the living area, stopped halfway and turned. "Are you coming?"

"Uh …" Against his better judgment, he followed her.

Wrapped up like a Grecian princess, she plopped onto the couch. "Sit. There is one last thing I want to ask."

He moseyed over and sat at the other end and rested his eyes while she began talking. His head tilted back and her voice trailed off.

≈≈≈

"Get up."

Charles fluttered his eyes and focused on a silhouette in front of him. After several rants of the same command, he realized it was Yokauve, who must have let himself in.

"Get up," he repeated. "You stand!"

Pulling Gladia's robe tight, Charles slowly rose and removed his glasses to rub his eyes. He looked over to Gladia, who brushed hair from her face. When he turned back, a racing fist popped his face and sent him backward. The room blurred and his jaw throbbed.

Gladia bolted upward and thrust her finger. "Get out! You don't hurt my friend. I will never see you again. Get out now!" Good thing Gladia knew how to project her voice like a drill sergeant: It kept Charles coherent.

Yokauve must have yelled back in Hebrew, because Charles didn't understand anything he said. Then the door shut.

"Are you okay? I am sorry." She lightly patted his face with her sheet. "He hit you hard. I will get you a cold towel and take you to the hospital."

"No, I'll be okay," he mumbled with his eyes closed.

≈≈≈

Gladia came back from the kitchen, dropped the wet cloth and lightly slapped Charles' face. "Wake up, Charles!" With adrenaline pumping, she ran outside and opened the car door. If she could carry encyclopedias up a ladder, she could get him into a vehicle.

Rushing to Bnei Zion Hospital, she began dragging him to the front entrance, yelling for help. An elderly doctor and nurse came out followed by an orderly pushing a gurney.

"A terrible man hit my friend!"

They lifted him and rushed inside. Yelling for an IV and cold pack, the doctor unlaced the pink robe and put a stethoscope to his chest.

"Why does he not wake, Doctor?" Gladia asked.

The physician lifted the scope. "Did he fall after he was struck?"

"He landed to my sofa."

"Are you sure? He has a small lump on the top of his head."

"Is he going to die?"

177

"I doubt it. He's breathing a little erratic, but that should stabilize with the oxygen." He looked at Gladia through his round glasses. "I will be back soon."

She leaned close to Charles' face, her hand on his chest so she could feel his heart beating. "Charles wake up." She had to tell him before he died. "Something I have to tell you. I should have said … when I tell you my parents were killed in the Arab revolt, I see them die." Her voice quivered. "I was twelve, and the British lose control to the Muslim Brotherhood in our village. When Arabs crash our door, my father hide me. They shouted, then stab Papa, and, and put a knife…." Squeezing her eyes tight, tears dripped onto his chest, "To Mother in her neck. I try to be quiet, but I cry. When they hear me, I run to Mother and bend down to stop her bleeding.

"Then Dov …" She whimpered. "He rushed in the door and point his rifle at me. I didn't know he was aiming at the Arab behind me, so I stand up when he shoot." She touched her chin. "That is how I get the scar. The bullet only hit my face a little and passed to kill the Arab man. Two more Arabs come out from the bedroom. Dov shoot them too.

"I lay on the floor with blood all over. Then my mother grab Dov on his leg and whisper, 'Promise to care for her.' Her last breath, she said it again. Dov said, 'I will, I promise!' My mama died with a little smile on her face when he said that. I miss her and Papa so much."

Gladia took the edge of the blanket and dried her tears from his chest.

"Dov took me to his home like he was my brother. He lost his family in the war, so I become his new sister. He gave me a home, and love. He got me in the Technion and paid the first year." She dried her face with the sheets. "They would be happy I know you. They would love you like I do." She squeezed his hand and wiggled it. "Now wake up. I need you!"

≈≈≈

Charles awoke wondering why a warm, heavy pillow lay on his chest. He soon realized it was Gladia's head, and when he rubbed her back, she jolted up and disappeared. Echoes of her loud cry for the nurse and doctor probably woke the whole hospital. She ran back to his side. "I love you!"

The doctor came running in, the nurse followed with a cart, clanging full of equipment. The doctor halted at the bed and smiled at Charles, then turned to Gladia. "I thought he stopped breathing the way you summoned us." He turned back to Charles. "Welcome back. I'm Doctor Busante."

"What happened?" Charles whispered. He removed the cold pack from his aching jaw, which hurt worse than his headache.

"You passed out after a man struck you this morning. Do you remember anything?"

Charles put his hand to his head. "My head hurts really bad. How did I get here?"

"Your girlfriend brought you here."

Strangling a towel, Gladia shot a half-smile.

"I still don't know how she got you in the car," Dr. Busante said. "Now that you're awake, we need to run some tests to find out why you lost consciousness for so long."

Gladia held his hand. "I am sorry he hit you." Her creased, reddened face resembled what he imagined a sweet wife's concern would look like. He'd never seen her so happy and worried at the same time.

"That's right. I got punched."

"The blow might have triggered the blackout," Dr. Busante said, "but not for three hours. Did you know about the small lump on your head?"

"This one on top?" Charles felt it. "Yeah. I noticed it a few months ago and hoped it would go away."

After several tests, they were escorted to a room and given turkey sandwiches. Finally, the nurse came in. "The doctor will see you in his office."

While following the nurse down the corridor, a memory came to mind that excited him. Gladia told Yokauve to never see her again. That was worth the sore face.

When they entered his office, Dr. Busante smiled. "Come in, sit down." He dipped a pen in ink. "I haven't drawn a conclusion yet. I need to ask some questions. You two seem close so hopefully your girlfriend can help."

Girlfriend. Charles liked the sound of that.

"Have you ever had any head injuries?"

"No."

"How about toxins? Does your father have any hobbies that used spray or liquid chemicals?"

"No." He wouldn't admit to the fumes he routinely inhaled from burning trash in the backyard on Sundays, when the neighbors were at church. Father was methodical about riding the house of excess boxes labeled "charity."

"How about headaches?"

"Yes, he has them all the time," Gladia piped up. "They are worse."

"How long have you been having headaches?"

"A long time. Probably two or three years."

"Did they start out weak, and now they're much stronger?"

"Yes." He looked at Gladia because his hand ached from her squeezing. "What is it, Doctor?" she asked.

"With the indications I have so far, I'm fairly certain you have a brain tumor."

She gasped, then lowered her head.

"Am I going to die?" A year ago, the news wouldn't have been welcomed, but with Gladia losing everyone she loved, it would devastate her.

"Not today, son. We need to find out if it's malignant. If we can find the cause, that would help." Dr. Busante charted notes. "How about grease? Did you grease your hair like other American kids?"

After numerous questions and Charles trying to evade the nightmares associated with the scalp treatment, Gladia gently elbowed him. "Tell him what the pharmacy man said."

Dr. Busante removed his glasses. "The pharmacist?"

"I … *ah* … tried to get a bottle refilled of … stuff my mother used to apply to my hair, but the pharmacist insisted it was number-three red hair dye."

"Did it turn your hair dark red?"

When Charles nodded, the doctor frowned. "That's not good." He rose and pulled some files out. "I know two other cases of tumors from hair dye: One is malignant, the other is not. That stuff is quite toxic." He thumbed through the files. "I want to send you to a specialist in Jerusalem."

Gladia sprang up and left, her sobs reverberating from the hallway. Dr. Busante handed him a referral card clipped to his file. "Dial this number right away." They shook hands. "Good luck, son."

He left the office feeling stupid. He thought he had intelligence, yet how could he have believed the lie about the "red medicine" all his life? Gladia met him and buried her head in his chest. When they reached her car, she stopped and held him. "I will die inside if you leave me. We need to call Moshe. He was a doctor."

"That's a good idea. And though I don't feel like I'm going to die, I'm glad you're with me right now."

"I will be with you the whole time."

He looked at the car. "In fact, I'm hungry again. Let's eat."

"Again? We just had turkey."

After he ate, they climbed into her car and she stared straight ahead. "I know why your parents use the dye." She started the car and headed down Main Street toward her house. "Arab irregulars learn how to look like everybody else, wherever they go. Sometimes you will not know the enemy until they speak."

They got out and walked into her house. "Your parents, they did not want you to look Arab in America, so they change your hair. We also learn if they keep you in the house, your skin will be more white like Americans. Dov tell me that the food you eat can make you anem … I forget the word for no iron in your body to make the skin more white."

"It's anemic."

"Yes, that is it." They sat on the sofa.

Charles' insides cringed. "Oh, my …" No wonder he'd often felt sickly. And his growth-spurt came when the hair dye ran out and he began eating meat. His parents were slowly killing him.

"What is wrong? Should I take you back to the hospital?"

"No. I'm just trying to process everything. I'm an Arab! You're not going to change how you feel about me. Right?" He studied her response, hoping that wasn't the reason she wasn't attracted to him: maybe she'd sensed him being the same descent as her parents' killers.

"No, Charles. I love you. And I don't hate Arabs. Just irregulars. Many Arabs were friends and neighbors of mine. But now, Arab irregulars pressure the peaceful ones to fight or leave Palestine. My father's good friend Emil, he was an Arab businessman from Jerusalem. Irregulars beat him because he told his village not to fight Jews, and not to join the Arab Legion."

She reached over and squeezed his hand. "It is not who you are born from. It is who you are." She smiled. "You and Dov are the best man I ever know."

He got up and paced the room to dissipate energy from her comments. She'd called him a man for the first time.

She sniffled. "I'm ... worried for you."

She rose and interrupted his pacing with a hug and gently caressed his back; She'd never caressed his back. "I love you so much. You know I get afraid because everyone I love is leaving ... I mean, has left me."

He felt her tears on his neck. "It's okay, like the doctor said, I'm not dying today. We have another saying in America: Let's take it one step at a time."

"Okay." She pulled back and puckered her lips like a pout. "You better not die tomorrow either."

She led him to Dov's room, but stopped at the threshold. "You should sleep now. I will go to the café and call Moshe." She kissed his cheek. "Then, we will ask him about the special doctor in Jerusalem."

He put his arm around her. "Thanks again for being with me."

She smiled. "Of course."

CHAPTER 21

July 1947

When Charles opened his eyes, the sun beamed streaks through his window on Gladia, who sat as a blurry image. He reached for his glasses and tightened his stomach to sit up, but dizziness sent him back to his pillow. "I thought you couldn't enter Dov's room."

She sighed. "I wanted to make sure you wake up okay before I go to work. When I spoke to Moshe last night, he say to watch you."

Charles squinted. "You haven't been here all night, have you?"

"Just each hour, I come in and check your breath with my hand. Then I go back to bed."

Charles didn't think his love could grow any more, but he was wrong. "I'm okay. If you have time to wait, I'll come to work with you."

She tried to bend her lips into a smile, but they flattened. "I will make you eggs while you get ready."

After chewing breakfast slowly, they drove to the library as he observed her locking eyes with him more often than usual.

After collecting books at his table, he caught her arm and gently tugged. "Wait. Moshe said he would have his physician see me. But there's something else. You're ... different."

"What do you mean?"

"I don't know, you look at me differently." He studied her for a reaction.

"Well I have, *ahh* ... affects."

"Affects?"

She nodded.

Two young women walked by and smirked. Gladia stiffened her body and stared at them. "You need help?" She turned back and shrugged, which she had learned from him. She met his eyes again. "I'm happy I have you."

"Me too!" This one time, he would play ignorant. He needed to know if she was only acting different because he might die. "What do you mean by *affect?*"

She blushed slightly. "Uhh, you know...."

"Describe what you mean, and I'll figure out the right word."

"I am not sure how...." When she averted her eyes, the main door opened and lit their area with the morning sun. "With you gone, I—"

Samuel stepped into the library; His presence reminded Charles of the anguish that betrayal brings. Charles recalled a scripture about forgiveness in Daniel 9:9: *The Lord is compassionate and forgiving even though we have sinned against Him.* Interesting to have a thought like that while Samuel approached. His first thought would have normally been one of father's derogatory chants.

"Charles, I found you. Hi, Gladia."

"Hello, Samuel."

Samuel scraped a chair across the floor and sat. "Gidi send me to find you."

"Who's Gidi?"

Samuel looked around. "He is our leader now that Dov is," he turned to Gladia, "not at work. Sorry." He gritted his teeth. "If I could, I would break him out!"

Gladia put her index finger over her lips. "*Shh* ... thank you, Samuel. Remember the library has no loud voices. How is your family? Is your father okay?"

He slapped his hand on the desk. "My mother said he got shot in the arm and beaten."

Charles' heart jumped. He still hadn't gotten over Jonathan or losing Jesse's respect. "Is he okay? How did he get attacked?"

"He tried to help a Jew from an Arab beating. That is *our duty*. He is lucky to be alive."

Charles had lost count of all the acts of terror since he arrived in Palestine. "I'm sick of the violence." In hindsight, Charles shouldn't have joined the Irgun. But then he looked over at Gladia, and couldn't imagine life without her.

She leaned forward. "Jesse. He is healing?"

"He is okay. Just his pride got damage." Samuel rolled his eyes at Charles. "But he is angry. I do not exist, and probably you do not either. He blames us for Jonathan's death, even though police bullets cut him down."

"We think about Jonathan all the time," Gladia said. "His parents, are they okay?"

Samuel shook his head. "I feel bad too. Maybe they never get over him." He looked over at Gladia "We know that pain, you and I."

Gladia dug her fingers into Charles' shoulder. Knowing she was fighting back pain from her parents' death, he patted her hand.

Samuel folded his hands and leaned toward Charles. "We need your thinking for a mission." His voice had lowered.

Charles knew he should decline. "What kind of mission?"

Samuel looked around and stood. "Come, we will go to the meeting place."

Charles swigged his tea in two gulps. "All right. Let's get this over with." He stood and embraced Gladia. "I will meet you at home?"

"Okay."

When they arrived at the old warehouse, Samuel looked around before entering. "Come upstairs so I can show you."

Samuel clunked up the stairs. Charles, smelling dust, thought back to the fateful day that spun adventure and turmoil into his life.

Samuel reached the top and turned. "Come up."

The men who used that room had caused a failed mission that took the one he'd wanted to adopt as his little brother. Stepping upward, he tried to imagine Jonathan's gleaming face at age fourteen, but his pasty corpse and deep bullet wounds were branded into his memory.

But refusing to at least listen to the mission wouldn't bring him back.

Samuel pointed to a chair. "Sit."

Charles crossed his arms and remained standing.

"We have a plan to recover our missing papers. Moshe told you about them, yes?"

Charles' gut knotted. "You mean our profiles seized by the Brits?"

Samuel nodded.

"He told me about it." If the Brits deciphered his records, he'd be deported and lose Gladia.

Samuel widened his eyes. "I cannot go back to prison!" He ducked under the table, then popped up and rolled a dusty blueprint out. "Here is the plan." Samuel traced his finger along the edge of a building, then stopped and tapped his finger.

Charles bent over to see what he was pointing at. He ran his eyes down to the legend and saw "King David Hotel." "I know that place! I've eaten there."

"Here is where they keep our papers. This man with a press pass; They think he reports news, but really he counts British security and looks in file cabinets. Then he tell us what he finds."

"Crafty." He sat, slightly intrigued.

Samuel leaned forward. "That is where we have to bow it."

He spoke so matter-of-factly, Charles had a hard time believing what he thought Samuel had just said. "You don't mean blow up the hotel?" He leaned back and narrowed his brows.

"Yes."

Charles rushed to his feet, knocking his chair over. "No, Samuel! That's stupid." He thrust his hands up. "I can't believe the Irgun would ask this of me." He stormed toward the door. "You're a bunch of terrorists!"

"We will telephone them so they will run before the blast. Just the south wing, where Brit headquarters are."

Charles turned when he reached the threshold. "Yeah, like the time you *accidentally* over-blew the SS *Patria*'s rudder and sunk two-hundred sixty-seven Jews? Count me out!"

"Count you out?" Samuel rose and kicked a chair over. "You will kill many more Jews if you do not help. And this is an order from Haganah, not Irgun."

"Save the tricky speech for someone else. I'm not getting involved."

Samuel picked up the chair. "We do without you, more people get bowed up. We need help, so people do not get hurt. Just the documents." He pointed to the chair. "Please, let me show you how come."

"I'm not looking at anything." Yet he couldn't stop starting at the documents.

Samuel motioned his hand. "It will not hurt if you look. I know you are curious." He patted the chair.

"So where's Borus and the others? Why are *you* the only one here telling me this?"

Samuel frowned. "Borus died yesterday with half of our group." He raised his shirt and revealed a blood-soaked bandage on his side. "And this mission is on a need-to-know-it basis." He thrust his finger at him. "You know that."

"You must have someone else."

"You are smart and know structure engineering. Our people say the hotel is too hard to guess where the bombs go and how much TNT to use. I tell them about you, and Moshe say to ask for your help."

Charles bowed his head. "You want a precision strike."

"Yes!" He scooted the plans toward Charles. "Look."

Charles paused and thought about other blundered explosions their men had detonated in the past. "Forget it. No matter how well you plan it, people are bound to get hurt." He turned toward the door.

"They have Gladia's address."

He halted, his back to Samuel.

"And her workplace. She could get five years. And you know what happens to women in prison."

If he could save Gladia, and maybe even someone else, it would be worth it. He took a deep breath and walked to the table. "Where did you get the blueprints?"

Samuel gave him a glazed-over look.

"Never mind." He squinted and examined the print, knowing he'd regret helping, but he couldn't stand seeing Gladia apprehended, himself being extradited and the Jewish dream of independence foiled.

He ran his finger over the main foundation supports, where several letter B's for "bombs" were written. "No! If you put explosives on those supports, it will collapse the central structures and probably demolish the whole building. Let me study this, so I can calculate precise hits." He looked up and furrowed his brows. "How do I know you'll call in the threat for a proper evacuation?"

"I promise. We have a woman. She learn what to say in three languages. She will call the hotel, the *Palestine Post*, and the French consulate, twenty minutes before. You can stay down the street if you want. But tonight you take Gladia and dance her there. You watch and tell us what you see. Then you meet me here to report."

Charles had a hard time believing Moshe ordered the strike. "I don't know how to dance, and I don't spy for the Irgun."

Samuel leaned in. "This is your chance. She can teach you, so you will be close to her."

"Okay, I can do that." He smirked. "But don't expect me back later unless there's something critical to report."

"Our leader Gideon—Gidi—he poses as a waiter. Do not give away his cover if you recognize him."

Charles walked away with a lump in his throat.

CHAPTER 22

Since he arrived home early, Charles prepared eggs and toast for dinner to surprise Gladia. When she walked in, he took her things and set them by the door.

Her eyes opened big when she took a whiff. "You cook dinner? It smells wonderful." When their eyes met, she paused. "Did Samuel have bad news?"

Charles sighed. "You certainly know how to read me."

"You have worry."

"They're planning something big." He took a deep breath. "He asked for my help, and I should have said no, but it's complicated."

"You can tell me after the mission, and we will see, yes?"

"Sure." He walked back to finish dinner.

"Why haven't you seen Moshe's doctor? I know your head hurts."

"His doctor's been in London. He said I could see him next week."

She walked into the kitchenette and turned the heat down. "You lie down, I will finish."

He nodded. "That would be nice."

She took the pan off the burner and placed it on the iron trivet, then made her way to the sofa. "You want me to rub your head?"

"That would be great." He put his legs down the couch and reclined on the pillow she placed on her lap. "Gladia?"

She looked down. "Yes?" With her face only a foot away, she ran her fingers through his hair.

He tried to conceal his grin as she invigorated his scalp, but then he eased her arms away and slipped out from underneath them. When he rose to his feet, he had to say something to distract her from what he was feeling. "The assignment requires something from you."

She looked up. "I will do it."

"I haven't even asked you yet."

"Whatever it may be, if it is with you, I will do it."

"Oh." How could he ask her if she'd had a change of heart without causing a disaster like last time?

"You didn't let me rub your head very long." She rose and stretched, with the most amazing posture.

"You *ahh* ... can finish dinner while I wash up."

When he came out of the washroom, she brought the pan to the table and scooped the steaming food out.

"So tell me the assignment. My part, nothing else," she said while sitting.

"I hope you believe me." He sat across from her. "I'm supposed to take you dancing at the King David Hotel, so I can observe the surroundings."

She smiled. "Sure. It is in the basement, called the Regency."

"But I told Samuel ..." Picturing her on the dance floor, brushing up against him, sounded really good.

She tilted her head. "What is wrong?"

He knew he had to be blushing from the pressure he felt in his cheeks. "I don't know how ... to dance." He glanced down so he wouldn't have to see her roll her eyes. But curiosity made him tilt his head back up.

She grinned big. "I can teach you!"

"You know how?"

"You are kidding me? I am Jewish." She lifted her hands. "You want me to teach you?"

What an amazing look of enthusiasm: gleaming eyes, arched brows, and a vivacious smile. "Yes." He motioned to the living room.

She giggled. "First we must eat."

When they sat, he gulped a few bites quickly, but another warning from David came to mind: *Slow down and relax around women.*

Her meal was only half finished when she patted her lips with a napkin. "You eat so fast." She scooted her plate toward him. "I know you want to finish mine."

"We can't let it go to waste." After he finished her leftovers in a few bites, she gracefully moved to the living area and put her hands out. "Come."

When he stood and walked toward her incredible pose, black dots sprinkled his vision. He found it difficult to look her in the eyes while placing his hands to hers.

"Okay. We step this way," she pulled his arms, "watch my feet. Then we go that way." She led him in a circular pattern. "Keep watching my feet, not my body."

He almost tripped at her "body" comment. "I love you," he blurted, not meaning to. He looked away but then met her eyes again.

"I do too...." She paused and the silence dazed him. "I guess we can go."

As they proceeded to Jerusalem, each time he tried to speak his rehearsed lines, he flashed back to the first painful letdown and changed the subject. Upon arrival, he hated how busy the hotel looked as she steered past a plethora of cars to park—the more people, the longer it would take to evacuate. On his first visit, he was excited meeting Golda Meir and witnessing the historic Dead Sea Scrolls. This time, looking at all the innocent faces had already ruined the evening. He had a tremendous urge to scream "Bomb!"

After descending into the basement and being escorted toward a table, he examining the ceiling and bumped her; She knocked the table.

193

"Are you okay?" She put the salt and pepper back in their place and looked up. "You are worried again."

"I don't know." He couldn't let her go to prison.

Gladia stood and put her napkin to Charles' cheek. "You are sweating. What is it?"

Charles squirmed. "We should go."

"Okay."

When they entered her car, he didn't want to talk. "I'm going to lay my head back and see if I can get my headache under control. Will you drive to the warehouse? I need to speak with Samuel."

He had to cancel the operation and smuggle Gladia out of Palestine, but when they arrived, Samuel wasn't there. When he returned to the car, he couldn't sit still, and on their way home, he punched the dashboard. "Gladia, can you skip work tomorrow? We need to be in Jerusalem in the morning."

"Because of the mission?"

"I hope not." But it would be just like Samuel to deceive him about the actual day.

She parked in her driveway and looked at him. "Then we should spend the day at the beach. I don't like how you look at the hotel, and run in the warehouse, then you come out with terror on your face."

He couldn't believe she just invited him to the beach for the day—another first. He refused to torture himself by picturing her in a bathing suit. "I know staying home is the wise thing to do but—"

"You want to be there so no one is hurt." She opened her door and they walked into the house.

"I shouldn't have gotten involved."

"Okay, we will go. But we must be careful and not get close."

CHAPTER 23

July 1946

Driving to Jerusalem, Charles kept his eyes on the rearview mirror, while Gladia kept glancing at him. She tilted the mirror back her way. "No one is following."

"I know."

"Try to be calm. I can rub your head if it hurts when we get there."

"It's that obvious?" He pointed forward. "Watch out!"

She screeched the tires behind a line of cars. "This is a new checkpoint."

He poked his head out to see how far ahead the drawbar was. "This is going to take forever."

Gladia shifted to park. "Moshe warned us. When we get close to victory, travel will be harder." She removed her gun from her purse and stuffed it in the seat below her knees. When she eyed his waist, he knew she was thinking about his gun, but she didn't bother to ask. A half hour of small nudges brought them to the guard tower.

"Out of the car!" a British soldier demanded.

Charles grimaced. "Why? You didn't ask anyone else to get—"

"Sure. We can get out." Gladia nodded.

When they stepped out in front of the strapping soldier, a line of cars behind watching, Charles removed his glasses and rubbed his forehead. "No disrespect intended, but your questioning ..." He raised his hands like a criminal being arrested. "Don't panic, I'm pulling my identification card out.

Yes, I'm American, riding with a Jew. We met at school, and no, we're not freedom fighters planning an attack."

The soldier gripped his gun. "Do you want to be detained?"

Charles shook his head. "I'm sorry. I've got a bad headache, and I've been harassed more times than I can count."

The soldier looked over their cards. "We're not here for your convenience. We are trying to keep order in this God-forsaken land."

What a strange comment: The land was supposed to be the Holy Land, not God-forsaken. "Well, you're not—" Gladia poked him.

The soldier returned their cards. "Just go."

The sun broke through the marine layer by the time they parked across the street from the hotel. Charles' stomach knotted at the sight of a tour bus pulling up.

Gladia rolled the window down. "It is getting warm already." She turned her body toward him. "Come. Lean on me and I will rub your headache."

He turned and leaned against her soft body. Her breathing made his speed up. He glanced at her flowing hair over his arms and then shut his eyes, knowing she would soothe him. Her long fingers ran up his neck first, then to his scalp making him tingle all over. To imagine her hands going anywhere else would be futile. He finally understood why people married.

When she shifted her body he opened his eyes.

"Something is happening, honey."

Charles jolted forward and turned. "What did you call me?"

"Look." She pointed. "They walk with the little bounce like Irgun and the robes are too short. The Arabs, they don't show ankles."

He put his cheek to hers and stared out the driver's window. "They're carrying big milk canisters!"

"Why does that matter?"

"Samuel said they were going to pack TNT in containers like those."

196

She turned, bringing their faces inches apart. He pulled back, already overly excited about her endearing word, and grasped the door lever.

"Don't. Let us wait." She rolled the window back up.

He released the lever. "I have to do something."

She latched onto his arm. "You cannot interfere, they will harm you."

He looked at the hotel. "They're inside."

She restrained his arm and showed him the back of her hand. "We must wait."

He took note of her deep stare. "You seem … you keep looking at me differently and…." He focused on his ring shimmering on her finger. "What's that?"

"You don't recognize it?"

"That's the ring I tried to give to you. I … thought it was lost."

"No. Not lost. I pick it up when you walk away and keep it in a box. I'm sorry about that time, I know it hurt."

"That's okay, I understand. You need *a man*." At least that's what David told him. "But why are you wearing it?"

"Why do you think?" She bit her lower lip.

He narrowed his brows, still unsure about their communication gap.

"What do you think it means?" She wiggled her brows.

He swallowed. After all this time of pain and uncertainty, he found it difficult to accept that she finally wanted him. "Is … are you saying—?"

"Yes!" she nodded vigorously.

His jaw dropped. "I can't believe it! I … don't know what to say."

She put her lips to his ear. "You can say you want me." She brushed her cheek against his. Chills ran down his neck, and with her lips inches away, his heart pounded.

A loud bang sounded. Charles snapped back and Gladia gasped. They both moved to her side of the window and looked out, cheek-to-cheek.

"Why would they set off a small bomb in the street?" She shook her head. "They never miss by that much."

"Oh no. It's going to happen! That's the pre-blast to scare everybody out of the hotel." He reached for his door handle. She grabbed his elbow. "No!"

He yanked his arm back. "I can't sit here and watch this."

"No, Charles, I cannot lose you." Her face reddened as she pulled him.

A massive blast shook the car. The windows clattered as they both slammed into the steering wheel, which sounded the horn. They ducked when wallops and thumps plopped on the roof and hood. Milky dust followed and clung to the windows. Gunshots echoed as several Irgun fled the scene—a bullet pierced the windshield and drove them to the floorboard.

After a spray of gunfire, eerie silence followed until someone banged on their window. They both rose to see a dust-covered security officer crouched over, legs spread, his pistol aimed at their faces. He wrenched the car door open. "Hands in the air where I can see them! Identification. Now!" He reached out his hand while holding his shaking gun at their faces. "Nice and slow."

They coughed while fumbling their papers.

The officer whisked their cards from their shaking hands. "Do you have weapons?"

"No, I'm an American. You can't—" Gladia swiftly placed her hand over his mouth.

"I can see you're American." The officer looked at Gladia's card and sneered. "But you're with a Jew." He waved his gun. "Get out. You're both under arrest for questioning. Hands out forward." He slapped cuffs on Charles. "Move. And careful lad, these guns go off easily." He pushed him forward with Gladia at his side.

After a few dozen paces through the rubble-filled street, Charles halted at the sight of several overturned cars. His heart pounded; the scene resembled a war zone. He looked at Gladia. Tears dripped down the white dust on her cheeks as she surveyed the devastation.

A breeze blew through the curtain of filth and exposed the building's missing corner. "Oh my!" Charles said. The officer remained silent at the sight of the ravaged structure as it came into full view. Charles put his cuffed hands to his cheeks, his open mouth collecting soot.

People screamed and ran in all directions, but as if in slow motion. About thirty steps ahead, an arm with no body attached rested on a chunk of wall. The officer brushed his uniform, cleared his throat and pushed them toward a woman pinned by a massive piece of the building.

Gladia ran to her. "Halt. I'll shoot!" The officer cocked his gun.

Charles inserted himself into the line of fire.

"Help me get this off her," Gladia yelled.

Charles ran to Gladia's side; the officer followed. The woman was pale and unresponsive, her limbs crooked under rocks and dirt.

The officer uncocked his gun and set it down, his eyes piercing Charles. "I will count to three, then we push. Go for the gun and you're dead." He girded himself. "One, two, three!"

They grunted and rolled the giant fragment off the crushed woman's chest. The officer lunged for his gun and straightened. Charles' legs almost gave out. The woman lay flattened like a giant, blood-smeared Raggedy Ann doll. Gladia held her hand to her mouth, more tears streaming.

Charles did this to her, as far as he was concerned. When he looked up from hearing the officer's command to regather, he cringed at seeing an Arab bus on its side. The first blast was designed to make people flee the area, but it seemed to have done the opposite.

The woman fluttered her eyes open. Her lips moved but only wheezes sounded. Her eyes widened when Gladia stooped and gently brushed pebbles and dust from her face.

"She is still alive," Gladia said to the stunned officer. "Do something!"

The officer holstered his pistol and cupped his hands. "Medic. Medic!" The plea for help echoed under the sirens and screaming, but rendered no reply. The officer drew his pistol at Charles. "There's nothing we can do for her. I can get help from the—"

"We can't leave her here!" Gladia protested.

The officer clamped Charles' arm with his free hand and aimed his gun at her face. "Move, or you're going to get a bullet."

Gladia held the woman's hand. "I'm not leaving her!"

He shoved the gun into Charles' side and cocked it. "Are you coming now?"

She tightened both fists, stood, and started walking. "You are a heartless man," she said over her shoulder.

"This way." He waved his gun to the right and ushered them down the street for what seemed like a half-hour trek. They were forced into a noisy jailhouse, through a maze of detainees complaining about their rights being violated. Suspects had been chain-cuffed to anything solid: desk legs, banisters and benches. Charles and Gladia were attached to a line of six other Jews cuffed under a staircase. The officer vanished.

The next several hours brought swollen wrists, aching feet and parched mouths. Charles rotated his head to ease his aching neck: Gladia slumped beside him, her head resting on his shoulder. She warned that more time would pass without food, water, or a bathroom break, to weaken them for interrogation. Finally, one by one, men dressed in suits had taken each Jew through two black double doors. Charles had almost nodded off when clinking keys rustled behind him. After unlocking their shackles, a Brit in a dark gray suit escorted them to a room with a bright light glaring from the far end of a table. A man's silhouette appeared at the other side while the escort clicked their restraints to the table legs.

"We need food and water," Gladia said, her free hand shading her eyes. "Charles' head, it is not well." With no chairs in sight, Charles bent over and laid his head at the edge of the table.

"You'll get what you want when you give us what we need." The man kicked the table, making Charles thrust upward. When he wobbled to maintain balance, Gladia leaned his way to steady him.

The man in the shadow lit a match, highlighting the tips of his wrinkled face. A bright orange glow from his lit cigarette revealed the rest of his bulky features. Then he blew a stream of bright-gray smoke through the beam of blinding light. Charles coughed and blinked to focus his vision. "I want to speak to the American consulate," he said, his voice raspy.

"Certainly, chap. But there's a three-day interim with all the ruckus going about."

"I need to call my Aunt Agatha," Gladia said. "She will worry."

"You can ring her, tomorrow."

"I have a right!"

"You have no bloody rights, Jew!" The cigarette glowed and more smoke billowed.

Charles wiped sweat from his forehead. "Why are no Arabs detained?"

The man chuckled. "Typical spoiled American. You don't belong here, muddling in our affairs. Besides, you're battling an unwinnable war. You're ill equipped, outnumbered … what's the use." He snuffed his cigarette on the table and blew out his last drag. "Arabs don't blow up British assets, chump, they're too busy taking *pot-shots* at you. If it weren't for us, they'd clean you out." He faded back into darkness. "We tallied fifty-seven dead so far, and we know you're caught up in the mess."

"Fifty-seven?" A cold ripple shot down Charles' spine. He wanted to scream out a confession, but being hanged wouldn't bring back the poor victims. Hopefully the man was bluffing, though the crushed woman's face already haunted him.

"Fifty-seven for now; That puts you in the class of Jack the Ripper." He slapped the table and advanced forward. "Who planned this attack?"

Charles didn't flinch at the man's bloated face and gnashing teeth. But now, he wasn't sure whom he disdained more: the Irgun or Father.

Gladia turned to Charles. "No Arabs arrested because they have oil. We have nothing to bribe them with—"

The man slapped the table again. "I'm sure there's *more dead* under the rubble, lassie. And you're going to pay for it!" He stomped past them.

"How long are you holding us?" Charles asked.

"He is gone." Gladia wiggled her shoulder to keep him propped up. "Your face is red and sweating." She pulled on her chain. "I wish my hands could reach you."

"I think I'm going to be sick." Experienced at manipulating his body while being bound, he maneuvered the chains and twisted his body, so he could partially lie on the table.

Gladia followed his example and wrestled her chains so she could kick the metal door. "We need a doctor!"

"Wait. The yelling makes it worse." Charles spoke with his eyes closed. "He'll probably be back soon. I saw his unsettled reaction when I mentioned the American consulate."

"Okay, I'm sorry. You need a pillow." She rustled her cuffs. "I will give you my dress."

"No, don't. I'll be okay."

"Do not die on me."

"I won't. I love you too much." A surge of vigor rushed through him when she rested her face onto the table next to his. "I want to be with you forever."

She lifted her face off the table. "Is that a *proposal?*"

"What?"

"You hear me."

"Yes, it is. Will you marry me?"

"Yes!" She grinned. "Now you have to stay alive."

Chills prickled him. He closed his eyes for a moment and tried to breathe. "We're getting married! That's all I need to get through this." He couldn't pass out now; it would be a nightmare if he woke up and realized she still just wanted to be friends. He'd never imagined proposing without even kissing her yet.

"We will get through this. If they don't hang us." Her voice trembled.

"*Shhh* ... I just realized, they're probably listening," he whispered. "That's why he left. They're not going to hang us. I'm an American and you're a woman."

"That does not seem to matter," she whispered back.

"Yi-hi-hya. It will be all right, you'll see."

"It's *yiheyeh*. I will not feel better until I talk to Agatha and we leave." She wrestled her chains and stretched her neck to place her cheek on his. "I'm scared, but happy too." She brushed her cheek along his and positioned her lips for a kiss, but the door opened and she jerked back.

An officer unchained her and took hold of her wrist. "Out."

Charles knew their next tactic would be to separate them and continue robbing their sleep, for intense questioning. He closed his eyes to prepare for the next round.

The door flung open and startled him awake. A man shoved Gladia into the room. The only thing he remembered was an interrogator constantly waking him for questions. "Your stories match a little too well," the man said.

Gladia's face reddened. "I said he needs a doctor! And he needs food and water, right now!" Her voice was raw.

The man came nose-to-nose with Charles. "We know you're involved! Your name has been on our list for months." He pivoted toward Gladia. "And you reside at the address of a captured Irgun criminal." The man smirked. "Dov Grunner will get what's coming to him."

Gladia tightened her lips and swung her chains.

"But you've wasted enough of our time." He waved his hand at a man behind them. "Go. You had better hope the gallows aren't waiting for you someday."

An officer unlocked their shackles. When they walked outside, they squinted at the brilliant July sun. The warm air burned against Charles' swollen wrists. He blinked several times to focus at the well-dressed heavyset woman approaching.

"Agatha! How did you know we are here?" Gladia asked. "They did not let me call."

Agatha pointed to a car. "I'll tell you later, let's get out of here."

She and Gladia helped Charles into the backseat. "He's dehydrated with heat exhaustion, let me get a cloth." Agatha moved to the front seat and rummaged around while Gladia scooted in next to him. With dark spots filling his outer vision again, he began slipping over until Gladia caught him and laid his head on her lap.

Agatha turned from the driver's seat. "I don't have anything to wipe his face with." She started the car and began driving.

Gladia adjusted his upper body and dried his face with her dress. "We need the store to get him food and water. And a doctor."

Agatha screeched the wheels around a corner. "Sorry, honey. Everything's closed due to the bombing. And if I yell, be prepared to duck down. Arabs like to take advantage of crisis and take shots at Jews."

"My car. There is water in it." Gladia started rubbing his arms as he looked up at her.

"If you show up there, you'll be arrested again," Agatha said. "And we're not going to get a doctor here. We'll have to return to headquarters to see our nurse, Josephina."

Gladia squirmed. "That is too far. And I hear them say Jerusalem road is blocked."

"I know, I'm taking the back roads through the villages."

"He needs help right now—"

"Duck!" Agatha hit the brakes.

Gladia laid her head on Charles. "What is it?"

Agatha stepped on the gas, made a sharp turn and raced onto a bumpy road. "Arabs just shot up an ambulance at a streetlight right in front of us. Gladia, the quickest way to get Charles help is to listen to me. That could have been us back there."

"Okay." She cuddled Charles' head like a mother nurturing a baby.

"The bumps hurt," Charles said. The smell of dust also made it difficult to breathe. To distract himself and stay awake, he decided to ask Agatha, "Your English is perfect, Agatha. Where are you from?"

"Milwaukee, Wisconsin. I was a law student here in Jerusalem at the Hebrew University. I worked with Gladia's parents, in communications for the Haganah. Then, they promoted me to legal counsel when I graduated."

"Charles, no more talk … Charles?" Gladia yelled, "He's dying, Auntie, hurry!"

Charles could still hear, but he had no strength to open his eyes or talk.

"I can't stop, this is a known hostile Arab village—"

"Pull over, he fainted. They will have water and food. He's wet all over."

Gladia's lap and loving care made him smile inside. He had to muscle enough strength to at least pry one eye open, to see his ring on her finger. But his quick look only revealed her sweaty face.

The car halted and the motor stalled. "This doesn't look good," Agatha said. "We're in the heart of Deir Yassin. Here comes a bunch of Arabs with pitchforks, axes, and machetes. I couldn't bring my gun to the disaster, and I know you don't have yours. At least a shot in the air would have helped." Agatha's keys rustled, but the engine kept cranking without starting.

Wanting to help, Charles blinked his eyes open, but couldn't move. He tried again to lift himself, but couldn't overcome the spinning backseat.

Gladia kissed his forehead. "Lock the doors, Agatha. Don't worry. God is with us. I know it." She squeezed his arms. "God, please rescue us right now!"

The mob had to look bad for her to pray. He'd never pictured himself dying on her lap.

"It's going to take more than prayers to get us out of this." Agatha tried to crank the motor again. "They look spooked. I'm sure they heard the explosion and received news about the hotel yesterday."

Multiple taps clicked the windows, accompanied by foreign babbling. Gladia cracked her window and spoke in Arabic, her voice shuddering. She must have been pleading for their lives.

Calm voices replied back in their dialect.

She rolled the window down. "They know what I say about Charles."

"Don't roll the window down," Agatha said.

"I think they are offering help." Gladia opened her door and continued speaking to them.

Two Arab men reached in, gently picked Charles up and carried him to a hut, where an older man was sitting on a straw-woven drum. It smelt dusty and smoky, but at least he could get an eye open.

Gladia continued muttering tidbits of Arabic while Charles felt a finger smear something gooey under his nose; he coughed while it warmed his chest.

A woman held a ceramic vase to his lips. The foul liquid almost choked him, but it made him sit up and breathe hard.

Across from him, an elderly woman caressed Gladia's face with her shawl, patting and dabbing her sweat and tears as a mother would. The intimate expressions on both their faces astonished Charles because Agatha marked the village aggressive. When things came into focus, he looked for Agatha, but didn't see her.

After more food and drinks, he stood without jittering and his headache became manageable. When the Arabs walked them to their vehicle, Agatha stepped out, openmouthed. When cloths filled with apples, nuts and bread were offered, he tried to refuse the gift, but Gladia shook her head, so he accepted it. He patted his trousers for his pocket watch to give in return, but it was missing. Gladia hugged the women and he shook hands while the older men opened the car doors for them.

Driving off, Agatha shook her head. "That was a miracle. I didn't know there were Arabs like that in this sector. Obviously, God is watching over you two."

Gladia placed her hands around Charles' head. "You lay down on my lap and let me care for you. You are okay now, yes?"

He lowered his head to her lap and closed his eyes. "I feel much better." Even more, he was the luckiest man on the planet to have Gladia as his wife. If this was what his friends meant when they told him God blesses those who bless the Jews, then he wanted to continue being a part of God's plan. He looked up and smiled. "This is the best place I've ever been."

"*Shh*, you rest now," she said.

"Gladia, I'm jealous! The way you two carry on …"

Gladia didn't respond, she continued to stroke Charles' hair.

After several more bumpy paths and turns, they made it to a paved street, and finally the headquarters. Agatha settled them into a room with a brown couch and volumes of books stacked against the walls, then left.

She walked back in with a frown a few minutes later. "Moshe received confirmation of the death toll. It's not what we expected."

Charles stood. "Are you going to tell us?"

CHAPTER 24

Charles dropped to the couch next to Gladia. Ninety-one confirmed dead. Mostly Jews, Arabs and British. Recalling Agatha's words, he kicked the coffee table. "Samuel promised they'd warn the establishment."

"We did," Agatha said. "One of our aides, Adina, phoned the warning, and a British officer replied, 'We don't take orders from Jews!'"

Charles slapped the armrest. Gladia jumped. "I helped kill those people! How am I supposed to live with that?"

"You saved lives!" Agatha said. "You know how Irgun bombings have backfired in the past. If you didn't help, the entire hotel could have collapsed, killing everyone."

"She is right," Gladia said. "You must not forget you save people."

He looked at Agatha. "You knew about my involvement?" He wondered how many others did.

Agatha came closer. "Imagine hundreds more dying if they didn't use your modified plans."

"That doesn't make me feel better."

"Well, it should."

Charles squinted. "So Moshe ordered this? Where is he?" He paced toward the door, but Agatha stood in front of him. "He left for a few days. There are bigger things at stake than what you know." She pulled a piece of paper from her satchel. "Moshe left you a memo." She reached for her glasses hanging from her neck. "'Dear Charles, on behalf of a grateful nation, thank

209

you. The Jewish Agency condemned the bombing, but it was for the public's ears. Our estimates calculate your involvement saved up to six hundred lives. You are a true hero!'"

≈≈≈

Charles had a few days to cool off and think about what his friends had said. Yet when Moshe summoned him, he struggled to restrain his indignation when he entered his office.

Moshe got up and shook his hand. "First things first; I heard about your splitting headaches. My personal physician is waiting to see you. We will spare no expense to help you get well." He motioned for him to sit. "And … about the hotel. I know it's a sensitive matter. While the deaths were horrific, the mission was a tremendous success."

Charles rolled his eyes. "A success? Was it worth ninety-one lives?" He choked back tears. "How do you keep a straight face? Or sleep at night?" He took a breath. "I have a woman's crushed body stuck in my memory!"

"I know it's hard." Moshe sat at the edge of his desk. "The mission hurts me too. Any rational institution would have evacuated the entire building, like we planned. That should give you an idea of who we're dealing with."

Charles crossed his arms. "This is not what I signed up for."

"We're in a war! Even your country killed to win victory from the British. Don't forget, without this mission, you would have been facing your father from a jail cell right now." Moshe went back to his chair. "Imagine how many more Jewish lives would be eliminated if we were hanged." He sighed. "Now imagine Palestine as an Islamic state—there'd never be a balance of power in this region."

Moshe looked intently at him. "Destroying those documents was an act of self-defense. After all, this land has been conquered many times over, and no one is shouting at the British for killing Turkish lives over it. And since we possessed this land long before them, why shouldn't we take it back? There is no Palestinian language, no Arab capitol or any organized Arabs who have set up any type of government here. This land, nor Jerusalem has ever been mentioned in their Koran; yet Jerusalem and Israel was written hundreds of times in our scriptures. So who has the most historical rights?"

Charles looked away from Moshe. "I'm not sleeping again—I can't think about anything but death—and I'm not eating much."

Moshe knocked on his desktop. "Please, look at me."

Charles looked.

"These are good things you're going through—normal reactions for a decent human being. This is what separates *you* from the enemy! I pray you never lose what you feel right now." He leaned in. "See the bags under my eyes? I haven't slept more than a few hours since it happened."

Charles knew it was true, but he just wanted to forget the whole mess.

Moshe rippled a paper on his desk. "God has caused something good to rise from this atrocity, making this event our last offense against the British."

Charles perked up. "You're ending the violence?"

"To the Brits? Yes. But our other enemies have us boxed in on all sides! If we don't take aggressive action immediately like our forefathers did, thousands will fall prey to Arabs and Nazis." Moshe stood. "And now, something monumental has risen from this anguish!"

"So you're not ending the violence...."

Charles fixed his attention on Moshe, who'd thrust a stiff finger in the air. "The British handed the fate of this land to the United Nations."

"Who are the United Nations, and why is that so significant?"

"The UN was established recently to become a world peacekeeping court. They can accept votes from member nations with hopefully less-ulterior motives than the British. We're praying for a partition of the land: half to the Arabs and half to the Jews. We're hoping a compromise like that will bring peace to this region."

A few taps made them both look at the door.

"Sorry to interrupt. I have thirty minutes prior to my departure for London."

Moshe waved. "Please come in. Charles, meet Doctor Pallid." He motioned toward the door. "Go ahead, Charles, we'll finish later."

The physician led Charles upstairs to a small medical office and examined him. Later, Moshe walked in with Gladia. Charles finished buttoning his shirt and greeted her. Moshe nodded. "I'm going to speak with the doctor in my office."

When Moshe returned, Gladia stepped forward. "What did the doctor say?"

"They need to run more tests."

Moshe looked at Charles. "I know a world-renowned oncologist, who resides in London. If you're up to it, I have a critical assignment there, requiring your skills."

"Thank you, Moshe," Gladia said.

Charles was relieved she didn't ask what an oncologist was. Knowing her though, she'd look it up at work and panic when he was gone. But he had to find out if he was terminally ill before they married, so she could decline—it was too wonderful to actually happen anyway.

"I knew you would take good care of him, Moshe. But," she looked at Charles, "no more assignments to foreign countries. Just see the doctor and come back."

Moshe stepped between them and placed his hands on their shoulders. "I understand. I've lost family and friends to this horrific war." He turned. "Charles, you've more than proved your loyalty to us. And I have to warn you, this assignment is risky." He patted Charles' shoulder twice. "Let's sit in my office so I can brief you. Then you can decide."

Charles followed Moshe into his office and sat: Gladia stood in the hallway. Moshe turned. "It's okay, Gladia. Come in and have a seat."

She stood by Charles, her posture rigid. Charles was divided. Even though it was because of Gladia that he volunteered in the first place, he didn't want to upset her. But an inner drive compelled him to hear Moshe out.

As he settled in his chair, Moshe's gaze shifted from Gladia to Charles. "First the risk. If caught with these documents," he took a breath, "you could be tried and hanged by the British."

Gladia stormed out. Charles loved her for that.

"But it's unlikely since you're an American citizen. And President Truman has petitioned the British parliament with some success." Moshe began assembling files in a folder. "No one will think any less of you if you decline, but need you on this one." He placed the files on his desk. "An American reporter named Kennedy furnished these documents from the Balfour Declaration of 1917, which contain British commitments to grant a Jewish state in Palestine. The Brits will be furious when this evidence has been presented to a world court—and no one will know about this unless it's delivered."

Taking on the British government certainly ranked higher than deceiving Father.

Gladia walked back in. "You must have others who can do it."

Charles looked at her. "Let him finish."

Moshe nodded. "Of course." He pulled out a telegram. "But here's why we need our best agent." He put his glasses on. "'We are pleased to confirm the United Nations have agreed to take the responsibility of Palestine's fate from the British, sincerely, Chaim Weitzman.'" He looked at Gladia. "We're the first major task the UN has agreed to take on. If we demonstrate our legitimate right to this land, it will be pivotal to establish this nation legally."

"Why is the assignment so dangerous?" Charles asked.

"These papers undermine the British argument against our right to this land: The Arabs have really tainted them. If the UN were to favor our claim, it would prove to the world that the British have wrongfully arrested and killed Jews." Moshe stood. "Also, the British labeled us *all* terrorists since the hotel bombing, so they've boosted their efforts to apprehend us."

He placed the documents into an envelope and sealed it. "These are originals." He shifted his eyes between them.

When Charles stood, Gladia came closer and lightly jabbed him.

Moshe's eyes followed her elbow as he held the envelope to his chest. "He won't be long, Gladia. A quick stopover to see my physician, then to New York and back."

"New York? I thought I was only going to London." After Charles' near arrest, Father would certainly be combing the city. But even though his pulse ran wild, this time he wouldn't allow Father's malevolent grin or dirty chants fill his thoughts anymore. With all apprehension aside, if the delivery could end the violence, it would be worth the risk. "I'll do it."

Gladia stiffened. "I must go with him!"

Moshe shook his head. "Sorry. You know we don't have a passport for you." He shifted to Charles. "First you will stop at the *Boston Post*. Ask for a reporter named Robert Kennedy, and let him copy these documents in your presence. He claims his brother John will be the future president of the United States, and we can use all the allies we can get."

Tears welling, Gladia clasped Charles' arm. "But I—"

"We'll get him back to you," Moshe said.

She pulled on Charles' arm. "I do not feel good with this. I can't take another ten months!"

Moshe walked over and put his arm around her. "He'll be back in a week." He stuffed the envelope down Charles' shirt. "Convincing anyone at the UN to favor our nation is your primary goal."

"I understand sir, I won't let you down."

"Excuse us, sir." She led him into the hallway. "Don't go," she whispered. "I have bad feelings about this."

"I'll be okay. Plus, I can see the best doctor available." He hugged her. "Our nation needs this delivery."

She tapered her brows with glossy eyes. "That is the first time you say 'our nation.' See the doctor, but not New York. We have not been alone for even a little time."

He rested his face on her shoulder. "I know and that makes this difficult. I can see us at the beach playing in the water, kissing and ..." He retracted his hands from her.

She squeezed him. "I won't sleep until you come back. I wish you had a *bad* way of delivering messages so they don't use you. You are zealous for this land like a Jew. I hate it!" Then her face morphed into a grin. "And I love you for it too." She smacked his lips with hers and winked with both eyes, not knowing that a wink was supposed to be done with one eye.

After she left, Moshe led Charles into the infirmary, unlocked a medicine cabinet and turned with three pills in his hand. "Do you know what cyanide is?"

Charles widened his eyes. "That's poison." It quickly jolted his thoughts out of the romantic beach scene.

"Keep one in your possession at all times." Moshe stared at him. "Open your hand." Moshe dropped the tablets onto his palm.

Charles stared at the shaking pills. His throat tightened as he thought about Gladia's intuition.

CHAPTER 25

Charles followed Moshe back to his office. "Wait a second. There's more to this mission than British documents isn't there?"

Moshe sat and chuckled. "All right, but this information stays in this office."

Charles nodded and closed the door.

"We have tangible proof of Arab leaders conspiring with Nazis to carry out Hitler's genocide. This evidence is critical for the UN to examine during their decision process. There's a photograph tucked in your packet, and a transcript of Amin Al-Husseini, the Arab Mufti of Jerusalem, meeting with Hitler about what they called 'the Jewish problem.'"

He was sorry he'd asked. "The public doesn't know this?" Good thing Gladia didn't know he'd be crossing Nazis.

"Controversy sells newspapers more than the truth. Even the American press often slants the truth to make us look like the enemy."

"Am I going to have Nazis on my tail after this?"

"They already know who you are."

Charles' stomach felt like it dropped to the floor.

"When Hitler commissioned his top officer, Heinrich Himmler, to infiltrate Palestine, they taught Arabs how to gather intelligence on Jews. When Nazis were at large after the war, Arabs provided them new identities, jobs and homes." Moshe got up to leave.

Charles crossed his arms and stood. "There's still more.... "

"I'll tell you when you return."

"I know it's about my parents."

"You don't want to know this right now."

"We both know I might not come back. Uncovering their secrets is what I originally came to Palestine for. They ruined my life and I have to know why." Part of Charles didn't want to know anymore.

"Look … you must know parental abuse is never the fault of the child."

"I have to know. Their secrets eat away at me everyday."

"Sit." He sat at his desk. "The man you call father, Roger Devonshire, is not who he claims to be."

Somehow that didn't surprise Charles.

"Peter Von Deisenberg is his real name."

Charles squinted. He'd always wondered why father's cufflinks had the initials P.V. engraved. "That's a German name."

"It's also the name of a Nazi."

Charles gasped for air. Images of Father's smug face were suddenly tied to the film reels of Nazis killing Jews. It must have been German his comrades were speaking at the midnight meetings.

Moshe punched his call button. "Nurse, I need a paper bag."

Charles held his hand up, "No, no, I'm all right." He took in a deep breath.

Moshe held the button. "Disregard, Nurse." He exhaled. "Let's finish this when you return."

"It's all makes sense but … I just can't fathom being the son of a Nazi."

"Charles, you've become like a son to me. I really shouldn't … you're not."

"What do you mean?"

"Your Arab mother had a forbidden love before you were born."

His eyes opened big. "My mother?"

"We don't know his name, but we believe your biological father was most likely Jewish or an American."

"Jewish?" Charles almost smiled. That would be the most ironic thing he'd ever heard. Maybe it was why he felt an inner drive to help Jews in the first place. "How could you possibly know this?"

"Von Deisenberg was either sterilized or had abstained from marital relations with your mother. Nazis took oaths not to impregnate other races that didn't possess pure white skin. That would have violated their vow to Aryanism."

Charles just realized that he'd heard the word "Aryan" before. He had an urge to step outside and break something. And then another forgotten memory: "Oh my goodness."

"You remember something?"

"My parents slept in separate beds ... a friendly woman, one who Mother wouldn't serve drinks to, was always at the meetings." Chills crept up his neck. "Blonde hair and white skin. He had a mistress!"

Moshe frowned. "I'm sorry you remembered that. Their marriage was probably arranged for the sake of a mission against Jews."

"You know more about my biological father...."

"We don't know for sure, but it's the only plausible reason your mother's brother, *your uncle*, would have had her first love ..." He cleared his throat.

Charles noticed Moshe pull his fingers into a fist and then open his hand. That subtle pattern usually meant Moshe was holding back something else—hopefully the final missing piece that could give Charles resolve.

"This is beginning to sound like a Hitchcock movie. But you know more, and you're not supposed to tell me." The information overwhelmed his racing mind. "So my uncle—"

"You have two uncles, actually. The younger is an Arab revolutionist leading numerous revolts against Jews. The older is an accountant and has no record of suspicious activity."

"Now I see why you didn't want to tell me." He stood, his head dizzy. "I always regretted being related to that imposter. Now I want to know who my real father is … or was." He stood and shook Moshe's hand. "I suppose you're not permitted to disclose that."

Moshe shook his head. "Not until we achieve our goal." The Sherut Yediot is the best counterespionage agency in the world. If they found out I leaked this to even you, a trusted agent, I'd lose my rank. But they don't know you like I do."

"That's fair. I can't begin to tell you what this means to me." What a relief: that evil man was not his father after all. "Can you at least give me his name? My real father?"

Moshe morphed his expression to an odd-looking grin. "What real father?" He turned. "We're surprised he didn't eliminate you—your uncle. You might have been the reason your mother was paired with a Nazi and reassigned to America."

Charles scratched his head.

"There's no possibility of Arab terror networks accepting Jewish or American babies, so we assume your mother pleaded for your life." Moshe stiffened. "There is one last thing."

Charles took in a breath. What else could there be?

"The Arabs have you on their wanted list, same as the Nazis."

Charles felt his cold sweat getting colder. "Gladia already suspected an Arab brother and his sister were tracking us."

"Then follow protocol: do not form a routine. We've done a good job confusing them with your fictitious name, Richard Anderson, but Nazis are crafty and their cohorts have learned well."

He clenched his fists. "Now it makes sense, how my parents raised me under lock and key—all their secrets and dirty lies …"

"Unfortunately, they were paired when Arabs eagerly desired Nazi methods of persecuting Jews. I'm sure that transfer of knowledge will haunt us the rest of our days."

"What type of duties would my parents be assigned to America?"

"Twofold probably. Nazi publicity officer, Joseph Goebbels, enlisted Von Deisenberg to carry out Hitler's propaganda, which was prolific in Los Angeles. Those pamphlets you spoke of were part of a massive distribution effort to convince Americans to hate Jews. Your mother was probably commissioned to spy on Zionist activities."

Their secret meetings finally revealed. "My goodness."

"Do you remember more?"

He lowered his forehead to his hand. "My mother sent and received telegrams every week. She'd burn them as soon as she read them."

Moshe nodded. "That would be another reason why they were sent to Los Angeles: Hollywood became a major target for Nazi and Arab spying, because Jews dominated the film industry."

"I've seen plenty of film reels. My father … or Von Deisenberg, used to make me watch. When I got older, he'd make me deliver boxes to stores where they sold pamphlets." He crouched over with a kink in his side. "I, *ahh* … he made me repeat things."

Moshe raised his palm. "You're not responsible for that."

Charles' eyes watered. "Thank you, I needed to hear that." As the missing links pieced together, dozens of opposing emotions swirled: and the temptation to resist forgiveness grew.

Moshe opened his door. "I've told you far too much. You need to rest before you depart."

CHAPTER 26

Freshly returned from New York and London, Charles walked into Moshe's office grinning. "Are you ready for incredible news?"

"I could use some right now."

"Chaim said confidence is high and the United Nations are going to recommend a partition for Palestine. We just need to convince a few more countries to get on board."

Moshe slapped his hands together. "Fabulous news. And great job on the delivery!" He shook Charles' hand, but only mustered a slight grin. The bags under his eyelids were puffier than usual.

"Are you okay, sir?" Charles also had a hard time receiving good reports since the hotel bombing. "Where's Gladia? She's never late to greet me."

"I don't know, Agatha told me she'd be here by two o'clock, and it's almost three. I figured she probably broke protocol and drove to the airport to meet you. A determined woman, that Gladia." He pressed a button. "Agatha, report to my office please."

Two taps struck the door and Agatha entered. "If it's about Gladia, she said she'd be late." She grinned. "Hi, Charles."

"Hello, Agatha." He squinted. "You sure? That doesn't sound like her."

"I agree, but that's what she said."

Agatha left. Moshe turned back to Charles. "This partition is exactly what we've been praying for."

He could tell Moshe was trying to help him take his mind off fussing over Gladia. "I know, my friend David said he's jealous. He works for Yaakov now."

"I'm glad to hear that. Your friend is working with one of our finest commanders. And how is Yaakov?"

"He sends his love. Said he can't imagine what it's like to command the Haganah under the heightened aggression." Charles tapped his fingers on his lap, eager to find his sweetheart—the beach sounded really good. He needed to distract himself. "I also heard Abba Eban address the UN: 'After two thousand years, it's time to accept Israel's nationhood, the only state in history which has the same territory, retains the same language and customs, maintains the same capitol, and upholds the same faith as it did prior to its demise two-thousand years ago.' His next statement caused murmuring: 'Some Arabs use the UN not as an instrument for solving conflicts, but an arena for waging them.'"

"I'm not surprised, you know how many peace talks we initiated that they cancelled?"

"I remember your frustration when we first met."

"Their pretenses are over—the gloves are off."

Charles glanced at his new English pocket watch. "She's never late. Do you mind if I go look for her?"

Moshe nodded and punched his call button. "Agatha, will you take Charles—"

Agatha walked into Moshe's office and jingled her keys. Charles stood, feeling a taste of what Gladia must have been feeling when he was off on missions.

When they entered her car, Agatha extended the butt of a pistol at him. He folded his arms. "What are you doing?"

"Gladia told me you continually violate procedure." She wiggled the gun. "Things are worse around here, and Gladia needs a partner who can protect her."

Charles had tremendous respect for Agatha; she loved Gladia. He accepted the handle and hid the pistol in his pocket. "There, you happy?" He stared back at her. "Where do you think she is?"

"I have an idea … hope I'm wrong." She took off, tires screeching.

"This isn't the road to Haifa. Where are you going?"

"You'll see." She accelerated.

"You're making me nervous, you never speed."

"She doesn't do well when you leave. We should have looked for her earlier."

Charles nodded. "She worries too much and thinks everybody she loves is going to die." He felt the same; the thought of her dying scared him.

Agatha turned. "I've never seen her like this with anyone."

"Really?"

"She's crazy in love with you, but I'm … it makes her anxious that she's not permitted to travel with you. When you're gone, she prepares a table with food, brings flowers from her garden, and keeps a pot of tea on, since no one knows when you return."

"I am the right man for her." He dabbed his eye with his sleeve, loving every word she just said. "No one can love her more than I do." He peered out at the road, hoping to see her car, then smacked the seat with his hand. "No more traveling."

He squinted at the rolling hills ahead. "Why are you going toward Atlit?"

"They said you were sharp."

"That's where Dov's being held."

"Yup." Agatha nodded.

His gut ached. "You don't think she's …"

223

Agatha's hands shook as she increased her speed again. When they rounded a turn, she gasped, "There she is!" She turned the vehicle to the shoulder. The car rocked and kicked up dirt as it slowed. They stopped behind Gladia's vehicle and ran through the lingering dust.

Gladia sat in the passenger seat, staring through a barbed-wire fence at the prison camp across a long field.

Agatha opened the driver's door. "Gladia, what are you doing?"

Charles opened the passenger door. "Gladia, are you all right?"

"Charles!" She removed a Sten gun from her lap and placed it on the seat. "I ..." She got out and embraced him.

"What are you doing?" he asked.

Gripping his belt loops, she lowered her forehead onto his shoulder. "I must have lost track. I think ... I thought you were coming later."

Looking down at the car seat made his heart patter. "Why are you here with the gun and ammo?" He'd never seen her irrational before. Everyone knew Dov had a death sentence coming, yet even the Haganah didn't dare try to penetrate Atlit.

"Hey!" Agatha animated her arms. "We need to get out of here. This is a highly patrolled area. Charles, you drive and follow me."

"*Ahh* ..." He'd only driven Yaakov's trucks inside the docks.

Agatha widened her eyes. "Let's go!"

He helped Gladia in and trotted to the driver's side. His hands shook on the wheel; Brits could come out of nowhere at any moment. He started the car, circled around and followed Agatha. He stared at the gun and noticed not one, but three metal boxes of rounds on the floorboard.

"There are grenades under the seat too," she said, matter-of-fact.

He shook his head. To have found her in a morgue that day would have shattered him—he'd have to watch her more carefully. If pulled over, they would both face prison for possessing the weapons. He should have tossed them, but munitions were in short supply.

"You should watch the road, you are wobbling the car." She appeared to be snapping out of her trance-like state. "The London doctor. I know what an oncologist is now. What did he say?"

Charles took a breath. "Let's go home, then I'll tell you."

She slid over and laid her head on his shoulder. "I am looking forward to our alone time." He tried to enjoy her snuggling, but had to regain control of the swerving her comment caused. When the turnoff to Haifa came, he honked and waved to Agatha. She waved back and headed toward Tel Aviv.

Upon arrival, Gladia had fallen asleep, so he picked her up and carried her into the house. After laying her on the couch, half-awake, he went out and stashed the munitions in her flimsy detached garage.

Back inside the house, he noted the table had everything Agatha described: except she didn't mention the gaily-wrapped box.

Gladia rose. "The doctor. What did he say?"

He dabbed her puffy, bloodshot eyes with his handkerchief and brushed her messy hair back. She hardly ever let her appearance show that much stress. "Are you going to tell me what that was back there?" The bow-tied box came into focus behind her, but that could wait.

She looked at him without her usual smile. "I have to know what the doctor said."

"Good news. It's not malignant." He smiled and hoped to see her do the same. "They don't want to operate, but it might come to that if the medicine doesn't shrink the tumor."

She sat on the couch and extended her arms. "Come to me."

This would be the moment he'd waited two years for, but something more pressing had to be settled: "Tell me what you were planning back there."

"I will tell you later. I promise."

They were finally alone and tonight was the time for their first serious kiss. He sat and leaned into her; her penetrating fingers began their magic on the back of his head, while he slipped his hands around her. As tingling chills ran down his neck, he neared his lips toward hers, but her eyes remained closed with little tears running. He wanted their first kiss to be special, so he eased back, praying his hormones would retreat too. It could be a lengthy process of convincing her to never try and free Dov.

"Relax. You are breathing too strong, she pulled him closer." She continued running the tips of her fingers in gentle circles over his scalp. "I will take the ache away if you can be calm."

His eyes closed, he smiled. "I love you so much. I could marry you right—"

The window smashed, spraying shards of glass as smoke hissed from a bouncing metal canister.

Coughing, Charles sprung to his feet and pulled Gladia's hand toward the back door.

"This way," she said, tugging to his left. The front and back doors crashed open.

They dashed to the toilet room, where she pulled up the floor rug and lifted a panel. "Dov's escape route. Jump in." They both made it under the house and replaced the cover before sounds of stomping boots overhead reached them.

They crawled on all fours under the house and through an opening that led them through thick bushes. Banging noises exploded, and as they sprinted across the street.

"It is Arab irregulars I think," Gladia whispered.

"Worse. Look at the man out front, keeping watch. He's holding a Luger pistol. He's German—Oh my gosh!" Shuddering chills wracked his body.

"*Shh* ... you are too loud. You recognize him from your trip?"

"That looks like my father!"

"Are you sure?"

"I can't tell, it's too dark." He stood halfway, hearing more bashing inside her house.

She pulled him as he tugged upward. "They will kill us. Come, we must contact Moshe."

Charles continued staring. "I knew he'd find me," he said through his teeth.

She gasped. "Look, in the backseat of their car."

"You were right. The brother and sister led them to us!" He looked at Gladia. "That girl deceived me."

"We are in war; Normal people can turn bad."

Three men emerged from the house as a blast rocked the dwelling.

"Oh, no!" Charles crouched and put his arm around Gladia while flames blew out her windows.

"No! My things." She buried her face in his chest.

They could feel heat from the blaze that enveloped her home. She gazed through the bushes, the glow of the flames lit her face. Crackling and snapping followed with embers and billowing smoke.

"Why would they burn your house down?"

She lifted her tear-streaked face. "They cannot find you, they are angry. The Arab riots are happening again. You should not have gone to the assignment. They want you dead for it."

"They want us all dead." He dried her cheeks with his shirttail. "It's okay, I'm here. No more traveling without you. Okay?" He led her away, down a wooded trail toward the city center.

She looked back to the glow in the sky. "If that is him, how can your father know you are here?"

"That evil man is not my father." Moshe's admonition of secrecy came to him.

She shook her head. "I am not understanding—"

"Just remember: He's relentless." They locked arms. "I'll explain another time."

Following the dark path to town, the flames brought back memories of his books burning. Von Deisenberg had wised up to Charles gaining knowledge to defend himself from mind games. That was the final clash that drove Charles to begin plotting a way out of Los Angeles.

When they made it to town, she led him to the back entrance of Café Ramiel to call. Agatha got on the line and told them to meet her at the old warehouse. A short walk through some dark alleys brought them there. Agatha pulled up. "What happened?" She asked. "You're dirty and look terrified."

They hurried into the car. "Please go, now!" Charles said.

Agatha's acceleration thrust them back in their seats.

Gladia turned to her. "Arabs and a German, they burn my house!" Her voice trembled. "We lost everything." Charles glanced down at his sack, happy he'd remembered it.

"That's horrible." Agatha looked at Gladia. "I doubt it was a German. They're not popular around the British, and many are being investigated for war crimes." She sped up. "Let's speak with Moshe. He'll know what to do."

CHAPTER 27

November 29, 1947

When they walked into headquarters, the nurse, Josephina, motioned to follow. "We were hoping you would witness this."

"Witness what?" Charles asked.

"Come quickly to the operations room, we're boosting the signal. The United Nations is about to announce the results of the partition vote."

The decision could be the biggest break in Jewish history. Holding her hand, Charles had a new resilience to the attack against Gladia's house; She was his confirmed soul mate now. They followed Josephina downstairs, where a dozen or so people sat on wooden buckets and potato sacks. Their statue-like faces stared at the center of attention: a black radio box filled with glowing tubes, perched on a crate of ammo. Other than static and the broken voice stemming from the weak frequency, silence prevailed.

A voice emitted from the radio and began to mutter over the crackling. Josephina raised her finger. "Here it comes, everybody; The most important news in Jewish history!"

> In a vote of 33 to 13, it has been decided that the majority members of the United Nations have passed UN Resolution 181 to favor the partition of the British Mandate of Palestine into two provisional states: one Jewish and one Arab.

The room erupted with shouts of, *"L'chaim—Tov me'od!"* Josephina and Agatha hurried to a cabinet and broke out wine, bread, and bowls of hummus.

The noise and celebration clouded the following chatter over the radio, so Charles pressed his ear against the speaker. He remembered the social climate in New York, and knew there had to be more to this monumental announcement. Malicious foes had made serious threats against anyone favoring this decision.

> Zionists have agreed to the partition, but Arab leaders from neighboring regions unanimously rejected it. Delegates are trying to reason with them, so peace can exist once and for all, but the Arabs' shocking statement was bold and deliberate: "No Jew shall have Palestine, and if they claim it, we shall massacre them and drive their dead bodies into the Mediterranean Sea!"

Charles put his hand to his chest and took a few breaths—that was a direct threat against him, Gladia and all his friends. He'd already calculated the odds of surviving all the near-misses they'd incurred, and knew the amplified aggression could soon catch up to them. The tenacity of Arab leaders publicly proclaiming death to all Jews made him reach for Gladia's hand and hurry her upstairs, with the intent of finally asking her to flee Palestine. His mind scrambled for the quickest route to London.

She stopped him at the top of the stairs, her hands shaking. "This land is ours! We must get Dov out now. He risked his life so we could see this day."

Charles led her to the main entry and grabbed her hands. "All of us would love to do that, but it would be a suicide mission. Atlit is a fortified—"

"He saved me!" She gripped his lapel, her blue eyes wild. "Now I must save him!"

Charles lowered his head, hating to see her anguish. His plan to flee would be impossible; when she made up her mind, no one could change it. And now he had to figure a way to impede her plan. Exasperated, he sent a request to God: *Lord, if you're there, stop her because I don't know how!*

Agatha came out of Moshe's office. "I'm sorry, you'll have to spend a few weeks here. Moshe is handling a dozen crises, and he's expecting a special American guest soon. Everything's too chaotic to relocate you." She put her hand to her cheek. "Unfortunately, reports of attacks have clogged our radio since the partition announcement. Moshe expects Arab aggression to be worse than those disastrous Arab revolts that took ..." She looked at Gladia.

Gladia sniffled and clenched his hand.

"I'm sorry honey, I shouldn't have mentioned that. This whole thing has got me bundled in knots."

"Me too," Charles said, exercising his fingers to loosen her grip a little. "How much more bad news can we take before *someone* snaps?" Charles darted his eyes toward Gladia so Agatha would help intervene.

Agatha sighed at Gladia. "I'm sorry, the universities have cancelled all classes. And of course the library is closed, so you're out of a job too. And ... we only have one room available."

Gladia shook her head. "That is not a problem. I will return to school when this is over, and I will sleep on the floor. Charles needs the bed for his headaches."

Charles would have to have a word with Agatha later. He looked at his precious girl and knew she was acting too calm. "No, Gladia. You're taking the bed."

"Ah, well ..." Agatha took a breath. "We had to remove it to make room for new immigrants. We can't build settlements fast enough."

"I can call friends in Jerusalem," Gladia said.

Agatha shook her head. "You know those roads are strictly off limits, except for military convoys. You and Charles will be here for a while."

≈≈≈

December 1947

Windows rattled from thunderous bombs, followed by rippling bullets. Charles bolted up from his floor mat and accidentally kicked Gladia. It reminded him why they weren't sleeping much. They got up and followed the scent of something delicious downstairs.

Charles yawned when he entered the kitchen; there were bowls dusted in flour, empty muffin tins and piles of squeezed orange skins. "Wow, Agatha. The muffins smell amazing."

"Thank you. Dig in, goodies like these won't last." After she poured orange juice, the fluid rippled from a nearby rumble. "Moshe said the Brits are doing very little about the attacks here in Tel Aviv. But there is some good news." Her tone brightened. "Eleven minutes after the UN granted our land, President Truman declared America's recognition of Israel."

Great news, but nobody was in a celebrating mood and Agatha's gleam dimmed. Gladia approached her. "There is something else, Auntie?"

Agatha buried her face in her hands. "Oh, look at me going on like a child." She raised her reddened face and wiped her eyes with her apron. "You two are the ones who are homeless."

Charles poured her juice, but a closer detonation jiggled the whole kitchen, causing him to spill it. He moved from under the light fixture to avoid dust trickling onto his hair. "We're not safe here."

Agatha wouldn't receive the half-empty glass. "There is no safer place, but that's not why I'm …" She embraced Gladia.

Charles watched them hugging, but couldn't read Agatha's grief. He shifted his thoughts to building a new home for his future bride, but knew it was impossible until the attacks lessened. He picked up Gladia's drink and stretched his arm toward her.

She shook her head. "We must break him out!"

"Gladia, no!" Agatha stilled her arms. "You know Dov would be furious if he saw you anywhere near that prison."

"It is making me crazy." She put her hands on Agatha's cheeks. "You love him too!"

"I'm not going to love anyone ever again," Agatha sobbed.

Charles rubbed Gladia's back. "I'm sorry. I'm out of ideas for saving him." Now it was up to God to save Gladia from doing something irrational.

Agatha wiped her eyes. "It feels like there's a knife in my heart. We've lost too many good people and I don't know how much more I can take!"

Charles frowned. "Even if we achieve victory, how do we stop Arabs from inciting more violence? I shuddered when you told me about schoolbooks that teach their children to hate Jews. I know what that can do to a child."

Moshe walked in, his wrinkles deep and eyes dim. "New orders, everyone. Even with the UN, the Americans, and Russia condemning the Arabs' rejection of Resolution 181, *all travel* is restricted to armored vehicles only." He put his hand on Gladia's shoulder. "I heard your cries for Dov. We already had a covert operation planned to attack Atlit, but Dov and other key personnel were moved when riots erupted in that sector last night. And we don't know their new location."

Gladia buried her face in Charles' chest and sobbed. Charles noticed Moshe's fingers squeezing and releasing again; he was bluffing about Dov. Charles loved him for the brilliant deception he displayed to save Gladia from getting herself killed. A sobering chill hit him because his prayer for Gladia to be saved had just been answered. Rabbi Jesse wasn't kidding when he said how God answered prayers in mysterious ways.

January 1948

Being sequestered at headquarters had robbed any chances of alone time. They soon grew weary from relentless hours of guard duty and distress calls over the radio. Also, mortars and rapid gunfire rendered no need for an alarm clock.

Each day began in the noisy communications room, where Charles learned to fine-tune radio signals and repair burnt-out tubes and wiring. One morning he peered through the vent fins from behind the metal rack that held the overheated radio transceiver—Gladia's face had turned rosy from rushing to his new matrix board, which logged incoming reports. "Are you okay, Gladia?"

She poked her head behind the rack. "I am hot, sweaty and tired." When incoming messages came, she'd label: "mortar fire relief" in red chalk—"send a platoon" in orange—"medical supplies" in yellow, and lesser problems in green. Charles had received a commendation for his invention to organize priorities more efficiently.

Moshe walked in with a tray of lemonade and set it on the dark walnut table where the microphones were. "You need a break?"

"Oh, bless you, sir." She picked up a glass and guzzled while a drop rolled down her neck. "This is Commander Dayan. We need two hundred Palmach in Jezreel, immediately." The blaring radio voice had rapid gunfire echoing behind it.

He'd never met the Palmach, the highest elite troops in the Haganah.

Moshe looked about. "Where is Amri? You can't do this alone!"

Gladia set her glass on the tray. "He got heat stroke, he is laying down."

"I'll get this one, Gladia." Moshe clicked the button on the radio. "Roger that, Commander." He looked at the large Collins transmitter. "What's the status for that unit, Charles? This one doesn't have the range to reach the Palmach."

Charles wiped sweat from his forehead. "A few minutes, sir. Almost have these tubes replaced." He peeked out at Moshe. "This machine is like a furnace."

"You two arrived just in time." Moshe stared at the wall. "You both did an amazing job with these color-coded priorities."

Gladia beamed. "Charles did it, and showed me how to write under them."

Charles came out from behind the transmitter. "All done, sir. I replaced the switch too...." He took a few steps and bumped the tray of drinks.

Moshe steadied him. "Easy, Charles. Here, sit down." He handed him a glass of lemonade. "Don't drink too fast."

Seeing Moshe's expressive grin, Charles took delight at accomplishing something that would save thousands of lives. He held the glass to his cheek. "I'm fine. It's just the heat." He stooped and plugged the unit in, then flipped a lever. It hummed as it lit up.

Moshe shook his head. "You never cease to amaze me. Here, take this." He extended another glass of lemonade and one to Gladia.

Charles licked his lips. "Thank you, sir." He chuckled. "It feels funny being served by you."

Moshe half smiled. "You remember what I said about leadership?" He raised his brows, waiting.

"Yes. 'Leaders lead by example.'" He swallowed a few more gulps. "Thank you for the drinks." He walked to Gladia and held her sweaty hand. "We're a team again, like we used to be."

"This is Commander Shaltiel," the radio blasted with thunderous booms in the background. "Taking heavy fire in Sector Four-C. Need twenty men on the western hill to flank the enemy in the Jordan Rift Valley. We need ammo badly."

Gladia's hand shook as she wrote the commander's needs in red. Charles slapped the intercom, his hand trembling too, from reports coming in like that hourly. "Barracks, report please." A moment passed, and he looked back. "We're out of fighters again." His heart sank when he thought about the hundred ships seized at sea—those arrivals would have given them thousands of new fighters to call on. The reality of being outnumbered and outgunned again brought discouraging expressions—though no one spoke. The pounding blasts outside were more frequent, getting closer, and the enemy-repelling Davika bombs were depleted. They had nothing left to intimidate the advancing Arabs when they neared headquarters. Charles resisted picturing their dead bodies being dumped into the Mediterranean.

Moshe took the microphone. "This is Commander Sneh. Relief is coming!" He released the latch. "I'm going in." He slapped the intercom button. "Agatha, I need the truck keys and Josephina to help with the emergency ammo crates."

Charles stood. "Commander, you're not supposed to—"

"I'll be darned if I'm going to let this turn into a Middle East Holocaust. This land is ours legally now, and we're claiming it!"

Just weeks after Hitler's death, Charles remembered Father bragging about another Holocaust. "Let me go, sir. You're too valuable."

"No, Charles! You promise...." Gladia's adamant face came close to his.

Moshe reached in a drawer and pulled out a Bible. "Raise your right hand."

Charles froze. He couldn't be serious about swearing him in to fill the commander's position.

Moshe wiggled the Bible. "Lives are at stake here."

Charles raised his right hand and placed his left on the book. Gladia gaped. Moshe took a deep breath. "Repeat after me."

Charles expanded his chest. Other than learning to shoot on a range, he had no combat experience. If the enemy reached headquarters, it would be their demise; even the guards outside were called into battle.

"I Charles Devonshire …" Moshe spoke with a formal tone.

Charles repeated, and as Agatha entered with keys in hand, Moshe was prompting him, "will assume full responsibility of this post under the title of Commander Devonshire." Hearing his temporary rank pronounced made him think about peers at school who wouldn't be laughing now.

Moshe's stare pierced Charles. "Hurry, Commander, I need to leave."

"*Ahh* … will assume full responsibility of this post …" When he finished, Gladia wiped her eyes and smiled for the first time in months.

Moshe snatched the keys from Agatha's hand. "Give Charles the emergency instructions." He hurried to the door and turned. "Pray I find some men."

Tension made Charles sit and pray for wisdom as he thought about the entire military resting on his decisions. One wrong command could kill hundreds of precious men and women. He pulled in a breath, wiped his sweaty face, and returned to the radio.

Agatha unlocked a drawer, removed a sealed packet and held it out to Charles with her lower lip trembling. "Here you are … Commander." She averted her gaze toward Moshe's exit.

Charles stared at the packet, certain Agatha didn't want someone half her age as her superior.

She jiggled it. "You have to read this—"

"This is Commander Shaltiel. Ten more wounded and no ammo. Haven't fired a shot for twenty minutes." Charles knew morale was under the ultimate test. However, reports came daily where the enemy could have conquered entire platoons, but they wouldn't advance for some unknown reason. Some of the commanders speculated how the enemy must have assumed their silence to be a trap. Each time, Charles could hear Rabbi Jesse: *God is watching over them.*

He pushed the call button. "Commander Sneh is coming, but you have permission to retreat at will."

"We should be dead by now! The Arab Legion has us cornered—there is no place to retreat. I see them in the distance, but something restrains them."

Charles stood and pondered that statement. Either the Jews were the luckiest people on earth, or Rabbi Jesse was ... *Yet in spite of their sins, if they repent, I will remember My covenant with their ancestors so as not to destroy them completely....*

His knees gave out. Sitting on the floor stunned, a compelling voice inside said he wasn't in command in the capacity he thought he was.

Gladia ran to him. "What is wrong? You look like you see a ghost." He flinched, snatched a note from her hand and jumped to the mic. "Stand by, Commander." He gazed over several squares of his matrix. "Gladia, pull ten of Commander Amir's men from Sector Two-D, send them to Sector five-B, and instruct them to flank the Valley of Megiddo—that should draw the enemy away from sector four." He looked up. "Huh. That place sounds familiar."

Agatha placed the packet on the radio table. "I'll tell you about Megiddo later. How can I help?"

He stood. "Take the radio while I study the matrix." He circled the room and looked at all the wires running along the walls, picking off the notes posted above them. "Gladia, let's reorganize these notes in alphabetical order and find out where the last of our supplies are."

"Mayday, Mayday!" The radio blasted. "This is Captain Yisrael. An Arab blew up a section of the Jewish Agency building! Our covert operative said the perpetrator admitted to the Brits about parking an American Embassy vehicle loaded with TNT—and the Brits congratulated him! The man's name is Daud. I will call in the bloke's whereabouts when I receive word of his destination."

Agatha dabbed her flushed face with a cloth and sat at the radio table. "That's horrible! Moshe will want to know about this. This very morning, he sent a bulletin out about the Arab League sending truckloads of soldiers from Jordan, Syria and Iraq. Thank goodness they don't know the location of this building."

CHAPTER 28

March 1948

After two back-to-back shifts in the stuffy basement, Charles and Gladia needed to change clothes.

When four elderly people entered, Agatha stood. "Ah, the retirees I called are here. Just in time for sup—" She wobbled, and slapped her hand on the table.

Gladia steadied her and wiped her cheeks with a rag. "You are not cooking tonight. You need the couch."

After acclimating the relief crew, Charles and Gladia helped Agatha up the steps. Leaving the insulated basement into the cooler air upstairs revealed louder mortar blasts. Charles inhaled through his nose. "Mmm. Is that spaghetti and meatballs I smell?" He hoped his question would distract Gladia and lighten her tense face.

Agatha fanned her cheeks with her hand. "Bless her. Josephina is still here, cooking." She straightened. "I'm okay, I just need some water." She patted Charles' arm. "Your nose is playing tricks on you; we haven't had meat for months now."

Gladia led Agatha toward the sofa and fanned her face. She glanced at Charles and motioned toward the toilet room. "I will get her water. You can clean up if you wish, commander." She fixed her gaze on him. "Your face is bright red. Does your head hurt?"

He almost laughed at her commander comment, but her adoring look made him romanticize their overdue beach date instead. "It hurts a little, but I'm all right." He walked the hallway past empty offices, picturing the staff filling battle positions, and hoped none of the secretaries or interns were in combat. When he entered the toilet room, the hanging platoon photos quickly reminded him of leading a dwindling twenty-five-thousand-member defense force.

He returned and watched Gladia nurture her auntie with pats from a damp cloth. He took her hand and led her to the front window to see the Mediterranean view.

"Wow," She locked fingers with him. "Look at the sun on the water. That is where we should be, walking the sand."

He marveled at her face as reflections from the waves shimmered in her eyes and illuminated her lips. "We have a saying back home."

"I love it. Tell me."

He enjoyed her eagerness to hear his quotes. "So close, yet so far away."

She squeezed his hand. "That is true."

He squeezed back. "As soon as it's safe, we'll walk that sand."

≈≈≈

Charles gasped a quick breath, thinking the enemy had captured him, until he saw Gladia stooped over, nudging him awake. Behind her, the window illuminated with a lavender glow. His big yawn attested to his lack of sleep because either Gladia's feet kicked him from sleeping head-to-toe, or the artillery whistling and exploding would jar them awake.

"I can't stay in this house one more minute, I will be crazy," she whispered. "It is finally quiet out there. Everyone is asleep, except the new guard. Since it is getting light, let us go to the beach sunrise and walk the sand."

He rubbed his eyes. "I don't know, Moshe said—"

"There are many Jews in this town. I feel safe for a little walk. It is right in front of us, and beautiful."

"The guard outside has strict orders."

She extended her hand. "She is a student like us. You are in command and can order us to go."

He smiled knowing she'd be relentless until he gave in. And this could be their first opportunity to embrace like dating couples do. It also might snap her out of depression, so he accepted her hand and stood.

Opening the door, the fresh breeze tingled his skin. She was right. The brisk air was just what they needed to ease the mounting stress of hearing brave commanders pleading for supplies and soldiers.

He looked down the foggy streets. "I don't know, it's *too* quiet. And the guard isn't at her post."

"I saw her go to the toilet room." She bumped shoulders with him. "I want to hold hands and walk the sand."

"I like the sound of that." If they could just find a home in a less violent area and have some alone time, maybe she could be happy again.

"Come. We will return before they wake." She pulled his hand.

While avoiding mortar holes, they strolled past houses with huge gashes on their walls, like Swiss cheese—a great indication for a rational person to turn back. But a few more minutes strolling hand-in-hand revealed the Mediterranean's glistening span. They stopped in awe as he took a cool breath in, trying to forget the destruction he'd just seen. "Wow!" they said in unison.

Gladia swung their arms like a swing and smiled at the predawn light. "You see? Is this not wonderful?"

"You're wonderful! I can be anywhere with you and feel like this. And, I have to admit this place makes you look radiant."

"What ever that word is, it sounds nice. You always say good things to me." Pulling his hand, she grinned. "I'm ... still not used to that."

Their chemistry caused him to stumble. Her lips looked cold and he could warm them, but the time wasn't right yet.

She broke hand contact and ran her fingers past the goose bumps on his neck. "You are cold?"

"A little, but the wind feels refreshing."

She wrapped her arm around him as they neared the sand, their hips rubbing. Seagulls seemed to invite them toward the water with their squawks; the roar of the crashing waves beckoned too: Come and marvel at God's creation! He tightened his arm around her to increase body friction. Just kissing and nothing more, he told himself. Well, a tight face-to-face hug wouldn't hurt either.

She looked at him while they strolled. "I like it when you see me. Others? Now I don't care how they look at me."

His ultimate mission accomplished. He'd made her feel beautiful for the first time since her injury. Her comment also sounded like an invitation; Yet everything to be just right.

When their shoes pressed in the sand, she stopped and took hers off. She pointed. "Take them off."

"My shoes?"

"No, the pants." She giggled.

The risky outing was worth hearing her laugh. He removed his shoes while the wind tousled their hair in all directions.

The cold sand tickled his toes while he tied their laces together. He flung their shoes over his shoulder, then ran ahead, sank to his knees, and started digging.

"What are you doing?" her voice echoed off the distant rocks. "That is a broken canoe. Why do you dig under it?"

He tossed their shoes inside. "Always provide an escape route. I learned that from Dov's passage in your house." He turned to her. "Isn't that amazing? No matter where he is, he still influences us." He realized he shouldn't have mentioned her brother. He studied her face to see if he just killed the romance.

"He does change people." She shrugged her shoulders. "You and Dov could have become brothers. I love that about you." That was the first time she'd mentioned his name without moist eyes or a crack in her voice.

He stood, slapped the sand from his hands, then interlaced fingers with her.

He determined to store up every endearing term she spoke, and as he peered down the coastline, he eyed the perfect spot. "Why don't we walk that way?"

She swayed their arms again as they strolled in front of the orange sun rising above the water. "I know this will sound crazy, but I wish I can meet your parents someday. Then, I will know you even better."

"I don't think—"

"I know it does not seem possible. So I pray that they change, and somehow you could reconcilly them."

"You mean reconcile?"

She nodded. "Yes. Re-con-cile."

"That would take a miracle."

"Yes, but scripture says all things are possible with God."

"I've certainly seen plenty of miracles. But, my parents changing?" He was aching to tell her what Moshe revealed about them.

She gently pulled his arm. "God can change anyone." When she turned, the gusty breeze blew her hair into her face. "It is nice you believe miracles now. When we met you doubted." They continued along the pounding waves with the rocky landscape just ahead. He hurried their pace because the daylight reminded him to relieve the retirees.

"This is the most I've ever heard you speak about God," he said.

"I am believing more again since I know you."

"Since you've known me? But I'm not very religious." He still grappled with accepting a God who would allow tragedies—namely, his upbringing and especially Jonathan's death. If the Jews really were God's *chosen* people to deliver His message to the world, why would He tease them about obtaining the land, knowing there was no hope of conquering so many enemies? He wanted her opinion, but the questions could spoil the moment.

"When you first come, you don't believe anything about God," she said. "But now you see miracles and scripture promises come true, and you believe someone powerful is helping us. And because of you, I see it is important to return to faith. I loved God with my parents. But when they got killed, I told Him to forget it. Now you come here and I change."

That was the greatest compliment he'd ever heard. "Wow, I did that?"

"Yes."

He lingered to watch the sun separate from the waterline. Its rays beamed behind her, causing a glow around the edges of her shape. Charles was ready to marry her right there.

She smiled and wiggled her fingers. "Come." This time she hummed a familiar tune as they resumed walking.

"I've never heard you hum. What is that song?"

She opened her mouth. "La, la … la …" She giggled. "You must know it. It is from an American movie with Bing Crosby."

He didn't want to sadden her by admitting he'd only seen three movies in his life, when David would help sneak him out of his "jail cell." "I recognize it, but I must admit, you have me stumped."

She laughed. "Finally, I know something you do not."

"Come on. What is it?"

She beamed a wide grin. "Not now. I am going to enjoy this."

He put his hands to his hips, mimicking one of her poses. "You'd better tell me or—"

"Or what?" She beamed a huge smile.

He lifted his lips and grinned with his teeth closed. "I'm going to grab you and kiss you all over!"

Her face lit like the rising sun behind her. "You will have to catch me first!" She scampered like a gazelle in the opposite direction.

He darted after her with two year's worth of love and passion, his heart pounding like a hammer slamming an anvil. Within a few hundred meters he closed in and grabbed her hips, and they tumbled to the sand laughing.

"Okay, I will tell you," she said, out of breath.

"Too late." He scooted against her and slipped his arm around her waist. "I'm so glad I caught you," he said, breathy. "You are stunningly beautiful and you drive me craz—"

"No!" She jolted up, knocking him back.

A knot kinked his chest. "No?"

Her face looked like she'd seen a murder behind him. "Look!"

Before he could swivel his upper body, multiple gunshots echoed. He turned back and saw men with robes running in their direction, their rifles recoiling with each shot. He jumped up, yanked her hand and rushed toward the rocks. "You run and hide under the canoe," he said. "I'll distract them."

"No, they will kill you," she yelled. "We go together."

"Gladia, go and hide!" He remembered her parents told her that too.

"I will not. We die together," She said kicking up sand.

He loved and hated her stubbornness. "All right, this way."

They ran in zigzag formation, according to their field training; Gunshots echoed off cliff rocks as bullets kicked up sand around them. A glance back revealed three men fanning out.

He led her behind the rocks away from the canoe.

"Why go this way?"

"Watch." He'd better be right or they would forfeit their lives. He refused to think about her fate if caught, so fighting to the death would be the only option.

Charles had already mapped a route from each landmark they walked. He led her in an arch formation around tall rocks, then he backtracked on top of their footprints. They doubled back, hit the sand chest-first and wiggled under the boat. Once inside, he filled the hole he'd made earlier.

"They will find us. This hiding is too easy." Even her whisper quaked under the reverberant wood.

"The obvious is what I'm counting on. I've studied how they think."

She put her index finger to her rounded lips. Their Arabic chatter drew closer, peaked, and thankfully trailed off.

After a long period of silence, they put their shoes on and started digging.

≈≈≈

When they walked into headquarters, faces hot, Charles heard voices.

"There you are." Agatha peeked out from the hall and motioned to follow, but then abruptly stopped. "Your faces are red." She shook her head. "Sand? What were you doing at the beach?"

"Long story," Charles said.

Agatha narrowed her eyes. "You're not supposed to be outside, you could be killed."

Gladia crossed her arms. "He's the commander, so he can order us for a walk."

"Not anymore. Moshe's back." Hands to her hips, "You followed procedure coming back?"

Charles took a breath and tried to relax. "Yes. We took the long way through the corridor, but there were no guards."

Agatha helped brush off their remaining sand and led them toward the meeting room at the end of the hall. "Our special guest is here and he's been asking for you." They entered, and Agatha approached a uniformed officer and a man in a suit. "Commander Yadin, it's such a pleasure to see you again. Moshe is in his office."

"Agatha. I'm delighted to see you as well. This is our distinguished guest Colonel Mickey Marcus, otherwise known as Michael Stone when he's in public. He's here to advise us on American techniques of battle strategies."

Colonel Marcus stepped up and extended a large hand. "Pleased to meet you, Agatha."

Agatha blushed. "The pleasure is mine, sir."

He shifted his tall muscular body. "Are these the fine youngsters I keep hearing about?"

"Yes, this is Gladia Limbauski, and Charles Devonshire."

Colonel Marcus extended his hand to Gladia and didn't even flinch at her scar. "A young lady freedom fighter. I'm impressed. We didn't see women near combat where I served."

Gladia smiled and shook his hand. "Thank you, sir."

He shifted his attention. "Charles, I'm delighted to hear about you too. I thought I was the only American helping to create this great nation, until they informed me about you and a few others. I envy your reputation among the Jews. It's not easy to integrate with these soldiers, even if with the title of colonel."

"Thank you, sir. I'm not sure who is receiving more … me, or them." Hearing Colonel Marcus express confidence in building the new nation surprised him. If the colonel knew something Charles didn't, he'd like to hear about it.

"Well Colonel," Commander Yadin said, "let's go visit Commander Sneh and then proceed downstairs to our operations room, where I will show you how we divided the land into eight sectors."

"Shoes!" The colonel lifted his foot. "What about the shoes?"

"What?" Commander Yadin squinted.

"I don't want to see one more operation until I know you've ordered new shoes for all your men!"

Yadin pivoted. "Agatha, could you be so kind as to check the files to see if we received funding for *new shoes*?" He shifted back. "I'll personally see to it." After exchanging goodbyes, they left the room.

"Too bad he's married … what a man!" Agatha said. "Our staff doesn't know what to make of him. He says things like, 'We must run this operation like an offensive war, not a defense agency.'" She blushed. "So bold and sure of himself." Agatha looked at Charles. "And he mentioned something similar to what you said."

Charles raised his brows. "Really?"

"The colonel's prime motivation is to help establish the first democratic government in the Middle East. One that recognizes freedom of speech, equality between men and women, free enterprise and freedom of religion."

Charles smiled at Agatha. Since she acted like Gladia's adopted mother, he desired her approval to marry Gladia. "Why did he comment about shoes?"

"He recently visited the Palmach special forces, in a hidden cave near Galilee. He was appalled at how undernourished and underdressed they were. All the men admired him when he promised new shoes and told them: 'I've never seen more high-spirited soldiers in my life. It's men like you that win wars, even if you are ill-equipped.'" Agatha sighed and turned toward the hallway. "I'll be back later."

Gladia leaned on Charles' shoulder. "I feel like I am in a cage again."

Heart twisting, he lowered his head to meet hers. "With the fighting so heavy, they probably can't relocate us for awhile." He took her hand and led her into the kitchen to search for two muffins. "I saw Moshe's notes. The Arabs have at least a sixty-to-one advantage over us. Things aren't looking good." He finally upheld his commitment to prepare her for a huge military upset.

She put her hand on her hip. "Many times, our people have battled enemies when it does not look good. If you read about Gideon, then you will not have that look on your face."

"Who's Gideon?" No muffins, so he brought out unleavened bread and set it on the kitchen table.

"You do not remember? I tell you about him in the scripture. It was on my paper. Judges Seven, verse nine?"

Charles remembered, but he'd wanted a logical answer why God would allow innocent people to be at such a disadvantage, like he was with his father. He wanted more proof to understand God's will in order to agree with it. He nodded for her to continue.

"Gideon fought thousands of Midianites with only three hundred men. God confused the enemy and Gideon win the battle."

Although that didn't seem feasible, commanders routinely called for munitions while the enemy halted for no reason. And he had to admit, according to Moshe's reports, the Jews should have been wiped out months ago. "I hope I'm wrong."

"If God does not help, then we die trying."

It still unnerved him to hear her talk about death as a way of life in Palestine. "Okay, I'll admit, making it this far has been miraculous."

CHAPTER 29

Charles and Gladia continued to operate the radio in double shifts due to shortages of personnel. Moshe walked in the communications room. "Moshe! What a delight to see you," Charles said. "It was difficult to walk in your shoes, but I did my best."

Moshe placed his hands on their shoulders. "The Haganah owes you both a debt of gratitude. Take a break, I have a relief team coming." He turned to Charles. "You are officially relieved as commander."

Charles sighed. "Thank goodness for that."

"Something is wrong," Gladia said. "Your mission. How was it?"

Moshe looked down and took a breath. "Charles, you're going to be proud, but sad about this. On my way back from resupplying Commander Shaltiel's platoon, I approached a small regiment guarding the rear of Lydda airport. I can't tell you the details, but I will tell you the last words of their leader … Aaron Bartimus."

Charles widened his eyes. "You met Rabbi Aaron?"

Moshe nodded, and Charles recalled the frail elderly prisoner of Cyprus. He never thought Aaron would collect on God's assurance to die in the Promised Land. Escaping that rat-hole would have taken months to dig out of.

"When I approached the men, Aaron commanded his sergeant, Vidal Sassoon, to stand down after I identified myself. It broke my heart to watch a sick old man standing so proud to defend his post while enduring a bullet

251

wound." Moshe cleared his throat. "When I ordered Aaron to lie down, I peeled off layers of hair covers used to dress his wound. I asked the sergeant where they got the unusual wound dressings, and he explained they were from his cosmetic school in England. I was impressed how a young man would leave his schooling to serve in the Palmach.

"Aaron remembered I had sent you for the mission that led to his escape. He was hacking, but managed to crack a little grin, and asked me to deliver a message to you."

Charles braced himself.

"'Please tell Charles, you helped fulfill God's declaration to let me die in the Promised Land. *Now* I am complete! Repent and know God, so He can richly bless you too.'" Moshe looked at Charles with tapered brows. "He died whispering those words."

"Excuse me." Charles quivered on his way to the washroom, gratified how Aaron's wish had been granted. He also marveled how Rabbi Jesse said God would reveal Himself to Charles in unexpected ways. Chills ran down his spine: He could no longer deny God not only existed, but really did keep His word to faithful servants like Aaron, who said he'd repented.

Leaving the toilet room, his chest tightened when he contemplated how he'd never confessed his sins to God; he stopped in the middle of the hallway to catch his breath. *Do not fear the enemy. The Lord God, who goes before His people, He shall fight for them. Repent and turn to Me, for I will be with you too.*

Charles looked behind him, then hurried down the hallway, rubbing at the goose bumps on his arms. When he returned, Moshe and Gladia were waiting. She looked at him. "Your face, it is white. Are you okay?"

He nodded slowly.

Moshe glanced at his watch, then finessed the knob of the radio to fine-tune the reception for the daily broadcast: "This will be a war of extermination and a momentous massacre," the announcer blurted. "The bold statement came from Azzam Pasha, secretary-general of the Arab League—"

Moshe flipped the radio switch off. "I don't know why I bother. They can't report anything positive: Like all the peace meetings we initiated—those aren't newsworthy. Do you have any idea how many Jewish leaders have gone on record with that same desire to exterminate Arabs?"

"Not many, right?" Charles asked.

"No Jewish leaders are on record to reciprocate genocide. We're frustrated with Arab leadership, but our general policy remains: We desire peace. Until now, we have been a defense agency, but our American friend, Colonel Marcus, has convinced us to change our strategy because our peace talks have obviously failed. Unlike local Arabs, their leaders are not interested in negotiating. The colonel predicts that behavior until the end of time."

Gladia looked at Charles. "That is why we fight. This is our home; Jews and peaceful Arabs should not have to leave."

Charles nodded. "Isn't there anything else that can be presented?"

Moshe stood. "Here's the root of our problem: Most Arabs and Jews want peace. It's the *radicals* on each side who incite violence, and who pressure locals to fight or die." He pulled a paper from his satchel. "The grand mufti, Al Husseini, broadcasted this message throughout Europe with Nazi funding: 'Arabs, arise and fight for your sacred rights. Kill Jews wherever you find them. This pleases God, history, and religion.'"

Gladia raised her index finger. "I am sorry to interrupt. Have you found us a place to live?"

"I'm sorry, Gladia. You've lived here longer than planned, but I need more time to find safe living quarters."

Her gaze plummeted. "We lose everything in the fire. I know you have bigger problems, but we have nothing."

Charles' heart sank. He wanted to sneak into Haifa, withdraw his money and find his own place without burdening the commander. But he'd escaped near death enough times to know the odds of returning alive weren't in his favor.

"Don't you worry. Big problems or not," Moshe sighed. "I won't allow you to be homeless for long."

The front door shut. Agatha came in with a wide grin. "He's here, sir."

"Splendid!" Moshe raised his arms. "Charles, I have a great surprise. It's the least I could do. Then I have urgent business." He turned toward the front entry. "Come in."

"Hey, buddy ... surprise!"

Charles lowered his jaw. "David? Oh my goodness! How did—?"

David stomped across the room and bear-hugged him. "When your home was attacked, Moshe sent a bulletin to find a personal security agent for you and ..." He released Charles and opened his arms. "Gladia! You're twice as beautiful as Charles described."

Laughing, she wrapped her arms around his barrel chest. "I'm glad to see you, David. This is wonderful you coming."

"I wouldn't miss this for anything." David released her and straightened. "When someone says my buddy's in trouble, I come runnin'."

Watching David talking with Gladia was exhilarating; Charles always wanted them to meet. But then, tension hit when he thought about the ramifications of his best friend in Palestine. Daring individuals like David and Dov often ended up dead, or arrested by the Brits. "How did Moshe find you?"

"He sent word to Yaakov for reinforcements. After you introduced us, I escorted his guests in New York. The next thing you know, presto, I'm on a plane to Palestine. I'm your security shadow until further notice."

"Maybe you can tell me about home." Gladia looked at Charles. "He does not talk much about it."

David grinned. "I can't blame him. But I'll tell you lots of things you probably don't know." He turned back to Charles. "Yaakov sends his love, and wanted you to know, over one hundred sailings have carried one-hundred-twenty-thousand Jewish immigrants."

"That's amazing!" Charles said. Too bad the Brits seized so many of them. "I want to hear about that later, but first we celebrate."

David shook his head. "Look at you. Still growing."

"This is fantastic seeing you, but what did your parents say about leaving school?" As much as Charles wanted David by his side again, he really wanted to send him on the next ship home.

David raised his palms to his waist. "That's the big surprise. At first, they were against me skipping next semester. But when I told them how close we are to establishing this nation, my father said, 'Son, you're a man now—and this is a man's decision.' Then he cried and said, 'I'm so proud of you. Go and do your duty. You bring great honor to your uncle Harry, God rest his soul.'" He turned to Gladia. "My uncle was murdered in the Nazi death march, just weeks before the Allied Forces freed the Jews."

Gladia put her hand on his shoulder. "I am sorry. I know how you feel."

"And what about your girl, Anna Lee?" Charles asked.

David took a large breath and exhaled it through closed teeth. "That darn girl must have overheard us at some point. She called the police, hoping there was a reward for you." His lips tightened. "I was so mad at her!"

"Any new pursuits from…?"

David flashed his palm up. "I'll tell you later."

Agatha walked back in. "Enough depressing talk. We must celebrate. Tonight we eat, drink and dance. Why don't you all go upstairs and wash while I prepare a feast."

They reached the top of the stairs and David turned. "There's a lot to learn here. This is a sophisticated—"

A rumble shook the upper floor. David ducked under a table. "Oh my goodness! Palestine has earthquakes too?" He looked up while holding his heaving chest.

Gladia looked at Charles. "We will have to tell him."

David squinted at Charles.

"That was probably a fifty-pounder … Mortar."

"Oh." When David stood, a massive blast followed and he dropped to the floor again with his arms over his head. "What was that? A hundred-pounder?"

Charles and Gladia laughed.

"Uhh … what are you laughing at?" David remained on the floor, pale. "That sounded like the world coming to an end."

Gladia smiled at Charles. "They made new ones and sound bigger." She turned to David. "That one had your name."

David got up, chest still pulsating.

"That was the Davika," Charles explained. "Whenever the enemy's near headquarters, we set off the most amazing invention in warfare. The Davika's a bomb that barely causes damage, but it's so intimidating, the enemy runs far from it. Thus, this building has never been under attack."

David took a deep breath and nodded. "What a stroke of brilliance! That thing left my heart on the floor."

CHAPTER 30

April 1948

Charles whiffed the aroma when Agatha entered with baskets, her breath huffing. David approached, hands extended. "Here, let me help you with that." Watching, Charles thought if she'd been ten or fifteen years younger, they'd make a good couple.

Agatha sidestepped him. "I got it." She placed the baskets on the brown leather sofa. "You can go downstairs and get the rest if you like."

David grinned. "There's more?"

Gladia peeked under a cloth. "Chicken! Where did you get meat?"

Agatha wiped her face with her apron. "When I found out Charles' best friend was coming, I pressed my sources." She uncovered a cloth from another basket. "Fresh biscuits, and butter ... yes, *butter* everyone!"

Gladia opened her eyes wide. "You have good friends."

Agatha handed her a corner of the red-striped tablecloth. They flapped it and spread it over the table. Gladia began pulling food from the baskets and placing it in neat sections. "This is a treat." She turned to Charles and held up a red apple. "Look, your favorite." She tossed it to him, then turned and hugged Agatha. "What would we do without you?"

David came back upstairs with a platter of wine, tea and cups. "I just met your cook and nurse, Josephina. She just told me there're problems with the mail?" He set the tray down.

Agatha nodded. "The British will be leaving, and refuse to let us assume government services. Effective April thirtieth, all mail service, cables, telegrams and other communications will stop; Thanks to pressure from Arabs." She pointed to Charles, who chomped his apple. "But your friend has big plans for that."

David chuckled. "I'm not surprised." He walked over and patted Charles' back. "I used to call him Einstein…."

Charles swallowed and opened his mouth. David held his hand up. "I know … there is only *one* Einstein." He tightened his brows. "So how am I supposed to contact my parents?"

Agatha walked closer. "No need to fuss. We have several American pilots who've been smuggling weapons from Europe. We hand them letters when they take furloughs back home."

David nodded. "Convenient."

A discharge shook the floor and David ducked; Agatha left without flinching. Charles remembered his buddy hated earthquakes in Los Angeles, so he knew he'd never get used to bombs.

Gladia poured wine and tea, while Agatha marched back in, set her bowl down and stared at her. "I just found out … Josephina said you two are getting married?" She raised her hands shoulder height. "Were you planning on telling me?"

"What?" David turned to Charles, eyes wide.

Charles looked at Gladia and beamed. "We were going to wait until the war was over, but nothing happens timely around here. One day you're happy, the next you're miserable. One moment you think it's safe, then you're scared to death. I came here single, and now I'm engaged." He chuckled. "I can't remember a normal day since I've been here."

Gladia walked to her purse. "I guess I can put this on." She slipped the antique ring over her finger.

Agatha ran to Gladia, her arms waving. "Oh my goodness gracious, a ring?" She hugged and swayed Gladia like she'd never let go. Looking over Gladia's shoulder, Agatha glowed as if she were getting married.

David hugged Charles. "This is a great surprise!"

Agatha stepped back with a wide smile. "Tell us how this proposal came about."

Gladia grinned at Charles. He certainly couldn't say they embraced on the worst day of his life. And he didn't want to describe the proposal, since they were both in chains when it came about. "It's the greatest thing …" He restrained a tear. "To ever happen to me." It had also been torture since they'd been deprived of developing intimacy. "It's complicated, since I'm not entirely sure how it came about."

"Well, you have a nice glow," David grinned. "I've never seen you like this!"

Gladia smiled. "We are both glowing, but more on the inside."

Charles interlocked their fingers, happy to see her smile. "This is a hard time to love someone so deeply, because we have a duty to fulfill, and she …" He smiled at her. "You worry too much about me."

"But what about home?" David asked. "You're coming back eventually aren't you?"

Gladia tugged Charles' arm. They hadn't discussed their long-term plans. "This place has changed my entire perspective on life," he said. "I'm learning about ideals and principles, and how the human spirit can draw strength from faith in God."

"That really doesn't sound like you." David's eyes darted between Gladia and Agatha.

Charles nodded. "You were right when you said I was miserable with life in Los Angeles." He shrugged. "I don't see myself going back."

David raised his brows. "Wow."

"Living here has shown me other things too: like Americans and Jews sharing similar ideals about democracy. How Jews and Christians believe in the same God: the God of Abraham. And both faiths believe the prophecies about dispersed Jews regathering to rebirth this nation."

"Wait a minute," Agatha said. "What do Christians have to do with our land? This will be a Jewish state."

Charles looked at her. "Several Christians at the docks in New York kept quoting one of *your* scriptures in Genesis twelve, verse three: *I will bless those who bless you (Israel), and curse those who treat them with contempt....* They also spoke about the *valley of the dry bones* in Ezekiel thirty-six."

Gladia motioned toward the table. "Why don't we sit and eat? You guys keep looking at the food."

Charles pulled out a chair for her. "I couldn't understand why Gentiles at the docks would risk their lives sailing to Palestine, since Jews and Christians didn't agree about their faith." He stared at Gladia. "Everyone knows why I joined. But now I serve for additional reasons. And I think God could do mighty things with this nation, like He did in America." He was surprised he'd just said those things, but wanted Jews to succeed, and Von Deisenberg's dream to die.

Gladia and David gaped at him as if they were watching a suspenseful movie, while Agatha narrowed her eyes.

He sighed at Agatha. "I'm just saying there are parallels between the founding of America and this nation being born. And why can't Jews and Christians work together for a mutual cause?"

Agatha crossed her arms. "I'm not going to believe in the New Testament in exchange for their help."

He tensed. "Is that what you think? I labored side-by-side with some very dedicated people, who believe this land belongs to the Jews! They also said something surprising; They love Jewish people dearly! What other group says that? When I asked why, they told me about Corrie ten Boom. Then they went on to explain how Jews were God's *chosen people*, to co-write and preserved the most important book of all time; A book they base all their beliefs in."

Agatha squinted. "Who is Corrie ten Boom?"

When Charles leaned forward, Gladia slipped her hand onto his leg and gave it a little shove. "You don't know who Corrie ten Boom is? The Christian woman who was sent to a death camp for hiding Jews from the Nazis?" He breathed a flustered sigh. "So they believe the Messiah has come, and you don't." He spread his palms out. "I think it's wise to look at what you *do* have in common with these Gentiles, not what you don't."

"I agree," David said. "We should view Christians as allies. They're obviously not on the side of the Arabs."

Agatha flinched. "Of course we will build our nation with anyone who's willing. But were not going to convert to their Jesus!" She pointed her finger at a portrait on the wall. "We believe our Messiah will be a man, not a man who says he's God—someone like David Ben-Gurion. He's our modern-day Moses."

Smiling, David took a big whiff of the aroma rising from the table. "Why don't we eat?" David's gift for soothing conflicts was always timely, like the day he talked four high-school bullies out of stuffing Charles into a trashcan.

Gladia plucked up a chicken leg and placed it on Charles' plate. "Yes. Let us eat."

Agatha looked at Charles. "Will you pass the bread please?" When he held out the loaf, she broke off a piece, then turned to Gladia. "Do you have a date for this glorious event?" Oddly, her tone and demeanor had shifted as if they never disagreed.

Although he needed no approval from Agatha, her blessing would be important to Gladia. "We haven't been able to think about a date with all the trouble going on." He raised his teacup.

"I'm ready!" She said.

"You are?" The cup teetered midair.

She wiggled her brows with the most sensual grin he'd ever seen.

David and Agatha hummed an audible acknowledgement.

Charles spilled a few drops as his mind replayed the wedding vision he'd had when they met. It made him wonder if God had planted that thought in his mind; he'd already witnessed undeniable evidence of other foretellings being fulfilled. Why not have a prophecy fulfilled in his own life?

"*She's ready*, Charles," David said with a sly grin. "Better not keep her waiting."

Agatha narrowed her brows at Charles. He sent her a firm nod and then smiled at Gladia. "Then let's set a date."

"I say we do it next week," Agatha said sarcastically.

Charles tried not to look surprised, but his brows rose. He wondered if Agatha was being genuine, or testing him.

"I know a wonderful synagogue with lots of room for our guests," Agatha said.

"Guests?" Charles looked at David and raised his shoulders.

"We are homeless." Gladia hadn't taken a bite yet, while David was half-finished. "We can't get married without a home."

"You just said you're ready." Agatha grinned. "Don't be concerned about that. Moshe will locate one when I tell him the news." She looked at Charles and stood. "We all could use an *event like this* to take our mind off things too." She left without finishing her plate, which was unusual.

Charles rose. "I'll be back after I visit the toilet." He decided to take the longer route past Moshe's office.

"They can't get married right now," Moshe's voice muffled behind his office door. "There's too much instability."

"Oh come on sir, they're young and in love."

"I thought you didn't approve of him."

"Well … he's certainly better than her last boyfriend. And she adores him!"

"I'm happy for them, but every strategic post the Brits vacate becomes an award to the fiercest army. Snipers are everywhere, and you can obviously hear all the near misses around this building."

"But, sir—"

"Unscrupulous enemies are after Charles because of his last assignment. I'm more concerned for their safety than their happiness for now."

Swallowing hard, Charles walked back upstairs, but couldn't finish his meal.

Agatha's boots echoed up the stairs but she paused at the door. "Moshe is working on your new place." She patted her chest. "As soon as he has something, we will get *you two married!*" She glanced at David. "I guess we have a best man, but who's going to be your maid of honor?"

Gladia rose and put her arm around Agatha. "I just happen to know an auntie who would fit that job to perfection."

"Really? I'd be honored. Oh my," she fluttered her hands, "we have a wedding to plan!"

Charles stood and raised his cup. "Let me propose a toast. To my bride, the most wonderful, beautiful woman walking the face of this planet." He kissed her cheek. "I love you more than life itself!"

"Here, here," David said.

"L'chaim!" the others shouted, while Gladia struggled to keep tears from falling.

The reality of getting married at nineteen made Charles think about school, his parents, and life expectancy. There'd be no issues with providing for his wife; he had thirty thousand dollars in a safety deposit box, if Barclays Bank survived the violence. But now he'd become a hazard to be with, and his challenge would be keeping Gladia from snipers, bombs, and fierce enemies.

≈≈≈

Several more days of unrelenting explosions had shaken both the headquarters and everyone's nerves. But no one was bothered when heavy stomps reverberated up the stairs. "Good news," Moshe said as he strode into the room. "I found a safe place for you in a kibbutz nearby. It's a small home with a garden in front, and a hut nearby for David."

David squinted. "What's a kinbuzz?"

Charles laughed. "That's right, we haven't schooled you with the essential Hebrew words yet." He put his hand out to Gladia. "Let my wife-to-be enlighten you."

She smiled. "It is a place ..." She put her finger to her cheek. "*Ah* ... it is hard to explain in English."

"It's a self-sufficient community of Jews who rely on themselves for living," Agatha said.

"Thank you, Moshe," Gladia said. "Where is it?"

"In a little village called Yehuda Meragusa, outside Jaffa near the coast." Moshe took a breath. "I'm glad we didn't transfer you to Jerusalem. The Arabs have laid siege and demolished water pipes to starve the residents. We lost one hundred armored cars and many good fighters, trying to dismantle their stronghold."

Gladia pulled a breath in. Later, Charles would ask Moshe to refrain from disclosing bad news about Jerusalem in her presence.

When Moshe left, Charles escorted Gladia downstairs to the front entry while Agatha and David took their turn cleaning. "I wish Moshe had found a place farther away," he said. "Since the irregulars chased us at the beach, they're probably still in the area hunting for us."

Gladia scanned the room. "I feel the same, but I cannot tell Moshe that we sneak out and—"

Moshe walked out of the kitchen; his eyes fixed on theirs. "What's wrong?"

"Nothing," Gladia said. "We are talking about the troubles."

"I have new assignments for both of you, and David. Our intelligence office in Tel Aviv has been asking for Charles."

David and Agatha passed by, their arms full of bowls and plates.

"Everyone wants Charles," Gladia said, snuggling up to him.

Moshe turned. "David, will you come in here please?"

David joined them. "Gladia and David. You'll be working with Charles to relay intelligence information over the shortwave in code."

David raised his brows. "Code?"

"Don't worry, Charles knows them. He will decipher and relay information to you for the English-speaking commanders, and to Gladia for the Hebrew-speaking officers. We're connected to every Jewish settlement in Palestine by wireless. I've chosen this assignment because it requires a high level of trust and attention between the three of you. David, these two are not to leave your sight. Keep your pistol with you at all times."

"I'll guard them with my life, sir."

"That's what I'm counting on." Moshe walked toward his office.

Agatha approached. "I'm going to the synagogue tomorrow to—"

The room quaked and a cup fell to the floor; only David reacted, putting his hands over his head. Agatha turned. "Charles, we have much to do in preparation for a Jewish wedding. Are you up to converting to Judaism?"

"Actually, I've been looking for the right time to announce something."

Gladia took his hand. "What is it?"

"I'm going to tell the three of you something you cannot repeat." He quieted his voice. "Moshe disclosed something he learned about my parents. I bothered him last night for permission to tell you." He chuckled. "I'm probably half-Jewish. Roger Devonshire isn't my biological father." This was the first time saying it aloud, and it was too wonderful to speak with a straight face.

"Charles, you don't have to be Jewish to marry Gladia," Agatha said.

"I know—"

"Wait. I believe it." Gladia raised her palm. "You have your mother's face, but your father … he is not like you. Not his face or how he acts."

"You've seen Charles' parents?" David asked.

"I saw a photograph."

"Oh … the one Charles found behind the mirror? I agree, Mr. Devonshire is nothing like Charles." David turned to him. "But how did you learn this? And how'd you know your real father was Jewish?"

"I can't give you details. But I know it's true. Especially the way Roger treated me." He frowned. "He had the same contempt toward me that Arab irregulars have toward Jews." The word Nazi was on the tip of his lips.

Agatha clapped her hands together. "This is fabulous news. But you're about to marry into our faith. We still need to prepare you for the ceremony."

CHAPTER 31

Charles woke up groggy the next morning, as he did every day since the last botched mission. But this time the room was empty of transitional refugees. Gladia sat against the wall, knitting.

Moshe came in but stopped after advancing a few steps, his face pale and brows tapered. Gladia put down her knitting and stood. Charles knew the familiar look too; an uneasy silence loomed.

"I just received disturbing news." Moshe approached Gladia with moist eyes. "Before you leave, I must tell you something." He placed his hands on her arms. "It's not good."

She folded her hands and blinked several times. Charles stood next to her, his gut tight.

Moshe made firm eye contact with her. "Dov's trial concluded at the military court in Jerusalem. He was charged with firing on policemen, and setting explosive charges with the intent of killing personnel 'on His Majesty's service.' When asked if he admitted his guilt, he recited a statement to the judges."

Gladia shivered a breath in.

Moshe unfolded a paper, "'I do not recognize your authority to try me. You came to Palestine for good reasons, but you have reneged on your original Balfour commitment, namely, to grant the Jews our God-given right to possess this land.'"

Charles tried not to tremble while holding Gladia. He pulled his handkerchief from his back pocket and dabbed her tears, then gave her a little jostle so she would exhale.

Moshe balled his hand and coughed into it. "'When the prevailing government in any country is not legal, when it becomes a regime of oppression and tyranny, it is the right of its citizens—more than that, it is their duty to fight this regime and topple it.'"

He crumpled the letter and shook his head. "Unfortunately, his statement had no effect on the judges, and the president of the court announced he'd been found guilty … they sentenced him to be hanged."

Gladia's knees gave out. Charles grasped at her, but her body slipped onto the floor. He dropped and cradled her head on his lap while she sobbed.

Looking at her, Moshe frowned. He gave Charles a gentle nod, then left.

"Why would Dov do this?" She raised her puffy eyes. "Does he not know how much I love him? I have no more family besides you now."

He picked her up and carried her downstairs to the couch.

Agatha came in, also in tears, and urged Gladia to eat. Gladia rose to a sitting position and shook her head. After returning with water, Agatha announced it was time to leave for their new home.

Gladia's already slender body had been thinning since Dov's detainment. And now with nothing to pack, she averted her eyes from everyone. With Charles' assets unreachable, and the Haganah funds stretched, they only had a few changes of surplus clothes Moshe had provided.

From the hall, the radio still echoed with familiar pleas for more ammo, supplies and medical emergencies. Charles didn't want to add to the dampened mood, so he refrained from asking about the status of the five surrounding nations, who were pressing in with far more weapons, troops and supplies than they had. The Jews' only advantage was plenty of gall and determination; two essentials the American colonel said could win a war.

Charles assumed that was a pep talk. Miracles or not, there was no logic in that kind of reasoning with the odds so heavily stacked against them.

Agatha and David approached. Their strained smiles must have been created for Gladia's sake. "Are you two ready?" Agatha's cheery tone sounded forced.

Charles shrugged. "Sure, I've got my knapsack."

Agatha sighed. "I'll get you to your bank as soon as it's safe, even if I have to requisition an armored vehicle."

He put his arm around Gladia. "Let's go see our new home." He held her tight and hoped she'd lift her face while they left. Maybe the wedding Agatha was pushing for would help.

As the car sped off, Agatha cracked her window and peeked back at Gladia. The misty breeze was chilly, but refreshing. Rounding a corner, she hit the brakes to avoid ramming a caravan of Arabs carrying suitcases, their long faces pointed toward Haifa port. Their slow trudging and tousled hair confirmed the Arab radio propaganda to get out of Palestine or die from Jewish raids.

"That's strange," he said. Even though he knew what the evacuation was about, Charles looked at Gladia and hoped she'd give her usual explanation.

"What are they doing out here?" David asked.

Agatha waited for a few teenagers who trailed the group, then turned onto highway 2. "They're evacuating from the public call of the Arab League." She glanced at David. "You might as well know; They're boasting an all-out slaughter of Jews and don't want them in the way when they come. But God will be our shield."

David knitted his brows. "What do you mean, 'when they come'? I've been hearing them all around us since I arrived."

Charles decided not to answer David, so he wouldn't depress Gladia any further. According to Moshe, the bulk of Arab troops were only waiting for the British to leave Palestine so they could initiate their anticipated "annihilation day."

After passing a few more streets, Agatha jetted down a dirt road that led to a village. Grass-pitched roofs cascaded for hundreds of meters. Charles nudged Gladia. "Look at that. It's the same type of brick laundry and bakery we saw in the other kibbutz: We can bake your favorite cornbread."

Gladia continued to stare out the opposite window.

Agatha stopped in the village square next to the bakery, its little chimney smoldered. David looked around. "All I see are a bunch of mud huts, but no people. Is there some kind of temple service going?"

Agatha opened her mouth as if to answer, but closed it and looked back at Gladia. "There's your home." Agatha shot her finger past David's chest, toward a wooded cottage. "Moshe rounded up a dozen men to assemble it, just for you. There's no heat or running water, but there are two rooms and a living area." She opened her door, got out, and poked her head in the rear passenger window. "It's the best we could do for now." She opened Gladia's door. "Are you coming, honey?"

David popped out of the front seat and pointed at the only hut that was still light brown. "Is that my hut over there?"

Agatha straightened. "I know it's not what you're used to."

David moseyed to the trunk and removed his suitcase. "It's fine. It'll be like camping." He touched the back door and extended his hand. "Come on, Gladia. I brought you gift from America. It wouldn't have made sense to give it until now."

"You got me something?" She accepted David's hand and rose.

Grinning, Charles climbed out the other side. His buddy's flair for cheering people up just lifted his spirits too.

"Yup," David pointed to his luggage. "Let's go inside and I'll show it to you."

Charles put his arm around Gladia and lipped a thank-you at David. They passed a few goats and clucking chickens on their way toward the house's wood-planked entry. Dirt and rocks filled the center square, while tall green grass slow danced from the breeze in the outskirts.

"This look like a movie set at MGM Studios?" Charles said.

David nodded. "It does. I didn't think anyone used adobe clay or thatched grass roofs anymore—except in Africa."

Agatha stopped and turned. "You guys have been on movie sets?"

David nodded. "Yeah. We lived right by Hollywood, California. I used to sneak over to Charles' house and pop off the screen to his bedroom window, since his parents ..." He looked at Charles.

Charles grinned, recalling the unique friendship they formed in high school. David rescued him from bullies and Charles tutored his new friend while they bonded. "It's okay. They know most of my history."

"Anyways, we saw lots of stuff like this at movie studios."

Within a short stroll, Charles blocked the front door and held out ten fingers. "Wait." He opened the door. Then he whisked Gladia off her feet, which made her gasp. "I want to dedicate this place to my wife-to-be." He kissed her cheek. "Gladia, may this home be filled with our love, and God protect this place from our enemies...." He didn't dare speak the rest of the sentence: *Because we're sure going to need it.*

Gladia lipped, *I love you.*

"I will love you all my days. You have my pledge to protect you and be yours always." Her reciprocation to his oath made him grateful that David enlightened him about how he thought too clinically when pursuing a woman.

When he'd set her down inside, Gladia browsed the living area and inspected the small green couch, then walked to the oak table and sat in one of the four wood chairs. She rose and half smiled on her way to the kitchenette, which housed a little sterno plate warmer and a chopping block.

He knew what David was thinking by the approving grin stretched across his face: *See? Build your body strong at the docks to attract her attention, and learn the ways of romance to capture her heart.*

Agatha dabbed her smeared makeup. "That's the most beautiful thing I've heard." She clutched David's arm. "I'm sorry honey, I need a little support right now."

David chuckled and put his arm around her. "I don't mind. Too bad I'm not ten years older." She blushed.

Charles looked at Gladia. "I love this place, but I'm not going to be able to communicate with the villagers, am I?" She taught him some basics, but learning their language was the only subject that had ever challenged him.

"You might not," Agatha said. "Most villagers speak Hebrew, and some know a little English."

Gladia walked to the nearest bedroom, Charles followed. "What do you think?" he asked.

"I am sorry. I should be happy after I complain so much. Dov would say stop being sad."

They walked back to the living area. "We each have a cot in our own rooms. And it was nice of Moshe to provide furnishings."

Gladia stood before David. "What did you get me from America?"

David unbuckled his suitcase, drew out a wood box and placed it on the table. He opened it and removed several pieces of fine cotton cloth, violet edged with white lace. He draped one over a chair. "They're curtains with a matching tablecloth."

Gladia put her hands to her cheeks. "They are beautiful!" She hurried over and buried her face in David's bosom while stretching her arms around him. Charles almost cried at the timely gift.

"My mother made them," David said.

Gladia handed Charles the curtain and unfolded the tablecloth. Agatha stepped forward and ran her hand across the scrolling patterns. "Oh my. Your mother is an artist. These are exquisite." They spread it over the table.

Gladia ran her fingers along the ruby edges that lined the inside of the white lace. She turned back, blinking her eyes. "I love them! We must hang the curtain right now. Then we will have a home."

David walked toward the door. "Be back in a jiffy. I purchased a curtain rod at the Tel Aviv mercantile yesterday."

Agatha bounced on her toes. "That's more like it. Time to celebrate!" She followed David toward the car.

Charles learned something new about Gladia. A bit of tender love and a few feminine items to surround her, and she could make a home for herself. He hoped the emotional medicine would help her.

David and Charles hung the curtain. "Look how the villagers stare at our car," David said, looking out the window. "There was no one when we pulled up. We probably look like rich folks who invaded their village."

Gladia stood between them and smoothed the fabric into place; her eyes scanned every inch. "I will talk with them. They will like us, you will see." She put her hands to her hips. "You see, Charles? You need to practice Hebrew."

≈≈≈

The next morning, Charles cracked the new curtain to see Agatha's car stirring dust as she pulled up. He and Gladia met her in the village square. The three laughed, seeing an old man off in the distance, trying to teach David to glean foliage with a sickle: probably for the thatch material that constructed their roofs. The man kept motioning his hands and shaking his head while David swung the tool wildly. Finally, the villager pointed to a youngster about half David's age, who took over and swung the aged tool like an expert.

Her eyes glowing, Agatha turned. "Great news! Now that you have a home, I've reserved the synagogue for Friday."

"This week?" Charles was still surprised at Agatha's eagerness. They didn't even have a bed yet.

Gladia smiled. "You ready, my lovely?"

He paused as his nerves fluttered around his belly. "Yes. I'm so happy to see you smile, but it's hard to imagine getting … did you ever think you'd be married at twenty-two?" He turned to Agatha. "Don't we need a marriage license?"

"In America, you'd have to obtain a license through the courts, which wouldn't be possible here, with your names on the watch list. However, the rabbi can grant you one at the synagogue because Palestine isn't a country, it's an area of the British mandate." She pointed her thumb behind her. "I have everything set for a Thursday walk-through. Then, you marry Friday, and we'll celebrate all weekend; Hopefully without interruptions." She sighed. "We can't risk inviting any guests though. And Moshe can't make it either."

"Surely he can break away for a few hours." Charles scowled. Celebrating would be difficult at a time like this, but they might not get another chance to marry for a long time.

"He's in a major crisis." Agatha said. "There's a ship off the coast of Haifa, called *Exodus*. The Brits seized it and towed it here. It's a big mess; thousands of Holocaust survivors aboard are resisting arrest. Their supplies are gone, and they're are willing to fight to the death to avoid another incarceration and enter this land." She pushed air through her teeth. "And, there are hundreds of fighters onboard." She rolled her eyes at David. "That's why the Brits hinder Aliya Bet and arrest Jews at sea: They certainly don't want our army fortified by grateful immigrants."

Charles found it unthinkable to be a Holocaust survivor with all their hopes up for new freedom, only to be robbed of it again. And now, if Jews made it to Palestine, they were handed a gun right off the vessel and asked to fight a daunting war just to survive. He stared at Agatha. "It should be illegal to detain innocent people in international waters."

"That's precisely what Moshe and I have said. He's furious! Several victims already died from malnutrition on the *Exodus*, some were injured by fighting the Brits, and they haven't even docked yet."

"We have all the people we need for this ceremony," Gladia said. "Moshe has a bigger problem with helping our people. We must pray for them." She placed her hand to her temple and looked downward. "But we have one more problem I did not think of."

Agatha rubbed Gladia's shoulder. "What's wrong, honey?"

"I just realize something. We cannot get to the bank and I do not have a dress."

Agatha scanned Gladia's body. "Oh my. I've been so occupied, I forgot too. Obviously you'll never fit in one of mine, and certainly not in Josephina's." She leaned back on her car and crossed her arms. "But I did notice that David's mother made curtains for three windows, and you only have one."

Gladia turned to Charles. "Would he get upset?"

Charles laughed. "David would do anything to make you happy." He cupped his hands. "Hey David." He waved at him. "I think he needed rescuing anyway."

They laughed, and Gladia faced Agatha. "We must gather food from your friends so we can feast to the top!"

Agatha frowned. "The food shortages are worse. I have to use a ration card like everybody else now. But I scavenged a few cans of corn, some whole wheat flour for bread, and seven eggs." She rubbed her hands together. "And of course, a big bowl of Josephina's hummus...." She cast her eyes down.

"What is wrong?" Gladia asked.

"Moshe's not exactly ... he said we have to travel in an armored car with an automatic weapon when going into the city. Snipers are everywhere." She looked around. "Many of these kibbutzes are being attacked too. You practiced your escape drills, right?"

CHAPTER 32

When Charles returned from mapping additional escape routes, he watched in amazement as his burly friend, under Gladia's direction, transplanted wildflowers to their front yard. Agatha drove up in a black vehicle with ugly bars over the windows and dented-steel reinforced sides. She rolled her window down. "Is everybody ready for some fun?" The car just didn't match the event.

Gladia frowned. "Maybe another time. I am sure you did not finish my dress in one day."

She cut the engine and nodded toward the backseat. Gladia jumped up. "You didn't!"

"Oh yes I did!" Agatha opened the back door and pulled out a paper-draped hanger. "Let's go inside and make sure it fits."

Charles and David followed until Agatha turned and held her hand out. "*Ahh* … no. You guys will not see her in this masterpiece until the big day."

≈≈≈

After the rehearsal without the rabbi, they drove back to their village. Before they stopped, David turned. "I have a problem; I couldn't get security for the ceremony. Even Josephina can't leave, because they lost the radio operator in battle. I should stand outside and keep watch during the wedding."

Gladia shook her head. "No. You are the best man. We must have you with us."

Agatha looked at David. "You're such a great friend. We'll be careful. Then, we'll come back here and celebrate discreetly."

≈≈≈

Sunrays poked into the front window when a car scuffed gravel outside. Charles sprang from his cot, which he had moved into the living area; Agatha wasn't due until ten o'clock for the noon ceremony. A cautious peek through a crack in the curtain allowed him to breathe calmly while Agatha climbed out of the ugliest vehicle he'd ever seen.

The commotion had interrupted his thoughts about the consummation. He should have been looking past that, to plan escape routes to and from the synagogue, but he couldn't help thinking about the miracle of marrying Gladia, and the excitement of what would come later. He still felt awkward though, when Agatha explained an ancient Jewish tradition: The best man was required to listen for proof of consummation and report it to the entire reception, which would only consist of Agatha. Knowing Gladia's projective voice, they could probably get their "proof" way out in the village square.

A knock vibrated the pine door. When Charles opened it and squinted into the sunlight, he hoped she wasn't early to announce an evacuation that would ruin his ultimate dream.

She came in with David following. "Good morning. I know I'm early."

Charles raised questioning brows at David.

"I'm on the lookout per Moshe's orders. Cars never come here, so if one pulls up like this, I need to know why. And I'm still on New York time, so I've been up awhile."

Charles loved David. Even back at school when his friend protected him from bullies, peers at school would ridicule David, since redheads seemed to carry a curse.

Gladia walked out, her eyes half open and hair ruffled. "Why is everyone here? It is not time yet." Even at her worst, she out did any girl at school.

Agatha bobbed her head. "I'm sorry, I couldn't sleep."

Charles motioned toward the table and chuckled. "If you brought breakfast, we'll forgive you."

"You know I always bring food." She craned her neck. "Hey Davey, wanna get the bag from my car?"

David rubbed his tummy and headed out. Charles turned to Gladia and mouthed, *Davey?* When Gladia scrunched her nose and grinned, his heart leaped to see her happy. Certainly, she'd need extensive support when Dov's sentence was carried out. But today was a good day to forget about their troubles. When light from the open door beamed on her too-tight pajamas, he turned away and wished their home had a cold shower.

David came back with a sack and unloaded buttermilk biscuits on the tablecloth. "Agatha. You certainly know how to take care of friends."

Agatha blushed. "I know how ..." She turned. "Let's eat."

Charles grinned at Gladia and wondered if she'd seen what he saw. Agatha was twice David's' age, but after the biscuits were gone, they interchanged arms while they planned alternate safe routes on a map. Then Agatha glanced at her watch. "It's time. Out you guys, so I can wash and prepare our beautiful bride."

Charles followed David outside. "I haven't seen your quarters yet. How about giving me a look."

After a short viewing of David's hut, a distant battle erupted in the north, so they took a security check around the perimeter, then returned to the hut so Charles could get dressed. It seemed like hours before Agatha finally opened their door. They stared at the empty threshold. Then Charles lost his breath at the sight of Gladia's angelic presence. "Wow ..." Even the echoing gunfire behind the hills softened.

The way her face beamed, the violet multi-tiered dress must have made her feel like a woman again. It contoured her curves well, and the cluster of miniature pink flowers she held matched her rosy cheeks.

She tilted her head. "You look like you find gold or something, but you don't say anything."

Charles tried to swallow the lump in his throat. "I see a lot more than any treasure could ever bring me …" He couldn't believe his ultimate desire stood in front of him. Everything about her was perfect. She loved and cared for him far beyond anything he'd ever imagined. She wanted to see the world, loved math and just like him, wanted a college degree.

"So you like it?" She ran her fingers down the velvet linings.

"Uhh … " He stepped forward, carefully wrapped his arms around her and closed his eyes. "I will never forget this moment," he whispered. He pulled back and kissed her. "You have completed me. I'm stunned by your beauty." He blinked quickly so a tear wouldn't drop to her dress.

Agatha came out, a white-laced veil draped over her arm. "No hugging! You're dropping rose petals." She pierced him with narrowed eyes. "You're lucky to even see her like this before the ceremony." Her lower lip quivered. "We have to get in and out fast. But at least we'll get you married. In a real temple, by a gracious rabbi."

On the way to the synagogue, surrounding booms reminded them to keep their eyes on trees and bushes. The new travel rule demanded no stopping for anything or anybody. David sighed. "Everyone have their pistols loaded?"

They all nodded. "Agatha. You drove this route on your way here, right?" David asked.

"Yes. It was all-clear."

Gladia looked down at her matching hand-purse. "I never imagine carrying a pistol to my wedding."

Agatha parked the car a few blocks away from the synagogue, and they left the vehicle peering in each direction.

On the final dash to the main entrance, the loose waistband on Charles' borrowed suit caused his gun to slide. He wiggled his ankle so it would plop to the ground. David picked it up and checked the safety. "I'll hold it."

Gladia locked arms with Charles as they walked up the steps. Her cheek creased, but she couldn't get a smile out as she took one last look behind them.

When David opened the doors, a young man spread his arms out. "*Ahh ... Charwos* and *Glaoudia*, you look too wonderful! You make beautiful a bride and a grooma. I am Daniel Tricoffski, synagogue facilitator. Rabbi Horowitz and his wife will be with you soon." Daniel frowned and motioned his hands to follow. "Sorry we cannot meet yesterday for rehearsal."

Charles knew what that frown meant. A rabbi in this area must have an enormous amount of funerals and emergencies to look after.

Daniel tried to regain his cheery demeanor with a partial smile. "Please sit. I will announce you are here."

His shoes clacked on the polished-oak planks. The walnut entry was larger than a house, and the beams between the stained-glass windows lifted toward the endless cathedral ceiling. It reminded Charles of where he'd met Gladia.

The rabbi entered the foyer with his wife and opened his arms like a choir director. "*Charlouse* and *Glaoudia*, you look wonderful!" He hugged them both together. "I am Rabbi Horowitz, and this my lovely wife, Mary. She will provide glorious music with the harp."

Everyone exchanged greetings. "Come, follow me." His voice boomed while he led them into the chapel, the sun streaking colorful lines through the stained-glass windows.

Daniel approached. "Rabbi, there is a problem. I hear noises out there. A gang of Arabs and a white man park across the street. They have guns, so I lock the doors."

Rabbi Horowitz stormed toward the window, his hands flying in the air. "What is this?"

Daniel ran toward the window, but David beat them and cocked his gun. "There's a large car and two motorbikes. Too many to fight off."

Banging and rattling emitted from the main doors.

"They're looking for me," Charles said. "Can you hide us somewhere?"

"Hide what?" the rabbi asked.

"Us, Rabbi!" Charles' heart pounded. He dreaded Gladia seeing Von Deisenberg's smug face if the white man was him.

Rabbi Horowitz gestured. "Down here, to the basement!" He led them behind the altar to a narrow stairwell.

The window smashed. "Where they are?" Arab accents boomed.

"Where is who?" Daniel's voice trailed off as they proceeded down the steps.

"David, my pistol?" Charles said.

David handed him his Berretta. Charles was glad to have it, even though his hand shook uncontrollably. Agatha and Gladia's firearms shook too. Charles pushed through cobwebs and began to survey the bricks. The vent window didn't shed enough light, so Agatha pulled a chain and clicked a hanging bulb.

David took a stance at the base of the stairwell and aimed his gun upward. "I'll shoot any Arab who comes down here."

"There is too many," Gladia cried. "I hear them breaking things up there."

"They sound furious," Agatha said.

"Form a shooting line," David barked. "Charles, behind me."

"Charles, what are you doing?" Gladia said. "We need you."

Charles examined each wall. Logic told him every problem had a solution. A bloody shootout with hardened terrorists was unacceptable.

"Charles," Agatha cried, "what are you doing? He's frozen, Gladia."

"Everyone," David called out. "Point your guns upstairs so we can maximize our firepow—" A woman's screams reverberated, followed by an old man's. Then, silence.

"They slaughtered the rabbi and his wife," David said. "It won't be long till they find us." He turned. "Charles!"

"Look at this structure. It's a nonbearing wall that doesn't really need to be here—"

"Charles, get over here!" David whispered.

"Help me remove this access panel on the wall."

"Why?" Agatha asked.

"This place has classic Middle Eastern architecture. That plank is probably an access into the water or electrical system. Come on, help me remove it."

While David guarded the stairs, the women helped him slide a table to the wall. Charles and Gladia hopped up and tugged the plank. It released with a ripping noise.

"My dress tore," Gladia said.

"Oh my ... that stinks," Agatha said. "I can smell it from down here."

Gladia contorted her face. "I don't know if I can go in there."

Charles poked his head in. "It's okay, it's just the sediment from a leaky water pipe." He smelled sewage also, but didn't want to alarm them.

"Hurry, I hear them near the altar." David lowered his voice.

"Gladia, you first. Throw the bouquet in."

She stiffened, mouth open. He knew it must have resembled the cupboard her parents told her to hide in on that fateful day.

Charles strapped his arms around her legs while rose petals floated to the floor. He lifted her in, legs kicking. When she dropped in, a tiny swishing stirred.

"It stinks." Her arm stretched out and clenched his lapel. "Get in here!"

Charles unfastened her hand and waved at Agatha. "Hurry."

Agatha wallowed onto the table, while Charles pulled on her arms. "I think I'm going to be sick," she said as she stood.

He strapped his arms around her substantial thighs. "It's just stagnant … water," he grunted. His cheeks flushed. "David, help …" She teetered on the opening, muffling her whimpers with her mouth closed.

David ran, hopped up and clutched her lower legs to plop her over. Unfortunately, she dropped headfirst and made quite a splash.

Charles peeked in. "Are you okay?" he whispered.

"Ohh, this is disgusting!" Her voice thundered in the darkness. "*Ahh*—"

"*Shh*…." Gladia fastened her hand over Agatha's mouth.

Charles heard a critter chirping down the dripping water pipe. "He's more scared than you are Agatha, and he's leaving." He removed his bowtie and clipped it to the bottom of the wooden plank, so they'd have a handle. He snatched David's and fastened it to the top. "Kick the table away when you bolster yourself up."

"This is brilliant, buddy, but it's bad in there," David whispered. "Get in, I'm right behind you. Hurry … I hear 'em jostling the door."

"Make sure you hand me the plank." Charles clicked the light off and hurtled in, landing shin-deep in cold water. Oozing mud seeped into his shoes. His heart sank at seeing Gladia's dress with rust and mud stains. He wanted to embrace her shivering, but he had to help David. "David, get those rose petals off the floor."

David scooped them, lifted the plank and handed it to Charles while he hoisted his body up. He kicked the table outward while balancing on the opening, but lost his balance and splashed everyone. He came up covered in muck.

Agatha hugged a pipe to steady herself. "I'm going to die in here!"

"Not so loud Agatha," Gladia said. "Pinch your nose like this."

It was a bad time to find out a friend was claustrophobic. Charles helped David with the plank. He cringed at the light still swaying, and prayed the cunning Nazi wouldn't notice.

"It's pitch—"

"*Shhh* ..." All three of them shushed Agatha, while hearing her slosh.

"Agatha, you must keep still," Gladia whispered. "Or we will die today."

Charles never thought anything could be worse than the closet his parents locked him into every Saturday night. When David bumped him, he struggled to hold the plank still. Then, sets of footsteps plopped down the steps. One slip and they were dead.

"No one here!" a muffled voice stammered with an Arab accent.

"Fools! You let them get away. Damn that rabbi for lying. I'll find that little runt and get my money back."

"No," Charles whispered. He knew that condescending voice.

"Charles, I can't steady it," David muttered. "It's slipping."

"Hold on, they're leaving."

"It's...."

"They're almost gone."

David wiggled. "Gladia help—"

The plank fell onto its edge and made a dull thud. They looked about, breaths panting. David pointed his dripping gun through the opening.

Agatha stirred. "I need out!"

Keeping his gun aimed, David pushed one palm in front of Agatha's face. He made them wait a few more minutes, then climbed out and carried the table over.

Charles helped the women into David's arms. After he climbed out, they trudged up the steps, dripping with rusty water. In horror, they saw the rabbi, his wife, and Daniel lying in front of the altar, surrounded by growing pools of blood. Everyone turned their faces away, but Charles knew the bloody scene would be burned into their memories forever. He saw his much-stronger hands strangling Von Deisenberg.

Agatha gagged. David peered out the window. "Looks clear. Let me scout the perimeter, then we can get out of here. Form a shooting line."

Gladia looked at her ravaged dress, then at the three victims. Her quivering lips were purple. Charles hugged her, knowing the dead bodies would be a reminder of her childhood tragedy. He held her cheeks and pulled her face to his. He opened his mouth, but no words could undo what he'd just put her through. To see their wedding devastated by Father made the same outrage from the diner mount—actually that man wasn't father—he was Von Deisenberg, an evil Nazi. "More death because of me." Ready to kick a few pews over and let his rage take over, he averted his sight from the militated bodies to get her out safely.

They scurried from the synagogue with pistols drawn, their drenched shoes squeaking down the wooden steps.

"Charles, Arabs killed them. You can tell by the knife markings," Agatha said. David came out from around the corner. "All clear, let's go!"

"Wait. We can't get in the vehicle like this." Agatha looked around. "Let's see if they have a garden hose."

David shook. "No! We leave now." He led them toward the vehicle. "Everybody in!"

Charles looked at David after the women climbed in. "He'll torture us until I tell him where my inheritance is, then when he has it ..." Von Deisenberg had punished him severely when he was finally caught spying on their secret meetings. From that point forward, Von Deisenberg informed

Charles, he'd join their group after he graduated or die. He agreed so he could buy time to plan his elaborate escape. His strategy had backfired though, since he put his friends under the same risk he'd been under.

Agatha started the engine and peeled away. "Surely he won't torture you, if you give him the money."

"If he doesn't kill me in the process, he'll try to force me back home, which would be just as bad." Charles grimaced. "Every interaction with him is non-negotiable—and he doesn't except loose ends."

Agatha shook her head. "He can't force you back. You're an adult now."

"You don't know this madman. He'll befriend the British or anyone who'll help him achieve his objectives, and ..." Charles blew a breath through his nostrils. "Now it makes when he slipped once and called me a half-breed; He must have known I'm half-Jewish."

"He's right, Agatha, Roger's unrelenting." David turned back to Charles. "I don't know how but we have to get rid of him."

"We can't just kill him," Charles said.

"We both know he'll never stop. And I'm sure he'll hunt me down for lying to him." David shifted his eyes to Gladia, and Charles knew what that meant. Gladia and Agatha's lives were at stake as well; He'd hold them hostage to force Charles to join the Nazis, which were prolific in Los Angeles.

"We can't leave. I'm sure he's got men watching the borders and airport," David said. "Palestine is small. He'll eventually find us."

"I'll think of someth—" Charles raised his index finger. "Wait a minute! Nazis are still heavily pursued by the British."

"What?" the others said in unison.

"Oops." Charles had promised not to leak that. "You're all going to have to forget I said that."

"We can't forget it, but we can certainly keep it between us," Agatha said. "That wouldn't matter since he was in America during the war. You can't have him arrested for just being a Nazi."

Maybe the Brits could be good for something after all. "He just murdered three innocent people. I'm going to figure out a way to exploit his weakness."

"His weakness?" Agatha said. "Sorry, but he murdered Jews, and Brits barely do anything when a we're the victim."

"He might not be a war criminal, but I'm going to figure out a way to have him apprehended; He'll commit more crimes."

On their way home, Gladia's face remained buried in her hands. Charles didn't know what to say. Nice people dead, her dress was ruined, they were cold, exhausted, discouraged and still unmarried. He placed his hand on her. "What can I do for you?"

She shook her head, but didn't raise it. "That poor rabbi and his wife and Daniel. Our wedding…. This is worst day ever." Her muffled voice broke.

Charles felt his blood boiling again. He leaned his head back and vowed right then not to ever let Gladia see an outburst.

Agatha frowned. "I'm so sorry. Moshe was right. I shouldn't have pushed for this wedding." Reaching the edge of town, her eyes widened in the direction of their kibbutz, then she slapped the wheel and swerved the car away from the path to their home. "We can't go back. We'll … report to headquarters, where it's safer."

Charles saw smoke rising from their village and shut his eyes: another home in flames. He was relieved Agatha had the wisdom not to mention it. He pictured the morgue and watched three more bodies accompany Jonathan, Dov, and over ninety faceless victims from the hotel. He slapped the seat. "I'm risking all of our lives! Just drop me off somewhere. I can't continue endangering all of you."

"We will do no such thing!" David said. "No one leaves my sight."

Gladia lifted her face and pulled at Charles' soiled jacket. "You promised to marry me."

CHAPTER 33

May 1948

They returned to headquarters damp, and removed their soiled footwear in the Spanish-tile entry room. Charles moved toward the linen cabinet to get dry towels, but Gladia put her hand on him. "The ring. I left it in my handbag."

Charles frowned, "You didn't—"

"It is in the basement, behind the furnace. I need it."

Agatha brought towels. "You can't take the road to the synagogue. That's how the enemy spotted us. I'm so stupid!" She put a towel down for their feet. "And the authorities will be there. It's pointless to give a testimony and expose ourselves, since we didn't witness the actual murders."

David furrowed his brows. "What do you mean, expose ourselves?"

Agatha took a breath. "Whenever a Jew is near a crime scene, the Brits tend to arrest and starve them while conducting an interrogation. You must have been informed about that. They could detain us for days, just to take a few more fighters off the streets."

David shook his head. "My briefing was a crash course."

"The only way to retrieve the ring is sneak in late at night," Charles said. "Let's wait. I have enough money to buy a new one when it's safe."

"That is sweet, but that ring is special." Gladia rubbed the dampness off his back with her towel. "I want to marry you before—"

He abruptly turned and faced her. Gladia's faith in prophecy had rubbed off on him, but her urgency to wed alarmed him. He again pictured her near Atlit with the Sten gun on her lap.

Her eyes glimmered. "I know back ways to Haifa. And I can get a dress from my boss Regina."

He couldn't say no; she deserved happiness, and he was determined to help her through her emotional trauma.

Agatha shook her head. "Out of the question. You both know Haifa's too hazardous. I'll make you another dress, and you can marry when Tel Aviv is secure."

Gladia put her towel down. "The way things are, it will never be safe."

Charles put his arm around Gladia. "Agatha, we need to do this."

Agatha gathered the towels. "Haifa is a fierce battleground because of its strategic shipping port. No one wants you married more than I do, but you'll simply have to wait."

≈≈≈

When Charles was shaken awake, he sat up and balled a fist.

Gladia's warm hand covered his lips. "Everyone is asleep."

He yawned and paused from the silence outside. "I'm not going to wake David. No need to endanger him too."

"He has orders to be with us all the time."

"Not this time." He stood and caressed her. "This is our risk. Let's get in and out as quick as possible."

She put his palm in the middle of her chest. "Feel my beating heart? I am scared, but excited."

Not wanting to act prematurely, he retracted his hand.

They snuck to the back office, where he found car keys and an updated map of enemy activity. They crept into the dim early morning, and found the auxiliary armored vehicle camouflaged behind bushes. Getting into the huge hunk of metal, Charles lit a match and scanned the map for safe routes.

He directed her to take backroads that wound through four villages, and when they arrived near the synagogue, the skyline's topaz gradient glowed over the hills. Gladia parked in an alley a few blocks away. They peered through the steel-armored slots and saw more Arab families caravanning with luggage stacked atop camels and donkeys, while others sporadically trudged the streets as if part of a funeral procession.

Charles put his hand on her lap. "Wait here. I'll get it."

"Careful and hurry back," she whispered.

His heart pumped rapidly while he moved along the shrubbery lining the street toward the crime scene. The doors were boarded up, so he slipped in through a broken window. The air inside was unbearable, so he hurried to the basement and clicked the light. The musty smell reminded him of Von Deisenberg's leather jacket, where he'd kept ample pamphlets to hand out. By fourth grade, he realized the power those papers had to taint the public's view of Jews. The chilling speech he heard was still fresh in his mind: *Propaganda is a great deal more than persuading people to believe something that isn't true. It is a technique that works below the surface of the mind.*

He took the purse and trotted back to the vehicle with a spike in his heart. It would take a long time to heal from the responsibility he carried for another catastrophe.

Gladia started the vehicle and Charles guided her to a rocky back road toward Haifa. "Are you okay?" she said. "You look sick."

"That was difficult." Quivering inside, he put her purse on the bench seat between them.

"Can I see it?"

He dug in her purse, opened the little box and pinched the ring between two fingertips. The diamond caught the morning sun and beamed like a miniature beacon. Her gleaming-eyed reaction made the risk worth the anguish.

"I love it. Thank you."

After bumping down a pitted dirt road, they came upon a highway to cross to maintain a northern heading. A little café with one car out front appeared, and she veered toward it.

"What are you doing?" He looked at her.

"I am hungry for breakfast. Let us eat there."

He surveyed the desolate area. "All right, I'm hungry too. I still have a few grush that Agatha gave me." He pointed. "Over there. Park behind that big trash container."

They got out, covered the vehicle with brush and made their way toward the entry. Opening the door, a bell jingled. A bald man pushed through double doors, chattered in Hebrew and motioned his hand to a table.

Charles enjoyed the poetic sounds when Gladia ordered breakfast in her native tongue. He pointed toward the back. "Let's sit by the rear exit."

When they sat, Gladia stretched her hands across the table. "I am in love with you more than I can say in English." Her supple fingers interlaced his. "I wish we were to marry right now."

As soon as he cracked a smile, flashes of the synagogue sent his lips to flattened again. He couldn't get the sinister grin on Von Deisenberg's face out of his mind, knowing he enjoyed slaying three Jews. He breathed deep and determined to battle the Nazi mind exploitations swirling.

"Something else is chipping away at you." She squeezed his fingers.

"Where did you learn that phrase?"

She tilted her head. "Phrase?"

He nodded. "The words …'chipping away.'"

"David tell me … told me."

"What else did he tell you?"

She broke hand contact and swiped a finger across her mouth. "My lips are sealed."

Charles sat back. "Wow." She said that like an American with no accent. He loved her intelligence, and her resolve to communicate with him better.

Her grin fled. "You tell me ... something else is in your mind. What is it?"

He released a breath. "I know I can tell you just about anything—but not this."

She straightened back as the food was set on the table and exchanged a few words with the proprietor. "You know I will get it from you. Save the trouble and say it."

He leaned in. "It's something I can never say to you—or any Jew for that matter." He took a whiff and looked down. "Let's eat." He'd finally told her no.

She pushed her plate forward and crossed her arms. He let out another breath and pushed his thumb to his plate, bumping her dish. "All right, I'll tell you. But it's not going to be pleasant."

She stared at him.

He repositioned his body. "This is difficult." He looked up and scanned the café. "He made me repeat things ... ever since I was four or five." He sipped his milk. "Every time I get a headache, those sickening words come back. Sometimes I wake up saying them." He released the tablecloth bunched up in his fist. "My worst fear is waking up next to you and realizing I'd chanted it in my sleep."

She tilted her head forward, a clear gesture she wanted him to continue. He looked at the scrambled eggs and toast, knowing they were getting cold. And he knew what she was thinking: Confronting his demons aloud would be the first step to recovery. But the awful things in his head could also send her into further depression.

He raised his hands and dropped them on the table. "All right, you want to hear it?" He rounded his lips to whisper. "'Jews are the reason we have high taxes, crime, and death.'" He looked for her reaction, but she didn't flinch. "'There's no peace until we exterminate Jews like little rats.'" The table began to shake—mostly from him. "'Jews are scum, it is our duty to get rid of them before they take over the world.'"

She maintained a straight face, but her hands trembled. For his healing, she took a verbal beating. And while he hated doing it, it would no longer be a shameful secret. He held back a rush of tears from enormous relief.

She jolted up and her chair fell; she dashed to his side and hugged him. "You see? You can be better now."

He lowered his head to hide tears. "I'm sorry. Those words repeat in my head like a skipping record." He lifted his flushed face and she patted it with a napkin. "It's not as bad as before, but it won't go away."

He slid her plate back to its place. "That's it. I'm not saying another word about it."

She released him, picked up her chair and sat. "That is not the first time I hear those words." He smiled inside, because he didn't have the urge to smash something, as he did in New York. Instead, he took another deep breath and felt his appetite return. He bit into his toast, not believing the words he repeated to a Jew, but relieved he'd shared another dark secret with his sweetheart. Hopefully she wouldn't pry him for the deepest one.

She buttered a piece of toast, scooped some egg onto it, and stretched it to his mouth. "I still think we should have taken David." She scooped more egg on her bread and took a bite.

"I know, but I can't see any more friends die: especially him."

She nodded. "He loves you very much. I can tell."

"Yeah, I love him too. He's the only real friend I ever had until I met you." Charles fed her the next bite from his plate. "We're best buddies and

I'm thrilled he's here, but I'm concerned. He's so fearless and carefree, but he doesn't know Palestine like we do."

"I agree. He is watching our safety and we must watch him too."

≈≈≈

The sun was fully up by the time they reached the outskirts of Haifa. Charles pointed toward a wide trail between some trees. "Don't go that way."

Gladia made a sharp turn to avoid the path that led to a massive whirlwind of dust. "How many do you think are under the dirt?"

He squinted. "It's got to be hundreds." Booms vibrated the floorboards, and the echoes of large-caliber machinegun fire unnerved him.

"Do you know where we are? Is Regina's home close?" he asked.

"Yes. That is the backside of Carmel Hill in front of us. The library is on the other side."

"The library? Agatha said the universities are closed."

She looked down. "I sneak a call to Regina, she sleeps in the back room because her house fell."

"You broke protocol? And you didn't tell me?" Now he really questioned her judgment. Any corner they turned could bring a band of Arabs looking to kill Jews and Americans. But she'd suffered more heartache then he ever had, and he sure made his share of risky decisions under duress.

"I am sorry. She will know how to find a rabbi to marry us in all this trouble. And, she is my size for a nice dress."

"She knows a rabbi? She's Arab."

"Yes, but she knows many Jews, like I know many Arabs."

Charles was relieved to see no enemy when they reached the peak of the hill. The Technion was intact, and right below them.

Gladia stopped between two trees that overlooked the college. "Can you see any trouble down there?"

"I'm surprised it's clear. But we better get in and out quickly."

She drove down the hill, and when they got out of the steel-clad vehicle, the noise of gunfire sounded close. They entered the library and Gladia halted. "No." She elbowed him. "Look ... I made a mistake."

Charles locked eyes with the twins. "They must be on watch detail. Get the car. I'll distract them. If you don't see me in a few minutes, meet me at the warehouse."

"Okay. Be careful."

After walking her to the front door, he turned back and almost ran into Gladia's former boss.

"Charles?" She peered over his shoulder. "Where did Gladia go? Her paycheck is here."

He noticed the brother was gone. "Regina ... I hope you can trust me. I need you to yell "Fire!"

"Why would I do that?"

"Never mind." When he rushed toward the parking lot, Arab irregulars rammed their vehicle, with Gladia in it.

Charles cupped his hands. "Leave!"

She revved the vehicle and ripped up the dirt hill. He was relieved to see her follow direction without insisting on waiting for him.

When the Arabs pursued him, he turned and bustled past the sister who screamed something he couldn't understand; Their car screeched, followed by closing doors and clunking steps.

His throbbing head slowed him, so he ran into the gym and hid himself in a locker. The stuffy compartment hampered breathing even more. When he heard them searching, with the succession of other lockers banging, he was certain they'd find him.

The smelly locker began to swirl as he felt along the walls, hoping to grab an object to jam the latch. Then his muscles and legs went limp, his body collapsed and slapped the wooden floor.

Dave Longeuay

CHAPTER 34

Gladia wrenched the wheel and screeched around the corner of Main and Fifth Avenue, nearly demolishing a horse cart before pulling up to the rear entrance of Haifa Pharmacy.

Inside, she bumped shelves while rummaging her handbag for a coin. She handed the fee to a man behind the counter, stood in the open booth and whirled the crank for the Red House: code name for Haganah Headquarters. When she heard David's voice she cried, "I need you here!"

"You're out of breath. What's wrong?"

Glancing at the man, she inhaled deeply.

"Where are you two? I woke up and you were gone."

"Something terrible happen. Maybe I killed Charles!" She glanced at the man's inquisitive face and lowered her voice. "We went to Haifa to … I did something foolish." She sniffled. "Arab irregulars, they capture Charles at Technion. I hide the car in the bushes, then followed them. They take him inside the back of Bortogios restaurant."

"Thank goodness you know where he's at."

"Probably they have a basement or quiet room where they keep him. Maybe they kill him if we don't get him out soon."

"Stay put. I'll take Agatha's car. Where are you?"

"Call Moshe and tell him to bring help."

"I can't. They're all on missions."

She smacked the counter. "You must hurry!" She glanced at the man again. His eyes widened before he turned away.

"Gladia. Where are you?"

"Haifa Pharmacy on Main and Fifth; In the back. Agatha, she will draw you a map. Hurry!"

"How many did you see?"

She looked up while unfolding the nightmare in her mind. "Four that took Charles in the car. They carry him in a big cloth." Her tears dripped on the counter. "The cloth, it was not moving when they carry him. Maybe they knocked him on the head to make him quiet. Please come fast."

"I'll think of something."

She could barely reattach the earpiece on the receiver. This could take David a long time—if he wasn't shot by snipers, caught in battle, or arrested by Brits for speeding and carrying a firearm. She wished she had a Thompson submachine gun. Her Walther P38 would get her in the door, but would do little good in a shootout with Arabs.

She walked out and paced the alley while squeezing the handle of the gun inside her purse.

≈≈≈

His heart skittering, David wanted to scout battle sites to pull in a few fighters. But he had no experience to approach the field correctly without being shot at, and there was no time. Charles' life was on the line. He pulled in the rear of the pharmacy and saw Gladia's frantic pacing, so he decided to hold back a lecture. When he got his buddy out, they'd certainly hear about it then.

Gladia hopped in. "Hurry." She shot her finger out. "This way."

He pushed the gas pedal and resisted the urge to reassure her everything would be fine. Bumping out of the alley, he followed her pointing finger. "Are we close?" He would die inside if anything happened to his buddy. And though he only had his pistol, a case of nine-millimeter rounds and two grenades, he didn't lack determination. While considering his odds, David and Goliath's showdown came to mind.

She rustled her hands. "Turn left. Park here, so we are not close." She pointed. "There it is, the red sign. 'Bortogios.'"

His mind raced for solutions, knowing he couldn't involve Gladia. "Let's call the police—"

"No. Our training say when police come for Arabs torturing Jews, they kill the Jew and shoot at the police."

David turned with gritted teeth. "You should've included me this morning." He pointed toward the highway. "Go back. Bring as many fighters as you can when they return from missions. Hopefully the radio's fixed by the time you get there so you can broadcast a plea for Charles' life."

The call would likely go unanswered unless Moshe heard it. If a unit survived a battle, they would move straight to another, so he was probably on his own. That thought made his hands shake while he stuffed ammo in his pockets and shuddered at the thought of a bloody shootout.

Gladia wiped another tear. "I need to help you." She opened her purse. "I know how to shoot—"

He put his hand over hers, thinking she was probably a better shot than him. "Go get help before he swallows … God forbid, if I'm caught, we're going to need troops." He noticed her looking past his shoulder. Hopefully she didn't catch what he'd almost said about Charles taking cyanide.

"Wait." She slouched. "The sister is crossing the street. She led Arabs and the German to burn Dov's house."

David grunted. "I'll peek in after she enters and see what I can learn." He started the car, got out, and leaned into the window. "Take the car to HQ, and *do not* come back alone." After she scooted to the driver's side, he placed his hand on her shoulder. "I'm going to save him, okay?"

She nodded. "I trust you. Please, be careful, David."

≈≈≈

Charles awoke to some sort of itchy material over his face, but left his head resting on his shoulder. A door squeaked and heavy steps clunked downward in perfect rhythm among a barrage of noises. The door shut, and it quieted again. The distinct smell of fried cauliflower and eggplant signaled the possibility of being in the basement of an Arab restaurant.

"The American. How come he sleeps?"

How strange to hear an Arab irregular speak good English, but with a strong accent. A voice replied in Arabic from Charles' left. "The smelling salts. Give it to him." Heavy clumps from big boots drew closer. "We must extract information before tomorrow. Then cut his throat."

Charles fought an urge to jolt, and hoped they wouldn't notice his shaking limbs. He visualized his corpse next to all his other friends in the cold morgue. Gladia would be there, weeping and falling deeper into depression.

Fingers pinched his hair and forced his head back. When his facecloth pulled upward, abrasive fingers squished his nose with an unbearable stench of ammonia. Blazing stings shot up his nostrils, but he hunkered inward, knowing any delay could help.

A voice from his left sputtered again in Arabic. Charles recognized three words: "He" and "not moving."

"Slap him! Pour ice water." The man with big boots said.

The sensation of a glass jug cracking his head made him jerk when the cold water splashed. "Back off!" He tried to stand but realized he was cuffed to a chair.

"*Ahh* ... finally. Welcome, Richard Anderson."

Follow procedure and play stupid. "What do you want?"

"You have information we need."

Terror gnawed his gut, from being in the presence of a ruthless killer. "Why don't you take this sack off my head?"

"We intend no harm. I will make you the good deal. You tell us what you say to United Nation and Chaim Weitzman, and we let you go."

Charles was astonished at how stupid the man was, addressing him with his fictitious name. He was well acquainted with manipulation tactics from his upbringing. From the deep sound of his voice and the heavy boots, the man seemed middle-aged and brawny. A familiar smell aggravated his senses too, like the stench of Mother's iron when she burnt Von Deisenberg's pants: that happened only once.

"We need to know what lies Jews told the United Nation. What countries they sway to get votes for partition? The documents you carried: what they said. You tell, and tonight you go home to the girl."

Charles gulped at the mention of Gladia. *Oh Lord, don't let her be near this place.* He regretted Moshe disclosing the sensitive documents in his UN courier packet, because he'd do anything for her safety. He also knew many other questions would be posed: especially where the Haganah kept their headquarters. And that could get his friends killed and cripple the Jewish command center.

"Okay, I'm mad at those Jews anyway. They haven't paid me in three weeks. I'm just a messenger, so how am I supposed to eat with no pay?" Charles tried to straighten but his cuffs forced him to slouch. "You can keep my hood on, but can you release my hands so I can relax and tell you what I know? I don't want to die for this stupid job."

"Foolish American ... looking for this?" The man rubbed a pill against Charles' chin, then pushed his face back.

"That's my headache medicine."

"It is your poison!" The man struck the side of Charles' head. "You fool. Every Jew carry one in the same pocket."

The knock sent waves of pain, accompanied with bright dots under the burlap mask. "I thought I didn't need that," he mumbled.

"I warn you, if you lie, we will hurt you." The steps drew closer and the outline of the big man towered over him. "You will tell. Easy or hard way."

Clunking shoes rushed down the steps and another man shrieked something in their foreign tongue. Charles regretted not taking basic Arabic classes sooner.

"I am busy!" The interrogator's tone sounded demeaning like Von Deisenberg's.

The man uttered the word "Jew," and Charles caught a glimpse of the outline of his hand pointing upstairs.

Oh Lord, let that be the Haganah, not Gladia. He realized another truth Rabbi Jesse taught: non-religious people only talked with God when their life was on the line. He was ready to give God his heart, mind and soul if He would spare Gladia being captured.

The interrogator stomped closer. "We have a Jew intruder. He friend of yours, Richard?"

"Can't be. I have no friends."

"This is good. Let us go see."

Sweating, Charles rocked his chair while all three sets of feet trampled up the steps. A few minutes later, light footsteps tapped their way down.

"Who's there?" Charles asked. "I know someone is in here—"

"It is me, Talia. Quiet. I will get you out."

The sister. "You led them to me! Why?"

"I am sorry." She uncovered his head and walked behind him. "I get you out ... oh no, they handcuff you. They always use rope." She faced him and shook her head. "They must want something important."

With his glasses missing, Charles squinted to focus her face. "Your English is better. Why would you try to save me? Is this another trick?"

"I just find out who you are. I am sorry." Talia's eyes welled in tears. She was either sincere, or the best actress he'd ever seen. Her passive gazes downward resembled Mother's demeanor. "My uncle, Amaud—"

"Wait." Charles flexed his arms. "Look for something to break these cuffs."

She looked around. "There is nothing here." The basement appeared bare except for a large wood table and chair, until he finally saw the item that generated the burning-iron odor: A modified warming rod for a hot plate sat smoldering on a metal holder.

He shifted his eyes to a black door on his left. "Look in there, hopefully it's a storage room. Hurry." His heart fluttered from the possibility of an escape and Gladia's life being at stake.

"He thinks your name is Richard Anderson," Talia said from the utility room. "I cannot see anything."

"Keep looking for a pipe, or pliers, any tools."

"When I watch you, I tell him your name is Charlous, but I did not know your last name until today."

"Is your uncle the leader?"

"Yes. But he got angry when he took your passport from my house."

"Where is he now? How many are with him?" He must be the one with the heavy boots.

"Your mother sent a telegram. She worries and say that you run away."

Charles shivered under his sweat. "How could you possibly know about my mother?"

"She sent the message to my father. He is Ishmael, her brother." Fumbling noises came from the little room. "Your mother mailed us a school picture and my father looked for your passport on the black market."

Charles opened his eyes wide. "I don't feel so good. Hurry."

"My father tell me today you are Charlous Devon-shi-re, my cousin. He likes Jews. But my uncle Amaud, he sneak in our house and steal your paper. He make me watch you, or I get ... I do not know the word."

She came out shrugging. "I cannot see anything to break them." She gazed around the room. "Today my father find your picture in my purse. I tell him you get captured and he said to let you go. But Uncle Amaud ... he will not believe you are family. He is outside with your friend from America."

"David is here?" Charles rocked the chair, and the cuffs cut him.

"Yes." She gazed downward. "I am sorry, they will kill him."

Charles grunted and thrust his body until the chair tilted. "Get me out of here!" Angry adrenaline made him yank his cuffs and kick furiously. If anything happened to David, he couldn't live with it.

"They will hear us," Talia said. "Only Amaud has the key to unlock you." She paced. "I do not know what to do."

He gritted his teeth and prayed Gladia wasn't next. "*Ahhhh* ... you're not helping!"

"I am sor—" When the door flew open upstairs, she scurried to pick up the cloth and covered his head.

"Don't go," he said quietly.

"What are you doing?" Amaud yelled.

"I ... I—"

"Get out, now!"

CHAPTER 35

When Amaud's boots clunked behind him, Charles' veil was yanked away to reveal his best friend, bound and gagged. The room dimmed again from the cover dragging back over his face.

Charles bit his lip—not David. He'd done everything in his power to avoid his buddy being involved, yet, here he was.

"Bring them. This place is not safe."

Charles felt his cuffs unlock and his arm yanked upward. When he stood, his legs cramped and he plunged.

"Get up, stupid." A big boot kicked his previously injured ribs.

After being yanked and led to another location, the smell of oiled machinery convinced him they'd entered a factory near the restaurant.

His feet almost came out from under him when they descended downstairs. When they stopped, two hands dug into his collarbones and forced him down on a seat. Cuffs tightened around his sore wrists and a few rustling grunts alerted him that David was there.

"Okay, we are all friends. Yes?" Amaud's voice reverberated as if they were in a large basement. The evil man sounded pleasant, just like the description concerning Arab irregulars who killed Jews with smiles on their faces. Capturing him and David must have made the interrogator's day, and torturing Americans would be two trophies any Arab terrorist could brag about for a long time.

"Now you tell me about the United Nation so your friend can live." Amaud's boots came closer. "Then we talk about Haganah location."

"Don't tell him anything, Charles." David's voice muffled through his gag. "He'll kill us anyway!"

"Cut his finger off."

"No!" Charles yanked his cuffs. Amaud didn't even sound agitated. What was the man capable of when angry?

Charles' veil came off. An Arab in a tan robe and sandals approached David with shears. When their eyes locked, David's image blurred from tears flooding Charles' vision. The wavy image of clippers lowered, while another man pulled his buddy's index finger straight.

Charles almost toppled from jolting. "No! Stop!"

The man flexed his wrist and snapped David's bone like a dry twig.

Charles hated himself for not insisting his friend go back to New York.

The gag muffled David's scream while he quaked in his chair. His face turned dark red and veins protruded. A cold sweat drenched Charles' face while he watched his friend's blood spurt airborne. "David, I'm sorry!"

Blood dripped on David's shoes and a puddle accumulated where his finger landed. His eyes rolled up and his convulsing lessened. Charles learned the purpose for the red-hot plate warmer, hearing sizzles as they cauterized the wound. David growled and shuddered like he'd been electrocuted. The smell of his burning flesh lowered Charles into deeper despair.

Charles hunched over and fought to maintain sanity so he could figure a way to save his friend. His mind swirled with rage against the barbarians torturing them. Only one thing caused his head to rise: Gladia. Then the itchy cloth went back over his face.

"Whew," Amaud said, "American Jew stinks. Yes, yes … you squirm, Richard. Now you know how we suffer." Amaud jabbed him in the gut. "Not so happy to fight someone else's battle, huh?" Amaud's cigar breath was strong. "Where is your comrades now?" He kicked Charles' leg. "Commander Sneh? He knows you are here. But he has no time for insignificant messenger."

Charles tuned out those words and focused on his surroundings to learn about his opponent. But his first concern was to listen for David's breathing.

"You tell me what I need so your friend does not lose more fingers." The threat in Amaud's voice intensified.

"I will tell you." There had to be something he could come up with to get David released—a bargain, a trade, something.

"That is better. Tell me first, what was in the document you take to the United Nation?"

"I don't get to see the documents, I just—"

"Another finger!"

"No, wait!" He had to make up something, and it better be convincing.

Amaud kicked his shin and slapped him on the side of the head. The man hit hard, like Von Deisenberg.

"Tell me what is on the documents!"

A misleading statement should help stall for time. "It was a secret plan to change the partition of Palestine." Charles put strain in his voice to sound convincing.

"We know that. You better know detail, or we will cut more fingers until your friend dies bleeding."

He couldn't have known that; there was no change in the partition. "I know everything you need."

"Tell me about Jerusalem."

"They knew Jerusalem would be difficult to divide, so the UN suggested the city be put under international trust so no group can rule it."

"Lie! We know Jews must have the city, and plan to destroy Dome of the Rock. Then they will put their temple there and take the whole world."

"Those are Nazi lies!"

"This is the last chance, or I take two fingers."

The man used the same verbiage as the Nazi pamphlets: "scum Jews" trying to "take over the world." Amaud just confirmed how Arabs were Nazi influenced. Everyone else knew Jewish leadership pursued peace and only wanted to govern one area: Israel.

"I think you want your friend to die." He removed his head cover and revealed a shiny stiletto an inch from David's throat.

Charles clanked his cuffs. "Don't harm him. I have valuable information."

"Then tell me; How and when are the Haganah planning to bomb the Dome of the Rock?"

Charles' mind raced for a convincing lie since there were no such plans. The classic Nazi propaganda, designed to add fuel to the hostility was obviously working. Nazis were notorious for stirring paranoia in anyone foolish enough to listen.

David looked at Charles with a weary squint and a strained grin. The expression didn't match his pain. Charles wanted to call out to—

David lunged forward; the knife pierced his jugular vein. Blood gushed from the wound as the man yanked the blade out of his neck.

Charles jerked his restraints. "No. David!" It was too soon for the suicide protocol.

"You fool! Patch him, so he do not die yet!" Amaud, only a few steps away, slapped his hand on the incision, but blood oozed past his fingers.

Charles convulsed as David swayed and kicked. When Amaud lost his grip from the erratic movements, blood spurted from David's neck like a little hose.

David's eyes rolled upward. Ripples of terror stole Charles' breath as he watched his best friend fade into pale sweat. "David," he screamed, "stay with me!" David slowed and blinked dimming eyes at Charles. His countenance said it all: *I love you, buddy. Live, marry Gladia. Take this nation.*

Wailing, Charles shuffled his chair forward, but David's eyelids closed and his body fell limp. When Amaud stepped away, Charles saw a dark red puddle flowing toward his shoes. David's blood smeared all over the enemy.

Amaud wiggled his hand at David. "Get that thing out of here!" He pulled the knife from the killer's hand. "You disgrace us with early death. Idiot." Amaud trampled through David's blood, and then kicked a table over.

The killer emerged from a storage closet with a green tarp, wrapped David's body, and stuffed him into a burlap sack; Then rolled him against the wall. Two others were called in: First they went to the closet, then carried mops and a pail to soak up the mess.

Amaud turned and noticed Charles' face uncovered. They both protracted an intense gaze at each other, then Charles tightened his abdomen and groaned. The pressure in his head felt like a ticking bomb with three seconds on its timer. Looking at the wrappings, he couldn't believe David had been discarded like trash. He'd no idea what to tell David's parents, if by some miracle he made it out alive.

Amaud ranted in Arabic. Charles recognized "American" and "bad information." Torturing hostages for leverage was important strategy to the enemy. Likely, Amaud complained to the killer that he could no longer get accurate information since he killed Charles' friend too soon.

It confirmed his training manual: If captured by Arabs, plan on dying and hope you have access to your last bullet or a cyanide pill. He had a new appreciation for the valor demonstrated by thousands of frontline Jews captured.

"I'm sorry you lose the friend," Amaud said. "We do not want him to die."

Charles always thought he was incapable of killing until today. "You mean you didn't intend he die so soon."

"Ha," Amaud scoffed.

Desperate to see Gladia again, he was ready to pour on his own manipulation strategies. "I'm your nephew!" he yelled with disgust.

"What?" Amaud froze and contorted his middle-aged, dark-tan face. "You must be delirium." He narrowed his eyes. "This is new trick of Haganah?"

"My name is Charles Devonshire, not Richard Anderson. You fool!" Insulting and demeaning the enemy was part of his tactic; He hoped.

Amaud marched over and slapped Charles' face. "Where did you get that name?"

Charles tensed. Not from the blow, but from the scent of David's blood that was now on his face.

Amaud latched onto Charles' lapel and shook him. "Tell me where you find that name!"

Charles found a weakness, and it had bought more time—anything to avoid losing Gladia.

"We have your passport and we know you travel to United Nations." Amaud wrung Charles' neck like a rag; The man's bulging face blurred as Charles pulled his chest for air, without success. The outer edges of his sight darkened. It was over.

"Where did you get that *name*?" Amaud spattered in his face after he released his stranglehold. "Tell me!"

Charles wheezed in a breath. "My mother …" Another short breath. "Gave it to me …"

"What is her name?"

The room shook like an earthquake from Amaud's yanking of Charles' collar. "Victoria Devonshire."

Amaud jolted back. "Wash his face! Now!" He advanced his squinting eyes closer like a slithering animal, trying to study Charles' features.

Noisy shoes thudded down the steps and a wave of cold liquid flooded him like a fire hose. He inhaled a shivering breath, while vapors of ammonia stretched his eyelids wide open.

"Comb his hair back."

Charles repulsed at the killer's hand touching him. Amaud peered at Charles. His tormenter's open mouth and wide eyes confessed; he must have seen the resemblance of his sister's face staring back at him.

"What is you father's name?"

Every yell resembled glass breaking inside Charles' head. "He's not my father."

Amaud thrust his finger at Charles. "His name!"

"Roger Devonshire." Charles' gravelly voice weakened. "But you probably call that evil Nazi Peter Von Deisenberg. God will judge him. And you."

Amaud straightened and turned away.

Talia had told the truth. Charles shivered with confirmation of another evil relative in his presence.

"Where did you live?" His voice calmer now, as though he'd accepted Charles' revelation.

"Los Angeles."

Amaud's bloodshot eyes bulged as he wiped David's blood off his black leather. His silence must have been unusual. His assistant, brows narrowed, stared at the interrogator's stiff gestures.

Finally, Amaud sat at the wood table and yelled at the man, who reacted with a submissive bow. Charles scanned the stairway behind Amaud, then looked for tools. He refocused on his opponent's vacant face, but Amaud wouldn't look at him. He'd learned about Arabs having strong devotions to family, and intended to exploit that next.

The assistant hollered a cluster of words while pointing at Charles. Amaud ranted back, probably scolding him, because the man darted upstairs. The door at the top didn't emit noises when it opened, so it was probably nighttime. Time for Charles to pour on the same manipulation he'd learned from Von Deisenberg. "You are my uncle, Amaud—"

"You shut up!" His face still turned away.

Good thing he didn't ask Charles how he knew Amaud's name; he didn't want to rat out his cousin. "I know you're supposed to kill me. But maybe now you're reconsidering because *I'm your sister's son.* Your Koran prohibits you from killing family. Yes?"

Amaud slammed his fist on the table. "I told you shut up!"

Charles had no idea if the Koran said that or not. "What would my mother's face look like if she found out you harmed her only son? Can you imagine her reaction?"

Amaud stood and rushed to the utility closet, returned with a cloth and stuffed it into Charles' mouth. "There." He pushed his finger in Charles' face. "*I decide* what to do. We have the bigger cause." He sat at the table and rested his head against his hand.

The stuffy room reeked a medley of foul odors, and sleep beckoned. Amaud's brows furrowed as though deep in thought. Time to keep quiet.

Finally, the sound he'd hoped for broke silence: heavy breathing, just above the threshold of snoring. Sensing his only chance for escape, he tightened his stomach, bent forward, and raised his chair from the bloodstained floor.

While inching toward the closet, he paused at the burlap sack that covered his buddy. His head rushed and the stillness of the lumpy sack made his chest contract.

He had plenty of experience getting out of bindings, but the hardest part of escaping would be the vision of David's death lunge repeating. Intellectually, Charles understood; Their training taught how Arabs routinely tortured one friend to pressure the other for information. They also enjoyed making a companion murder his partner in exchange to live, but David diffused that tactic.

He pushed open the utility door with his head, and managed to wedge the handle of a mop between the handcuff chain and the chair, but the maneuver sent excruciating pain up his arms. He dropped the mop handle, which clunked against a bucket. The noise was loud, so he prepared for a raging Arab to burst in and slit his throat.

After more twisting with the mopstick, the handcuff chain started to loosen, but his wrists went numb. Ignoring the pain and working the handle, it finally snapped.

He opened the door and carried the chair back, while Amaud snored. He labored up the steps, but a crick in his leg dropped him. When he crawled, the locked metal door made him bow his head, knowing where the key was.

David would've told him to smash the chair over his uncle's head, but Charles felt too sore and weak to attack. He quietly descended, and stretched his stiff legs behind Amaud to look for the murder weapon. A drawer with bloodstains on the knob had to be the location, but the snoring man's body blocked it.

He carefully limped the distance from Amaud's position to his chair and counted steps. He sat and stretched his hands back to make it look as though he was still cuffed to the chair—he needed time to regain strength and determine a plan—there were still Arabs upstairs making shuffling noises.

His second-worst enemy was his conscience, which was busy accusing him of David's death. The exhausting mental torment caused him to fight against his sagging eyelids.

CHAPTER 36

May 14, 1948

The clamor of Arabic words spraying like machine-gun fire startled Charles awake. He jolted and flexed his sore arms free as the man pointed upstairs and continued shouting.

"Slow down," Amaud said.

Charles hid his hands and inclined his ears to distant noises: like a parade's cheering, with car horns blasting and gunshots echoing. Soon after, the Shofar horn blew excessively, which was unusual, since Jews faced a penalty of jail for sounding their ceremonial pipe. The Brits, after all, didn't want to offend Arabs, though they never worried about offending Jews.

Charles returned his attention to the man who still spewed out words faster than his accelerated breaths. This time he understood: "Jews," "celebrate," "American," "kill him." He shivered, hearing his own execution threat, then recalled the British were slated to leave Palestine soon: Rumors had spread that David Ben-Gurion would declare Israel a nation when the last soldier removed his foot from their land. Sitting in confinement within hearing range of Israel's rebirth would certainly finalize the torture. At that moment, Charles wished he'd taken Amaud's life the night before.

"I bet the Jews are declaring their nation," he said. Of course the commotion had to be something else; the Haganah had lost too many fighters, had a tiny air force of four planes, no navy and zero Allied support.

"Shut up ... liar." The tenor of denial resonated in Amaud's tone.

317

Charles' breathing intensified when Amaud opened the drawer and stabbed the blade onto the tabletop. Leaving it there, he walked over to Charles, and the room went dark from the sack being pulled over his face.

"Sounds like the Jews have won their nation back. It's over. Better to release me before they find us."

"You go nowhere." Amaud didn't sound condescending. When something metal like the knife plunked onto the table, he envisioned Amaud removing his head cover, showing his ugly teeth, and slicing Charles' throat. Charles went over his calculated paces from his opponent's position to his own chair.

Lord, Gladia needs me. If you get me out of this, I'll do anything you ask.

Amaud's chair scraped the floor. "I am sorry, my sister." His boots grew louder, and Charles pictured David's murder weapon coming. Tucking his legs, he threw himself back to lift the chair's front legs off the ground. When he heard the last step, he plummeted the chair leg toward Amaud's foot—and missed.

His mask whisked off; Sure enough, the blade recoiled, but Amaud didn't show his gritted teeth. He took advantage of his uncle's pause, sprang upward and head-bumped Amaud's chin.

With a big grunt, his enemy fell like Goliath, his head slamming the concrete while the blade clanged across the floor. With his adversary lying dazed, Charles picked up the knife and slashed the throat of David's killer. Shaking profusely, he dropped the bloody weapon onto Amaud's chest and watched him gurgle into death; His dying eyes resemble Mother's.

He steadied his trembling hand on his forehead. "What did I do?" He stepped back to avoid a stream of blood chasing his shoes.

It was self-defense. He had to remember that.

Footsteps above sobered him, and he heard Amaud's name called. Heavy equipment scraped across the upper floor while he searched Amaud's pockets, found the key and removed the broken cuffs from his bleeding wrists. Glancing down, he grimaced. He'd heard about people dying with their eyes open, but no training could have prepared him for a face-to-face killing.

He looked at the burlap sack and wiped a few tears. "You didn't die in vain, my friend. You're still going to save me." He cupped his hands in the bloody pool by Amaud's neck and quickly spread blood up the first few steps. Cleaning his hands on Amaud's pants, he hastened to David's body.

Footsteps pattered the stairway as he stuffed himself inside the sack next to his friend. He tightened the opening, counting on confusion and shock to avoid detection.

High-pitched voices began yelling and resounded back up the stairwell. He breathed again. In the quiet that followed, he fought the pulling of his eyelids as his empty stomach growled. He had to muster strength to escape, so he could find Gladia and give David a proper burial, but then firm hands yanked the sack and startled him. The handlers grunted as they dragged him and David up the steps. Each bump sent sharp pains to his lower back and wrists. Then the motion stopped.

Bits of light crept through little rips in the material and showed rifles and ammo crates, stacked between sewing machines and fabric rolls. Arabic voices surrounded him and his heart raced. The frantic chatter and clacking of weaponry suggested an attack plan underway.

A strong tug at his feet and head lifted them, and he and David were soon thrown airborne into another small compartment. Charles felt his backside sticking out, but a swift kick sandwiched him against David's cold tarp covering. He let out a moan while being squished and bent, and then prayed the warehouse racket obscured his outburst. Some kind of lid slammed over them and everything went dark.

A car's engine started and vibrated him; he and David had been thrown into a trunk. When the vehicle sped off, he prepared himself to be weighted down and tossed into the Jordan River, or possibly thrown into a bonfire.

After numerous bumps and twisting turns, the car stopped but remained running. The trunk popped open, and a noise creaked like a trapdoor opening. They were raised up, then dropped onto something softer than a hard floor. The slam of metal above caused darkness again, and the muffled engine revved and faded away.

The new stenches reeked like a refuse bin. He wiggled his way out of the sack, propped the trapdoor open, and saw Arabs working at an oil refinery in the distance. Better to wait until dark to make his move.

When he sat back, a sliver of light revealed David partly exposed, his neck taped up like a scarf. He scooted some rubbish away from his friend's pale, blood-smeared face and wrapped him better. After tying the top of the sack, he kicked a pile of rubbage and shredded a cardboard box with teeth gritted. Then he looked upon David's form, his hand over his mouth. He fought back tears so he could think of a proper burial site, and again, what he'd say to David's parents.

CHAPTER 37

Charles woke and opened the squeaky lid; the cool evening breeze dissipated the stench, bringing with it a barrage of party noises. He eased himself over the wall of the bin and plunked onto the pavement. Pulling himself up, he limped through a parking area toward the neon lights. When he turned a corner, the streets were filled with Jews singing, dancing, and yelling joyously. Overstuffed trucks had smiling people handing out bottles, waving the Jewish flag, all in the absence of British guards and tanks.

Finally, he recognized students from the library, loitering in front of a dance hall. "What's all the excitement about?" He had to hear the words for himself.

One student squinted. "Are you the only one that hasn't heard?"

"Hey ... you don't look too well. Are you sick?" another asked.

Charles held his belly. "I could use some food if you have any, but first I have to know what this celebration is."

The young man extended a bottle. "The British left Palestine. David Ben-Gurion proclaimed the *State of Israel!* We are finally free." The young man pulled another bottle from a crate and lifted it. "La Heim!"

"I have to get to Tel Aviv." Charles wandered while the buildings and people tilted and blurred. The shouts of joy didn't have much significance, since Gladia's safety could be at risk. His shoes dragged like lead weights, then he remembered their emergency rendezvous spot. Hopefully she'd made it to the porch of the library safely.

321

Heading north, he avoided another entourage of local Arabs carrying suitcases and babies. They kept moving their faces left to right, as if they feared being shot by irregulars—they never displayed anxiety around the Haganah. There was no need to evacuate; the Jewish Agency had repeatedly announced fairness and equal citizenship to all residents of Palestine. Arabs even had job offers from the new Jewish government.

Crossing the street at the edge of town, he ducked between two cars to avoid irregulars, scoffing at a group of Arab farmers. He peeked over the car hood to see one of the elders drop his luggage and face the two combatants, who were waving guns and shouting "Cowards!" in Arabic. Now he was an eyewitness to irregulars taunting locals to harm Jews.

After ducking into alleys and hiding behind vehicles to avoid teenage spotters who traveled with snipers, Charles found the library and sighed. Thank goodness it wasn't looted, as some of the Jewish shops in town had been. He peeked through the large side windows, but the room was dark. He trotted to the back and found Gladia lying still on a bench. She'd better not be dead. "Gladia, wake up!"

"Charles!" She rose, eyes droopy, and clung to him. Her body shook from profuse crying. "I thought you were dead."

He could barely breathe. "I'm devastated." His voice broke. Unfortunately, he better understood her agony about loved ones dying.

She pulled back. "How did you get away? What is this blood and dirt on you?" She began prodding his body.

Moaning, he hunched over.

"Oh my! Your hands, they are bleeding." She pulled her dress up and wrapped his wrists, gently rubbing away some of the dried blood. "What happened?"

His lips quivered as he looked about. He pulled his hands back so her dress would cover her slip. "David …"

Her forehead creased. "Where is he?"

Tears streaming, he laid his head to her shoulder.

She cried with him while a mortar soared and boomed nearby. Then she pressed her body to his, her lips moving on his neck.

It was the wrong time, but after all they'd been through, he went in for their first real kiss. Maybe it could ease the agony for a moment; It felt so good, he couldn't stop. Every bruise burned during their heated exchange, but it was worth it. Feeling the vibrations of near-misses, he suspected the first kiss could be their last.

When their lips gently separated, she placed her soft palms on his face. "I want to be with you before they—"

A loud blast showered clusters of rocks and gravel; they couldn't dodge bombs forever.

He brushed her stained dress. "We're going to make it back!" Fed up, he grabbed her hand, but within a few paces the ground reeled while black and red dots spotted his vision.

She led him back to the bench. "Sit down, you are faint."

Sulfur and smoke burned his throat as another mortar screamed overhead and struck the gymnasium, catapulting concrete boulders at them. They ducked under the bench as smashing chunks littered the seat above them. He rose and gripped her arm, then limped with her toward the parking lot. "We have to get David's body."

When they reached her vehicle, it was sprayed with dust and rubble. Gladia started the car while he turned to three students who were clearing chunks of asphalt from their vehicle's trunk. Radio chatter billowed out their windows. "Any news about the enemy's positions?" Charles asked.

A young man showed the whites of his eyes. "You didn't hear the broadcast?" He was an American.

323

His leftover adrenaline from the passionate kiss kept Charles standing. "No."

"Five Arab countries are attacking from all sides, and they've infiltrated all of Palestine—it's all-out war and we're trapped in the middle!" The young man kicked his car tire. "Declaring Israel was a big mistake! We can't start our car. Can you give us a lift to the American consulate? They announced an evacuation to Lydda airport, for Americans."

"We're going back to Tel Aviv," Charles said.

"Then you'll die there."

Five bombers screamed overhead from the direction of Egypt. Everyone hit the ground as the roar vibrated across their backs. The fighters brought back a fond memory of Dov, when he'd bragged about Jews obtaining the only four planes that made up their air force: a dummy film company posed to create a newsreel of the English-made Beaufighters. Jews filmed them taking off from an English airport, only to never return.

After the growling engines faded, they lifted themselves from the pavement, while Gladia revved her motor.

"Here, listen for yourself." The young man sat in his car and reached toward his volume knob. "It repeats every ten minutes."

> Egypt, Jordan, Iraq, Lebanon, and Syria have joined forces to eliminate every Jew that refuses to leave the battle-ridden plains of Palestine ... or dare we call it Israel? You don't have to be Jewish to die today. All collaborators will be executed on sight according to the Arab Legion.

"Charles," Gladia yelled.

He climbed into her car. "We can take you to Tel Aviv, after we stop at the refinery," he said.

"We're not going there. The report said Tel Aviv's surrounded."

Charles turned to Gladia. "Go!"

She pushed the gas pedal and dodged holes the size of swimming pools. The backstreets were unusually bare, and she missed the turnpike toward the refinery. "There is a towel in the back."

He pointed at the highway. "You missed the turn."

"We will get David's body and return to Tel Aviv. Moshe will give him an honorable burial with a medal of bravery if we make it."

"That's good, but why are you heading away from the refinery?"

She pulled her car into the bushes and cut the lights.

"What are you—?"

A truckload of Arabs passed. They no longer disguised themselves to look like farmers; their rifles pointed upward.

She pulled a towel from the back and set it on his lap. "I know this will seem crazy. I have a shock ... I mean a surprise for you."

He squinted at her.

"Will you trust me?"

He couldn't say no as usual, even though her judgments lately were questionable. "Of course. What is it?"

She looked about, flipped the lights and bumped over brush onto the street. "We will have to go there before I can tell." She pasted the charred remains of her house without even looking, which was strange, since the disaster had added to her depression.

He recoiled every time he turned to her, because every muscle ached. "What are you doing?"

She tried to crack a smile. "You said you would trust me, right?"

He took a deep breath as she turned down Rabbi Jesse's street. "I do, but once a rabbi tears his clothes and disowns a person, there's no convincing him otherwise ... right?"

She stopped in front of the Rosenthals' and honked.

Jesse trotted out first, arms open; the whole family followed. The Rabbi showed his familiar joyful face with a tear streaming. "Charles!"

Charles couldn't contain his rush of tears, and climbed out with a new reason to smile. "Rabbi … Jesse!" They embraced.

Charles stepped back and winced, while Gladia put a supporting arm around him. He looked into the faces of each of the half-smiling family members and basked in the moment of having them back. "I don't understand." Dozens of fond memories flashed.

Jesse spread his hands out. "Your gracious girl explained everything. I'm sorry I believed Samuel about your involvement with Jonathan's death."

"I loved Jonathan." Charles tried to brush off his soiled clothes.

"We know," Jesse said. "When Gladia told us the trouble you were in, our whole congregation gathered and prayed for your escape." He touched Charles' cheek. "By standing here, you have proven how God performs miracles by answering prayers."

Charles, remember what you promised if you were freed.

He stared upward, baffled at why God allowed David to sacrifice his life so he could live.

Elizabeth stepped forward with a young girl next to her. "Okay. It's time to clean this young man, feed him, and prepare for his wedding."

Charles jostled and stared at Gladia's illuminated countenance. "What?" He couldn't possibly enjoy a ceremony without David at his side.

She nudged him. "This is my surprise. Rabbi Jesse said he would marry us."

Charles' mouth opened. "Now?" He ran his eyes across all their faces. "Shouldn't everybody be evacuating?"

Jesse had an unusually relaxed grin, a calm Charles hadn't seen on anyone in a long time. "There is no place to retreat to and all exits are blocked by the enemy." He spread his hands out toward his family. "We have asked God to spare us, and believe He will do just that."

A chill ran through Charles; If God could deliver Jews from the holocaust and assemble a scattered people in a war-torn land, and raise them to build the only democratic nation in the Middle East, He could certainly deliver anyone from anything.

"I would be honored to marry you." Jesse nodded toward the house. "If you're returning to the Haganah, this could be your last opportunity."

Charles marveled at Jesse's faith. The rabbi hadn't been wrong yet.

Elizabeth and Ruth stepped forward, their faces unusually pleasant for the threat surrounding their families. "Well … shall we get you ready?" Elizabeth's hand extended, her nod invited him in, though his grimy clothes had to be repulsive. And with all the mortars whistling and vibrating the ground under their feet, one could land on their house any moment.

David would've told him to get in there and marry her. He smiled at Gladia. "Okay. I guess … we're getting married!"

The family applauded. When they entered, everyone parted ways throughout the house. Jonathan would have been at Charles' side, helping him take off his soiled shoes.

Ruth and Elizabeth took measurements before he retreated to the toilet room. After bathing, eating and dressing, he entered the family room. Although he felt clean, the aches and pains hadn't washed away. He looked down with amazement at how nicely his suit fit. The family dished out pats on his back, but it was hard to accept the glee: David's murder scene kept flashing.

Ruth came and struck a hissing stick match to light a menorah, which illuminated the living room with a golden glow after Jacob dimmed the lights.

Everyone did an admirable job of ignoring the booms outside. Charles should have been burying David's body and at his post, but if the enemy plowed through the doors, at least he'd go out with the one whom he was destined to be with.

A knock pounded the door. He flinched. It couldn't be the enemy. They wouldn't have knocked.

Ruth smiled. "Charles, will you answer that?"

He froze. Jacob tapped his shoulder. "It's okay. Open it."

He walked over and pulled it open. "Moshe ... Agatha! I can't believe you're here." When they entered, he hugged them, but then tilted his head down.

Moshe patted his back. "We got the call when you arrived and heard the tragic news about David. I'm so sorry. He will be given a hero's burial and a medal of honor."

"We ... will all miss him." Agatha's voice cracked; she dabbed her eyes with a handkerchief.

Charles nodded. "I'm glad to see you both, but you must have pressing duties."

"You are my pressing duty!" Moshe advanced in the entryway and waved at the family. "Gladia put out the distress call and we raided Bortogios, but you'd been moved."

Charles didn't want to hinder the war by using the commander's time. Right outside the door, Israel's fate was at stake. "I had no idea you'd drop everything to rescue me."

"You're more valuable than you'll ever know." Moshe cleared his throat. "There's one more task, then I'm off." He turned and nodded at Ruth.

Charles' heart pattered when Ruth went upstairs.

Rabbi Jesse held his hand out. "This way, Charles." He walked him to a small oak pulpit. Agatha stood arm-in-arm with Annie and couldn't keep her face dry, but at least her crying drowned out some of the racket outside.

Charles' eyes watered when Gladia descended the steps in a white satin gown. The look she beamed at him was as if they were being wed in the peaceful garden he'd imagined long ago. She glided to Moshe's extended elbow.

Her face radiated from the candles' glow as she and Moshe strolled his way. As she drew nearer, an amazing calm tucked away life's anxieties. If ever he imagined an angel, her advance toward him would be the vision of it.

Jesse stretched tall. "Who gives this woman in holy matrimony?"

"I do." Moshe handed her to Charles and nodded.

Charles and Gladia locked arms and listened to Rabbi Jesse officiate the ceremony. Once pronounced husband and wife, Gladia broke into a cry of joy when she faced Charles.

"You may kiss your bride," Jesse said.

Charles kissed her while the whole family cheered, his knees nearly giving out. It was hard to see when he pulled back and looked upon his bride's tear-streaked face. "We're married on Israel's first day of independence!"

"La Heim!" the family shouted.

Charles was ready to take his bride upstairs, but he saw Moshe slip two pistols into Gladia's purse by the door. He had to gird himself and take care of his duties, so they could have a future together. And possessing a firearm would never again be a problem.

Moshe took him aside while Elizabeth removed flowers from Gladia's hair. Charles drew a map so they could retrieve David's body on the happiest and most miserable day of his life; then Gladia joined them.

Moshe hugged them both. "I'm sorry, I have a country to protect." He put his hands on each of their shoulders. "Do not let me see you at your posts for at least three days. That's an order!"

Next …
The sequel: *Reborn*!

Will Charles and Gladia have an opportunity to enjoy a honeymoon in the midst of an impossible war? And how could an underground army with no tanks, four planes and a bleak supply of arms defeat hundreds of thousands of battle-hardened angry Arabs?

Visit **www.rebirthofisrael.com** to learn more about the exciting sequels and other fascinating facts about this miracle nation.

Download Rebirth's press release to share with friends.

Read more about the characters and watch videos from this era.

Get your free Israel fact information ebooklet. Sharing "Rebirth" and learning more about Israel's contributions to the world will help educate others to support this great nation and promote peace in the Middle East.

All these things and more are on Rebirth's website.

ABOUT THE AUTHOR

Dave Longeuay has been writing since 1978. He's written poems, lyrics and music since his teenage years and in 1989, wrote his first book, *The End Times*. In 1980 he founded Public Recording, and built a thriving multimedia studio where he still produces all kinds of audio and video projects. He also wrote, co-wrote, and produced hundreds of popular songs for local musicians in Southern California, as well as numerous radio scripts for a wide variety of commercials and videos for his clients.

His writing skills broadened to compose dozens of scripts for a wide range of music videos, infomercials, commercials, and dozens of corporate products. His most notable independent work was writing, producing, shooting, and editing a documentary about missionaries. He personally filmed and directed the documentary in Uganda Africa, New Castle England, and Rosarito Mexico. Dave enjoys supporting his missionary friends at: **sgwm.com**

"I have a passion for writing and telling stories to inspire people worldwide. Please remember to pray for peace in the Middle East and remember to support Israel and missionaries abroad."

www.rebirthofisrael.com

www.rebirthofisrael.blogspot.com

www.publicrecording.com

Did the Jews really invite thousands of Arab residents to become Israeli citizens?

"The Arab states which had encouraged the Palestine Arabs to leave their homes temporarily in order to be out of the way of the Arab invasion armies, have failed to keep their promise to help these refugees."

—The Jordanian daily newspaper Falastin, February 19, 1949

"The mass evacuation, prompted partly by fear, partly by order of the Arab leaders, left the Arab quarter of Haifa a ghost city…. By withdrawing Arab workers they hoped to paralyze Haifa."

—Time Magazine, May 3, 1948 page 25

"The Arabs of Haifa fled in spite of the fact that the Jewish authorities guaranteed their safety and rights as citizens of Israel."

—Monsignor George Hakim, Greek Catholic Bishop of Galilee

'It was clearly intimated by the Arab-Palestinian Higher Executive that Arabs who remained in Haifa and accepted Jewish protection would be regarded as renegades."

—London Economist October 2, 1948

If these sources are true, then Arab population in Israel would be significant today. So how many Arab-Israeli citizens reside in Israel today?

Over 1.5 million: more than 20% of Israel's population are Arabs.